Louisa Heaton lives on Hayling Island, Hampshire, with her husband, four children and a small zoo. She has worked in various roles in the health industry—most recently four years as a Community First Responder, answering 999 calls. When not writing Louisa enjoys other creative pursuits, including reading, quilting and patchwork—usually instead of the things she *ought* to be doing!

Born and raised on the Wirral Peninsula in England, **Charlotte Hawkes** is mum to two intrepid boys who love her to play building block games with them and who object loudly to the amount of time she spends on the computer. When she isn't writing—or building with blocks—she is company director for a small Anglo/French construction firm. Charlotte loves to hear from readers, and you can contact her at her website: charlotte-hawkes.com.

PREGNANT BY THE SINGLE DAD DOC

LOUISA HEATON

THE ARMY DOC'S BABY SECRET

CHARLOTTE HAWKES

MILLS & BOON

First Published in Great Britain 2019
by Mills & Boon, an imprint of HarperCollins*Publishers*
1 London Bridge Street, London, SE1 9GF

Pregnant by the Single Dad Doc © 2019 by Louisa Heaton

The Army Doc's Baby Secret © 2019 by Charlotte Hawkes

ISBN: 978-0-263-26983-3

MIX
Paper from
responsible sources
FSC™ C007454

This book is produced from independently certified FSC™ paper
to ensure responsible forest management.
For more information visit www.harpercollins.co.uk/green.

Printed and bound in Spain
by CPI, Barcelona

PREGNANT BY THE SINGLE DAD DOC

LOUISA HEATON

MILLS & BOON

This is for all the lovely editors who have helped me
shape my stories, Charlotte, Nic, Grace, Sareeta
and Sara. I couldn't have done it without you!

CHAPTER ONE

WITH HER NOSE almost pressed up against the glass, Ellie stared at the row of incubators. Inside babies, some no bigger than the palm of her hand, lay covered in wires, tubes and nappies and hats that seemed far more suited to bigger, stronger babies. Dwarfing them even more.

She tried to swallow, but her mouth and her throat were dry. Her heart was hammering in her chest, and her legs were feeling as though if she didn't sit down within the next ten seconds she was going to collapse.

Ellie pressed her hand to the glass to steady herself, trying not to look at the faces of the parents who sat by each baby. She didn't want to see the pain on their faces and be reminded of her own grief. At least these parents still had hope.

Being here was bad. But it was something she was just going to have to get through if she wanted to achieve her dream of becoming a doctor. The university had placed her here—in the NICU. The Neonatal Intensive Care Unit at Queen's Hospital. So she didn't have a choice.

It was just a few weeks.

I can do this.

This part of the hospital had been nicknamed 'The Nest', because all the premature babies looked like scrawny, pink newborn birds. Here they got rest, warmth, food and protection, in the hope that one day they'd fledge and leave The Nest to go to their new homes with their families.

This was a place of hope. These families would not do well if they sensed her fear, so she turned away from the glass and sank down into one of the chairs as she awaited her mentor, Dr Richard Wilson.

She'd spoken to him on the phone just last week. He'd sounded a kindly old chap. Patient, sympathetic, friendly. Which was nice, considering some of the other mentors she'd been paired with during her training. He'd spoken to her at great length about what he hoped she would get from her placement with him, where she was in her training, what year of study she was in, which wards she'd worked on before, what he would expect from her. All standard stuff, but he had sounded different. Like a kindly grandfather.

She'd almost considered telling him about Samuel, but her nerves had got the better of her, and she hadn't been sure she'd get through it without crying, so she'd decided to delay until she'd been here a while and could judge the best time to tell her story. Because he would be bound to ask questions about it. He'd want to know about her experience as a patient. What had driven her to make the choices she faced today.

Finding it hard to swallow, she dug in her bag for her bottle of water, rummaging past all the other items. Phone. Purse. Tissues with a soothing aloe vera balm in case she lost control of her tears and didn't want to look like Rudolph afterwards. Pens. Notebook. A 2014 copy of the *BNF* that a kindly pharmacist had given her free of charge. It listed all drugs and medicines, what they were used for and what their interactions were, and she didn't want to look stupid. Tampons, just in case, a packet of painkillers and emergency chocolate...

Ah! The water bottle.

She struggled to open the lid, almost burning her palm as it came unscrewed, and then she took a giant swallow.

That's so much better.

Putting the lid back on, she stashed it in her bag and checked her appearance once more. She wanted to make a good impression on Dr Wilson. Show him that she meant business and that she was here to learn and get the most from her placement—even if this department *did* scare the hell out of her.

She sat there trying to steel herself, knowing that if she could just get through this first day, then the next day would be easier. And the one after that. And then she'd get into the flow. Perhaps see that this place wasn't as scary as she believed it to be. She would get past this placement and look back at her time on it and laugh that she'd been so scared in the first place!

It was ridiculous, the state of her nerves! Allowing herself so get so worked up.

It's stupid. It's—

'Ellie?'

She heard incredulity in a man's voice and turned to see who'd recognised her, expecting it to be a case of mistaken identity. But it wasn't. Not at all.

Shocked, she got to her feet. *'Logan?'* Ellie couldn't believe her eyes. Old, painful memories whizzed by at the speed of light. Was it really him?

Her brain scrambled to try and work out how long it had been since they'd last seen each other, but her mind couldn't compute and the numbers remained unreachable. Was she overjoyed? *Yes.* Was she apprehensive? *Oh, yes.* It had been *years.* Years since she had last seen him and he'd broken her heart by telling her that he thought it best if they were just friends.

Did I ever really get over you? No.

He'd devastated her that day. Had ended all her dreams

of the future back then. But perhaps that had simply served to begin making her who she was today. Stronger. More independent. Perhaps she should thank him for that first strike against her heart? It had made her ready for all the others.

Physically, he looked different. Changed from the gangly youth of their teens into a broader, more solid-looking *man*. Wider at the shoulders, with a squareness of jaw that was now more pronounced. The years had been good to him and he'd clearly thrived without her.

Would he look at her and think the same? Probably not. She wasn't the entrepreneur she'd always said she'd be. She wasn't at the top of some corporate ladder, wearing a power suit and waving a platinum card. She'd gone back to the beginning. Was a student again. She was on the bottom rung of the career ladder when she'd always aspired to be at the top.

She noticed he wore a name badge clipped to his belt—a sign that he worked in this hospital, identifying him as a member of staff. A doctor, of course. He'd left her behind to become one. His father was an oncologist, his mother had been... She struggled for the memory. Oh, yes. An obstetrician. When Logan had left her to pursue his dream of medical school she hadn't known what speciality he wanted to pursue. She hoped it wasn't this one.

'What are you doing here?' she asked, hoping he was just passing through. Maybe he was dropping off some notes for a patient and then he would be gone again. Hopefully to work in the department that was furthest from this one. Gerontology, perhaps?

'I saw the name in the diary, but I didn't think it would be *you*.'

In the diary? Why was he looking in the department's diary? Surely that was private to Dr Wilson and his staff?

A sense of dread began to filter its way into her body,

but she didn't want it to show on her face. She looked up and down the corridor, past the black and white artistic photographs of babies, past the noticeboard filled with old notices that should probably have been taken down years ago. Looking—hoping—to see Dr Wilson appear.

Perhaps if she concentrated really hard she could magic him up?

But the corridor remained resolutely empty and she turned back to face Logan, her cheeks hot, smiling politely. 'I'm here for Dr Wilson.'

Logan nodded. 'You're the new medical student?'

Her smile was almost a rictus, and she couldn't stand there talking to him any longer because it hurt too much already and... *Oh, Logan!*

'Yes. I am. So, if you could just excuse me? I need to let Dr Wilson know that I'm here. I don't want him to think that I'm late.'

And if I say his name often enough it might summon him.

She pushed past him, glad to find that, yes, indeed her legs *were* still working, and were even remarkably coordinated.

But as she passed him their shoulders brushed, and she inhaled a pleasurable scent of soap and sandalwood, and it was like being catapulted back to when she was eighteen years old and in his bedroom, sitting cross-legged on his bed, laughing at him because he was trying on different kinds of body spray for their date night. And then she'd got up from the bed and pulled him close to inhale the scent of his skin...

'Dr Wilson isn't here.'

His voice stopped her in her tracks and she closed her eyes in despair. Heart pounding hard against her ribs, she turned back to look at him. 'No? But he's meant to be meeting me. He's my mentor.'

Logan looked uncomfortable. 'He's not. His wife…she died this weekend.'

Oh.

That was dreadful news. Terrible! What was she to do? She'd have to ring her university. Tell them she needed to be assigned another mentor.

Shocked, she began to rummage in her bag.

'What are you doing?'

'I need to phone my tutor so they can assign me to someone else.'

Where was the damned phone? It had been there just a minute ago, when she'd dug inside to find her water. It must have gone all the way to the bottom and—

'They already have.'

She looked up at him, frowning. 'Who?'

But she already knew the answer just by looking at his face. A face that looked both guilty and apprehensive. A face that she had once kissed all over in bright red lipstick whilst he slept and then taken a picture of to give him as a card on Valentine's Day. A face that she had once caressed just to see how it went from smooth to bristly around his mouth.

'It's me. I'm your new mentor.'

Her heart sank.

Ellie Jones.

It felt strange, standing there just looking at her again. As if time meant nothing—as if all those years without her had been compressed into a microsecond of time. Her hair was a little longer, but still that dark so-black-it-was-almost-blue colour. Her eyes looked wary. Tired. As if she'd seen enough bad things in the world, thank you very much. Or perhaps it was just the way she was looking at *him*?

He was very much aware that he had broken her heart once, ruined her expectations of life and let her down. So perhaps she was suspicious as to how he could be the best mentor for her? He hadn't meant to break her heart. He thought he'd done the right thing for them both and she couldn't possibly know just how much their break-up had affected him.

But he was determined, here and now, to be the best mentor she could possibly have. As far as he was concerned the past was in the past, and though he'd hurt her once he would never do so again! He was going to push her hard during this placement, so that when she left she would realise that he had tried to make up to her for his failure in the past.

It was the least he could do. If she wanted to be a doctor, then he'd make her one. The best doctor she could be.

But can I stand to see her walk away from me again?

She'd never mentioned wanting to be a doctor before. He would have remembered something like that. Hadn't she wanted to run her own business? What had changed in her life to make her pursue this path? Because it wasn't easy. Not by a long shot. But if this was what she wanted then he would give it to her.

'I'll show you where you can put your things.'

She nodded, uncertain, clearly still hesitant.

Perhaps he ought to clear the air? State his intentions?

He turned. 'Look, Ellie, I know this isn't an ideal situation for us both, but I'm going to make sure you get the best education whilst you're on this unit with me, okay? You're here to learn and I'm here to teach. That's all it's going to be. All right?'

He hoped he could remain true to his word without letting in those pesky emotions he knew were still running so close to the surface.

Rooted to the ground, she simply stared up at him. *That's all it's going to be?* What else did he think was going to happen? That she was going to fall in love with him all over again? Or that it had already happened?

He had to be crazy if he thought that. She didn't need him stating the facts of the case as if she were some simpering spinster who thought there might be a chance of romance in the air simply because they'd been in love before.

It got her hackles up.

He'd walked her to a locker, where she'd left her things, taking only a notebook and pen with her that she could slide into her trouser pocket if she needed her hands free to perform or assist with a procedure. And now she was almost running to keep up with him.

'What's the number one reason babies end up in the NICU?'

Logan was giving her a lightning tour of the unit, asking questions as he went, not giving her any time to linger or think too much. So be it. Fine. She was here to learn. She'd show him how much it meant to her.

'Prematurity.'

'And the number one condition we see?'

She hesitated and he stopped to stare at her, waiting for a suitable answer. Had his eyes always been so blue? So intense? It was hypnotic to be under his gaze once again.

'Newborn jaundice?'

He considered her answer but his gaze was still scanning her face, as if he was familiarising himself with her features. 'Tell me about jaundice. What causes it in a newborn?'

She didn't know if it was different for newborns, but when she'd been on a general surgery ward there had been a patient there who had had jaundice.

'Er...high levels of bilirubin?'

'Are you asking me or telling me?'

'Telling you.'

He nodded. 'Good. In this place, more than any other in

the hospital with maybe the exception of Paediatrics, we have to be clear and firm about our diagnoses when discussing our patients with their parents. They don't want to hear *hesitation*. They don't want to hear *doubt*. They need to hear confidence and assuredness. Yes?'

She nodded.

'Okay, so what's bilirubin?'

She rifled through the files in her brain, trying to find the most efficient way of delivering an answer that sounded assured. 'A by-product of the breakdown of red blood cells.'

He began walking and again she followed fast on his heels, admiring the waistcoat that tightly encircled his middle, his flat stomach, his broad shoulders…

'And how would we notice it?'

'Yellowing of the skin—usually hands and feet. Eyes. Er…dark urine.'

'And what causes it in babies, specifically?' Now he stopped at a door that led into another room filled with incubators. Behind him she saw a row of them, one or two nurses and a few stressed-looking parents.

'The…er…liver isn't fully developed in a neonate, so it isn't as effective at removing the bilirubin from the blood.'

He nodded. 'Good. You've been reading up for this placement?'

She let out a breath. 'As much as I could along with… you know…doing assignments and things.'

'Stay on top of it. It's essential.'

'I will.'

She was a little annoyed that he was being this way— telling her what to do, being standoffish and abrupt—but she didn't want to say anything because he was now her mentor and, quite frankly, she'd had worse. But because of their personal history it niggled that *he* was the one telling *her* what to do.

'There are two babies in this next bay with jaundice, both being treated with fibre optic phototherapy. We have blankets that are laced with fibre optic cables, which shine directly onto the babies' backs. What contra-indications should we be aware of?'

She didn't know. There'd not been anything about that in the text she'd read earlier. 'Um…'

He answered for her. 'Temperature needs to be checked, and we must also make sure they don't get dehydrated.'

Of course! It was obvious now that she thought about it, and she felt like kicking herself for not knowing the answer in front of him. Her cheeks flushed red, but he didn't see because he was pushing the door open and showing her where she could wash her hands.

'Right—over here we have Bailey Newport and his mum, Sam.'

Ellie gave a nervous smile to the mum.

'Bailey is one of a set of triplets, born prematurely at thirty-two weeks. Sam had an emergency C-section, due to the threat of pre-eclampsia, but we only had one free cot, so her husband Tom is with the other two babies at St Richard's. We're hoping to get the family together as quickly as we can, but right now it's impossible to do so.'

Sam gave them a patient smile. 'It's difficult, but we take it in turns to be with each baby as much as we can. I'm expressing, but…'

Her voice trailed away as she looked down at her son and Ellie felt as if someone had punched her in the gut. Her baby was small. Thin, scrawny limbs, his body covered, it seemed, by wires and tubes. His tiny little hands scrunched up tight.

Witnessing hurt and pain like this would be the most difficult part of this placement, and she had to grit her teeth really hard and concentrate on her breathing so that she didn't let it overwhelm her.

'Bailey's taking his mum's milk well. He's one of the babies we have using the phototherapy, but his bilirubin levels are coming down nicely and we hope we can wean him off that soon.'

'That's good. Have you been able to hold him yet?' she asked Sam. She knew that was what any new mother wanted more than anything.

'Just the once. Everyone's so busy…we sometimes don't get the chance to.'

Logan looked at her directly. 'Perhaps you'd like to help Sam hold Bailey right now?'

'Really? I'd love to.'

'Okay, let's wash our hands first.'

'Ooh! Me too!' Sam beamed.

As Sam did that Logan stood on the opposite side of the incubator from Ellie and they looked at each other over the top of it. His hot gaze was full of questions and uncertainty and she wondered what he was thinking? Was he glad that she was here? As his student? Or was he troubled by it? He seemed to be looking at her as if he was really struggling with it.

She didn't think she would fall in love with him again. She wasn't after falling in love with *anyone*—not after what had happened between her and Daniel. But he could at least look at her fondly, as if he remembered the times they'd shared. As if she was his friend. He seemed to be looking at a space just off to her left now. As if he couldn't quite meet her gaze directly.

When Sam had washed her hands, she and Logan did the same and then he showed her how to open up the incubator, so that Bailey and all his tubes and wires could be safely transferred over to Mum and nothing would be caught, or twisted, or blocked.

She nodded and stood by his side, aware of his closeness, listening to his sensible instructions and trying not to think too much about how close they had been and how this was going to be the first baby she'd held since Samuel.

He'd been bigger than Bailey. Full-term, almost. Bailey seemed tiny in comparison and she didn't want to hurt him.

When the moment came she picked him up reverently, as if he was a precious Crown Jewel she was transferring to a safe, holding her breath until the transfer was done and she'd smilingly laid him in his mother's embrace.

Sam's face lit up with joy. 'Hello, little man. It's Mummy.' She glanced up with happiness, her eyes welling with tears as she looked to Ellie and Logan with gratitude. 'Thank you *so much*!'

Ellie could have stood there all day, feeling all the feelings, just watching this mother with her precious son, experiencing *that moment*. There was nothing else like it. Such a powerful image…a mother holding her child.

She'd had a similar moment herself, only hers had not been tinged with joy but with grief.

Feeling her own tears well up, she hurriedly blinked them away, wiping her eyes just in case.

Logan saw Ellie try to hide her tears and he was rocked to his core, fighting the urge to hold her. To comfort her. The Ellie he'd known had never been so emotional or sentimental. She'd been determined and strong, batting away the troubles of life with a confident smile on her face and a *you can't hurt me* shield.

It was something he'd always admired about her— especially when her father had become sick and needed that heart transplant. He'd marvelled at her stoic attitude, amazed at her strength as her father's health had continued to dwindle until the call eventually came to say that there was a heart for him.

Back then he would have crumbled under such similar circumstances, but thankfully his parents had been blessed with fine health. Something they were taking full advantage of now, in their retirement years, travelling the globe. The last he'd heard from them they'd been in Bali and had sent him a postcard of the beach there.

Perhaps it was this place? The NICU? It was a stressful environment for anyone to be in. No one wanted their family to need to come here. No one wanted to see babies covered in wires and needing machines to breathe for them, or tubes to feed them. He had to fight the feeling to reach out and wrap his arms around her and soothe her upset.

Trying to remember his own first day on the NICU, Logan thought back to his own emotions and feelings and recalled how apprehensive he'd been, how fragile the babies had seemed, how complicated it had all looked. Had he wanted to cry? No, but...

Then there'd been the day that Rachel was born. And he'd *had* to come here. Not as a doctor, but as a parent...

Perhaps instead of soothing Ellie, he ought to be toughening her up?

'Ellie, could I have a quick word outside?'

He turned to leave, squirting his hands with antiseptic gel as he did so, rubbing the alcohol cleanser into his skin and waiting for her to join him. His heart was thudding, and he knew he'd sounded stern, but he hadn't been able to help it. Her being here had thrown him into turmoil.

Ellie closed the door quietly behind her and looked at him questioningly.

'I know this is a difficult place to be,' he said, searching for the right words, not wanting to come across as harsh. 'But it's best for everyone if the medical staff—doctors, nurses and assistants—maintain some kind of emotional distance.'

'Yes, you're right.'

He almost didn't hear her whispered reply, so determined was he to make sure that she understood. 'You can't get attached in here. You can care—just not too much. Or a job like this could destroy you. Do you understand?'

She frowned. 'Is that how *you* do it? By being emotionally distant?'

Was she referring to now? Or to the past? He couldn't quite tell. One way it would seem like a genuine enquiry, the other like a slight. A comment on an inherent fault in his being. But he refused to apologise for either.

'It's the only way to survive. So why don't you take a moment to regroup and then join me in Bay Two? There's a case of gastroschisis I think you should see.'

He watched her go, wondering. Had he been too sharp? Too terse? He didn't want to be. Having her back with him like this was…*wonderful.*

It reminded him of how much he'd missed her.

Ellie stared at her reflection in the mirror, angry at herself for allowing her weakness to escape. She wanted to blame Logan, but she couldn't. She'd wanted him to treat her like any other medical student and he was. He was simply doing his job, and if she'd got emotional in any other ward her mentor would have advised her to maintain her distance there, too.

No. This was her own damned fault. Her own damned emotions. She slammed her hand against the sink in frustration, shaking her head, keeping eye contact with herself as she gave herself a really good telling-off.

Get a grip! You're stronger than this. Do you want Logan, of all people, to think of you as incapable?

Nothing had ever been able to bring her down like this. *Nothing!*

Until Samuel. And then something had changed within her. The floodgates of emotion had opened and it seemed that now every little thing could bring her to tears. Films, books... Emotional adverts—especially all those Christmas ones that told a little story. Or the ones begging for money for starving children, or children with no clean water to drink. Something about their faces... The sorrowful music... The silent tears that spoke of a pain that couldn't be heard. She felt it all like daggers in her heart, making her feel useless and hopeless. Weak and pathetic.

Her mum had told her she would change when she became a mum herself and she'd been right.

Ellie grabbed a couple of paper towels and dabbed at her face until it was dry. Then she took a couple of deep breaths to steady herself. To calm down. She couldn't afford a moment like this again.

'Right, then, Ellie. You can do this, all right?' she said aloud, and out of nowhere came a memory of something she'd read about standing in the 'power pose'. Wide-legged stance, hands on hips, shoulders back, chin raised. Like a superhero. How it could instil belief and confidence.

So she did that for a moment, because it was easier than having to do some kind of *haka*, which would have been noisier and slightly more embarrassing.

Her reflection smiled back at her.

The power pose was working.

Accepting his place at medical school had been a double-edged sword for Logan. His unconditional offer from Edinburgh had been fantastic, but it had also been difficult. Becoming a doctor was all he'd ever wanted to do. His parents were doctors, and he'd known he'd wanted to do that all his life.

He just hadn't expected that when it happened he'd have to leave behind the woman he loved.

She'd been sitting on his bed, flicking through a magazine, completely unaware that he had momentous news to share.

'I checked UCAS today.'

She'd looked up, dropped the magazine. Sat up straight. 'And?'

'I got an unconditional offer.'

Her face had lit up and she'd screamed with delight, bouncing on his bed as if it was a trampoline before jumping off and throwing her arms around him. 'That's amazing!'

He'd held her tightly, inhaling the scent of her hair, trying to take in every detail about her. Knowing he had to tell her the next part. The difficult part.

'It's Edinburgh.'

He'd felt her freeze in his arms.

She'd pulled back to look at him, confused. *'Edinburgh? I thought you applied to colleges here in London?'*

'I did. But Edinburgh's the one to offer me a place. Remember we went up there on the train with Mum and Dad for that interview day?'

'But I thought that you said it was too far away?'

'I did, but…' And then he'd felt a small surge of anger that he was having to defend this. 'We can still see each other. It just won't be as often as we'd like.'

'No. It won't be.'

He'd looked away. Not happy to see the look of hurt on her face. He didn't enjoy seeing her sad. 'We can make it work,' he'd offered, hoping that they could.

They were so young to have fallen in love, and they were being thrown by this, and he hadn't been sure what the best course of action would be to stop her from hurting.

After he'd left—after he'd spent his first term away—he'd felt their separation more keenly. When he'd spoken to her on the phone he'd been able to hear the pain in her voice. How much she'd missed him…how much he'd missed her.

But what could he have done about it? He'd been so

busy! Inundated by assignments, lectures and placements, he'd known there was no chance of him travelling all the way back to London, and no way she could come up to him either, because he needed to work.

He'd hated listening to her cry as they said goodbye each time. He'd wanted to do something to ease her pain, to try and make it easier for her, but the distance between them had made it hard. Each phone call they'd shared had been another stab wound. He hadn't been able to wrap his arms around her. He hadn't been able to kiss her or stroke her hair the way he usually would when she was upset.

He'd begun to think about setting her free. About whether he was being cruel to continue with the relationship, knowing that she'd be waiting for him for *years*. Ellie had dreams of her own. How could she follow them if she was waiting for him? He hadn't *wanted* to lose her. He hadn't *wanted* to walk away. What if she met someone else? But he had felt it might be the kindest thing—even if it hurt them both in the short term.

He'd called her on the phone. 'We need to talk.'

A heavy silence. 'About what?'

'About us,' he'd said, quietly. 'I don't think this is working. I've thought about this long and hard, Ellie, and I think it's best if we…'

'If we what?' Her voice had sounded timid.

'If we just stay friends.' It had broken his own heart to say it. To cut the cord. To let her go. But he had done it for her. So she could have a life.

'Why?'

'It's impossible, what we're doing. You're just *waiting for me*, Ellie, and that's wrong. You're waiting for me to finish med school. And even after that I'll have to work, and being a junior doctor is long hours and overtime, day and night shifts all rolled into one. We'd hardly see each other. And then I'd be working hard to get into a specialism, so you'd have to wait for me to finish that. I can't leave you hanging on like this—it's not fair.'

Each word had been like a scar on his heart. He'd loved Ellie so much! But he'd had to do it.

He couldn't expect her to wait for him. They were going to be apart for *five years*! And they were both so young, with so much ahead of them. It had been wrong of him to think that they could do this.

Ellie had cried down the phone, begging and pleading with him to change his mind, and although it pained him to let her go, he'd known it was the right thing for her.

When the call had finally been over, he'd put his head in his hands and just felt exhausted. He'd loved Ellie—he really had. But she needed to live her life, too. Not waste it. And he'd wanted her to be happy. Short-term pain for long-term gain, and if at the end of five years he returned home and the spark was still there then maybe they could revisit what they both wanted.

That was what he'd genuinely thought.

But five years later he'd already met Jo. And she'd been a junior doctor, like him, and she'd understood the life and was going through the same thing, and they'd just clicked, and…

And now Ellie was back and he was in turmoil. His emotions were all over the place at just seeing her.

She still had that long, wavy black hair. It concealed her face now, as she concentrated on getting a butterfly needle into the crook of the baby's arm.

'Adjust the angle. A little lower. That's it.'

The needle slid into position and she attached the va-cutainers to get the required blood samples.

She had steady hands. That was good. And she'd found the vein first time, which was sometimes hard to do on babies because they were so small.

He watched her finish off and cover the needle entry

point with a small wad of cotton wool that she taped into position. 'Okay, get those sent off to Pathology as soon as you've filled in the patient details.'

Ellie gave him a brief smile and he watched her walk away to the desk. Why couldn't he stop staring at her? Just having her there was remarkable, but he found himself wanting to be closer. To touch her. Make sure that she was real.

He'd made the right decision in leaving her years ago—he knew he had. There'd been no other choice.

That was years ago. Nothing you can do about it now except give her the best education you can.

She looked up, caught his eye, and he gave her a brief smile. Fate had thrown them back together again, and if that wasn't some sort of sign that this was a chance for him to make amends then he didn't know what was.

He'd set her free once. Now he would do so again. But this time when she left in a few weeks she would *thank* him.

CHAPTER TWO

'THIS IS LILY MAE BURKE. Born at twenty-seven weeks, she weighed one and a half pounds.'

Ellie gazed down at the tiny baby swamped, it seemed, by wires and tubes, wearing a yellow knitted hat that was almost too big and a nappy that seemed the same. Her eyes were covered by gauze pads and a tube was taped to her mouth, with a thinner one running into her left nostril. She looked lighter than a feather, but she was sleeping peacefully. Someone had placed a pink teddy in the far corner of her incubator.

'What happened?'

'Her mother went into an early labour at twenty-one weeks. They were able to stop the contractions and she went home—only to wake one night a few weeks later to find her bedsheets soaked through and with the urge to push. We couldn't stop the labour a second time.'

'Was it cervical insufficiency?'

'We believe so.'

'How's the mother?'

'Jeanette is here most days—you'll probably meet her later. We've been getting them to do some skin-to-skin therapy, which they both seem to enjoy.'

Skin-to-skin was something Ellie wished *she'd* had the opportunity to do—one thing for Samuel before he...

The thought almost made the tears come, but there was no room for that here. She needed to hold it together.

Logan moved on to the next incubator. 'This is Aanchal Sealy. A twin born at twenty-eight weeks. He's the bigger twin and suffered from Twin-to-Twin Transfusion Syndrome. Do you know what that is?'

Ellie nodded. 'A condition that can affect identical twins who share a placenta. One twin gets more blood volume than the other.'

He nodded. Pleased. 'That's right. And alongside Aanchal is her sister Devyani—the smaller twin.'

'By how much?'

'Two whole pounds.'

'That's a lot.'

'It is. Do you know the mortality rate?'

She shook her head. 'No.'

'Sixty to one hundred percent. Do you know the dangers for each twin?'

She thought for a moment. Before coming here she'd tried to read a few of her textbooks and learn about some of the more common conditions she might come across. 'Er...the bigger twin could have heart problems.'

'That's right. What kind?'

'Heart failure.' She tried to sound sure of her answers.

'Good—you've been doing your homework.'

'Did the mother have surgery before the birth to try and adjust the blood-flow?'

'Yes, she did. An umbilical cord occlusion to try and ligate the cord and interrupt the flow of blood between the two foetuses. It has an eighty-five percent survival rate, but a five percent chance of causing cerebral palsy.'

'Does Aanchal or Devyani have cerebral palsy?'

'We can't be sure just yet.'

Logan moved on to the fourth and final baby in this room. 'And this fine fellow is Matthew Wentworth, born at thirty weeks. He's had a few problems with his oxygen levels, so we're keeping him in a high-flow oxygen box.'

Matthew was much bigger than the others. He almost looked healthy in comparison, but she knew that looks could be deceptive.

She looked about the room—at the equipment, the machines. It was all so overwhelming. So frightening.

Samuel had never made it to a room such as this. But she wished that he had. Because if he'd made it there he might have had a chance.

These babies—they all had a chance at life. Hope was still alive for each and every one of them, and she envied them—then felt guilty for doing so. The parents of these babies probably wished they'd never had to come here, and here she was wishing she'd had the chance to. Wasn't that terrible?

Logan's dark brown eyes were staring into her soul, as if trying to read her, and she had to look away. The intensity of his gaze was too much. He'd looked at her like that before, but back then she'd been able to settle into his arms, or kiss him, or squeeze him tight. Not now, though.

How did he cope with this? Seeing all these babies who could grow up with disabilities, knowing how hard their lives and the lives of their parents might be. How did he cope, knowing that? Where did he find the strength?

What if there was an emergency? What if one of the many alarms on these incubators started to sound? What then? Would she be able to stay and watch as they tried to fight for a child's life?

I can do this. I've already survived the worst that life can throw at me and I'm still standing.

'How do you do it?' she asked him. 'Deal with this every day?'

'It's my job.'

'I know…but why choose *this* as a specialism?'

He looked around them at the incubators, at the babies, his gaze softening as he stared at their tiny bodies. 'They're so helpless, these babies. How could I ever walk away from them? Choose something else? They can't talk—they can't say what they need. You have to know. You have to be certain of what you're doing and have conviction in your actions. These babies need us. Once I'd spent a rotation here I knew I wouldn't ever want to do anything else.'

He had a faraway look in his eyes and she got the feeling that he wasn't just talking about the babies here. He meant something else. Something she wasn't privy to.

Would she always be a stranger in his life now? Or would her time here create a friendship between them so that they could go back to talking to each other about anything, the way they'd used to?

She'd missed him so much after he'd left for medical school. He'd broken her heart, and as well as losing her boyfriend she'd also lost her best friend. There'd been so much she'd missed telling him in the days after he'd broken it off. And she'd hated that empty feeling she'd felt inside because she couldn't just pick up the phone and tell him what was going on in her life.

'It's lunch. You should take the opportunity to eat whilst you can. I'd like you to have enough strength for surgery this afternoon.'

'I'm going into *surgery*?'

'Just to observe. We're hoping to help the gastroschisis baby get all her organs back in her abdomen, where they should be.'

She nodded. 'That's brilliant news.'

'Be back for two o clock.'

Ellie decided to offer an olive branch—to try and make things less awkward. 'You could join me? It would be good to catch up, wouldn't it?'

She saw the indecision in his eyes. 'Maybe another time. I have someone I need to see.'

'Oh, right. Okay.'

And she watched him walk away.

Perhaps hoping for friendship was hoping for too much?

Logan sat opposite his daughter, smiling as he listened to her tell him about blood. Specifically how many pints there were in the body and what constituents made it.

'Plasma, red blood cells, white blood cells, platelets…' She listed them off, holding her fingers out in front of her as she counted and explained their jobs.

It was a topic that anyone might talk about in a hospital and not have anyone stare, but here in a small coffee shop, just down the road from the hospital, his six-year-old daughter Rachel was drawing a few looks from some older members of the community, who appeared to be a little disturbed at her topic of conversation.

He was used to it, of course. This was one of Rachel's favourite topics. The human body and how it worked— its components and what jobs they did. It was something she'd become fascinated by ever since she'd truly begun to understand that her mother had died, and her autism had sent her down a road of trying to understand *why* her mother's body had failed.

He'd found it quite morbid to begin with. Disturbing and upsetting. So he got why strangers might find it odd. But he almost found comfort in it now, the same way Rachel did, as they settled in to a familiar, reassuring conversation in which there were no surprises and Rachel could control it, knowing the outcome.

First she would talk about blood. Then she would talk about the heart. And then she would talk about what stopped a heart and specifically what happened after the heart stopped beating.

He could see so much of her mother in her features. Rachel had Jo's eyes. Blue, like the sky on a clear, hot summer's day. And her hair was the colour of straw—not dark, like his. Sometimes when she talked, happily chatting away about her favourite subject, he would see Jo in her and would suddenly become aware of his loss—almost as if it was fresh once again—and he would have to take a moment just to breathe and remind himself that it had been years ago.

He felt guilty about Jo. He'd loved her—he was sure of that. But had it been the kind of love he'd felt for Ellie?

Ellie was from years ago and now she'd come back into his life. Jo would never come back, but Ellie had. He wondered what she would make of Rachel? Of him being a father?

She'd asked him why he did the job he did, but he'd not been able to tell her the whole truth. That in every child he tried to save he saw Rachel. That with every baby rushed to his department he recalled what it had felt like to be a lost parent, trailing in afterwards, hoping and praying that someone had the expertise to fix his child and make everything all right.

He'd have given his own life for Rachel, so he knew *exactly* what all those parents felt when they walked through into The Nest. Terrified and afraid…making bargains with God. He had an insight that the other doctors in Neonatal didn't have, and that was why he did this job. That was why he chose to be a mentor and teach medical students— because they needed more doctors who could save these tiny babies. To give these brand-new baby humans a future. To give them time to enjoy life.

He'd never expected he would see Ellie again, even though he'd moved back to London. So much had happened in their time apart he'd figured she wouldn't want him walking back into her life. They'd be moving in different circles. London was such a vast place and he'd just assumed she would have moved on.

Back then she'd talked about travelling the globe, seeing the world, and he'd hoped that by setting her free he would have helped her do that. Yet now she was training to become a doctor. What had provoked that?

Life hadn't even touched her. Except, maybe, for her eyes. Those beautiful eyes of hers, a cloudy blue, seemed to look right into his soul. Her eyes told a story and he wondered if it was a story he wanted to hear? She looked a little sad. The brightness and optimism that had flowed from her, that he had once enjoyed, was gone, and in its place was a reserve he had never seen there before.

His own life had thrown trauma at him in the years they had been apart. What had happened to *her*? What had she lived through—if anything?

Ellie had seemed hesitant. Was it *him*? Was it meeting him again after all these years? Perhaps, it was just shock and surprise.

He'd wanted to reach out when he came back, but it had already been five long years then, and life had got in the way, and as his life had progressed with Jo he'd felt sure that it was better for both of them if he kept his distance. He'd told himself that she would have moved on too, and that getting in touch would simply be reopening old wounds. It would have seemed odd to get back in touch just to cause her more heartache...to stir up old feelings that she must have moved on from.

He'd not wanted to seem as if he was rubbing her face in it. Not that he'd suspected in any shape or form that she was single and still waiting for him, anyway. Ellie was beautiful. He'd hoped that she'd found someone, too.

He sipped at his tea and smiled at his beautiful daughter as she continued to detail the areas of the heart. Atria. Ventricles. Mitral valve. Tricuspid valve. He heard the way she always paused before saying *sinus node* and wondered, as he always did, if she would become a doctor one day.

'And then…' she paused, considering, looking up at him. It was a strange, unexpected break in her routine. 'Daddy, how do you break someone's heart?'

He almost choked on his lunch. He had to cough, wipe his mouth on a napkin. He leaned forward, wondering where the question had come from? 'Why?'

'This girl at Verity's said that her dad had broken her mother's heart.' There was another pause as she frowned. 'How do you *do* that? The heart isn't made of glass, or china. It's muscle. It's meant to be strong, not weak.'

How *did* you break a heart?

I bet a lot of us could answer this one.

Ellie was putting on scrubs, preparing for surgery with Logan. She'd spent her lunch break reading up about gastroschisis as she'd tried to eat a sandwich, finding herself falling down rabbit holes of research as she often did, reading about one situation and sparking an interest in another.

The baby in question had a silo pouch currently covering her intestines, and she knew that after the surgery she would remain in NICU for several weeks. The intestines had been floating in amniotic fluid for months, so they would be swollen and not working very well. The baby would only be discharged once she was taking feeds well, putting on weight and excreting normally.

The surgery today was to insert the last remaining part of the intestines, remove the silo pouch and repair the defect that had caused the gastroschisis in the first place.

She was just putting her clothes into a locker when one of the nurses entered.

'Hi, it's Ellie, right? Clare. Very pleased to meet you.' Clare shook her hand. 'Is this your first surgery?'

'My first on this placement.'

'You've done some before? That's good. So I don't have to worry about you fainting, then?'

Ellie smiled. 'No.'

'Dr Riley is a good surgeon. He'll teach you a lot.'

'He already has.'

There must have been something in her tone, because Clare cocked her head to one side.

'Do you know each other?'

'From years ago. We knew each other when we were young.'

'Oh. Right. What was he like back then? Still handsome?'

Ellie tried not to smile, but couldn't help it. 'Oh, yes.'

'I *knew* it. I bet every girl in school was after him.'

'I only met him at college, doing A levels.'

'The wild years, huh?' Clare stripped out of her clothes and got into a set of scrubs. 'Before he settled down?'

Ellie looked at Clare. He'd 'settled down'? What did *that* mean? Was he married? Living with someone? For some strange reason the knowledge was disappointing. Almost upsetting. But what had she expected? That he was still single? She guessed she might have *assumed* he'd be with someone, but as she hadn't known for sure it hadn't hurt. But now...? Now that she was being told for definite...? Well, that was an entirely different beast.

She didn't want to appear to Clare as if she didn't know, so she went along with it. 'Yeah.'

'It's kind of sweet how he goes to eat lunch with Rachel when he can.'

Rachel. She's called Rachel.

Ellie slowly wrapped up her hair and placed it inside a surgical cap carefully, taking her time as she allowed this new nugget of knowledge to seep into her brain.

Rachel.

He meets her for lunch as often as he can.

That's kind of romantic. They must love each other very much.

And she felt jealous. A sudden wave of jealousy hit her smack in the solar plexus, making her feel almost dizzy and faint with the strength of it. Jealous that he had someone to love. Jealous that he had someone he could wrap his arms around and hold. Jealous that someone else now held the heart she herself had once thought was hers.

'Yes. It's very sweet,' she said, thinking it was anything but.

He could feel her watching him. Those wide blue eyes were watching his every move from over her surgical face mask. He felt tempted to look up and see, but after his lunch with Rachel and her questions about breaking someone's heart he felt guilty about doing so. He knew exactly how he'd broken Ellie's.

Luckily there was an operation to concentrate on: getting the last of Baby Darcy's intestines back into her body and the hole in her abdominal wall repaired. This would hopefully be her final surgery and would get rid of the horrible silo bag that she'd had attached to her since birth.

'How was Rachel?' she asked.

His hands paused. How the hell did she know about Rachel? He hadn't told her a thing. Had she spotted him at lunchtime with his daughter? Or was this just a case of the damned hospital grapevine at work? Probably the latter. However, he still felt irritated by it. That he hadn't been the one to tell her. And this was hardly the place to be bringing up something so damned personal!

'I'm not sure that's what we need to be concentrating on right now, Miss Jones.'

There and then he knew there was a change in the atmosphere in the operating room. Knew that those around him were all looking at him with questioning glances. Because normally he was happy to talk about his daughter and her progress. He was proud of Rachel.

He met her gaze. 'I'm sorry—that was rude of me. Rachel was very well, thank you.'

The tension eased somewhat and he continued with his work, even though he still felt bad. And he'd called her *Miss Jones*. Talk about creating an issue when there didn't need to be one! Now she'd probably spend the rest of the day calling him Dr Riley rather than Logan. He needed to change that. And quickly.

'Can you see what I'm doing here, Ellie? More light, please,' he instructed the theatre technician, standing to one side.

Ellie moved forward to see better.

'What are the complications of a silo—do you know?'

'Er…infection and fascial dehiscence.'

'Good. You've been reading up.' He looked up at her and smiled. 'On your lunch break?'

He was pleased to see her eyes crease at the corners, indicating a smile back.

She nodded. 'Best time to cram.'

'Removing the silo now… What are we looking for?'

'We're checking that the bowel looks healthy.'

'Yes. I'm going to stretch the defect now, to reduce this final section of bowel.' He carefully placed his fingers inside the defect, checking all around, before pushing the last of the bowel inside. 'Ellie would you like to irrigate the bowel and abdomen?'

She nodded quickly and he could tell that she was grateful to do something towards the surgery.

He organised the skin for closure, starting opposite the umbilicus, sealing off small bleeds with the cautery and separating the fascia, explaining what he was doing and why.

'I'm creating a purse string suture. Irrigate the wound

again, please.' *Good.* She was doing well. Her hands were steady and sure. No hesitation. 'Now I'll make a new umbilicus.' He created another purse string on the outer skin.

'It's so quick,' she said, glancing up at the clock. 'Barely twenty-five minutes.'

'And Baby remained stable throughout, which is the best thing,' he said, stepping away from the table and pulling off his gloves. 'How did you find that, Ellie?'

She pulled off her surgical mask as they went into the scrub room and her face was a mask of awe and wonder. 'Amazing! You made it look easy.'

He basked in her praise. 'You might be doing it yourself one day.'

Ellie nodded. 'Maybe.'

'Have you decided on a specialism yet?'

'I'm not sure. I'd like to do transplants—I know that.'

That was a good choice—though he was a little disappointed she didn't want to choose his speciality. 'General surgery? That's good.'

'You sound like you don't approve.'

'I do. Is that because of your dad?' Her father had had a heart transplant; he remembered that.

Ellie looked away. 'I guess...' She began washing her hands.

Logan stood watching her for a moment. He'd never felt so far away from her as he did at that moment. As if she was unreachable and he didn't know why. Maybe it was the way he'd spoken to her earlier? He wanted to put that right. Hated being at odds with her.

'I'm sorry about how rude I was to you at the beginning of surgery.'

She glanced at him. Gave a brief smile. 'It's okay. I was being nosy and it wasn't very professional of me.'

'Not nosy at all. It's just... I wanted to be the one to tell you about Rachel.'

'No one was gossiping about you.'

'I know. It's just…she's my daughter and I'm very protective of her.'

Ellie turned to look at him. 'Your *daughter*?'

'Yes.'

She laughed. 'I thought she was your—' She stopped speaking, blushed and grabbed some paper towels to dry her hands with. 'How old is she?'

'Six. Going on sixty.'

Ellie smiled and pulled off her cap. 'I'd love to meet her one day.'

'She has Asperger's,' he blurted out, not sure why he was explaining, but it was out now. However, Rachel having Asperger's was only one part of who she was—he shouldn't have labelled her as if that was *all* she was. 'And she's sweet and kind. And many other wonderful things besides.'

Ellie smiled. 'She sounds lovely.'

The rest of the day had passed almost in a blur. Doing half-hourly obs on the gastroschisis baby… Running around after the others… She hadn't got to see Logan at all after they'd done a consult in A&E. She'd wanted to talk to him more, after her little mistake about who Rachel was, but she'd ended up going home without seeing him again.

His *daughter*! *Not* his wife, or partner, or whatever she'd suspected her to be. But that still meant there was a mother to his child. Where was *she*? How come he didn't meet his partner for lunch?

She could be busy. Working hard.

I don't even know what she does. She could be a high-flying surgeon like Logan.

Of course she would be. Logan liked successful people. He'd been surrounded by them his entire life. Both his parents were doctors, he had an uncle who practised law, and a cousin who had created his first app aged just sixteen and was probably a multi-millionaire by now.

I'm happy for him.

She forced a smile to her face, telling herself this was true, but she was having a hard time with it. A small, self-ish part of her had wanted him to be stuck in some kind of limbo, too. Her life had been ripped apart and now she was starting again—why wasn't he? She felt so far behind everyone else now. Constantly playing catch-up.

But why did she constantly give herself a hard time? Was it because everything she tried failed? Her relation-ship with Logan had collapsed out of nowhere. Being a mother had ended tragically. Her marriage to Daniel had collapsed too. Her business had failed.

But now she was trying to be a doctor, and there was no way she was going to fail at *that*!

Somehow, and without remembering climbing the stairs, she found herself in the doorway to Samuel's bed-room. Everything was as she'd left it. In limbo. Half done. Two of the walls still needed painting. The crib was still in its flat-pack. A lonely teddy bear sat in the windowsill, waiting to be loved.

It all just looked so…*sad*.

But what was the point in finishing?

Ellie closed the door and went back downstairs to make herself some dinner. She'd barely had time to eat today, what with the surgery, and then rounds, and then she and Logan had been called down to A&E to assess a patient who might have been going into early labour. Thankfully, she hadn't. The maternity unit had managed to stop her contractions with tocolytics and Ellie had got to inject her with steroids to help with maturing the baby's lungs, just in case.

It had felt good today to be hands-on—first in surgery, then doing obs during rounds, and then later with that emergency patient. She finally felt as if she was moving *forward*—that she was achieving something. And Logan was actually a very good teacher.

She remembered how he'd drilled her on the way back up in the lift.

'Why do we inject with corticosteroids?'

'It helps the baby's lungs mature.'

'What else?'

'Brain function.'

'What would happen if we didn't?'

'An early delivery would mean the baby might be more likely to suffer respiratory distress syndrome or other complications.'

'Side effects of giving steroids?'

'I'm not sure.'

'Studies have shown that there are no adverse effects on the baby, but if more than one course is given studies do show that some babies can be a little smaller, though there are no long-term consequences. How far apart do we give the injections?'

'Twenty-four hours.'

Standing in that closed confined space with him had made her realise how her body still reacted to him. It was as if it remembered. As if it wanted to feel him against her once again. It had been a terrifying and delicious feeling all at once.

She liked it that he drilled her with questions—even over some of the simpler things they did. He was being thorough, making sure she understood the basics—because if you didn't understand the reasoning behind those, how could you understand the more complicated issues? And his questions took her thoughts away from how it had felt to hold him. To kiss him. To have him kiss her back…

She liked being tested. Liked getting the answers right. It felt good. And distractions were helpful.

Downstairs, as her ready meal of lasagne cooked in the microwave, she picked up her book on neonatal medicine and began reading from where she'd stopped at breakfast that morning.

She was happy that Logan had a daughter. That he had a happy, healthy child. He was lucky to have someone to hold in his arms.

She missed that. Being able to hold someone. To squeeze them tight, love them, knowing that they loved you back just as much.

He was lucky.

Very lucky indeed.

CHAPTER THREE

'*Don't touch me!*' Rachel screamed.

Logan backed off, hands palm upwards. How had he forgotten? She didn't like bodily contact, she didn't like to be touched, and he'd stupidly, unthinkingly, bent down to kiss the top of her head as he'd left her at Verity's.

Rachel was looking at him like a cornered animal, scared, her eyes darting all around. His gut twisted to see her so upset. And he'd been the one to cause it.

'I'm sorry. I didn't mean it. I forgot. I'm sorry.' He turned to Verity. 'I'm going to be late—are you going to be okay?'

'We'll be fine. You go. She'll calm down.'

He nodded, smiling a thank-you. Verity was an absolute godsend for him. A childminder who specialised in children with autism and special needs, and she was just down the road from the hospital, too. She ran a strict ship, full of routine, and all the kids enjoyed it during the long summer school holidays, but she also allowed him to turn up sometimes at lunch, to take Rachel out for the hour, so he could see her in the day.

It wouldn't be long until she was back at school, and then that would change, but for now he could do it. He hoped that if he got to see her later today she would have forgotten his little misdemeanour and they'd be able to go back to talking about blood, as they often did.

He gave his daughter a wave from the door, but she didn't see it, still in the process of calming down from his thoughtless contact. Briefly he wondered what it would be like to give his daughter a hug goodbye, like other parents did when they dropped their children off at school.

I guess I'll never know.

As he walked to work he thought back to when Rachel was a baby, and how it had felt to hold her then. Even then she'd cried, and he'd thought it was because she was crying for the mother she didn't have. That he wasn't doing it right. That he was a bad father who couldn't soothe his own daughter.

She'd been way behind on her developmental milestones, hadn't talked until she was two and a half, and because he was a doctor it had been incredibly frustrating for him. Until a paediatrician had suggested she might be autistic. Then it had been as if a veil had been lifted, and he'd finally understood her.

It had been better for Rachel after that. Not for him, though.

When he got into The Nest he saw Ellie standing at Reception, laughing with a nurse, and he envied her her simple life. Carefree. No children. Starting a new chapter in her life.

He was suddenly hit by a wave of nostalgia, of longing for how it had used to be, sitting in his bedroom, laughing and chatting, holding her in his arms, loving the feel of her, the warmth of her smile, the way that she laughed. It was infectious, her laugh. He'd like to hear it again. But most of all he missed his friend, and having her this close again was agonising, because he wanted to tell her everything.

About Rachel…about this morning at Verity's.

About Jo.

He ached for the *ease* that they'd once had.

'Ellie?'

She looked up, saw him and smiled, and it felt just like before.

He was out here in the world, feeling all alone, and he knew that she had once loved him. Cared deeply. She'd listen. He knew it. He needed someone in his corner.

Up close, she looked to him as if she was waiting for instructions. Keen. Eager to learn. Ready for whatever came next.

Such beautiful blue eyes. So trusting.

And suddenly he couldn't do it. Couldn't burden her. No matter how much he wanted to. He had to do this alone, as he always had.

'I want you on Darcy's case today. The gastroschisis baby? She's all yours. I want hourly observations. Report them back to me. Her Mum will be in later and I thought you could get her to give Darcy a bed bath. She'd like that. Get her hands-on. Parents like contact with their children.'

She looked pleased. Thrilled, in fact, to have a case of her own. 'I will. Thank you. Are you okay?'

He nodded. 'Tough morning.'

'With Rachel?'

How to answer? He didn't want to blame his daughter for what had been his own mistake. 'No, it was me. I screwed up.' He grimaced.

She smiled. 'I'm sure your wife will forgive you,' she said, and she turned to go and check on her patient.

She doesn't know about Jo.

He sank down into a seat, his head in his hands, knowing he had to tell her. But how to do so without coming across as if he was looking for sympathy? Because he wasn't. He was looking for…*understanding.* Ellie had used to have that in bucketloads. She'd been a good listener.

He recalled the time that he'd been so annoyed at not passing his driving test first time, convinced that the test invigilator had been unnecessarily strict, and she had listened patiently as he'd ranted and raved about the unfairness of it all.

And then another time she'd held his hand and listened as he told her stories about his grandmother, when she'd passed away. She'd even gone with him to the funeral and not once had she let go of him. Always there. Always ready. And when they'd stood by the graveside and he'd been bereft of words she'd stood with him, her head upon his shoulder, just waiting for him to be ready to go. She'd laid one hand upon his arm, gently stroking it, just letting him know that she was there for him.

She'd always supported him—and what had he done for her? He'd abandoned her. Left her behind. Disappeared for years and not got in touch. And now he expected her to still be the friend she'd once been? How selfish was that? He'd never put his needs before hers.

He placed his bag and his jacket in his office and looked at the single photo on his desk. One of Jo. She'd been facing away from him on the beach promenade and he'd lifted his camera just as she'd turned to look at him, one hand behind her ear, holding back her hair, which the wind was blowing everywhere. It was a perfect shot. Her smile captured in an instant. Her eyes looking directly at him, full of love and affection.

I failed you, too. Never loved you the way that I should have.

Was he destined to fail all the women in his life? Ellie. Jo. Rachel. When would he ever get it right?

Draping his stethoscope around his neck, he sucked in a deep breath and tried to pull himself together. He might screw up personally, but professionally he had lots of little babies depending upon him—and that he knew he could get right!

At least he would try.

* * *

'She shouldn't be here.'

Ellie looked up in surprise. Darcy's mother had arrived, entering the ward almost silently. She had been about to change Darcy's nappy, but if her mother was here perhaps she would like to do it instead?

Logan's words about parents needing contact with their babies rang in her ears, so she closed the incubator and stepped back. 'No one expects their baby to come to the NICU.'

'I didn't mean that. I meant by rights she shouldn't be *here*. At all.'

Ellie frowned. 'How do you mean?'

'Darcy's father is a married man. I didn't know that when I met him. I thought he was free and single, like me. Perfect. The perfect guy. I thought we were in love... that things were moving forward for us. Then I found out I was pregnant, and when I told him he told me he was already married. Happily!'

Darcy's mother looked up at Ellie with a rueful gaze.

'If Patrick hadn't cheated on his wife then Darcy wouldn't be here, and I wouldn't have to sit day by day beside her, wondering if my baby is going to be okay. Do you know, when I found out she had gastroschisis I thought I was being punished? For cheating.'

Ellie didn't know what to say. She gazed at Darcy's mother, seeing the hurt, the pain, the loss of her dream. The dream of having a perfectly healthy child with a man she'd thought loved her. Instead she was here alone, coping with the stresses that came with a child in Neonatal Intensive Care. All alone.

She wasn't sure of the best way to answer as a medical student. Perhaps if she were a doctor then she would know the professional way to respond. Perhaps there was a class instructing students on the best way to manage something like this?

But she did know how to respond as a parent. She understood the emotions of loss and fear and loneliness. So she stepped around the incubator and pulled the woman towards her in a hug. 'It's okay. It's going to be okay. I don't know what the future holds for Darcy, but right now she's doing really well. The operation worked wonderfully, there were no complications, and there's no reason at all why Darcy shouldn't grow up with any problems at all. She's sleeping and she's breathing well. She's a good weight, and right now she's got a wet nappy that we can change. Do you want to do it?'

Darcy's mother nodded, a tear slipping down her cheek. 'Yes. I would. Thank you. And I'm sorry for just blurting that out. I do that sometimes.'

'You're under stress. It's understandable to reach out.'

The woman nodded.

'I'm Ellie, by the way. It's nice to meet you.'

'Gemma. Thank you. You're very kind.'

'I just understand, that's all.' Ellie passed Gemma a paper tissue from the box that sat on the shelf beside her. She watched as Gemma dabbed at her eyes and blew her nose. 'It's difficult to see them like this, isn't it?'

'It's not how you imagine your first few days as a parent.'

'No... Do you understand all that's going on? Is there something you're not sure of? I could get Dr Riley who performed the operation to come and talk to you again.'

'Oh, I wouldn't want to bother him. I'm sure he's busy.'

'Never too busy to reassure a parent. Let's change Darcy's nappy and then I'll fetch him for you.'

'Thanks.'

Ellie fetched the items they would need and then helped Gemma change Darcy's nappy, lifting her gently to insert the new nappy underneath, and then she performed her first set of observations on her patient. Happy that she was stable, she set off to find Logan.

Hopefully he would be able to reassure Darcy's mother that she was doing okay and that there was a plan in place for any possible contingencies. Often in hospital patients were left waiting, not knowing what was going on, and their frustration was often passed on to their friends and relations. They often felt as if they were not privy to the doctor's decisions and processes, and Ellie knew it was important that Gemma felt that she was a part of that. Part of Darcy's progress. It would help to make her feel more in control, knowing what was happening to her daughter and why.

She spotted Logan on the phone and waited for him to finish his conversation so that she could ask him to talk to Gemma.

He looked up at her and met her gaze, and she felt the familiar stir of attraction in her gut. This man was part of her past—somewhere she didn't tend to visit—and it felt surprisingly strange that he was now going to be a large part of her immediate future, responsible for her success in this new endeavour. She had vowed never to let another man have control of her life again, and yet here she was.

She gave him a polite smile and waited.

It's only six weeks. Not long at all.

He put down the phone. 'You okay?'

'Yes. I have Darcy's first observations, but I was also wondering if you could come and talk to her mother? She's a little upset and I think she needs a bit of reassuring.'

He nodded. 'Okay. Why don't you come with me? It will be good for you to see how we handle situations like these.'

She didn't tell him that she already knew. That she had once been that tearful mother. Lost and alone. She didn't want to tell him that though his words would bring a modicum of comfort to the mother, they would never be enough until Gemma's baby was out of the NICU, healthy, and in Gemma's arms at home, living a normal life.

She dutifully followed him back into the room and quietly listened as Logan did his best.

He was good—she could give him that. He sat Gemma down and carefully explained exactly where Darcy was in her treatment. Then he explained how Darcy had ended up in her situation, and that it wasn't her fault in any way, and then he took her over to the incubator and carefully, slowly, went through what each of the machines was doing, what all the tubes were for, what everything was measuring and when he expected to see some improvement. He made sure that Gemma understood that Darcy was strong and was doing as well as could be expected at that moment in time, so soon after surgery.

'Does that help?' he asked finally.

Gemma nodded. 'Yes.'

'If you ever feel you don't know what's happening, please ask any one of us and we will do what we can to reassure you. I don't ever want you to feel that you can't ask. All of us here are dedicated to making sure that Darcy goes home with you a happy, healthy little girl.'

He placed his hand upon her shoulder and gave her a reassuring smile.

Ellie followed him out of the room, using a squirt of hand sanitiser as she passed it at the door and rubbing her hands together. 'You were very good with her,' she said. 'I think she felt a little better at the end.'

'Communication is key here. In this unit there can't be any misunderstandings. The parents are often at their wits' end and we need to make sure they know what's going on with their children. Can you imagine what it would be like to be in that sort of limbo?'

She nodded. This ought to be the perfect moment to

tell him about Samuel. But she felt it would be wrong. She was here to learn, not to get personal. And she thought that if she started it would be incredibly difficult for her to stop. The urge to tell him everything would be almost overwhelming.

I've been there! she wanted to say. *I know how it feels!* And she knew how easy he was to talk to. But they didn't have that kind of relationship any more.

Instead, she just presented him with Darcy's file. 'These are her latest observations. Kidneys are working well.'

He ran his gaze over them. 'What else do they tell us?'

She met his eyes. 'That everything's going as expected.'

He agreed again. But his gaze, as he looked at her, seemed to say something else.

'So, tell me what you know about the problems faced by babies born prematurely.'

Ellie thought for a moment. 'There are many problems. The earlier they are born, the more likely they are to have difficulties.'

'Such as?'

Logan was determined to keep asking her questions about work. If he asked professional questions then he wasn't telling her personal stuff she didn't need to hear.

'Problems with breathing, temperature control.'

'Good. What else?'

'Developmental delays. Intestinal issues, infection, hearing loss?'

He nodded, pleased. She knew more than some others they had in the department. In fact, she was doing really well. Working hard, looking after Darcy, as well as helping out with some of the other patients when called to do so.

'How are you managing the workload? University, placement, assignments?'

She smiled. 'It's a lot, but I'm getting there. Thankfully I don't have any distractions at home.'

He stared at her, intrigued by the small nugget of information she'd offered. 'You still live at home?'

'I moved out years ago. I've been living on my own for some time now.'

On her own.

Logan felt that the next most natural question would be, *Did you never meet anyone?* He hoped she had. Because he didn't want to think she'd been alone. Because surely it was impossible that there hadn't been a significant other in her life? Ellie was beautiful. Kind and caring. Loving.

He felt awkward, as if he somehow still owed her something for the way he had ended things. An explanation? An apology? It didn't feel right, having to be business-like with her. This awkwardness between them was uncomfortable. Once upon a time Logan had felt so at ease whenever he was with Ellie. Now that seemed to be gone, and surprisingly it hurt.

'Still plenty of time for that, I guess.'

She smiled. 'Well, my work and my studies are what's important right now, so…'

'Yes, of course they are. No time for…'

Romance? Anything else?

'No.'

Clare appeared at their sides then. 'I was about to insert the NG tube into Baby Sealy Number One but I thought it might be a good procedure for Ellie to do. What do you think?'

He welcomed the interruption. Their conversation was sending his thoughts into a direction he wasn't sure he wanted them to go. Did he still harbour feelings for Ellie? Of course he did. He felt confused and conflicted around her. But after Jo he'd vowed never to get involved with anyone ever again.

Ellie's different, though, isn't she? I've never stopped loving her.

'That's a great idea. Check Darcy's obs again, and if everything's fine then help Clare, okay?'

Ellie nodded. 'Sounds like a plan.'

'Do you know why we're inserting a tube?' Clare had asked.

'I'm assuming to help with feeds?'

'Aanchal Sealy is only twenty-eight weeks and therefore doesn't yet have a sucking reflex. She has also demonstrated difficulty with swallowing, so a tube going directly into her stomach will help her feed and maintain her weight gain.'

'Okay.'

'Once you've gathered the equipment you need, you must wash your hands. Have you been taught an effective way to do this properly?'

'Yes. We were taught that in our first week.'

'Good. So, with our patient straight, we have to measure the desired length of NG tube to be inserted. We measure from the bridge of the nose to the earlobe, then down to below the xiphisternum. Do you know what that is?'

The xiphisternum? Ellie assumed it was somewhere in the middle of the chest, but where was it exactly? 'No.'

'It's the lowest part of the sternum.' Sarah pointed at the baby's chest. 'Then we lubricate the tip of the tube and insert through the nostril.'

'Okay.'

'You have to hold the baby steady as she might struggle a little as you gently advance the NG tube through the nasopharynx. But this is the most uncomfortable part for the baby, so don't go too slowly.'

Ellie gripped the tube in her hand and steadied her breathing as she advanced it into the baby's nostril. Aanchal squirmed and tried to wriggle, but with Clare holding her firmly she managed to get it in first try!

'That's excellent! Well done. Now, once you get to the right length you can fix the tube to the cheek with a dressing.' She handed Ellie a pre-cut strip of tape. 'Remove the guide wire and you should be done!'

Ellie beamed with pride. Her first neonatal naso-gastric tube! This was what it was all about. Treating patients. Achieving targets. She'd looked in the induction pack that she'd received on her first day here and there was a list of clinical skills that she had to achieve before she left her placement. Cannulas, catheters, basic observations, drawing blood... She was slowly beginning to work through them and get them signed off. It was a real sign of how she was progressing in her career and it reminded her that she needed to focus on that, and not so much on Logan.

'Thanks, Clare.'

'Hey, no problem.'

'How long have you been a neonatal nurse?'

'A few years.'

'You must have seen it all?'

'There are days when you think you can't be surprised any more, but then you are. I guess that's medicine for you.'

'What's been your most difficult case?'

Sarah thought for a moment. 'Dr Riley's daughter.'

Ellie was stunned. *'Rachel?'*

Clare nodded. 'All cases are difficult, but when it's one of your own it's...' She shook her head as if she still couldn't quite believe it. 'She had such a tragic start to her life. Emotions were incredibly high. But that's the way of the world, isn't it? Bad things can happen to anyone.'

Ellie wanted to ask more, but some parents arrived at that moment and Clare got up to greet them and walked away.

Ellie washed her hands, wondering what had happened

to Rachel. What the tragic start to her life had been? If she really wanted to know she would have to ask Logan. But somehow it didn't seem quite right, and she knew she'd keep her questions and her thoughts to herself.

Clearly something bad had happened, but if he wanted her to know wouldn't he tell her?

At the end of the day, Ellie set out for home at the same time as Logan. They travelled down in the lift together and when the doors pinged open looked at each other uncertainly.

'Well, I guess I'll see you tomorrow?'

Ellie nodded. 'Yes. Definitely.'

'Good. Well, have a good night.'

'You, too.'

As he walked away she looked at him. He was drawing up his collar to keep out the light rain that was falling and she wondered what he was walking home to. Perhaps his wife was a good listener and she would help soothe his worries and his cares? They must work as a team, looking after Rachel. Was it difficult? Autism was a spectrum, and she had no idea how affected his daughter was. The mention of Asperger's indicated she was high-functioning, so maybe she was extremely intelligent even if her social cues were a little off.

I wonder who she looks like?

Did his daughter look like him? What would it feel like to see her? To look for those similarities? It had been awesome to see her own features in Samuel's face. Strange, but also powerful. It had bonded him to her in a way she hadn't expected, with such force it had almost taken her breath away. So to lose him so quickly had been...

Ellie pulled her umbrella out of her bag and popped it open. With one last look at Logan's retreating form, she headed in the other direction.

* * *

The baby was small—barely a pound in weight. Ellie stood back as Logan and his team swarmed around their new patient. She watched intently, trying to take it all in. She saw Logan place his stethoscope in his ears and listen to the baby's chest before he began issuing orders.

It was frightening to stand back, knowing that she could do nothing but watch. She wanted to help so much! But all she could do was stay out of the way, hugging the wall.

The team were busy with the new arrival for a good fifteen minutes. At first she thought it all seemed a little chaotic, but the more she watched, the more she noticed that everyone knew exactly what to do and when, and that Logan was leading his team calmly and efficiently. Everybody listened. Everyone respected each other and the jobs they had to do. And when it was over the baby was in an incubator, attached to a ventilator and in a stable condition.

Logan came over to her. 'I'm sorry I didn't get the opportunity to explain what was happening there. Stabilising a patient takes priority over teaching and time was critical.'

'That's okay. I could see that. What happens next?' She looked at the baby, which was pinky red. It looked so small, and she couldn't quite get over the fact that this baby was brand-new—minutes old—already facing a future filled with uncertainties.

'We'll do observations to start with, and then, when mum and dad get up here, we can talk them through what we need to be worrying about. The baby might need a scan.'

Logan went to the sink and began to wash his hands, then dried them with green paper towels.

'A brain scan?'

'To make sure there have been no bleeds on the brain. This patient is critical.'

'Right…'

She didn't know what to do. This sounded serious. So far there'd been no emergencies in the NICU while she'd been there. What would she do? How would she cope if a baby died? Would she be able to hold it together? Somehow she'd have to find the strength, because her thoughts had to be for the baby's parents rather than herself.

She found herself staring at the tiny baby in its incubator, praying silently to herself that he'd make it through.

'These are the difficult moments. They can be hard to witness. If you think you can't handle it, then I'd rather you weren't around when the parents arrive.'

'I can handle it,' she said with determination. 'How do *you* do it?'

His eyes darkened. 'Practice.'

The urge to pull him close was strong. To wrap her arms around him and keep him safe in her arms. The feeling was so strong she almost swayed.

'You okay?' he asked, reaching for her arm.

His hand upon her had a startling effect. As if she was being seared by his touch. She couldn't bear it and pulled herself free. 'I'm fine.'

But her voice was shaky and uncertain and suddenly Logan was staring at her and misreading the situation.

'Better take five minutes. Go on. I can do this.'

'I'm okay, Logan.'

He smiled, his face full of empathy and kindness. 'I know. But take a break anyway.'

Twenty minutes later he found her in the staff room, cradling a mug of tea in her hands that looked as if it had gone cold. She looked troubled, and he felt the need to try and bolster her self-confidence.

'It's okay to get upset.' He sat opposite her, removing

his stethoscope from around his neck and placing it on the table. 'In private, at any rate.'

'How do you *do* it, Logan? How do you look after these tiny babies? After what happened with your daughter?'

He blinked. 'You know about what happened to Rachel?'

'No. Someone said she came here, but not why.'

He nodded, thinking about telling her. He wanted to. And this would be the perfect time to explain everything. Yesterday he had wanted to tell her so much, yet he hadn't wanted to burden her. Maybe now it was time?

'I met Jo when I came back from Edinburgh. We were both junior doctors, and both working in A&E to begin with, so we spent a lot of time together.'

'She's your wife?'

He almost winced at the present tense. 'Jo got pregnant with Rachel. We had a very quick, very small wedding. Both of us wanted to be married before our daughter arrived.'

He glanced at Ellie to gauge how she was reacting to this. She seemed absorbed in the story, so he continued.

'One day we were driving home after a busy shift together and another driver...he had been up all night drinking... ploughed into our vehicle, side-on. He flipped us up, over and over, and the car came to rest on its roof.

'Oh, my God...'

'My seatbelt had jammed. I was hanging upside down. So was Jo, but she...' He paused, seeing the horrific image in his head. 'She had blood trickling down her face...'

Ellie closed her eyes, as if she could feel his hurt and distress. *'Logan...'*

'They got me out first. The firemen. It took them a lot longer to get her out, and by the time they did she was...' He rubbed at his eyes.

In that moment Ellie got up from her chair and came to sit beside him. She draped her arm around his shoulder.

He sank into her, appreciating her warmth. Her comfort.

'There was nothing to be done for Jo, but she was just past twenty-four weeks pregnant and I thought there might be a chance for our daughter. I had to do it. I had to try and give her a chance at life. Just weeks ago I'd seen her at the scan—heart beating, hiccupping. She was a *person*. She was alive and she deserved to live.'

'What did you do?'

'I told them to do a Caesarean.'

He was aware of her silence as she took in this news. He knew that she might disagree with his actions—knew that some people thought it was the wrong thing to do—but he'd already thought of himself as a father, and he'd lost the mother of his child. He wouldn't lose his baby, too. Not when she had the chance to survive.

'You're so brave…' She slipped her hand into his.

He stared at their interlinked fingers for a moment in disbelief that he was holding her hand again. 'I wasn't brave. I was desperate.'

'You did the right thing. You fought for your child. It's what any parent would choose to do. Isn't that what we see every day, here in this place?'

He nodded, staring into her cloudy blue eyes, and allowed himself a moment to lose himself in them.

CHAPTER FOUR

Sitting there peacefully, looking deeply into his eyes, Ellie felt as if time hadn't passed at all. As if they'd never been apart. As if they'd always been like this. Connected. As one.

He felt so right. Comfortable. Familiar. She had to remind herself that they *had* been apart for many years. And that it seemed his life had not been the pleasure cruise she'd imagined it had, but that he'd faced tragedy. Just as she had.

It would be so easy for her to lean forward and kiss him…

The thought made her start. She couldn't allow that to happen.

She stood up abruptly. 'I'll make you a cup of tea.'

He said nothing.

She felt bad for walking away from him, for creating distance, but she had to remind herself that he wasn't hers any more. He wasn't her boyfriend. She was here as his friend and nothing more, and friends sympathised and friends made cups of tea. It was the British way of things. A cure-all for all ills.

If only it was really a cure-all. We could have tea IVs and everyone would get better.

But it wasn't that simple, was it? It never was. The moment they had just shared was over and she had to push him away again. Unreachable. Untouchable. He was just her mentor. Who had shared his story with her.

What, if anything, could she learn from that? That life threw curveballs? That no matter how hard you worked, no matter how much good you did in life, it could all be taken from you in a moment?

As she poured hot water over the teabags she thought of Samuel. How happy she and Daniel had been that she was pregnant. How everything had been going right for them. The business was good. Their home was coming together, its renovations almost finished.

And then the scan had ripped their happy, ordered world apart...

'Here you go.' She placed the mug into his hands and sat opposite him, taking in a huge, steadying breath. *Focus.*

'I'm sorry. I shouldn't have told you all that. But... But a part of me kept telling me that I *ought* to tell you— because, well, because we're friends still, aren't we?'

She nodded.

'And friends don't keep things from each other.'

'No.'

She thought of Samuel. Had the memory of lying there in that theatre bed as the midwife walked away with him in her arms, never to be seen again. Knowing what they were about to do.

The burden of her own secret weighed heavy in her heart. She wanted to tell him. But this was *his* time. His moment. His sad story. She wasn't about to tell him hers. It would come across as if she were trying to say, *You think that's sad? Well, listen to this!*

Not that he *would* think that, of course, but that was how she'd worry that it would come across.

'I'd like you to meet her.' Logan looked across at her, staring intently into her eyes.

She blinked. 'Rachel?'

He smiled. 'Yes. I think you'd like her.'

Meet his daughter? Wow. That was… Hell, she didn't know how the idea of that made her feel. Meeting his daughter would make them more than mentor and student, wouldn't it? She'd be getting involved again. Taking huge steps back into his personal life.

'I don't know, Logan…' she said. But the real reason she had doubts was that she wondered if it would hurt too much. The fact that, despite his tragedy, he still had a child and she didn't. Would it be too much? The jealousy? The envy?

It was a silly fear, and she knew it was silly even as she felt it, but it didn't make it any less real. She was happy for him. She *was*. He had someone. He had survived with someone to love and that was *good*.

'You think it will be overstepping the boundaries?'

'No. Yes. I don't… It's just…' She couldn't think how to voice her concerns.

What would it be like to meet her? To see all the choices he had made after leaving Ellie behind? How he had moved on. How he had lived without her. It would be weird. But also it would make them closer again, and although she wanted that very much, she worried about what it would mean for her future.

She had a purpose. A dream she was chasing. If she got dragged into Logan's orbit again would she remain there? Or be able to break away?

'You'd get on, you and Rachel. She's funny. She's intelligent. The most clever, articulate six-year-old you could ever wish to meet. Plus, she loves talking about medicine, so maybe you two could chat about your studies, or whatever…'

He smiled and…

Oh, my gosh, it's just so hard to say no.

He was trying. Trying to invite her in. Trying to show

that she could be more than just his student. Trying to show that the past they'd shared still mattered to him and that he wanted her in his life. That after the six weeks were up in this placement this visit would still connect them.

And a small part of her *wanted* to meet his daughter—the way she would have wanted him to meet Samuel. To see Logan in her.

'Okay.'

He smiled back. 'Good. Okay… Well, I guess the next question is when are you free?'

Ellie shrugged. 'Well, most nights I'm studying, but I suppose I could take a night off. I'm sure my mentor wouldn't mind.'

'Then how about tonight? It's pizza night Chez Riley. Very casual, very relaxed. What's your opinion on having pineapple on pizza?'

'At your house? Oh, right. Well, I guess I don't object— as long as there's ham, too.'

'Good. That's good. Well, what about six o clock? And I'll introduce you to my biology-focused daughter.'

'Sure.'

He reached into his pocket to pull out a small pad of paper and scribbled something down. 'This is my address.'

She glanced at it. Number seven Cherry Blossom Avenue. It sounded a happy place. The type of address anyone would be thrilled to have.

'I'll be there.'

It was just an ordinary house—Georgian windows, topiaries in pots on either side of the front door. There was a sweeping driveway, but no car. Tall hedges on either side sheltered it from neighbouring eyes.

She stood there for a moment just looking at it. Gazing up at the windows and imagining the life that might be behind them. Logan and Rachel. A father and his daughter. Family.

She'd brought flowers—she'd popped into a florist's on the way there and asked them to make up a quick bouquet. Now she held it in front of her almost like a shield. Why was she so nervous? Why was she so apprehensive about stepping over the front doorstep?

Because it will change everything.

There was a car parked on the road outside and she used its windows to check her reflection. Typically, there'd been a brief rain shower on her way here and she looked damp, her hair flat against her head. She tried to run her fingers through it to give it a little lift, a little body, but her hair was thick and heavy and it sat on top of her head like a used mop. She let out a frustrated sigh, standing up straight again, and headed towards the front door.

Her right hand hovered over the door-knocker for just a moment, and she had to tell herself quietly that she was being ridiculous. There was nothing to be afraid of here. This was just two friends catching up. That was all.

She knocked. Part of her expected Rachel to answer the door. Wasn't that what children did? Raced to the front door ahead of their parents because it was fun? But it was Logan who answered.

He opened the door, stepping back with a smile and welcoming her in. Seeing him made her heart skip a beat, as it always did.

'Did you find us okay?' He looked awkward, then laughed. 'What am I saying? Of course you did—you're here. Ignore me. I'm just nervous.'

Ellie smiled. 'Snap.' And then she passed him the bouquet. 'These are for you.'

He accepted gracefully. 'They're wonderful. Thank you.'

'No problem.'

'Let me take your coat.'

She shrugged out of it and passed it to him and Logan hung it next to some others. One of which was bright red.

Logan saw her notice it. 'It's her favourite colour—red. Because it's like blood.'

Ellie's eyebrows rose. 'Okay… Well, that's good, because I've got a little something for Rachel too.'

Logan began to explain. 'She's not really one for toys…'

Ellie pulled from her bag the gift, which had been wrapped in coloured paper.

'What is it?'

'You'll have to wait and see,' Ellie said with a smile. 'Where is Rachel? I can't wait to meet her.'

'She's in the sitting room.'

He seemed to have a nice house. From what she could see it was neat and clean. Very minimalist. The walls were a light grey, the skirting boards and frames glossy white. A large mirror in the hall reflected the coat rack and the two pairs of shoes that sat neatly by the front door. One pair big, the other small.

Ellie could hear that the television was on, but when they went into the sitting room she saw that Rachel was not watching children's television, but a documentary about someone who was infected by the leishmaniasis parasite. She turned to look at Logan with an amused smile on her face, and in return he shrugged.

'It's what she likes.'

'Then I think I've got her the right gift.'

Logan bent down to pick up the TV remote and pressed 'pause'. 'Rachel, our guest is here. Remember I told you about Ellie?'

Rachel turned to face her and Ellie was struck by how much she looked like her father. They had the same eyes. Dark and alert, twinkling with intelligence.

'Are you a doctor?'

'Not yet. But I will be one day. Your father is helping me.'

'I am going to be a doctor one day.'

'That's good. That you know what you want to be. I
didn't know when *I* was six.'

'Do you have autism?' Rachel asked.

Ellie shook her head. No.

'That's why you didn't know when you were six, then.
You didn't have a superpower like me.'

Ellie laughed. 'No. No superpowers for me. But I have
brought a gift.'

She held out the wrapped parcel towards Rachel. For
a moment she didn't think the young girl would take it,
but Rachel looked to her father, who gave her a nod of
permission.

Rachel placed the gift on her lap and instead of ripping
through the paper carefully sought out where the pieces
of the sticky tape were and carefully picked it undone, revealing the human anatomy jigsaw puzzle that had been
hidden underneath.

Rachel gaze at it in awe, then beamed a smile at her father. 'Look! You can see all the nerves! The muscles! The
bones! They're all labelled!'

Logan nodded, smiling. 'I can see that.' He looked at
Ellie. 'You picked the right gift. How did you know you
could even get these?'

'You won't believe this, but one of my university lectur-
ers mentioned you could get them as a study aid.'

'It's perfect. Thank you. What do you say, Rachel?'

'Thank you, Ellie.' Rachel immediately got down on
the floor, kneeling by the glass coffee table, and tipped
out the pieces onto its surface.

'That should keep her busy until dinner. Can I get you
a drink?'

She nodded. 'Whatever you're having is fine by me.'

'I've got a pot of coffee. It's usually a permanent fixture in this house. You take it white with one sugar, don't you?'

'You remember?'

'I remember lots of things.'

She sucked in a breath. What else did he remember? How they'd used to lie entwined in each other's bodies? How they'd used to make each other laugh? How they'd used to kiss each other so hard they almost couldn't breathe?

He walked her into the kitchen and grabbed two mugs from a mug tree. He poured in coffee, then milk, added sugar and passed one of the drinks over, indicating that she should sit down so they could talk.

'She looks like you, Logan.'

'You think so?'

'Very much.' She took a sip from her mug. 'You must be very proud of her.'

'I am. I just wish things weren't so hard for her.'

'How so?'

'Not having her mother. I worry that I'm not enough for her. Whether I'll give the right advice. She doesn't have many friends at school.'

'Is she in mainstream?'

He nodded. 'We try to talk about her Asperger's as a positive thing, and it is. I talk about famous people, both past and present, who had the same thing, and what they managed to achieve, so she can see that the whole world is her oyster, but...'

'But?'

'What if it's not? I want her to be happy.'

'She seems content.'

'You've only known her five minutes.'

Ellie nodded. That was true. What did she know about anything? She sat there not knowing what to say. Perhaps this had been a bad idea? She'd almost called to cancel, then realised she didn't have Logan's telephone number. And now she was here, and it was awkward, because she still had deep feelings for this man and though he was less than a metre away they felt so far apart.

'Finished!'

They both turned to look at Rachel, who stood in the doorway smiling.

Ellie was surprised. 'Already? It had a hundred pieces!'

'It was easy. Come look.' And she turned and disappeared.

Logan and Ellie got up to follow and stood in surprise in the sitting room to see the completed jigsaw laid out on the coffee table.

Ellie gaped. 'Wow! That's amazing, Rachel. *You're* amazing.'

Rachel seemed pleased with her praise. 'I told you. I have a superpower.'

She nodded. 'Yes. You certainly do.'

They made the pizza themselves—Logan and Rachel. He'd bought a pre-made base, but they added all the toppings themselves—*passata*, ham, pineapple, green peppers, sweetcorn, cherry tomatoes, mushroom. No cheese.

'You don't like cheese?' Ellie asked them both.

'No. And the base is gluten-free, by the way.'

'Okay. That's fine by me.'

Logan and his daughter had clearly made pizza together before. They worked as a well-oiled team—Logan chopping and prepping as Rachel spread everything out on the pizza base in perfectly organised spirals. She was very precise as to how she placed everything, her little face screwed up in concentration.

'What kind of doctor do you want to be?' Rachel asked her. 'My daddy saves babies.'

'Well, I'm doing that too, at the moment, but I'm hoping to work with transplant teams.'

Rachel nodded. 'Organ donation.'

'That's right.' It felt strange to be having a conversation that was so grown up with a child who was so young, but that was the beauty of autism. It was full of surprises.

'Are *you* an organ donor?' Rachel asked.

'Yes.'

'That's a good thing.'

'Yes.'

Logan smiled at the two of them as he chopped salad, ready to go with the pizza, and Ellie caught his eye. At first she was pleased at his pleasure and then she was afraid of it.

'What type of doctor do *you* want to be when you grow up, Rachel?'

'I don't know yet.'

'Well, you have plenty of time to work that out. Logan, is there anything else I can do to help?'

'Er… We need the table set. Rachel, why don't you show Ellie where everything is and help her?'

And soon they all were quietly busy, preparing for their dinner together, and Ellie found herself looking at Logan and Rachael in moments when they didn't notice, just enjoying the feeling of being part of something.

Was this what it felt like to be a family? She'd never got a chance to experience it with Daniel. It had just been the two of them, and even though they'd started to prepare a nursery for Samuel the decoration had stopped halfway through after that damning diagnosis.

Grief and pain had stopped everything in its tracks. Not just the decorating, but their relationship, too. Neither of them had known how to talk to the other and they'd spent the rest of their time together existing alongside each other, but not living.

This moment she was sharing with Logan and his daughter was giving her all the good feelings. It felt warm and comforting. Reassuring. *Nice*. They each had a purpose, they each knew their role, and they could rely on each other to get it done. There was a cosy atmosphere, and the smell of the pizza cooking in the oven filled the kitchen with a delicious aroma.

'Smells great,' she said.

Logan peered into the oven. 'Another five minutes, I'd say.'

He looked happy in the kitchen. 'Do you like cooking?' she asked.

He shrugged. 'It never used to be my thing. But Rachel only likes certain foods, so we know what we're going to have each and every day.'

Ellie nodded. She understood that a lot of people who had autism liked order and repetition. It made them feel secure if they knew what was going to happen. It was a feeling she could understand. Everything in life was so uncertain—if you could control some things that firmly, why wouldn't you?

Perhaps I ought to make myself a weekly menu and stick to it? Then there'd be some certainty in my life.

'What drink would everyone like with dinner?'

Ellie filled the glasses. Orange juice for Rachel. Plain water for her and Logan. Then she sat down as he pulled the pizza from the oven and laid it on a wooden board in the centre of the table, before cutting it into slices.

'This looks delicious.'

'Wait till you taste it.' Logan served out the slices and then passed her the salad bowl.

She took a small amount and waited for Logan and Rachel to do the same before she started. Logan was right. It *was* delicious!

Who'd have thought that pizza without cheese could taste so nice?

'So, Ellie, what happened to all those ideas you had of running your own business?' asked Logan.

She dabbed at her mouth with a napkin, giving herself time to pause. This wasn't the moment to mention Samuel. 'I followed them. I had my own coffee shop and book store.'

He looked interested. 'Here in London?'

'Yes.'

'And...do you still have it?'

She looked away, forced a smile. 'No.'

'You gave it up to pursue medicine?'

It seemed the easiest way to get out of explaining. Especially with Rachel at the table. 'Yes.'

'What was it called? I might have been in and not known about it.'

'Stories on the Side. It was in Finsbury Park.'

He looked at her in surprise and awe. 'That's amazing! Couldn't you have kept it going with a trusted manager? So that you'd have an extra income coming in whilst you're training?' He must have seen the look of discomfort on her face, because then he said, 'I'm sorry. I'm prying. I shouldn't do that. It's not my place.'

Ellie smiled. No it wasn't. Not any more. But it was getting harder and harder to remember the need to resist him. 'Do you think you ever went in there?'

Logan seemed to think about it. 'I'm not sure I did. Sorry.'

'That's okay. It was quite small, and it wasn't there for very long.'

'Was it successful?'

'In the time it was there? Yes.'

To start with, anyway. Then Samuel had died and her business had crumbled to nothing.

'And your parents? How are they? Dad still doing okay?'

She nodded. 'He's done brilliantly since the transplant.'

'Your dad had a transplant?' asked Rachel. 'What kind?'

'His heart.'

Rachel seemed to think about this. 'That's the best kind. Getting a new heart. Do you think it means that you would fall in love with all new things that you didn't before?'

Ellie smiled at her. 'I don't know. Some people say that they do. That before a heart operation they didn't like classical music, but then afterwards they suddenly did. It's strange, isn't it?'

'The heart has four chambers.'

'That's right.'

'Here we go…' Logan smiled. 'Get ready for it.'

And off Rachel went on her usual monologue about how the heart worked, the parts of the heart and how it pumped blood.

Ellie gathered from his reaction that this was something he'd sat through many times before and it was an unstoppable description that they just had to let Rachel finish. She was astounded at the little girl's knowledge, and truly believed that if she carried on this way she would very easily become a doctor.

By the time Logan's daughter had finished talking dinner was over and they all helped clear away. Rachel disappeared to her bedroom with her new jigsaw puzzle and left Logan and Ellie alone downstairs to talk.

'Thank you for dinner. It was wonderful,' said Ellie. 'And thank you for opening up your home to me. I thought it might be weird, or difficult, but it hasn't been.'

He nodded. 'Me too. It's odd, isn't it? That with some people, no matter how much time has passed since you saw them last, you can just carry on as if you'd only just parted five minutes before?'

She smiled. 'True.'

'Can I get you another coffee, or tea? Something stronger?'

'Tea will be fine.'

'All right. I won't be a sec.' And he disappeared back into the kitchen.

Ellie took the time to have a proper look at his sitting room, and saw for the first time a picture on the mantelpiece of a woman who just had to be Rachel's mother. She was dressed as a bride. It was a wedding day picture. It was odd to look at it, knowing that at one point in time Ellie had believed *she'd* be the one to marry Logan.

Jo's dress was elegant. Off the shoulder, narrow bodice and a full tulle skirt. Her hair was swept up and off her face and she was smiling shyly at the camera, but looking very happy indeed. Content. It was a look that said, *I know I'm going to be happy for the rest of my life.*

How long had she and Logan been together before the car accident? Just a few years? It had to be. Ellie hoped that she had had some of the happiness she'd believed she was getting. Logan was a good man.

'Tea.' He came in carrying a tray holding a pot and biscuits, hesitating when he saw her standing by the mantelpiece.

Ellie felt awkward, being caught looking at the picture of Jo. 'She was very beautiful.'

He laid the tray down on the coffee table where Rachel had earlier completed her jigsaw. 'Yes.'

'I'm sorry you lost her.'

'I'm sorry, too.'

'Were you happy? Before...?' She had to ask. Curiosity and her need to know were more powerful than anything else.

He sighed. 'Very much so. What about you, Ellie? Have *you* been happy? Has life treated you well?'

Now would be the perfect time to tell him about Samuel. About everything that had happened.

But she could see it in his face. The need to hear that she had been okay without him. And they'd had such a wonderful night so far. She really didn't want to ruin that. She liked this closeness that they'd rediscovered. Why spoil all that when everything was going so well? Besides, she didn't fancy crying her eyes out in front of him as she told her story, and she knew that would happen because she'd never got through Samuel's story without bawling her eyes out.

Was it imperative that he knew? How would it benefit him? It would only make him sad. It would only make him feel sorry for her, and she didn't want his pity.

Tonight she felt that she had got her friend back. Logan Riley. The man she'd once loved. The man she wanted to talk to and spend time with. She didn't want any of that to change. Not when it was all so new. So fragile.

She plastered a broad smile across her face and sat down next to him on the couch. 'It has.'

He looked her in the eyes, as if he were searching to see if she were telling him the truth. But it seemed he'd come to the conclusion that she *was* being truthful and he smiled back. 'Good. I'm glad to hear it.'

His gaze dropped to her mouth before rising back to her eyes. Her own gaze couldn't help but mirror his.

She smiled...

'What's going on?' Ellie looked apprehensive as she saw all the hustle and bustle going on in the small hospital room.

Logan could see she was wondering who all these people were, gathering equipment together, unhooking machines.

'It's Bailey Newport. One of the triplets. St Richard's have got a space in their NICU so we're transporting him over there to join his siblings.'

'Oh, right.'

'I'm going over with the transport. Want to tag along to see how these things are done? But if you want to stay here, I don't mind.'

She seemed to be fighting an internal battle with herself. 'Sure, I'll go with you. It'll be interesting.'

'We're using specialist neonatal transport, so we don't have to take all our gear with us—there are monitors on board.'

She nodded. 'Okay. So St Richard's don't send a team to fetch a patient?'

'No, it's policy here that we accompany our own patients to a new hospital.'

'Is Sam coming with us?' Sam was Bailey's mother.

'Yes, she'll be riding up front.'

'Do I need to do anything? Can I help?'

He looked about them. 'I think we're about done, but you can keep an eye on the monitors on the way down. Any decelerations or changes in the numbers, you flag it straight away. Here's his file. Get familiar with his stats.' He passed it over.

'Are we expecting there to be any issues?' She opened the file and began to flick through.

'Well, Bailey has been stable since his birth, but neonates can surprise you—compensating for ages before suddenly crashing—so I don't want us to be laid-back about this. I consider every neonatal transport high-risk until they're safe and sound in their new hospital.'

'Understood.'

'Be ready to go in five.'

He made sure Bailey's mother had collected all their belongings and helped carry a couple of her bags. When the driver and a nurse were ready to go he notified the registrar that they were off and would be back as soon as they could be.

'Great. I'll get this section cleaned down and prepped for our next patient,' the registrar replied.

Ellie looked up from Bailey's file. 'We have someone already?'

'Not yet—but it pays to be prepared.'

Logan followed his team down the corridor, down in the lift and out to the bay outside the hospital, where Bailey Newport was latched into position in the back of the neonatal transport.

Ellie stood back as the team connected up the wires and cables and the machinery leapt into life, and as their own equipment was handed back to a porter to return for cleaning before being used again.

He watched her make a note of Bailey's observations, and when he finally got in himself she gave him a thumbs-up. 'We're good to go.'

Logan signalled to the driver. 'All stable here. When you're ready…'

The engine rumbled into life beneath them and the vehicle began to move off.

'How long should it take us to get to St Richard's?'

'Forty minutes. Give or take for traffic.'

They were rocked from side to side as the vehicle went over some speed bumps, and then it was rolling down the hill to the junction that would take them to the ring road.

'Rachel still loves your gift, by the way. I think she completed the jigsaw five or six times before I could get her to go to bed.'

Ellie smiled. 'I almost bought myself one. With more pieces. But then I figured I could revise better from books rather than scratching around for a piece I might lose and driving myself crazy.'

She looked at the monitors and noted down Bailey's stats.

'All good?' He could see that it was, but he wanted her to tell him.

'He's doing well. Perfect patient so far.'

'That's how we like them.'

She smiled at him and he smiled back.

It felt different being at work with her today, after last night. He felt that having invited her into his home to meet his daughter, and after they'd chatted in a relaxed setting, he had somehow removed some of the barriers they'd both had up before. Ellie knew about Jo now, and she and Rachel had got on really well.

He'd known that they would, but actually to watch them interact with each other had been really nice. For so long it had just been him and Rachel every night. He didn't often invite people over from work. He liked to keep his personal life personal. But Ellie was different, wasn't she? And he strongly felt that their working relationship could only improve even more as time went on.

It had felt good to be with Ellie again. He hadn't realised just how much he'd missed her, but now that she was back he ached to spend more time with her. To make her smile. To make her laugh. He wanted to make her happy.

Not that there was any chance of anything romantic going on. Of course not. They were just friends.

He could see through the partition that they were getting onto the motorway now. He checked that Bailey's IV drip was still feeding through at the correct rate, and then he donned a pair of gloves and stood up to use his stethoscope to manually check the baby's heart-rate.

Sam turned in her seat at the front. 'Everything okay?'

'We're good. Just double-checking.'

Sam smiled nervously and turned round again. 'Traffic's heavy.'

Logan sat back in his seat and strapped himself in. 'Chest sounds nice and clear.'

The driver called through. 'Coming up on a traffic jam, guys. Sit tight.'

'Will do.' Logan glanced at Ellie and raised his eyebrows in a way that said, *Typical.* Traffic was always bad, coming this way. But he let out a long sigh and rolled his neck, trying to relax as the vehicle slowly came to a stop. 'Let's take this moment to do a full check on our patient.'

He and Ellie both unclipped themselves from their seats and stood up to monitor Bailey. But before they could check anything they were suddenly and loudly knocked off their feet as the rear of the vehicle came crashing inwards with a screech of metal.

And all they could do was wait for the world to stop.

CHAPTER FIVE

ELLIE WAS THROWN hard into Logan, and both of them slammed into the back of the ambulance, bouncing off the rear doors and then being whacked again in the other direction.

She heard screams, and the whine and groan of metal, then shouts and yelling from outside as a high-pitched sound issued in both her ears.

What the hell had happened?

She felt disorientated, lying in a crumpled heap, face-down on the floor of the ambulance. Everything in her body was trembling with adrenaline and she had to take a moment to do a silent inventory. She could wiggle her toes, move her hands, and she was breathing. Her left shoulder hurt, and something was trickling down her forehead.

She went to touch it and discovered she was bleeding. Terrified, she turned to look up at the incubator. It had been locked into place, and so hadn't moved, but Bailey hadn't been wearing a seatbelt.

She scrambled to her feet, wincing at the pain in her shoulder. Bailey was crying, crumpled up at the bottom of the incubator, and she lifted up its lid to straighten him out and check his limbs, giving him a head-to-toe assessment. Her hands were shaking madly as she checked his skull, his neck, his chest, arms and legs. She found a stethoscope and listened to his chest and abdomen. Remarkably all sounded normal except for his heartbeat, which was a little fast.

'Logan? Logan, are you with me?'

She was aware of him groaning as he got up from the floor beside her.

'How's Bailey?' That was his first question, then she saw him reach out towards her face. 'You're bleeding.'

She pulled away. There was no time for that now. 'I'm fine. Go and check on the others.'

He steadied her hand. 'Let me look at Bailey. You check on Sam and the driver. Then see what the hell happened and if anyone needs help.'

She could hear in his voice that he was just as shaken up by events as she was. Passing him the stethoscope, she grabbed a pair of gloves, put them on and shouted through to the front of the ambulance.

'Sam? Are you okay?'

Sam was unconscious and the driver was clutching his chest. *Heart attack?*

'Tell me what's going on. What do you feel?'

'I'm okay. I just hit the steering wheel. Probably a cracked rib or something. Check the mother.'

'I'll need to climb through to you. The doors are ruined back here. Tell me—is she breathing?'

He looked. 'Yes. I think so.'

'Count her breaths for me, and if you can reach straighten up her airway.' Sam's head had flopped forward, so her chin was on her chest.

Ellie had no idea if what she was doing was right. All she could think of were the basics in emergency first aid. Something she'd learned ages ago, sitting in a drab lecture hall with hundreds of others. She'd made copious notes, and she thought she knew the correct way to do things, but she'd never found herself in this situation before.

'Do you have a phone? Does the radio still work? Call this in. Get police, fire and ambulance.'

The driver nodded. 'Will do.'

With one hand he supported Sam's head, whilst with the other he tried to use his radio to call the accident in.

Ellie couldn't get through the small partition wearing her fleecy jacket so she took it off, wincing at the angle her shoulder had to be in as she somehow managed to squeeze through the gap, falling onto the central console.

She got to her feet and held Sam's head upright. 'Logan, how's the baby?'

'He's doing all right. But we need to get him out of this vehicle. With all this oxygen on board we don't want to be in here if this thing goes up.'

She froze. *Of course.* The ambulance would be carrying oxygen tanks. That was *very bad.* But she didn't have enough hands. She needed to keep Sam's airway open.

Outside she could hear yelling, and someone, somewhere, was crying. Her mind was racing a mile a minute. 'Do we have any cervical collars back there?'

There was a pause, then. 'No. This is neonatal transport, not a traditional ambulance.'

'Damn.' She twisted and turned, trying to look through the windows to see if there was anyone about who could help them. There were people. People clambering from their vehicles, others standing on the roadside, their hands clapped over their mouths in utter shock. One or two were on their phones, hopefully calling for help. At least no one was taking pictures. *Yet.*

Ellie banged on the window to get their attention. 'We need help in here!'

Logan held baby Bailey in his arms and glanced at the small hole Ellie had crawled through to get into the front of the vehicle. If he wanted to get off this ambulance then he would have to fit through it, too. There was no other way off. And he needed the tank of oxygen in front of him so he could keep administering oxygen to his patient.

He knew that ambulances always carried a stock of oxygen tanks in another compartment. There could be three or more full tanks of oxygen elsewhere, just waiting for something terrible to happen.

Technically, because the back of the vehicle had taken the brunt of the impact and the engine was at the front, the likelihood of an explosion was low, but he didn't want to take any chances at all.

He stuck his head through the gap to the driver. 'Hey, I never got your name.'

'Mick.'

'Hi, Mick. I need you to do something for me.'

'Anything.'

'I need you to take the baby. I'll pass him through, and then his oxygen. Support his head. I've wrapped him in blankets, so we shouldn't have to worry about his temperature, but I need you to take him and then get out of this vehicle. I'll follow after you.'

'All right.'

Mick held out his hands for the baby and gently took him in his arms, adjusting his grip until he felt comfortable, and then he took hold of the oxygen tank as that came through, too.

'Now, get out and get as far away from this vehicle as you can. Do you hear me?'

'Yes. But what do I do if there's a problem?'

'I'll be right behind you—don't worry.'

'Okay.' Mick pushed open the driver's door, letting in the sounds of the outside world, and clambered out.

Logan peered at Ellie. 'How's she doing?'

'I'm not sure. There's a crack on the glass here. I think

she hit her head pretty hard.' Her voice had a tremor. 'There's blood in her ear canal.'

That wasn't good. 'Is she still breathing?'

'Yes. But her colour isn't good and her heart-rate is dropping.'

Damn. 'I'm coming through.'

He struggled out of his jacket, tossing it behind him, and then began to try and pull himself through the small partition. It was a very tight squeeze. Not meant for him.

He thought at one point that he was going to get stuck, and that he'd have the humiliating experience of needing a fire crew to cut him free, but he finally made it through, tumbling onto the central console the way Ellie had.

'We need to get out of here,' he said.

She looked at him over her shoulder. 'You go. Take care of Bailey. I'll look after his mother.'

There was no way he was leaving her behind. 'This thing could blow up, Ellie. There are oxygen tanks!'

'I can't leave her, Logan! She'll die if I don't maintain her airway.'

He couldn't believe she was going to disobey him! Or that she was willing to risk her life like this! 'And *you* could die if you don't get off this vehicle!'

'I'm *not* leaving!'

'Then let's swap places.'

She shook her head. 'No. You have a child. Rachel's already lost one parent—don't let her lose another! And Bailey needs you. If something goes wrong with him before another ambulance crew gets here he'll need you and your expertise—not me and mine. This way makes sense. We'll be okay. They'll be here soon.'

Her words struck home. Exactly as she'd intended them to. Ellie always had cut to the chase. And it hurt because it was the truth. He couldn't leave Rachel an orphan. But that didn't make this any easier. His wife had died in a car accident and he'd had to leave her behind, and now here he was being forced to make the same choice with Ellie.

'And what if this thing blows before they get here?'

She gave him a nervous smile. 'Let's hope that it doesn't.'

He stared at her, trying to work her out. What she was doing was either incredibly brave and self-sacrificing or incredibly stupid. He wasn't sure which one he wanted it to be. The idea that he could stand by on the side of the road and watch this ambulance go up in flames was not a pretty one. He'd lost his wife that way. To lose Ellie too would be...

Beside her, he noticed a small fire extinguisher and grabbed it. 'I'm going to drench the electrics and the engine, just in case.'

'Do what you have to—but do it quick.'

He didn't want to leave her, but he knew he had to check on Bailey. 'Stay safe, Ellie.'

She met his gaze. 'You too, Logan.'

He growled with anger at having to leave her, and he had to force himself from the vehicle. When he got out he gave a brief look around.

There was a solid traffic jam up ahead, after a huge HGV had rammed the back of their ambulance. He couldn't see the driver, so he assumed he was okay. A mass of people were beginning to gather, at a loss as to what to do.

'Has anyone got a cervical head collar?' He knew it was a hopeless request, but if they could get Sam out of the ambulance, and therefore Ellie, too, he'd feel a whole lot better about things.

Everyone just looked blankly at him, and he grimaced as he clambered onto the bonnet of a car to see where Mick had headed with the baby. He saw him—a small figure sitting at the roadside on a patch of grass, cuddling his bundle and adjusting the oxygen mask on Bailey's face.

Okay. Logan quickly read the fire extinguisher instructions, then popped the bonnet on the ambulance and sprayed the engine with the foam. He couldn't see any leaking petrol or oil, so that was good, but he didn't want to take any chances.

He gave the vehicle one last agonised look, then tore himself away, shuffling through the people and the cars until he made it to the verge where Mick sat.

'How's he doing?'

'Okay, I think. He cried a little, but he's gone back to sleep.'

'Let me check him.'

And that was when he realised he didn't have his stethoscope, or anything else he would usually rely on. It was all in the ambulance. He glanced back at the vehicle, his anger rising at the fact that this whole thing had happened and that he'd had to leave Ellie behind. He didn't want to tear his gaze away, somehow feeling that if he kept staring at the ambulance then Ellie and Sam would be okay.

But he didn't have any time for anger. Bailey came first. He had to protect his patient.

He laid his ear against Bailey's chest and held his wristwatch in front of his face as he counted heartbeats for ten seconds.

He smiled. Something to feel good about. Bailey was doing well. His rate was the same as it had been before the crash. 'Pass me the baby.'

Mick handed him over. 'I ought to try and get people off the road,' he said. 'Emergency services will be here soon.'

Logan stared at their crumpled vehicle and at the figures he could see hunched in the front of it. Ellie was still holding Sam's airway open with her hands.

'Let's hope so.'

He didn't know what he'd feel if things got a lot worse than they already were. *Why* was Ellie being so careless with her own life? He didn't know whether to be furious with her or to admire her.

So he chose the latter.

The second Logan left the ambulance Ellie truly felt the full force of her adrenaline. She was holding Sam's airway clear with her hands and arms, as she kept her head upright, and they really began to tremble.

She couldn't quite believe she'd sent him away. But what else could she have done? Left him in the ambulance with Sam? When he was a father to a little girl who needed him? Who would be devastated by the loss of a second parent if anything went wrong?

She hoped and prayed that it wouldn't.

She whispered her prayers out loud. 'Please don't blow up this truck. I'm still in it. And so is this poor woman. And she's a mother, too. To *three* babies! If you're up there, Lord, please look kindly upon us. Haven't we already been through enough?'

Her words must have brought Sam back to semi-consciousness, because her eyes rolled and she began to mutter, her eyelids flickering.

'Sam? Hey, Sam. It's me—Ellie. Remember? We're still on the ambulance. There's been an accident, but you're okay. I just need you to stay still for me.'

'Baby... Bailey...'

'He's all right. He's fine. And we're going to be okay, too. But I need you to hold still. Hold still for me, okay?'

But Sam kept trying to move, pushing at her and waving her arms about. Was she being combative because of her head injury? It must be a closed head injury if that was the case. The blood coming from her ear was the only sign.

Ellie struggled to hold on to her, turning her head away so that she didn't get hit in the face by Sam's flailing arms.

And then she began to hear sirens.

Oh, thank God!

'Help's coming, Sam. They're nearly here.'

The sound of their approach gave Ellie an extra boost of strength and a feeling of confidence that things were all going to be okay. She trusted in the fact that Logan had sprayed the engine with the fire extinguisher, and she felt sure that he would have told her if the truck was dripping petrol. He would have dragged them out kicking and screaming if necessary. But he hadn't. So she was taking that as a good sign. The chance of this thing blowing up was low. It *had* to be.

What had hit them, though? Something big… It had completely crumpled the back of the ambulance and knocked them flying off their feet.

As the sirens got louder she managed a quick glance out of the side mirrors and saw the ambulance crews in their hi-vis clothing making their way closer, their green bags of equipment hoisted over their shoulders.

Thank God!

'Help's here, Sam. We're going to be okay.'

The paramedics had got Sam out on a back board and loaded her into an ambulance to take her to the very hospital the rest of her family was in—St Richard's.

Ellie had tried to help as much as she could, but eventually she'd realised she was just getting in the way and so she'd stood back and watched, feeling very strange at the turn of events.

She might have died! An HGV had struck the back of their vehicle and by rights they should have been shunted across the motorway into another lane, or crushed beneath its weight. The driver of the HGV had suffered a cardiac arrest and was now on his way to Theatre to have a blockage removed, from what she'd heard.

Now she stood in the hospital corridor, feeling at a loss

as to what to do next. Feeling stunned. The enormity of what she'd just survived was sinking in.

'Ellie!'

She turned at the sound of his voice, feeling a rush of relief, a surge of joy in her heart at seeing Logan again, standing there waiting for her. He looked ruffled and stressed, and his hair was going every which way, as if he'd been constantly running his hands through it. She couldn't read his expression, and didn't know whether he was about to tell her off or take her in his arms.

Tears sprang to her eyes. *'Logan!'*

He walked right up to her, his eyes searching hers, looking for...what?

'I don't know whether to shout at you or just hold you.'

He stood right in front of her and she looked up at him, tears falling freely. 'Hold me!' It was what she needed in that moment more than anything else.

He reached out, pulled her in towards him and clasped her tightly, kissing the top of her head, whispering into her hair. 'I don't know what I would have done if I'd have lost you, Ellie Jones.'

She wrapped her arms tight around him, letting her tears sink into his shirt, breathing him in, sinking against him, relishing the familiar form, absorbing him. She'd missed him so much!

'I was so scared...' he whispered into her hair, his protective arms still around her.

'Me, too.'

'Having to leave you in that ambulance...'

She looked up at him. 'We were okay. We were all right.'

'Never have I ever...' He seemed unable to finish what he wanted to say.

Her heart pounded as he raised his hand as if to stroke her face. Then he hesitated, as if she were forbidden, but his gaze dropped to her lips and she whispered his name, and before she knew what was happening he was pulling her close and kissing her! Kissing her as she'd never been kissed before. Her arms went up around his neck and she surprised herself by kissing him back!

Whether it was just relief at still being alive, she didn't know, but she *did* know she needed this. This passion. This life! For so long she'd been trundling along in low gear. Just existing. Not really living. Feeling no highs, no lows. After what had happened with Samuel, and then Daniel, and her business collapsing, she had conditioned herself to be numb. Existing in a state of nothingness.

The accident had been a flare. A wake-up call. A reminder that she *was* alive. She needed to recognise that fact. Yes, she had put her life at risk, but she'd known it was the right thing to do. Because she hadn't been able leave that mother alone in that ambulance. She had three babies who depended upon her, and she had known they couldn't lose their mother the way Rachel had lost hers.

That sort of devastation changed people. Changed who they were. Who they *could* be. She knew that losing Samuel had changed her, but she'd realised that she still wanted to live. Still wanted to feel and experience life to its fullest. And that meant taking chances. That meant feeling adrenaline. That meant *living*.

She and Logan had loved one another once. And whether the remnants of that love were still there or not they were exactly what each other needed right now. They'd both felt it ever since they'd met up again at the hospital, and it didn't matter that she was in the arms of her mentor right now—because right now he wasn't her mentor. Wasn't her boss. He was just Logan and she had once loved him.

That meant something.

He meant something.

It was as if he had always been in her life and she'd been on hiatus—waiting for him to come back into it. Seeing him in Neonatal Intensive Care had been a surprise, but it had also been *expected*, in a way. She'd always known he'd come back—it had been just a matter of time before they ran into each other again. Especially with the new career path she had chosen.

They fumbled backwards against the door to an on-call room…pushed it open. The room was empty, not being used, and there was a freshly made bed. He lowered her down upon it, his hands in her hair, on her body, hungry to touch, hungry for her.

It felt good to be in his arms again. It felt so right. This was why it had hurt so much when he had left her to go away to medical school—because she'd felt as if she'd been losing a part of herself.

Only now she was back in his embrace and he felt so good. Tasted so good.

Urgently, they began to peel away each other's clothes, needing to feel the touch of skin upon skin. The contact of body against body. Heat against heat.

'Logan—stop.'

He pulled back, breathless. 'What is it?'

She laughed. 'Lock the door!'

He smiled and stepped out of his trousers and socks, turning the lock on the door before joining her on the bed.

He looked magnificent. Tall and broad and muscular. Strong. And clearly he wanted her as much as she wanted him right now.

No, not wanted. *Needed.* She needed him. Perhaps she always had? They'd been apart, but maybe it had always been inevitable that they would find one another again.

His lips caressed the softness of the skin at her throat. The gentleness of his kiss mixed with the heat of him and the hardness of his body was a delicious combination, and she gasped as he entered her, urging him on, pulling him towards her, breathing his name.

Oh, how she had missed this!

When they were younger it had been good between them, but this was on a whole other level.

Perhaps it was because of the accident? The need to celebrate being alive after being so close to death? She didn't know. And right there and then she didn't care. All she could think about was the feel of his lips, his hands, his body moving above her. *In* her.

He felt so good. Everything in her was awakening to his touch. Responding to him as she always had. She'd been asleep too long. Her body was singing with happiness and joy as he stroked and licked and kissed, the heat within her building to an exciting crescendo.

She came, crying out as she did so, and his movements became more urgent as his own climax swiftly followed hers.

Ellie couldn't help it. She smiled, then laughed with relief, holding him to her as he slowed and stilled, his lips against her neck, gently kissing her, before he lifted his head to look into her eyes.

'You always did drive me crazy, Ellie Jones.'

She lay in his arms on the hospital bed and he couldn't help but turn and kiss the top of her head. To have her here with him… Safe, no longer in that ambulance, but *here*, and secure, no longer in danger… She had *no idea* how that made him feel.

She's back where she's always belonged. In my arms.

He'd watched them pull Sam from the ambulance and peered over the heads of the crowd, waiting to see Ellie come pushing through, looking for him. But she hadn't, and he'd begun to fear the worst. Had something happened? Was Ellie somehow still trapped inside?

At St Richard's he had escorted Bailey up to the NICU, informed Sam's husband of what had happened, and then stayed for an update on the other two triplets, feeling that he must stay to continue their care.

Once the team had fully taken over he had headed down towards A&E, to see if he could locate Ellie—and then he'd found her, just standing in the hospital corridor, looking lost and numb, with three butterfly stitches near her hairline.

His palpable relief at seeing her standing there in one piece, whole and alive, had almost been too much! His feelings for her had come from out of nowhere and then he'd just needed her in his arms. Needed to feel her, to make sure that she really was alive, that she was his Ellie and...

And now they'd made love. It had been such a long time since he had felt such bliss. Such serenity. Felt that everything was right with the world again.

The last time he had lain with her in a bed, staring up at a ceiling, it had been when they were in their late teens. So much had changed—so much had passed in that time—but now the two of them had been... He couldn't think of the right word. It was like returning home.

'This is weird, isn't it?' he said.

Ellie laughed. 'A little.'

'This morning I thought it would be just another day in The Nest. A normal day.'

'Well, that's the thing with life. You never know when it's going to screw with you.'

'You'd have thought it's played with me enough.' He suffered a brief flashback to Jo's accident. How he'd been dragged, kicking and screaming, away from the vehicle. Then he thought how he'd had to tear himself away today, from that ambulance...

She propped herself up on her elbow and turned to face him, her dark hair sweeping over the broad expanse of his shoulder. She was so beautiful it made his heart ache.

'I'm sorry I made you leave me, Logan. But I *had* to.'

He felt her hair tickle his skin, liking the sensation. Loving the way her face was so near to his, her lips still swollen from his kisses.

'I know.' He stroked her face, tucking her hair behind her ear. 'It didn't make it any easier, though.'

'And Sam's okay?'

'Yes. Concussion, but okay.'

'And Bailey's fine?'

Logan nodded. 'Yes. And he's back with his siblings now, as he should be.'

'That's good. And us…? Where should we be?'

He smiled. 'Probably not in here like this. They'll be expecting us back at Queen's.'

She smiled, nodded, laying her head back against his shoulder. 'Not yet, though. Let's stay here a while longer. It feels so good to be back here with you. It feels *right*. Is that strange?'

So she felt it too?

Suddenly it struck him, as if he'd been hit over the head by a baseball bat, that he was lying here in a bed with *Ellie*. His student. His ex-girlfriend. That he'd stepped over a line that he shouldn't have and jeopardised their professional relationship.

It didn't matter that he'd wanted this for a long time— and, more than that, had allowed himself to *feel* again. To let his love for Ellie flow. To allow all those old emotions he'd held back years ago to be free again. To mean something.

There was so much more at stake now. He had a child. A career he loved. She was at the start of a great new beginning in her own life. Was he risking both their futures? Would he hold her back again? He didn't think he would, but how did he *know*? He'd ruined her life before and it was all so much more complicated now.

'We ought to get moving.' Guilt propelled him out

of bed and he began pulling on his trousers, picking up her clothes and passing them to her so that she could get dressed, too.

'Thanks. Are you okay?' she asked.

He fastened his zip, his button. Began to button his shirt. 'Sure.'

She sat on the edge of the bed, holding her shirt against her bare breasts, looking confused, and then her eyes widened as she realised something. 'You're worried that we didn't use protection. It's okay—I'm on the pill.'

He turned to face her. Nodded. 'Are you okay?'

She smiled. 'I'm fine.'

Logan felt the bubble burst. The adrenaline rush was gone and the implications of their actions were beginning to be felt. He needed to get back to the hospital. To his daughter. To his neat and ordered life where nothing ever changed. Where he felt *sure* of everything.

He was very much aware that he'd muddied the waters. He had enough to think about with Rachel. Up to now she'd been his one and only focus in life apart from work.

What he'd just done with Ellie was a grave mistake— no matter how much he'd wanted it. He'd been selfish. Stepped over the line. Gone beyond the boundaries of being a boss. A mentor. He couldn't carry on in that role for her now, could he? But if he asked to have her transferred to someone else it would reflect badly on *her*. It was unfair, but that was the way of things. People would ask questions. And this wasn't her fault. He should be *protecting* her.

Now that they'd slept together, would she want more from him than he could give? Like before? He wasn't sure what he could offer her. Rachel took up so much of his time. As did work. From the very first day he'd sat by his daughter's incubator he'd vowed to put her first in everything. Which would make Ellie second—or third. She didn't deserve to be anyone's second priority. She deserved to be their *first*.

I can't say anything. But I can re-establish our rules. How it must be.

They'd managed it before. He just needed to have stronger willpower, that was all. Do nothing that would throw them back into each other's arms.

He could create distance without hurting her, right?

CHAPTER SIX

THEY GOT A taxi back to their own hospital in complete silence.

Ellie kept looking at Logan, trying to judge his mood, trying to gauge whether speaking about what had just happened would help at all. But she was wary of starting on something private like that, with the taxi driver listening from the front. So she kept quiet, staring out of the window.

Being with Logan had been wonderful. Being in his arms had been more than she could ever have hoped for. They'd both needed it after all they'd been through. Her desire and the need she'd felt to be with him had overridden any worries she'd had beforehand about her education and her future and what getting involved with Logan might mean.

'I think it might be best if you took the rest of the day off,' Logan said as the taxi brought them to a stop outside the hospital, breaking the silence for the first time. 'Take time to recover. Your stitches… You've had a knock.'

'Okay…' She guessed that made sense. She *could* feel a tiny bit of a headache, and some general aches and pains from being thrown around the ambulance.

'We've both been through a lot. It's been a stressful day. It would be unfair of me to expect you to carry on working.'

Unfair because of the accident? Or unfair because

they'd slept together and now he was having regrets? His tone seemed to indicate that it was quite clear that what had happened had been a one-off and should never happen again.

'Will you still be my mentor, Logan?'

He looked at her. Uncertain.

'Because I want you to be.' She leaned in. Lowered her voice. 'What happened today shouldn't have any bearing on the future. It was one moment. That's all. It's done now.'

'If that's what you want?'

She smiled at him, to indicate that it was. But a small part of her was disappointed that he was so clearly regretting what had happened between them. She told herself that it didn't matter, because she didn't need this kind of complication either. She had a future to think about. A career in medicine. Did she want to throw it away because of this?

In her unexpectedly free afternoon she took some flowers to Samuel's grave and laid them against his headstone. There was no sign that anyone else had visited. Her old flowers were still there, so she took them away and placed them in the bin, annoyed that Daniel seemed to have forgotten his son. Just because they'd separated, and he'd begun a new life with someone, it didn't mean that he could just forget his child had ever existed.

Daniel had moved on.

Had she?

I think I might have taken a huge step backwards.

Logan sensed rather than saw Ellie come into the room. He felt a tension, a palpability, as he heard the door close quietly behind him and he just *knew* it was her.

He didn't turn around. He continued taping a new nasogastric tube to his tiny patient's face and then removed the debris, closed the incubator and tossed the trash into the clinical waste bin before washing his hands. He glanced over briefly to see where she was and saw her standing before the baby, one hand against the incubator.

'A new patient?' she asked.

'Twenty-nine weeks.' He hadn't intended to sound so gruff, but he knew he had. It wasn't because of Ellie. It was the baby. 'Anencephaly. Do you know what that is?'

She looked up at him, her face sad. 'I think I can see what it is.'

'Yeah... Basically it means that the neural tube that should have closed to form the spinal cord and brain hasn't closed properly and the patient is therefore born with most or all the brain tissue missing.'

'You've passed a feeding tube—what's the outlook?'

'It's a fatal condition. Most babies born with it are still-born, but some can live for hours, days or weeks. This little girl is still alive, and there's no reason why she should starve.'

Ellie almost seemed to back away, as if being so close to a baby who would die soon might somehow affect *her*. He didn't blame her for being taken aback.

'We'll keep her warm and hydrated, do as much as we can. If you're going to find this one tough you can step out.' He almost *wanted* her to step out. Then he could get on with his work without feeling guilty every time he looked at her. He already had a headache after no sleep the previous night.

'Does she have a name?' she asked.

'Ava.'

Ellie nodded, as if it somehow suited the baby. As if it was the *right* name. 'I'll stay.'

He tried not to let out a sigh. 'Okay.'

'What else can we do for her? Can she hear us?'

'Probably not. But it wouldn't hurt if you wanted to talk to her.'

Ellie looked at him. 'I'd like to talk to you.'

He felt his face tighten. 'I've…err…got quite a bit I need to be getting on with.'

She stood in front of him. 'I don't want things to change between us.'

Neither did he. 'Nor do I.'

'But I can already feel you pulling away from me.'

He shook his head. 'I don't want to jeopardise your future.'

'Really? I need us to be *friends*, Logan. Can we be that at least?'

He nodded. 'Always.'

She looked back down to Ava, opened the incubator and reached in to hold the baby's hand, to stroke its fingers. 'Are the parents on their way up?'

He paused. This was the bit he was struggling with. 'They don't want to see her.'

Ellie turned. Shocked. *'What?'*

'They think it would be too upsetting for them.'

'But they can't *do* that! They can't abandon her because they're *scared*!'

He didn't like her raising her voice in the NICU. 'Keep your voice down, Ellie. These babies don't need to hear grown-ups getting stressed. You know we don't get to say how the parents of these babies behave. They deal with it in their own way and we're here for them when they're ready.'

Ellie looked exasperated. 'But…but it's *their baby*. Their *child*. They can't leave her. They're making a terrible mistake!'

'We can't know what they're going through.'

She looked as if she was going to respond. She'd opened her mouth to retaliate. But he held up his hand, silencing her.

'Parents might make choices for their babies that we don't agree with, but it is *their* choice—not ours. We do our part by taking care of our patients for as long as we are able and that is *all* we are required to do. We're not social workers, we're not health visitors, and we're not judges. We're doctors and the babies are our patients—not the parents.'

Tears were in Ellie's eyes. Of anger? Distress? 'But she's going to be all alone…'

'Why don't you stay with her? I'll get on with everything else. You stay here. It'll help me out, knowing you're keeping an eye on her.'

What he didn't say was that it would make him feel better, knowing he had a trusted member of staff with this patient, and also it would give him some breathing space. He was finding it terribly hard to think clearly with her around now that he'd slept with her again. It was as if being in the same room with her made his senses tingle. Made him hyper-alert to her presence. His body craved the touch and the feel of her once again, whilst his brain told him to keep away.

He would pop in every now and again—get Ava's obs, give instructions on how Ellie ought to change her meds or fluids, and then go again.

She nodded. 'I will stay.' She reached for a stool and pulled it up so that she could sit down and still hold little Ava's hand.

He watched her for a moment, admiring her determination in the sight of this hopeless case. It was going to be tough for her. The first death of a patient always was. But perhaps she needed to experience it so that she fully understood this place and what it meant to save the lives of those they *could* save.

At the exit, he turned. 'Ellie…?'

'Yes?'

He wanted to tell her—warn her how much this was going to hurt. But perhaps he didn't need to. She was a grown woman. She *knew* how this was going to end and yet she still wanted to do it. He could admire her for that. And he felt guilty for cutting her off earlier.

'You're doing a good thing.'

'Someone has to.'

'Half-hourly obs. Alert me the second her saturations begin to drop. I don't want you going through this on your own.'

She looked at him with tears in her eyes but said nothing.

Ava lived for ten hours and seventeen minutes with only Ellie at her side. Then Logan and a nurse joined her, and they all sat and waited for the end. When it came, it was as silent as her life. One moment she was breathing—the next she wasn't.

Ellie held her own breath, waiting for Ava's next one. When it didn't come, and the machines announced their continuous tone, indicating asystole, she looked up at Logan, hoping that somehow he could make it not be true.

But Logan simply got up and listened to Ava's chest for a few moments, then silently draped his stethoscope back around his neck and gently closed the incubator. 'We'll need to inform the parents.'

Ellie was angry, felt tears dripping down her face. 'Why? They didn't care enough to be here!'

'Ellie—'

'What? She lived, Logan! She *lived*! For *hours*. They could have spent that time with her. Instead she had to spend her life with strangers! People she didn't know. Voices she didn't recognise.'

She had begun to cry and she couldn't stop it. She just felt so much rage towards those parents who hadn't made it to the NICU to sit with their dying child. Something she would have given anything to do for Samuel. They had wasted that opportunity and part of her wondered if they'd spend a lifetime full of regret thinking about that decision.

'She wasn't in any pain and she felt the comfort of human touch. Yours, Ellie. *You* gave her that.'

How could he understand? He had his daughter. He'd never felt the loss that she had.

'But was that enough? She should have had skin to skin... She should have had that!'

'She wouldn't have known what it was.'

'How do we *know* that?'

'She didn't have a brain, Ellie! That's how. She didn't have a sensory pathway the way everyone else has. She wouldn't have known.'

'But you fed her so she wouldn't starve. Hunger—that's a sensation.'

Logan stared back at her. 'It was her basic human right. Ellie, I'm sorry you had to see this. It's hard, the first patient death, I know...'

She knew he had no idea of what it was like to lose a child. 'I want to be the one to tell the parents.'

'I can't let you do that.'

'Why? Because I'm too emotional? Because you think that I'll say too much? That I'll accuse them of something?'

He shook his head. 'No. Because it's not protocol for medical students to pass on such news.'

'Maybe I could observe, then?'

'It's not something you want to see. Not until you have to.'

She glared at him. It was as if he was blocking everything she wanted.

'I'm trying to *protect* you, Ellie. Please try and see that.'

Ellie didn't want to see anything. She simply pushed past him and headed for the staff rest room. She needed a moment to think and process and grieve for a little girl she'd barely known.

How many young lives were lost like that? There was no word for a parent who had lost their child. Why *was* that? Was it too terrible to contemplate? Or was it because a simple word would not be enough to describe the devastation and grief that a parent felt and carried with them throughout life?

She wanted to punch a wall. Or throw the mugs across the room. To scream at the top of her voice. To sink to her knees and cry.

How could she understand a world that allowed such cruelty?

Ellie leant back against a wall and slid down to the ground, staring blindly across at the lockers. Tears crept silently from her eyes and she knew she'd never forget the little girl whose hand she had held for such a short time.

Sleep tight, Ava.

Work became quite uncomfortable for Logan after Ava's demise. It was as if the death of the baby had turned Ellie into some kind of robot. Either that or the fact that they'd slept together had changed their dynamic—though she had said, hadn't she, that she wanted to be friends?

He would ask her to do something and she would do it, but there was no conversation, no chat, no expression, and he was worried that maybe Ava's passing had affected her too much.

'Ellie, could I have a quick word?'

Ellie nodded and followed him into his office. He indicated that she should take a seat, which she did, staring down at his desk, not making eye contact.

'How are you doing?'

'Fine.'

He didn't believe her, and he was worried. 'You don't seem fine.'

'In what way?'

'You just seem a little…off.'

'Am I working to your standards?'

He gave a nod.

'Doing everything you ask of me?'

Another nod.

'Then what's the problem?'

'You're terse. Abrupt. You hardly ever crack a smile—'

She smiled then. 'I'm sorry—are you telling me to *smile* more? Don't you realise how terribly patronising that sounds?'

'You're misinterpreting my words.'

'So make them clear for me, then.'

He stared at her. 'Okay. If that's how you want it. Since Ava—since *us*—you've had a different demeanour. You do your work, and you do it capably, but that is it. There is no engagement, there is no enquiry, nor any interest in expanding your learning. You no longer seem fired up by your studies. You do the bare minimum and then you go home.'

She looked at him then. Finally met his gaze. 'Are you failing me on my placement?'

'No. Not at all. But I *am* hoping to light a fire beneath you.' He smiled at her, to show her that he meant his words kindly. 'You need to get your light back, Ellie. You can't let one death defeat you.' He leaned forward, his voice low. 'And you can't let what happened between us change you. I'm trying to tell you like a friend would. *Talk* to me.'

She shook her head. 'It's not about one death.'

It *wasn't* about Ava? 'Then what is it about?'

Were her eyes welling up? What was hurting her? Something he was failing to see? If she didn't tell him, then how could he help her? Because he truly *did* want to soothe her soul. Had he been too abrupt? Had *he* caused this? He didn't want to cause her any pain. He'd done that once already.

'You wouldn't understand,' she said.

'How do you know that?'

'Because you told me no one could if they hadn't gone through it themselves.'

And she got up and left his office, wiping away tears.

Logan stared at the door she'd left open behind her, pondering her words. What did *that* mean? When had he said that? And in what context? If he could remember, it might give him some clue.

She was trying to say she'd been through something that *he* hadn't. But what? He'd been there when Ava died too. She'd said, *'It's not about* one *death.'*

So who else had died?

What *was* it that he didn't know?

Her alarm woke her. Groaning, she blindly reached out to grab her phone and switch off the irritating noise, then flopped back against her pillow. Normally she woke up before her alarm, but she'd been feeling extra tired these last few days, and what with all the stresses and strains of the last few weeks—ever since the crash, really—she guessed her body just needed some extra time to rest.

She stared up at the ceiling, mentally preparing herself for getting out of bed and thinking of all she had to do before work. Get washed and dressed. Pack a lunch. Clean the kitchen. Have breakfast.

Ugh...breakfast.

Usually she'd have some jam on toast, or a bagel, or some cereal, but the idea of food today was not doing her stomach any favours.

What did I eat last night?

Then she remembered. She'd grabbed a takeaway on the way home. Chinese. Chicken *chow mein* with seaweed and crispy beef. She'd been ravenous and had almost eaten the whole thing.

No wonder I don't fancy breakfast.

Sitting up, she swung her legs out of bed and breathed out a sigh as her stomach gurgled.

I really mustn't eat so late again. It's not good for me.

Ellie got up and washed her face, brushed her teeth. In the mirror she looked a little pale, but what medical student didn't? All the work and then the studying, the late nights poring over textbooks and cramming for the next day, would take its toll on anyone. Especially when they didn't eat very healthily. Plus, it didn't help that she had such dark hair. It made her skin look paler than it normally would, but on the plus side it looked great at Halloween.

Downstairs, she began to brew some coffee and pottered about, clearing away the debris from last night. But by the time the coffee was ready she really didn't fancy it, and ended up pouring herself some orange juice instead. *Much better.* The acidity and sharpness was just what she needed.

She belched loudly, and then listened as her stomach gurgled some more. That didn't sound good. Heading back upstairs, she was about to get dressed when she felt bile rush into the back of her throat and had to bolt for the bathroom.

It soon passed, but she stood there for a moment, worrying that she had food poisoning. Had the chicken been cooked properly last night? She couldn't afford to take any time off. She rummaged through her bathroom cabinet and found some indigestion tablets, took some of those.

She took the bus to work, and when she got out at her stop the fresh air made her feel a lot better. She strode along quite happily, determined that today was going to be a fresh start.

Logan's talk the other day had comforted her a little. He'd *noticed*. Noticed that she was finding everything a bit hard lately. But no more. She couldn't allow what had happened to derail her future. It had already been disrupted enough, and she was doing her best with the options she had left to her.

She couldn't be with Logan. Not like that. He was a distraction. And if she couldn't be a mother then she would damn well make sure she was the best doctor there could be. Helping others, giving all kinds of people—children, babies, grown-ups—the chance to carry on. To live.

Because life was short, and for some it never even got started. She'd been off with everyone lately and he'd raised it with her. She had no doubt that if she had been anyone else she would have had a warning by now. Her friendship with Logan had prevented that. He'd been a friend once and he deserved her to be a friend now, so…maybe an apology? Or an explanation?

At work, she knocked on his office door and waited, but heard nothing. Hesitantly, she opened the door, but his office was empty, so she headed to the staff room, glancing into the wards as she passed them.

He was making coffee in the small kitchenette. Just seeing him made her heart yearn. She stamped down hard on it.

'Logan! Morning! Could I have a quick word with you, please?'

He turned and smiled. 'Of course!' Then he frowned. 'Hey, are you all right? You look incredibly pale.'

'I'm fine! Dodgy takeaway, I think, but I'm powering through.'

When he showed such concern for her wellbeing she had to fight the feelings it produced. Feelings of wanting to fall into his arms once again and let him care for her.

'All right… How can I help?'

'I just want to apologise for my attitude of late. You were absolutely right to call me out on it and I can promise you that from here on in you'll notice a vast improvement.'

Logan smiled. 'Okay. Can I get you a coffee?'

He wafted his full mug in front of her. The scent of it went up her nose and turned her stomach.

'Ooh, no thanks. Do we have any juice?'

'On a health kick?'

She laughed, dipping past him to open the fridge and look inside. There was a purple grape drink, so she had a glass of that.

'There's a surgery first thing that we could observe. Are you up for that?' Logan asked.

Of course she was! And she was glad they'd moved past his concern. Focusing on her studies, on her career, the future—*that* was what she should be thinking about.

'Absolutely! What is it?'

'It's a planned Caesarean section. Thirty-four weeks. The mother has got gestational diabetes and the baby is quite large. It's just not safe for her to continue or to deliver vaginally.'

She nodded, remembering reading about how some babies could have low blood sugar after birth, with possible jaundice or breathing difficulties.

'Has she been given steroids for the baby's lungs?'

'I believe so.'

'Okay. What time is it scheduled for?'

'In thirty minutes.'

'Great. I'll look forward to it.'

He peered at her. 'You sure you're all right?'

Don't look into his eyes. 'Of course!'

He scrubbed alongside Ellie. With her dark hair swept up in the scrubs cap, and her face mainly hidden by the mask, her blue eyes looked very wide and large. She'd always had such expressive eyes. Years ago he'd spent hours just staring into them, and he hated it that he couldn't do that now.

They headed in, and the operating obstetric surgeon, Max, checked that everybody was ready and the patient was comfortable. Her partner sat beside her, gowned up and looking terrified.

'Are we all ready to begin? Charlotte—I'm going to make a start.'

Charlotte nodded nervously.

'Can you feel this? Or this?' The surgeon pinched at her skin with forceps.

Charlotte shook her head. 'No.'

'All right—let's go.'

'Max, is it all right if my medical student steps up for a better view? I don't think she's seen a Caesarean section yet.'

Max nodded. 'Be my guest. What's your name?'

'Ellie Jones.'

'Ah…me and Miss Jones! I've always wanted to say that.'

Ellie turned to look at Logan, smiling behind her mask, and he smiled back. It was good for Ellie to see that it could sometimes be quite relaxed in surgery. Everyone knew what they were doing and everyone had a job. All she had to do was witness it and soak it all in.

'Make sure you ask Max some questions, Ellie. Keep him on his toes.'

Max raised an eyebrow as he worked beneath the theatre lights. 'As you can see, Miss Jones, I am currently making my way through the subcutaneous fat…'

Ellie leaned forward for a better view.

Logan hoped she would make the most of the experience. She'd been really good in surgery before, with the gastroschisis case.

'And now I'm cutting through the rectus sheath. Do you know what that is?'

'Err…no. Sorry.'

'It's the sheath that contains the transverse abdominal, external and internal oblique muscles.'

'Ah…okay.'

Logan heard her clear her throat and glanced at her as he detected a weird movement. Had she swayed a little? But, staring at her now he thought she seemed as steady as a rock, so perhaps he was fretting unnecessarily?

Besides, he had his own equipment to check and get ready—ready to receive the baby when necessary.

Max continued with his commentary. 'This is the peritoneum, and here you can see the abdominal cavity. Can you see it? Have a good look.'

Ellie bent forward. 'Err…yes.' She gulped.

Logan waited with the paediatrician to receive the baby. They would assess it together, and hopefully it would be all right to go to its mother and stay there. They would check its observations half-hourly, to monitor the blood glucose, but he was hoping for a good outcome.

Ellie could feel sweat beading her forehead. She was beginning to feel a little light-headed and regretted not managing any breakfast that morning. Mind you, she hadn't been expecting to go straight into surgery!

She glanced up to look at Max, the surgeon, who was concentrating hard, and then she glanced at Logan. He was saying something to the paediatrician, checking the equipment again as he waited for the baby to arrive.

Ellie was trying her hardest not to think of the smells and sights assailing her senses. The coppery rich scent of blood, the stink of the cauterising blade as it burnt flesh, the look of the yellow globulous fat and the redness of the blood and the…

She blinked, feeling a little unsteady. Her stomach was beginning to roll.

Panicking, she eyed the door to the scrub room. Could she leave? Would that be bad form? Would it raise questions? She didn't want to get a reputation as a student who couldn't make it through a short surgery. She needed to stay! How long did C-sections take anyway? Thirty minutes? Forty? She could last for that, right?

Just concentrate on something else…

'I'm now about to incise the uterus…'

Logan watched as, almost in slow motion, Ellie swayed violently and then went crashing to the floor, taking with her a tray of instruments.

'Ellie!' He wanted to take care of her, but Max had got the baby out at this point, and he knew it had to be his first priority, so he shouted at a nurse. 'Take care of Ellie! Get her on a trolley and keep me updated!'

The baby was crying. He was large and pink, lustily using his lungs, and Logan was aware in his peripheral vision that someone was hoisting Ellie up onto a trolley and wheeling her from the theatre.

He didn't have time to worry about her there and then. He needed to assess the baby. But the paediatrician seemed happy with his oxygen and APGAR score.

'I think he can go to Mum.'

'Do you need me?' he asked urgently, fighting the urge to just run from the theatre right now and check on Ellie.

'We'll be okay. Go and check on your student.'

Max turned to look at him. 'Better get one with a stronger stomach, Dr Riley!'

Logan ignored the jibe and went rushing out, pulling off his gloves, mask and gown and tossing them into the trash. Outside in the corridor he saw her, still perched on the trolley bed, looking pale and washed out.

'Ellie! Are you okay?'

She groaned. 'I guess that takeaway isn't doing me any favours… Ugh, I think I'm going to be sick…'

He fetched her a bowl and held it in front of her, but she

didn't throw up—which was good. 'Maybe you should go home if you're this ill.'

'No, I'm good… I'm okay. It was just…'

Her face went a little green and he held up the bowl again, but she pushed it away. He smiled, relieved that it seemed to be something simple like a stomach upset and not anything more serious.

'Maybe don't use that takeaway again, huh?'

She managed a pasty, clammy smile and belched. 'Maybe not.'

'Maybe you should have an IV? Get some fluids on board?'

'Maybe… I've not been able to eat anything this morning.'

'Well, there you go, then. That's your issue. Best not to go into surgery with an empty stomach.'

'I'm sorry I embarrassed you in front of your colleagues.'

'You didn't.'

'I bet I did. I'll apologise later.'

'Don't worry about it.' He laid his hand on her arm, rubbed it. 'You just get better.'

She looked up at him with those wide blue eyes of hers—eyes that he would happily wallow in if he could.

'I'll try.'

Ellie was mortified. She had never, ever fainted in surgery before. Hadn't even come close to it! Surgery fascinated her. Seeing someone's insides was like being given a special preview of something magical and fantastic. A hidden world. To pass out like that was embarrassing! She wanted to be a *surgeon*, for crying out loud!

Logan was right. She ought to have tried to eat something before surgery. But she'd felt so rotten earlier, and then nausea had really hit her hard as she'd watched the surgeon cut through those fatty layers…

Ellie groaned, just thinking about it, and lay back against the trolley, feeling a clamminess against her skin. Perhaps she should accept an IV? Because right there and then she didn't imagine she'd be ready to eat for a while.

It was weird, but the last time she'd felt this sick she'd been pregnant with Samuel—but she couldn't be pregnant because she was on the pill. She pulled her phone from her pocket and looked up the efficacy rates of the contraceptive pill. She knew they were pretty high, but right now, when she was feeling this rough, it wouldn't hurt to reassure herself, right?

More than ninety-nine percent effective. Good! She read on. *If taken regularly.* Which she did. Didn't she? Okay, sometimes she'd come home from work and flop right into bed. But she always tried to remember to take it before going to sleep. It hadn't been a huge priority as she hadn't been sleeping with anyone. Perhaps she had missed one…maybe two…

Surely not?

But the possibility that she'd made a mistake kept niggling at her. And the nausea that kept coming in waves made the worrying worse.

She couldn't be. That would be just ridiculous! For her to fall pregnant from just one encounter.

Technically, she was a few days overdue. But she'd never had a regular cycle! That was another advantage of being on the pill. It regulated her cycle and stopped her periods from being so heavy, too! Otherwise some months it could be twenty-eight days long, others over thirty!

There never seemed to be any rhyme or reason to it— it was just the way it was with her. Being a few days late meant nothing! It certainly didn't mean she was pregnant!

I'm reading too much into this. I'm panicking because of Samuel. I'm fine! Of course I'm fine!

But the niggling voice wouldn't go away.

Of course there was an easy way to settle it. *Just take a test.* It would be over in a minute and she'd be able to see with her own eyes just how silly she was being.

Ellie swung her legs over the side of the trolley and stood up gingerly. Maybe her blood pressure was low, because she felt a little dizzy, but she put that down to having just passed out, not for any other reason.

There were bound to be pregnancy test kits in the hospital. All she had to do was find one.

Easy, right?

CHAPTER SEVEN

'SHOULDN'T YOU BE taking it easy?' Logan caught her making her way through The Nest. 'You look really washed out.'

Seeing him froze her into position, but she managed a weak smile. 'I thought I'd get some fresh air.'

'Okay. Want me to come with you? In case you pass out again?'

He genuinely looked concerned, and she wasn't sure how to deal with his concern when all she wanted was to take the test and put her mind at ease. She certainly didn't need the father of her possible child showing her kindness. Not at a time like this, when everything was so uncertain. He had *no idea* of the turmoil battling it out in her mind.

Being pregnant would *not* be good. It would *not* be welcome. She had vowed never to get pregnant again. Not after what had happened to Samuel. The risk that it could happen again was too great even to contemplate...

'No, no. You stay here. You're needed here.' She swallowed. 'The babies need you. Not me. I'm just...' she pointed in the direction of the exit '...going that way. I won't be long, and then I'll be back, good as new.' Another weak smile.

'All right. Try and eat something—it might help.'

She nodded. 'Yes. I will. Yes...'

Why was he looking at her like that? As if he *cared*?

As if he was really worried about her? There was no need for that. She wasn't any of his business. At least she hoped not. If she were pregnant, then—

No. Don't even consider it.

She grabbed her jacket from her locker. It was getting cold outside. It would look odd if she said she was going out but didn't take her coat. She used her ID card to go through to Labour and Delivery, nodding a greeting at one of the midwives she vaguely recognised and asking where her equipment cupboard was?

'What can I get you?'

Her cheeks coloured. 'I have a mother in Neonatal. Thinks she might be pregnant and—'

'A mother?' The midwife laughed. 'Isn't it a bit soon for her to be thinking she's pregnant if her child is in Neonatal?'

Ellie blinked, not having thought through her quick lie thoroughly. 'Er...well, yes—you'd think that, but the baby has been in Neonatal for a couple of months and...'

'Ah, I understand. Well, we don't have pregnancy tests on this unit. Women are usually already pregnant by the time they get here! But you could try the Fertility Clinic.'

'Where's that?'

'Down this corridor, through the double doors and it's the first door on your left.'

'Thanks. I just want to put her mind at rest, you know?'

'Sure. She must be pretty stressed, having one in Neonatal and thinking there's another on the way.'

Ellie nodded. 'Stress plays havoc with a woman's cycle. I'm sure she's not, but I said I'd try to help.'

'I hope she gets what she wants.'

Well, what Ellie wanted was to take this test and prove to herself that she wasn't pregnant! But the evidence was beginning to mount up the more she thought about it. A late period, passing out, feeling sick, avoiding coffee, tiredness... And didn't she often need to pee, now that she came to think about it?

It's psychosomatic. I'm imagining things!

The mind was a powerful thing. If you believed something enough you could make yourself feel that way.

She began muttering to herself as she made her way to the Fertility Clinic. Her cheeks were flushed, her heart was pounding and her light-headedness was not helping matters.

It's the chicken. It's food poisoning. It's got to be. It's got to be!

She felt like a thief, an interloper in the Fertility Clinic. This was a place where women came because they *wanted* to get pregnant, and here she was, walking its halls and praying that she wasn't. She hoped she wasn't leaving behind any bad vibes for anyone else. She wanted to get in and then out again, so she could go and hide in a toilet and reassure herself that all was as it should be.

She found the testing kits and slipped one into her pocket, then slipped out of the clinic again.

This felt weird. Weird and crazy. She'd never thought she'd have to take one of these tests ever again.

She remembered finding out about Samuel. She'd been at home alone. Daniel had already left for work and she'd been about to go too. The book store and coffee shop was doing really well. They'd just been featured in the *Evening Standard* as one of *the* most hip and happening places to be seen.

She'd been hoping back then that she *was* pregnant. There'd not been many obvious signs, except for the absence of a period, and when the stick had shown her two blue lines she'd been ecstatic! Scared, but thrilled. Their whole world was about to change.

She'd vowed to work for as long as she could, so she could take a decent amount of maternity leave before returning to the shop, or to do the baby-wearing thing and put her baby in a sling. Would that be possible? She hadn't known. She'd guessed as long as she didn't serve hot drinks it would be safe.

To think that was my greatest concern—hot drinks.

How little she had known…

Ellie slipped into the nearest toilet and closed the cubicle door after her, pulling the test from her pocket and staring at it for a moment.

That little bit of paper was going to tell her everything. Either it would put the world right again or it was about to tip the whole thing upside down.

'Don't be positive…don't be positive…' she whispered as she used the test strip and then laid it on the back of the toilet as she got dressed.

Nervously she picked it up and stared at it, her heart thundering and making her feel as if she was going to pass out again.

Ellie stared at the strip in disbelief. 'Oh.'

Logan was on the phone to a consultant in A&E when he saw Ellie come back onto the neonatal ward. She still looked pale, and there was something weird about the way she was moving. As if she was stunned. Or as if she'd just heard some bad news or something?

His heart immediately ached.

He was really worried about her as he watched her go into the staff room and wondered if he ought to have told her to go home. She was certainly off today. Not her usual self. Things hadn't been right with her for a while. She was definitely withholding something from him and he didn't like it.

He returned his attention to the phone. 'Sure. Yes. I'll come down and talk to her in the next few minutes. What are the complications with her baby?'

'Thank you, Dr Riley. I'm not sure, to be honest. The woman is upset and crying but she says there are issues...'

'Okay. I'll be down as soon as I can.'

He put down the phone and got up to see if Ellie was all right. He really needed to know that she was okay. It was as if his head was muddled. He was being torn between wanting to do his best as a doctor and a teacher, and also just wanting to be with Ellie. Get her to talk to him about what was going on.

There was definitely something, and he hated it that she was dealing with it on her own when he was around to help her. But would he be helping her as a mentor, or something else? He couldn't stop thinking about their time together after the accident. How right she'd felt in his arms.

He could take her with him down to A&E—maybe they could talk along the way? Then she could observe his chat with this prospective new mother who was apparently experiencing contractions at twenty-three weeks.

The consultant had said they didn't seem regular, and they were hopeful they could stop them, but it wouldn't hurt for him to just go down and reassure the woman that they'd always have a room in Neonatal and would be ready for her baby if need be.

Hopefully not. Twenty-three weeks was awfully early to deliver...

He went to the staff room and noticed that Ellie was just standing in the kitchenette, staring at the floor.

'Did it help?'

'Huh?'

'The fresh air? Did it help?'

She looked at him as if he'd just said, *Purple elephants are playing bassoons in space.* As if what he'd said didn't make any sense whatsoever. Either that or she hadn't really heard him, and that was kind of hurtful.

'Er...sort of.'

'Good. Well, we've got a consult down in A&E. If you're up to it, I'd like you to come along.'

She nodded. 'Sure.'

'Are you okay? You seem a little…spacey.'

Ellie blinked and forced a smile. 'I'm fine.'

'All right. Be ready in ten minutes? I've just got to check on the Williams baby first.'

'Okay.'

He decided to trust her. Something was wrong, but he couldn't work out what it was and he had to trust that she would tell him if she needed to. Was it just her illness? Or something else? She still hadn't told him what she'd meant the other day with her cryptic comment about it *not being about one death*. And now she was ill. She had fainted in surgery and she hadn't been right since they'd slept together.

Also—although he wasn't sure—it looked as if she might have been crying. Her eyes looked a little red. But maybe that was tiredness, if she'd been up all night with a dodgy stomach.

Even if he didn't know what was going on, he did trust that Ellie wouldn't put her education or her patients at risk. But at the same time he wanted to scoop her up, carry her out of here, lay her on her bed at home and take care of her. Do what he always should have done.

Be by her side.

He had no doubt that she would prove him right when they went downstairs for the consult. She would spring back to life with a patient in front of her and become the curious, interested, productive Ellie that he knew and loved.

It would be nice to have that Ellie back. He'd missed her. It had been a huge shock to have her walk back into his life like this, but now that she was here, and he'd got used to it, he actually really loved it. It felt as if she was here for *him*. And he liked that. It was his guilty pleasure.

Together they walked down to the lift and he pressed the button for the ground floor. They were alone. 'Are you sure you're okay?' he asked.

She nodded. 'Yes.'

'You seem distracted. Still feeling ill?'

She looked up at him. 'I'm not feeling ill any more. I'm fine. Who are we going to see?'

'A pregnant woman in A&E has come in with some early contractions. Apparently there are already some complications with the pregnancy, but the consultant couldn't get anything more out of her, so we don't have any details. Perhaps you'd like to have a try? She might feel better talking to a woman.'

Ellie nodded. 'Okay. How many weeks is she?'

'Twenty-three.'

She grimaced. 'That's early. No wonder she's scared.'

'I'll do the initial introduction, but then I'd like you to take over and find out what the other issues are, okay?'

He figured that if he threw her in at the deep end to take control of a consult, it might bring back the hard-working, attentive student he recognised.

'Right.'

He reached out, stroked her arm. 'You can do it. I believe in you.'

She managed a weak smile. 'Thanks.'

Mrs Rowena Cook was sitting on a bed in a cubicle, her face pale, tear-stained. She was hooked up to a drip containing some medication that they hoped would stop the contractions.

Logan closed the curtain behind them. 'Mrs Cook— I'm Dr Riley, I'm a neonatal consultant, and this is Ellie Jones, a third-year medical student. They tell me you've been having some early contractions?'

Rowena nodded and dabbed at her eyes with a tissue. 'Yes...'

Logan turned to look at Ellie, expecting her to continue with the questioning.

She stepped forward. 'How long have you been having contractions?'

'For about three hours.'

'How often?'

'About every twenty minutes.'

Logan nodded. Good. Ellie was doing what he'd expected.

'And how long has each contraction been lasting?'

'About half a minute. They're painful. Crampy. I'm sure they're not Braxton Hicks.'

'Okay. The first doctor who saw you said that you mentioned some complications with your pregnancy. Can you tell me what those are?'

Rowena's eyes filled with tears and she sniffed and dabbed at her eyes again. 'She has ectopia cordis.'

Logan saw Ellie turn to look at him with questioning eyes. She didn't know what it was and he had no time to explain. This was serious.

He stepped forward. 'When was your last scan?'

'Two weeks ago.'

'Okay. We do have the facilities to take care of a baby with her condition, but I'd like to make sure I have the best minds on board in case of an early arrival. Hopefully you won't need us just yet, but I'd like to get you to take a walk around Neonatal when you can—just so you're familiar with everything if you have to come to us. It can be a bit scary. If you'll give me a moment, I'll call a specialist friend of mine and chat through your case with him.'

Rowena nodded and he indicated to Ellie that she should follow him out. They headed towards the A&E doctor who had examined Rowena.

'Ectopia cordis.'

'What *is* that?' asked Ellie.

'It means the baby's heart is either partially or totally outside of the chest.'

'Oh, my God.' She looked sick. 'Can it be fixed?'

'Yes…but it's risky.'

'Is the baby's life at risk?'

Logan looked at her and gave a brief nod. 'I'm afraid so.'

He didn't notice the look on Ellie's face as he began to chat with the A&E doctor, talking over Rowena's case. He had to focus on how he was going to help his patient and her baby.

'Are her contractions slowing at all?' he asked the consultant.

'We think so. Since we started her drip the contractions have gone to more than thirty minutes apart.'

'Let's hope they stop, then. I'd hate for a baby with such a condition to be born at twenty-three weeks. The longer the baby stays in the womb, the better its chances.'

'Logan…'

He looked at Ellie then, and saw her face, and he just *knew* that she needed to talk to him. In private.

He waited for the other doctor to go and then he turned to face her. 'What is it?'

She looked strained. Awkward. 'We need to talk.'

'Okay. We're alone right now. Whatever it is, you need to tell me, Ellie, because—'

'I'm pregnant.' She looked at him with her eyes filling with tears, but he almost couldn't process that—because she'd said she was *pregnant* and that wasn't right. It couldn't be!

'*What?*'

'I'm pregnant.'

'Pregnant.'

He continued to stare at her, his mind spinning away in

all directions as his thoughts bombarded him. She meant pregnant with his baby. But she'd said that she was on the pill. She'd said... He leant back against the wall in shock. He already had a daughter, and he loved her, but autism was a risk. Could he cope with another child with a disability?

'How?'

'I don't know. I might have missed a pill. Maybe two.'

'*How* did you miss taking them?'

'I was exhausted! Or upset! Or... I don't know! I had that bad headache after the accident. I took painkillers but I think I forgot my contraceptive!'

He gently pulled her into a side room. *She was pregnant? With his child? Was this why she'd passed out?* 'When did you find out?'

'About ten minutes ago.'

'And that's why you're so...?' He waved a hand in her general direction and she nodded.

'Yes. I think so.'

He ran his hands through his hair. *Ellie. Pregnant with his baby!* Once upon a time this would have been a dream situation! But now...? Now he couldn't think straight. They had a new patient and the possibility of a very fragile baby coming into the world. He needed to sort that out first. He knew they would have to discuss this later.

Softly, he said, 'We need to get back to work.'

'We need to talk—'

'Later.' He reached up to wipe away a tear that had trickled down her cheek.

'When?'

'Tonight? You could come round to mine. After Rachel's gone to bed? About eight?'

She nodded.

'We'll be okay. We can deal with this. All right?'

He let out a heavy breath and walked back in the direction of A&E, aware that Ellie was following closely behind.

Ellie knocked on his front door lightly, not wanting to be too loud and wake up Rachel. As much as she liked Rachel, she didn't need the little girl to be around for this conversation.

The day had passed in a weird kind of bubble. As if the rest of the world was still carrying on as normal, but she and Logan were pushing forward through the day with this huge news hanging around their necks and only they knew.

She had to tell him everything, right? Why should it be just *her* burden to carry? Besides, she was terrified to go through this alone. *Again.*

No. She needed to tell him. Needed to know if he would support her. If this time it would be different between them.

Logan opened his door and smiled at her. 'Come in.'

'Is Rachel asleep?'

'She should be by now.'

'Good. That's good.'

'Can I get you a drink?'

'Just water, thanks.'

'Okay. Take a seat. I'll just be a minute.'

She sank down onto his sofa. She was about to derail his life completely and he had no idea. He thought her pregnancy was the big news—well, it wasn't. She shivered.

Eventually he came back in with two glasses of water. He set them down on the table in front of them and went to sit on the couch opposite.

'There's something I haven't told you, Logan.'

He stared at her, frowning. 'What else is there?'

'I… I haven't been strictly honest with you. About my past. But you need to know about it. You need to know how things stand.'

'How what things stand? What's going on, Ellie?'

She could hear the fear in his voice and she hated it—because she didn't need fear. She needed strength from him. He'd let her down once and so had Daniel, by walking away when it got too much. Would Logan walk away from her again? Ellie was terrified that he would.

'I got married years ago…to a man called Daniel.'

'You were *married*? What happened?'

'The business we had together was thriving. Everything was going brilliantly—until I got pregnant.'

Logan blinked and stared, his mouth slightly open with shock.

'It seemed a normal pregnancy at first. I didn't get very big, but I put that down to the fact that it was my first and I've always been kind of slight, so…'

She reached for the water and took a sip, aware that he was waiting for the rest of the story. She knew she had to be brave. Even though it was make or break.

'I had a scan and they discovered that the baby—a boy—had bilateral renal agenesis.' She looked at him to gauge the impact of her words.

He closed his eyes as if in pain. 'Ellie…'

'We were told it was fatal. That he wouldn't live after birth and that I should have a termination of the pregnancy.'

He reached for her hand and she looked at their fingers entwined, grateful for his touch.

'What did you do?' he asked.

'We were both very upset. Our perfect world was shattered. Our baby had no kidneys! That was why I was small—he wasn't producing urine, and there was almost no amniotic fluid. Daniel wanted me to go ahead with the termination right away. He didn't see the point in letting the pregnancy continue only for our son to die after birth. He didn't see the point in putting us through that.'

'So you ended it?' His voice was gentle.

She felt her eyes well up, almost as if she were going through it for the first time. 'No.'

Logan frowned.

'I couldn't let him go like that! Like his existence meant nothing! Like he was nobody. Without a burial or anything. I needed to know that Samuel had meant something.'

'Samuel? That was his name?'

She nodded, feeling the tears trickle down her cheeks as she reached into her pocket to pull out Samuel's ultrasound picture and pass it to Logan. She watched as he focused on the picture, his eyes softening.

'Yes. Daniel and I argued. A lot. He disagreed with my decision, but I hoped that I could change his mind when I told him why.'

'What was your decision?'

'To carry Samuel to term so that legally he would be a person and then allow the doctors to use him as a donor. They told me that if he reached a good weight then they could use his corneas and heart valves. I knew I could carry on then—if my baby boy had a purpose and he could save someone else's life.'

'*God, Ellie...*'

'I got to hold him for a few moments after he was born. He looked perfect. Just asleep, that's all. And then they took him.'

Logan reached for her hand again and squeezed her fingers tight.

'I never wanted to get pregnant again because of the risk of having another baby with renal agenesis.'

'Did you and Daniel get any genetic testing?'

'Daniel wanted nothing to do with us. He didn't come with me to the hospital when I went into labour and I came home alone. He blamed me for being selfish and I blamed him for abandoning me. The marriage didn't last long after that.'

'That's why you decided on medicine?'

'Partly. To be part of a transplant team. To see the end result of what that kind of work does. I need to *see* it, Logan! I need to have hope…to know that my choice was the right one. I need to prove it to myself.'

'Only now you're pregnant. And that complicates everything.'

She nodded. 'And you need to know the risks. I can do this alone, Logan. I've done it once before and I could do it again if I had to. But I would like to think that you will be supporting me, as it's your baby too.'

He looked down at the ground, clearly overwhelmed by all that she'd said. 'I need time to let this sink in, but of course I'll be there for you. Whatever happens. You won't have to go through it alone.'

'Really? I will carry this baby and I will find out if it's okay. If it's not, well… You needed to know. From the very start.'

He breathed out. 'Okay.'

She got up to leave. 'I'll go now. I think I've ruined your evening enough.'

'Ellie.' He stopped her from going, his hand on her arm, and looked deeply into her eyes. 'You could never ruin anything. It's a shock, yes, but we can get through this— you and me. All right?'

She blinked back tears. Nodded.

He couldn't think straight after she'd gone. His mind was going round and round in circles, arguing one way and then the other. Bilateral renal agenesis was fatal. A baby couldn't survive outside the womb without kidneys. Ellie had kept her baby alive through the magic that was the umbilical cord and placenta. They had worked effectively to sustain Samuel.

But Ellie had lost her baby!

He hadn't been able to tell Ellie that it wasn't just the renal agenesis he was worried about. Rachel had autism. Okay, she was high functioning, and he'd been told she would have been autistic whether her mother had been in a dramatic accident or not—but did that mean he carried faulty genes? Ellie had enough on her plate to worry her senseless. Not reminding her of Rachel's diagnosis had simply seemed the right thing to do.

He'd always imagined that it would just be him and Rachel from now on. He hadn't wanted to be part of another relationship. But he didn't want to lose Ellie. Not again. Not now that she was back in his life.

But even if this baby was healthy, what would they do? Parent separately? Would he become one of those part-time fathers who only saw his child on alternate weekends? How would *that* work with Rachel? She liked routine. How would she understand all that was going on? A half-sibling who appeared only once in a blue moon?

Rachel. His heart ached for her and the confusion this would cause. He could already anticipate his exhaustion from her endless questions and the conversations that would go round and round and round as she analysed it all, trying to work it out. What had happened and where she stood in all this.

Would she understand what being a half-sister meant? He could talk to Rachel about the complexities of the human body, but when it came to talking about love and relationships, abstract ideas without form or shape, would she understand those?

He couldn't help but think about Ellie and all that she had gone through. How she had kept this huge thing to herself. All those times he'd asked her if she was all right in The Nest, working with the babies, and all those times she had lied to him and told him she was fine.

How *could* she be fine?

She had lost her son! He had died! No wonder she had gone a little crazy over baby Ava, had been so angry at the parents for not taking the time to see their baby. He could understand her reaction now, because in her eyes she would have loved *any* extra time with her baby.

He tried to imagine her going through such a thing alone. Abandoned. Her husband unable to deal with the thought of his son being used for organ donation. Had Daniel not understood the courage that his wife had had to make such a decision? What sort of man walked away from his wife when she was going through such a thing?

Logan felt a surge of anger, imagining what he might say or do if he ever met Daniel. His fists clenched and his stomach twisted and he had to take a deep breath to calm down.

Ellie had been so brave. And now he'd told her he would be there for her. But how? Hadn't he just derailed the future she saw for herself yet again? He wasn't sure what he and Ellie were to each other any more. He wanted to be there for her…but what about if he lost her? What if they lost this baby?

Could he go through the pain of that kind of loss again?

CHAPTER EIGHT

ELLIE WENT HOME and immediately found herself in Samuel's half-finished room. How long she stood in the doorway she didn't know, but when she realised she needed to do something, rather than just stand there and stare, she realised that her cheeks were wet with tears.

Tears for Samuel. For her marriage. For what had happened with Logan and now this new pregnancy.

A new concern.

A new fear.

She'd told him she was brave enough to do this alone, but *was* she? She'd barely made it through before. Walking out of the hospital with empty arms and a partially deflated belly had been like leaving a piece of her heart behind.

She'd known she'd never be the same again. And then, just days later, just when she'd thought she couldn't cry any more, her milk had come in—for a baby who wasn't around to drink it.

She'd debated expressing it and donating it, but had quickly realised that if she started doing so she wouldn't know when to stop. So she had just endured the pain and the ache and then, treacherously, mastitis had kicked in—as if her body thought she hadn't been punished enough.

And every day she had sat in an empty home, wondering how she was going to get through the future all alone.

But the thing that had sustained her, that had kept her

going, had been knowing that Samuel's heart valves had saved a life. That his eyes had allowed another baby to see. It had been the only lifebelt of hope that she'd been able to cling to.

And now another baby grew in her womb. It was tiny, but it was clinging to life, and whilst it did she would do all that she could to help it. She could do nothing else. As terrified as she was, she knew that she had to fight for this child too. It was what a mother did—and in her heart of hearts she *was* a mother! Even if she had no child to hold.

Logan had reassured her somewhat. He'd been kind. Sympathetic. And he had said he would be able to get her through this. He hadn't run from it the way Daniel had. Logan had opened his arms and allowed her to feel safe within them. She felt hope in her heart that he wouldn't let her down like before. Life had changed for him, too.

'I can do this,' she said to the empty room, her gaze falling upon the unconstructed cot. She wondered if she would ever get to build it. If she would ever get to finish painting the walls. If she would ever get to see her baby wearing the Babygros she had bought years ago.

Would it be wrong to put a new baby in Samuel's clothes? She didn't think so. Lots of children got hand-me-downs, didn't they? From their older siblings? It would just be the same thing.

'Maybe I'm thinking too far ahead. I still don't know if you'll be all right,' she said aloud.

Her hand lay protectively against her stomach and she exhaled a heavy breath, wondering if her belly would grow. She guessed that would be a sign, wouldn't it? She hadn't got very big with Samuel due to the lack of amniotic fluid.

There was a full-length mirror on her wardrobe door. Ellie went to her bedroom and stood in front of it, turning to the side, smoothing her hand over the swell of her abdomen. Was it larger than normal? It looked as if it might be. But what guarantee was that? She knew that if you'd carried a baby before you often got bigger quicker, so…

The one thing her stomach *did* tell her, though, was that she was hungry, so she headed downstairs to the kitchen to grab something to eat.

As she prepped a salad to have with some cold potatoes she had in the fridge, her phone rang.

'Hello?'

'Ellie?'

'Logan!'

It felt good to hear his voice. She was smiling without realising it. But then a darker thought emerged. What was he ringing for? To tell her that he'd changed his mind? That she was on her own again? Her stomach griped painfully.

'I just wanted to check you got home okay,' he said.

'Oh. Right. Yes, I did. Thank you.'

'Great.'

A pause. 'I guess I dropped a bombshell, didn't I?' she asked.

He laughed, but there was no humour in it. 'I haven't stopped thinking about it.'

'You're concerned. You have a right to be.'

'I'm concerned about Rachel in all of this.'

She nodded. Of course. He was a father. 'We could talk to her. Explain to her what's happening so she understands. She likes human biology, right? She should be okay.'

'I hope so.'

She knew it would be complicated, but they had months to work this out. Months to explore their feelings.

What *were* her feelings towards him? They were tangled. Complicated. She'd loved him before and that love had never quite gone away. Now they were back working together. Had slept together. Conceived a child. And yet he was still her boss. Still her mentor. But he had a pull, a hold on her heart that she couldn't fight.

She wanted to give it wholeheartedly to him. To trust him. To know that he would be there. But she was scared. He'd let her down once before when she'd thought they were strong.

'I'm not Daniel,' Logan said suddenly. 'I'm not walking away from you.'

The reassurance was exactly what she needed. Her knees almost buckled. She hadn't realised how tense she'd become, and now she released her grip on the knife she had in her other hand and laid it down gently upon the work surface.

'Thank you.' Her voice was like the squeak of a tiny mouse as tears leapt unbidden to her eyes. Tears of relief. Tears of happiness. For now, anyway. They still had many mountains to climb. Many rocky paths to traverse.

'But I want to keep this quiet for a while. In case of… Well, you know what I'm talking about.'

He meant the first trimester. They might not even make it through that first hurdle. 'Of course.'

'And we'll need to arrange your thirteen-week scan. That should give us some idea of what's going on.'

'Okay.'

She liked it that he was taking control suddenly. Liked it that he had somehow made up his mind as to which side of the fence he was falling. She clutched the phone, wishing he was there with her right now. Just to hold her in his arms and make her feel safe. Protected.

Loved.

CHAPTER NINE

ELLIE WOKE TO waves of nausea and staggered sleepily towards the bathroom, hoping she wasn't about to throw up all over her bedroom floor. Thankfully she made it, and washed her face afterwards, swilling her mouth out with water and blinking tiredly at her reflection.

I look awful. Where's that glow everyone talks about?

Downstairs, dressed and ready for work, she stared at the contents of her fridge and her cupboards for inspiration. She needed to eat, but what would stay down? There was a packet of plain biscuits, half empty, so she grabbed a couple of those and tentatively ate them. It seemed to help, so then she had a glass of juice and headed on out to work.

She felt apprehensive. Working with Logan would no longer be student and mentor but two adults who had made a baby, and she, at least, was struggling with her feelings.

How would Logan be with her today? She'd dropped an awful lot of information on him yesterday and now he'd had time to sleep on it. Had he changed his mind? Got cold feet? She felt ridiculous, doubting him when he'd said he'd be there for her, but she couldn't help it. And as she got closer to the hospital she found herself mentally preparing for him to have backed away—because that was what she was used to.

'Morning, Ellie!' other staff members called out, and she said hello back.

'You look tired. Late night?' one asked.

'Something like that...' she said.

Logan wasn't in the staff room, and she sat waiting for the team of doctors and nurses on the night shift to arrive and do the hand-over. When they did Logan still hadn't appeared. She tried to push it from her mind, telling herself it didn't mean anything. He might just be delayed in traffic or something. But it was typical that the one person she wanted to see and speak to the most wasn't here.

She made notes on her hand-over sheet and when it was over got up to do her rounds on the patients. To check in, check observations and familiarise herself with everyone's cases.

But it was difficult. Everything she did was overshadowed by worry about the health of the baby inside her womb. About whether Logan was going to bolt. He'd left her once before—he could easily do it again.

Her nausea was coming in waves—much more than she'd ever had with Samuel—and she wondered if it meant that her baby was a girl rather than another boy. She'd heard someone say that the sickness could be different depending on the sex of the baby. It was probably rubbish, though. An old wives' tale.

In her peripheral vision she saw a man walk by and she looked up.

It wasn't him. It was someone else.

'Looking for someone?'

It was Sarah, one of the nurses. Ellie hadn't even noticed that she was in the room.

'Dr Riley.'

'I heard he was in surgery. Some emergency...'

'Right. Okay. I'll catch him when he comes out.'

Ellie felt ridiculous. What had she been expecting? For him to come rushing in first thing to find her? To ask her how she felt today? To place his hand on her abdomen and say *Hello, baby*? It wasn't as if they were *together*. They weren't *a couple*.

This was just so confusing! She'd loved him madly when she was younger and he had walked away to pursue his career, breaking her heart. She had mourned this man, hoping that one day he would come back into her life. And now he had, and they had slept together, and now she was pregnant with his baby.

How was she *supposed* to feel about him? Had her feelings for him ever stopped? But she wasn't eighteen any more. She wasn't a lovesick teenager any more. She'd moved on. So had he.

And yet…

Maybe it was pregnancy hormones playing tricks with her mind. Was she really still seeking that happy-ever-after she'd dreamed of for both of them so many years ago? Logan cared for her. Was being so sensitive. He clearly still had feelings for her, and that was making her feel they might have a chance at a happy future.

But perhaps she was being stupid, hoping for a happy-ever-after, because he hadn't said outright that he wanted to be with her romantically, and she had no idea if this pregnancy would produce a healthy child at the end of it. If she even made it that far, of course.

And, despite what he'd promised, would she ever feel she could truly trust his word? He'd told her once before that he loved her. That she was his world. And then he'd gone to Edinburgh and within months he had ended it. He'd discarded her like a pair of shoes that no longer fitted.

She'd thought back then that he had loved her, but clearly she'd been wrong. Could she trust her instincts where Logan was concerned? He'd found it so easy to walk away from her. He'd never looked back. Never written. Never called. He'd made a clean break and that had been it. Surely if she'd meant *anything* to him there would have been something?

Ellie washed her hands at the sink, slowly and thoroughly. Taking her time before she had to assess the next baby. As she did so she told herself firmly that she had to remind herself that just because he'd said he would be there for her it did not mean they would be romantically involved. She was pregnant and this was serious. The two of them had to work together to get through this. But it would be co-parenting. That was all.

No point in trying to muddle through romantic feelings, too.

Logan had woken late to find Rachel already downstairs, getting anxious that life wasn't running to schedule. He'd had to handle one major blow-up, then get her to school, and then he'd got caught in traffic. By the time he got to work he felt hassled and stressed.

Last night had given him so much to take in. He knew about bilateral renal agenesis, but he'd found himself researching it on the internet, trying to discover if there was any risk for the new baby that Ellie was carrying.

Poor Ellie, having gone through that alone. What fortitude she must have! Such strength!

He'd never expected this. Not now. Once, maybe. He'd thought they'd always be together—until the realities of being so far away from each other and for so long had made him set her free. It hadn't been easy. His studies had suffered terribly afterwards as he'd fought the pain of her loss.

He'd got through it by telling himself he had done the sensible thing, but now...?

Now he wasn't sure.

He'd wanted her. He could admit that. The moment after

the accident when he'd held her again, had lain with her in his arms, had been a dream come true.

Ellie.

His feelings for her were so confusing! He'd never really stopped loving her. Sleeping with her, holding her, loving her again so freely had simply made their situation worse.

He'd *needed* her. They'd both been in an accident which, had it been any worse, might have claimed their lives. It had almost been like a wake-up call. He'd been going through life on auto-pilot. Working. Being Dad. But when had he last been *himself*?

The *real* him, Logan Riley, had craved her, had needed the comfort he had known he would find in her arms, and it had been frantic and magical and oh, so amazing! Yes, the guilt had kicked in afterwards—but was that true guilt or just selfishness?

Ellie had given him everything he'd needed and he had soaked it up like a sponge, hungry for more. Perhaps it was that hunger for more that had made him feel so confused? Because if he asked for more wasn't he putting himself at risk of loving again? *Losing* again? Letting her down by not being good enough?

Getting involved with Ellie could mean losing her. Losing their baby. Was he strong enough for that?

Logan sat at his desk and pondered the situation. If this baby was all right—if it even got past the first trimester—then they would be starting a family together. Another family that would tilt his world on its axis.

And how on earth would he cope with that? Just being in the hospital now made him feel that he wanted to go search her out, ask her how she was feeling. Pull her close. Hold her tight. Protect her.

He wanted to make sure she was looking after herself. Dammit. Stupidly, he even felt as if he wanted to lay his hand on her belly!

They'd had one uncontrollable, passionate, amazing moment in which they had both probably lost their minds, but they could be sensible *now* and make sure that would never happen again. It couldn't. Not until they knew what was happening.

So now he felt as if they were circling each other, testing the water, trying to decide how they should proceed.

Would they ever work that out?

Because he didn't want a future of treading on eggshells.

When it was the end of the day they left together and stood awkwardly by the lift, waiting for it to take them down.

'Did you have a good day today?' he asked.

She noticed as he glanced at her that his gaze dropped to her belly for a brief millisecond, before he coloured and looked away again, stabbing at the lift button in the hope of making it arrive quicker.

'It was good, yes. The lady we saw in A&E the other day came up. They stopped her contractions, but she came for a tour of The Nest anyway.'

'Oh, that's good! The longer babies stay inside, the better.'

He smiled, then looked awkward, obviously considering the situation between them. So much was being unsaid. There was so much they both wanted and needed to say, but they were holding back from one another.

It hadn't been awkward like this between them before. Was this how it was going to be from now on? Because she didn't need him being uncomfortable around her. She needed to know that she could talk to him. That they could talk to each other. After all, they were in this together.

'Logan. Are you having second thoughts about this?'

He quickly turned to look at her, an appalled look upon his face. 'No!'

'Good. Because we need to feel that we're able to be in the same space with each other without it being awkward. If we can't communicate, then how is this going to work?'

The lift pinged its arrival and when the doors slid open there were already three other people inside, so the opportunity for Logan to answer was not there.

They got in and rode the lift in silence.

Ellie could feel tears pricking at her eyes—which wasn't fair, because she felt as if she was being the strong one here, and yet she was going to cry, and everyone assumed that a crying woman was somehow weak. She looked away from everyone, trying to take deep breaths, trying to control her racing thoughts, until the doors pinged open once again and everyone got out.

Logan grabbed her arm and drew her to one side. 'We can talk to one another.'

'You've avoided me all day.'

'I've been in back-to-back surgeries.'

'Couldn't I have been in them *with* you? You're meant to be my teacher, and all day I've done nothing but record observations and change nappies. I want an education as well.'

Logan looked suitably mortified. 'I'm sorry. I didn't think of that—even though you've been on my mind all day. I want to care for you, but I don't know how to *be* with you. What *am* I? Just your mentor? Some guy who might have to co-parent with you? It *feels* like more than that. I *want* more than that. And yet...'

She could hear the yearning in his voice. 'You're all those things and more. We need to find a way to make this work. I've been left on my own too many times!'

'I know. And I'm sorry.' He reached to stroke her hair and then stopped himself.

She wiped away a tear. 'I won't break.'

'That's not what I'm worried about.'

'What *are* you worried about?'

Logan looked uncomfortable. He shuffled his feet, looking around them at all the milling staff and visitors, the odd patient wheeling an IV so they could go outside and smoke. He knew he had to get these words out, because they were killing him inside.

'I'm worried that if I allow myself to love you I could lose you. I could lose the baby, too. And I'm worried that if I start touching you I won't ever want to stop.'

She stared at him, her breath caught in her throat.

The words had just come out. One minute he was staring at her, his heart breaking because he'd upset her, and the next he was telling her he might not be able to stop himself from touching her!

What on earth was going on in his brain?

He made to walk away, his cheeks flushed red, angry with himself for saying such stupid things, for stepping over the line.

She called his name.

'Logan!'

He turned.

'Come to dinner tonight. Just you and me. We need to spend some time alone. Time outside of work, somewhere we won't get interrupted or distracted. Please?'

He could see she meant it sincerely. It was in her eyes. The desire for him to say yes. Perhaps it was a good idea? Though he wasn't sure if he'd be able to find someone to sit with Rachel. Sometimes Mrs Bennett his next-door neighbour could, but it was late notice.

'Err... I could try to get a sitter...'

'I could make my Ellie special?'

He smiled, remembering. 'Spaghetti? I'll be there.'

She touched his arm. 'Thank you.'

It was just a brief touch. A short acknowledgement to

show that she understood the hoops he jumped through on a daily basis. A touch to let him know just how much she'd heard him just now.

'What's your address?'

She told him and he noted it down in his mobile.

'Can you be there for around six?'

He nodded and then pulled her close. Embraced her in a warm bear hug. He knew it wasn't easy for her either, and that she was putting herself out on a line here. He needed her to know that he knew that.

He'd been right. He *didn't* want to let go of her now he'd touched her, but he knew he had to and so he stepped back awkwardly, nodded and began to walk away. He was getting as far away as possible from her as he could—because if he stayed any longer he might do something stupid... like kiss her.

And she wouldn't want that.

Would she?

At a quarter to six her doorbell rang and Ellie almost jumped out of her skin. She'd been checking her reflection in the mirror, wondering if the outfit she'd put on was too...date-ish.

She wanted to feel relaxed. Comfortable in her own home. But this was an important night for her and Logan, and for some reason she felt like she wanted to look beautiful. How often did she get to dress up and go out? *Never*, was the answer. There'd been nothing like that since Samuel.

But in the back of her wardrobe had been this lovely midnight-blue wraparound dress, which felt comfortable around her middle and didn't show off too much cleavage. She'd spent twenty minutes debating whether to wear flats or heels and had then decided on bare feet—so that had meant another ten minutes of painting her toenails and waiting for them to dry.

She'd washed her hair and straightened it, put on a full face of make-up that was designed to make her look 'natural' and then dithered a bit longer on whether dangly earrings were called for or not?

This is crazy. We're just going to be chatting. He'll probably turn up in jeans!

She told herself it wouldn't matter if he did. Because *she* felt like dressing up a bit and why not?

She opened the door with a big smile and butterflies in her belly. 'Logan! Hi, do come on in.'

Logan held a bunch of flowers in his hand and he passed them to her, dropping a peck on her cheek. 'You look lovely.'

She tried not to think about taking his face in her hands and kissing him properly. That wasn't what the evening was about, even if that was her urge.

'These flowers are beautiful. Thank you. I'll put them in a vase in a moment. Why don't we go straight through to the kitchen? I need to get the pasta on.'

Logan closed the front door and she smiled to herself as she headed into the kitchen—because he hadn't turned up in jeans. Logan was smartly dressed too. Dark trousers… white shirt slightly open at the collar. He was freshly shaved but had forgone cologne, knowing that it might upset her newly heightened senses.

Putting the flowers to one side, she washed her hands and added dried pasta to the already bubbling water. The kitchen smelled of garlic, the garlic bread having been in the oven on low for a couple of minutes already.

'Can I get you a drink?'

'Whatever you're having is fine by me,' answered Logan.

She grabbed the flowers again and put them in the sink,

then made the drinks and gave the pasta a stir, so it didn't stick to the bottom of the pan. She put a low heat under the pasta sauce.

'This won't be long. Then we could maybe eat in the lounge? There's a small table in there.'

Logan nodded. 'Please tell me you've expanded your repertoire and don't eat pasta *every* night?'

She smiled. 'I can boil an egg now, too.' There was an awkward pause when she didn't know what to say. Then, 'Quick tour?'

'Lead the way.'

Ellie showed him the lounge, then the bathroom, the spare bedroom, and then she hesitated at Samuel's door. She felt her mouth go dry. She'd never shown anyone this room. Not since he'd died.

'This was going to be Samuel's room.' She pushed open the door and stepped in so that he could follow her.

She saw him look around. Noticed him take in the still flat-packed crib leaning sadly against one of the two unpainted walls.

He glanced at her and then walked over to the windowsill, picked up the blue teddy bear that she'd hoped to take with her to the hospital on the day of his birth and put in his bassinet.

It had never made it there.

She'd never felt embarrassed at having left his room this way. It had simply paused in its purpose, the way she had in her life, and it had seemed wrong to take anything away.

Would Logan think she was terribly sad for having left it this way?

'How long ago were you…?' He looked down at her belly.

'It's been four years.'

'I'm sorry. Will this be the new baby's room?'

'Yes. It was always meant to be a nursery.'

He laid the teddy bear back upon the windowsill. 'Perhaps I could help you get it ready? I quite enjoy painting, and I've always enjoyed the puzzle of a flat-pack project.'

He smiled at her and she felt her heart thud loudly in her chest. He wasn't pitying her! Or blaming her for keeping this room as a...a shrine. Although that wasn't the right word, was it?

'You'll get good light in through this window and it's cosy. It will be perfect.'

'Thanks. I'd like that. Very much.'

After that she took him back to the kitchen, forgoing a detour to show him her bedroom. That seemed a little unwise, considering what he'd said when they'd been at work. Considering her feelings for him, too.

It would be so easy to fall back into his arms again. But she still wasn't sure what they were to each other, and she needed clarity before anything else happened. They both did. But he was here now, and that was what counted at the moment.

Back in the kitchen, she gave the pasta a stir. It was nearly done. She checked on the garlic bread and then asked Logan to help her set the table in the lounge.

They worked together quickly, and every time she looked up at him he smiled at her. She felt herself colour. *What was happening?*

Her hand went absently to her stomach.

He saw the movement. 'How do you feel?'

'Sick. Hungry. Tired.'

'That's good!'

'It feels worse than last time. *Does* it get worse with subsequent pregnancies?'

'I think each one is different.'

'I guess I should be thankful it's not hyperemesis gravidarum.'

He nodded and smiled. 'Have you been in touch with your doctors?'

'I gave them a call. They said I should hear something about the scan in the next couple of weeks. My GP is very good.'

'That's great. I think it's best we try to be positive, don't you?'

She nodded, wishing that she *could* be positive. But she would always hold a piece of her heart back until she knew for sure. She wouldn't be able to be fully happy until she had a healthy, happy baby safely in her arms. That was the dream, wasn't it?

He helped her serve up the food, cutting the garlic bread into slices whilst she served the pasta and the sauce. She was enjoying this domesticity with Logan. It was what might have been. What could yet be.

They sat down together and Ellie realised just how much she had missed this. Eating with someone else. Dining together like they had before. It was so lovely! And the enjoyment of it brought a small tear to her eye.

'Are you all right?' Logan asked.

She laughed. 'I'm fine! Pregnancy hormones!' She swirled her fork in the pasta and smiled at him.

The first scan would tell them so much. If the baby was growing properly. If its tiny heart was beating. Its kidneys intact… She could only hope.

'This is lovely,' said Logan. 'It was always one of my favourites.'

'You used to tell me you loved it back then.'

'You've managed to elevate it a bit.'

'It's just a different sauce.'

Why couldn't she take his compliment? Why was it making her feel so awkward?

They ate in silence for a moment, and then, when she couldn't bear it any more, she put down her fork and looked at him. 'I'm scared, Logan.'

He stared at her for a moment, and then he reached

across the table and took her hand. 'I'm here. I'm not going anywhere.'

She nodded in understanding, but the tears were already threatening to fall. 'You loved me once and then you left me. I'm trying to believe you're going to be here for this, but... I'm struggling.'

He squeezed her hand in his. 'I can't go back and put that right. What's done is done. But I'm going to try and make sure I do this right.'

'Try...?'

He smiled. 'I won't let you down. You need to trust me.'

She wanted to.

She wanted to very much indeed.

CHAPTER TEN

THEY WERE HAVING a lovely evening together. One of the nicest evenings that Logan could remember for a long time.

'Do you remember that time we went on that walk down the canal towpath and you almost fell in the water because you were showing off?' she asked.

Logan laughed, nodding. 'Oh, yes! I was such an idiot. Trying to make you see how cool I was. We hadn't been going out long at that point, had we?'

Ellie shook her head, her eyes alight with mirth.

'I can remember thinking what a good idea it would be to show you that I could balance my way across the lock. Show you that I wasn't scared,' he went on.

'You would have done it effortlessly if it hadn't have been for that goose honking!'

She laughed. It felt good to laugh with her. To reminisce.

'We do stupid things when we're young.'

'I'm not sure we do that many clever things when we're older.'

Logan thought about that and sipped his drink. 'Perhaps not. We're grown-ups, and we work in medicine, and yet we've still managed to have an accidental pregnancy.'

Ellie looked down and away.

'Oh, I didn't mean it was your fault,' he said. 'I just... Forget that, please? It came out wrong.'

She smiled. 'You're forgiven. So, how are we going to play this situation we now find ourselves in?'

He let out a sigh. 'I don't know...'

'We're friends...but I don't know what else we are. Our history together muddies the water.'

'We *are* friends,' he agreed. 'But we're more than friends, too. I don't know how to explain it.'

How could he when he couldn't explain it to himself? He knew what he wanted them to be, but what if he couldn't be what she needed when push came to shove? The last time he'd been with her he'd broken her heart *and* his own. He couldn't be that man again.

'We're both single now. We loved each other once but it didn't work out.'

She looked at him as if she needed him to say something—something that would reassure her that this time it would be different. But how could he know for sure?

'It wasn't because something went wrong with *us*, though. It was geography and timing.'

'And today it's history. So what do we do now? How do we move this further? Take it one day at a time? See where it leads us?'

At least she had the bravery to ask the question outright. To ask if they were going to try to be a couple again.

'Are you saying you want us to be together?' Logan asked, hoping beyond hope that she *was* saying that. That she wanted that.

But how scary would that be? Because then he'd have to totally step up and give her his heart—which he wanted to do! Of course he did! But he also wanted to move with caution this time, so as not to get it wrong.

He looked at Ellie and was suddenly struck by the warmth in her eyes. She cared about him. He could see that.

'I don't know.'

His gaze dropped to her belly and he wondered what secrets were contained within and whether their baby would live to see the brightness of the day.

The baby was a mystery. One that terrified him. Nowadays he and Ellie had modern technology to help guide them, let them know what they should do. But that first ultrasound was weeks away yet.

What if their baby *did* have bilateral renal agenesis? What then? Would he be strong enough, supportive enough to be with her if she carried on with the pregnancy? Knowing what grief awaited them both?

I don't know. I want to be.

It was too hard a decision to make just yet. He needed certainty. He needed to know the answers that would be provided by the ultrasound scan—because if everything was all right with the baby then he could tell Ellie just how much she meant to him.

Perhaps it would be better if he didn't think too much about the pregnancy in case disappointment and upset awaited him?

Logan looked directly into Ellie's eyes and could see how apprehensive she was. Already she was pinning all her hopes on this new pregnancy, hoping beyond hope that this time the baby would be all right and she could finally bring it home to that half-finished nursery down the hall.

What if she didn't? To lose a second child would break her in two—and what would it do to *them*? That was what scared him. Would she blame him? Would he lose her? Because he already had a family would she find it unbearable that she couldn't have one? Could he bear to lose her twice in one lifetime?

Loving Ellie would either bring him utter joy or total heartbreak.

'I've had a lovely evening, Ellie. Thank you. I think we needed this.'

She nodded. 'Me too. I had fun.'

'You should come to us next time. Or maybe we could go for a walk? Rachel likes the park.'

Ellie could imagine. 'I'd like that.'

'Small steps whilst we figure this thing out?'

'Yes.'

She was glad that he was still sorting out this situation between them. It was a difficult line to walk, with so many added complications.

'And of course I'll let you know when I get sent my scan date, so we can both put it in our diaries. You *will* come to the scan, won't you?'

Please say that you will. She couldn't bear the idea of going alone and hearing any bad news by herself.

He nodded. 'Of course. Well… I'd best be going.' He stood up. 'Can I use your bathroom before I go?'

'Sure.'

She watched him go and realised as he walked away that she really liked having them here. She knew that when he was gone the flat would seem terribly empty and lifeless.

Ellie looked down at her belly and caressed it. A new future might be growing inside her. A new hope. Someone who would make them incredibly happy or grief-stricken once again. In a way, it was the same thing for her and Logan. If they gave each other a chance, tried again, it could go right. But it might also go oh, so wrong.

He came back from the bathroom and grabbed his jacket. 'Thanks again, Ellie. It's been a good night.'

'I'll walk you out to your car.'

She tried not to feel sad. Tried not to feel as if she was letting him slip away as he opened the front door to leave her. Tried to feel optimistic that she would see him again soon at work. That this wasn't a permanent goodbye, just *au revoir*.

He turned in the doorway.

Ellie looked up into his eyes and felt a burning desire rush through her. A need so raw and simple for this man before her that she almost couldn't breathe.

She saw his gaze drop to her mouth and suddenly he was moving towards her, closing the gap between them hesitantly, uncertain, but doing it anyway.

Because neither of them could fight it.

And his lips met hers.

This kiss was different from the one when they'd thrown themselves at each other in the hospital. That kiss had been full of desperate passion and desire and an *I must have you now* adrenaline boost.

This kiss was gentle and tentative. Slow and measured. And she felt its warmth and the slow spread of it through her body as she was awakened to the desires within her.

This kiss took her breath.

And then he broke it off suddenly and stepped away. 'I'd…er…better go. Early start.'

She nodded, trying to smile. 'Of course.'

But her lips were still burning from his touch, her body was screaming to be touched too, and her blood was pounding its way through her veins.

Her fingers touched her lips as he got into his car and started the engine, and then her hand was at her throat as she realised what it might mean.

Were they getting back together?

So many questions. And this evening hadn't answered any of them. It had only created more.

Logan drove away, lifting his hand to wave before he went out of sight.

But that kiss… *Boy, that was something!*

She smiled to herself, biting her bottom lip, and turned to hurry indoors.

* * *

Logan could have kicked himself for kissing her.

I was supposed to be keeping my distance! It was meant to be a peck on the cheek. A thank-you!

But he'd been staring into those blue eyes of hers and he didn't know what had happened. Maybe it was the fact that they'd been talking about their relationship, how close they were to being together again...

He'd spent the whole night being sensible and keeping his distance, and yet there was a piece of him growing inside her—*their baby*—and he'd suddenly been overwhelmed by a feeling of such closeness and intimacy and love for her. He'd wanted to kiss her and he hadn't been able to stop himself.

And she'd kissed him back. That was the scariest thing. As if she'd *wanted* him to kiss her and she was enjoying it.

But, as he kept telling himself, they weren't together. They were just two people who'd made a baby by accident. That was all, right? So what was with all these feelings he was experiencing? Washing over him like waves? When he was with her he couldn't stop looking at her, and when they were apart his thoughts were of her.

It's probably just because of the baby.

Ellie had so much to worry about right now. She had to be in turmoil. He needed to give her some space until they were through it. Give her fewer complications to worry about.

This pregnancy could be a second chance for both him *and* Ellie, but the best thing he could do now would be to support her as a friend. By creating some emotional distance for himself he would be better able to protect her if it all went wrong. By loving her, letting himself get close, he'd risk devastation for them both, and she would need someone strong to lean on.

The pain he felt, knowing he had to hold back, was as raw as the pain he'd felt upon seeing his newborn daughter in Special Care—not knowing if she would survive. Not knowing if he should love her as much as he did because of how much it would hurt if he lost her. It was like a weight upon his chest. A cold lump of fear in his gut.

Can I hold myself back from her again?

He told himself—firmly this time—that he needed to begin distancing himself properly. If only to protect and support her heart if it all went wrong.

Despite the morning sickness Ellie woke up feeling bright and optimistic. She had a packet of biscuits at the side of her bed and she nibbled on those to get the nausea under control before she got up and headed downstairs.

Coffee and tea were still off the menu, so she poured herself a glass of apple juice and grabbed a breakfast bar for the trip into work. She'd discovered that if she ate little and often it seemed to help the most. Getting hungry was a big no-no.

But for some reason the sickness seemed a bit easier to handle today. It wasn't because it was actually any less—it still had the capacity to bring her to her knees if she let it—it was more that she herself felt stronger, and she put a lot of that down to the fact that Logan had kissed her. So gently. So tenderly. And with such devotion that she'd felt he cared. That she wasn't doing this alone.

She'd got so used to just relying upon herself, because it was safer that way, but this new way of living felt good, and she remembered now how it felt to know that she had someone she could lean on.

Logan.

Who'd have thought it? That after all these years they

would reconnect in such a way and have a baby together. Perhaps it had always been meant to be? Perhaps they'd both needed to go off in different directions in life in order to truly appreciate what they had now?

Once she got to work she clipped on her ID card and headed to the hand-over session.

Logan was already there, and she smiled at him and said good morning as she came in. He didn't really react, but she put it down to the fact that he was deep in discussion with another colleague. And she couldn't sit next to him because all the seats were taken.

She sat and listened and then, fully cognisant of what was going on in the department, got up to start her shift. She waited for Logan to be free.

'Hi.' She smiled at him.

'Hey.'

'What are you going to have me do today?' She was feeling optimistic.

'Well, I guess later we'll need to catch up on your placement file—make sure it's all up to date and see if there are any procedures or elements of patient care you haven't done yet.'

'I haven't followed a baby through to being discharged out of The Nest. Either to home or to Paediatrics. I know that.'

He nodded. 'Okay. The Carling baby is due to be discharged today—once we've done the car seat test.'

'The car seat test?'

'We put the baby in a car seat and leave it in for thirty minutes, to make sure their oxygen saturations stay at high levels.'

'Oh, okay.'

'Maybe you could be in charge of that, and then I can show you how to discharge a patient?'

'All right.'

He smiled to indicate that their conversation was over and then walked away from her, heading towards his office. She figured he was always busy at the hand-over of shift and must have a lot to do—unlike her. She had an easier workload.

She went to take a set of observations on baby Marcus Carling, so she'd have a base set of numbers before she had to do the car seat test.

His parents were already there, with the car seat they'd been asked to bring in, and she smiled at them both. 'Morning, Jess… David. How are you today?'

Jess smiled nervously. 'Anxious.'

'About the test?'

'That and taking him home.'

She stroked Jess's arm. 'That's the best part.'

'*And* the most terrifying. We won't have all of you guys looking after him…making sure he's okay.'

'But you have to comfort yourself with the fact that since he came into The Nest his oxygen levels haven't dropped the way they did after birth.'

Marcus had been born at thirty-six weeks. He'd been blue, with the cord wrapped three times around his neck, but they'd managed to revive him and get him breathing. Then, about an hour after birth, he'd begun to look hypoxic and his parents had pressed the emergency buzzer in a panic.

Since then baby Marcus had been monitored for three days in The Nest and his oxygen saturations had been fine—not even dropping when he had his feeds. He was looking good and it was safe for him to go home. The car seat test *had* to go well.

'We've bought an oxygen monitor, just in case. You probably think we're being over-cautious, maybe paranoid, but—'

'I don't think that at all. I think it's a sensible step for you to take.'

'It will make us feel safer,' David said. 'What with us both being first-time parents.'

Ellie nodded. 'Of course. Let's see how he's doing first, and then we'll get him into the car seat—okay?'

'For thirty minutes?' Jess asked.

'Yes. If he manages that without dropping his levels— we'll have a monitor on him at all times—then he can go home.'

She began to take her readings, assessing him for colour and form, tone and alertness. Compared to some of the other babies in The Nest Marcus looked sturdy and healthy. As if he shouldn't be there at all.

'Do you have kids?' asked Jess.

'I have a son.' It had just slipped out, and she blinked hard, realising what she'd admitted for the first time.

'How old is he?'

She smiled, pulling her stethoscope from inside her ears. 'He's still a baby.' It hurt to tell this half-truth, but she couldn't show it.

'So you know how scary it is to take a baby home for the first time? Any tips you can share?'

Ellie hoped she wouldn't cry. Her emotions were all over the place right now. 'Sleep when they sleep. Rest as much as you can. Eat well.'

'Sounds doable,' said David.

She smiled, knowing that she'd never got the chance to do any of those things. Would she this time? Was this baby going to make it?

'Okay, shall we start the car seat test?'

David nodded and got the seat ready, placing it on the floor and preparing the safety straps, pulling them out to wrap around Marcus.

'Okay, Mum, when you're ready?' Ellie stepped back, holding the monitor she would wrap around Marcus's toe.

Jess knelt down, kissing Marcus on the forehead, before placing him in the seat, adjusting his arms and legs through the straps and clicking the safety buckle.

'You gotta ace this—you hear me?' she whispered, then stood up and wrapped her arms around her husband.

Ellie attached the monitor and checked the read-out. All looked good.

She sat back and waited.

Logan observed her from his office. She didn't see him. She was too busy talking to the Carlings. He guessed the car seat test had gone well, because it looked as if it was smiles all round, and Jess Carling was beaming, having scooped up baby Marcus into her arms.

He was smiling a little himself. It always made him pleased when parents could finally take their baby home. It meant that everything was right with the world and all was as it should be. Babies should be with their parents—not trapped on a hospital ward.

Had he now created a situation in which he and Ellie would be sitting anxiously by a cot?

He blamed himself. He'd caused this by giving in to his desires. Kissing her. Sleeping with her.

What on earth was I playing at? I should have been her mentor and protected her. Put her feelings first.

He'd told her he would be there for her and he would. But he also had to remember that he had Rachel to think about. He couldn't start a relationship with Ellie when they didn't know how this pregnancy would go, and it would be the wrong thing to do to get involved just because of it.

What did it even *mean*, anyway? It was proof that they'd slept together, but it wasn't physical evidence that they'd have a fool-proof romantic future!

He couldn't deny that he loved Ellie. He probably always would. But he couldn't be involved with her romantically just yet. That wasn't what she needed. She needed him to be strong. There were so many hurdles they had to get over first—before he could allow himself to think of anything else.

She said she'd do the same thing again if she knew their baby wouldn't survive.

He really hoped that neither of them would have to face that possibility. To watch her go through that would tear him apart. And to experience it himself...? Well, he had no idea how he'd feel, but he *did* know how he'd felt when he'd not known if Rachel would live. That had been horrendous.

And although she'd said she was strong enough to do it...*he* wasn't.

Ellie waved off the Carlings, feeling happy tears prick at the backs of her eyes as she watched them walk away with baby Marcus in his car seat. They were going home with their baby, which was exactly as it should be.

She was happy for them. She *was*. But she was also envious, not knowing if she would ever experience the same thrill for herself. She could hardly imagine how it must feel, but she supposed it must feel wondrous. You'd feel ecstatic and nervous and exhausted all at the same time!

'He made it, then?'

She turned to smile at Logan, glad that he was there with her to see it happen. 'Yes, he did brilliantly.'

'Are you crying?'

She laughed, a little embarrassed. What could she do with these hormones running rampant? 'Maybe a little.'

She felt a need for his arms around her at that moment. Just a little something to show that he cared. So she moved to wrap her arms around him, going up on tiptoe to give him a kiss.

He stepped away, looking awkward, looking up and down the corridor to make sure they were alone. 'What are you *doing*?'

Confused, Ellie looked up at him, not sure what was going on. 'I was just going to…to kiss you.'

'I don't think we should do that here. I'm sorry if I've given you the wrong messages, or the wrong impression of what's happening between us, but we shouldn't be doing this. Not really. *Slowly*, we said.'

His words, and his physical retreat from her, hit her like a sledgehammer. 'What do you mean? I thought we'd had a lovely night last night? We *kissed*! It was…it was the most wonderful thing I—'

'It was a mistake. I should never have done it and I apologise.'

'What?' Surely what he was saying couldn't be true? He'd kissed her last night! And that kiss hadn't been a goodbye kiss between friends, or a peck on the cheek. It had been deep and sensual and it had *meant* something!

'I'm here for you, Ellie, but…'

She held up her hand, stopping him from speaking. The tears were falling freely now. 'I should have guessed. I mean, you've done this sort of thing before. I should have known. You have a track record, don't you? Of letting me down?'

He shook his head. *'Ellie—'*

'Please—don't. I just can't believe you'd do this to me again!' And she pushed by him, running to the toilets so she could break her heart in private.

What a fool she had been! To think that just because he'd kissed her, just because they were having a baby, they were more than friends.

I've embarrassed myself!

And, worse, she had done so at work! Where she was supposed to be making a future for herself. He was her mentor—how the hell was she supposed to learn anything from him *now*, without there being an atmosphere?

I can't stay here. I can't look him in the eye. Not today.

She wiped her eyes with tissue and then left the safety of the bathroom and headed to the staff room.

One of the nurses was in there. 'Hi. I'm just making a cup of tea for a mum. Want one?' The nurse did a double-take. 'Hey, are you all right?'

'No. I don't feel well. I'm going home.'

'Have you told Dr Riley?'

'No. If he asks can you tell him that I've gone and that it's probably best if he doesn't call.'

The nurse looked confused. 'Er...okay...'

Ellie grabbed everything from her locker and raced from the department, hoping she wouldn't meet Logan on her way out. She didn't want to see him. He'd made everything quite clear.

She'd been a fool not to see it before. His hesitation. His uncertainty. He'd been having doubts but had been too afraid to tell her! Daniel had walked away and now Logan was doing it too. *Again!* They were apart. Not a couple, as she'd hoped they were. And now, no matter what happened to this baby she had in her belly, she was going to have to do it alone—as she'd suspected.

How could he do this to me?

Logan was frustrated that she hadn't let him explain. But to let her kiss him? At *work*? It was the one thing he wanted to do more than anything, but how could he let it happen when he was trying so hard to keep her at arms' length until he knew what was happening with the baby, so he could support them?

He loved her! Deeply. She couldn't possibly understand

how much! He did, and it was hurting him to push her away, but he was doing it so he could protect her heart. Support her if the worst happened.

Because if there was something wrong with this baby he'd need to be able to deal with it, and his feelings, without having to worry about letting Ellie down. If they lost this baby he'd be a basket case. It would tear him in two. But Ellie would need someone strong around her.

He'd kissed her last night and he shouldn't have. But his friendship with her, his feelings for her, had kept dragging him back, and he'd needed the connection he'd felt with her. He'd thoroughly enjoyed last night, but he knew he'd enjoyed it too much, knew that when he was with her he couldn't stop himself from gazing at her face, from being mesmerised by her lips, by the feelings he felt within his own body whenever she was near.

Physically, his body betrayed him. Emotionally...? He didn't want to think about that. Right now he wanted to focus on the anger he felt with himself. If he focused on that, then he wouldn't have to think about how her large blue eyes had welled up with tears and how she'd run away from him.

He knew this was all his fault.

Focus on that!

He threw himself into his work, only discovering some time later that Ellie had gone home. 'Feeling ill', the nurse said, but it was clear from the nurse's face that she suspected it might be for some other reason.

'She said best not to call her.' The nurse raised an eyebrow.

'Right. Thank you.'

His duties done for now, he headed into his office and closed the door, sinking down into his seat and holding his head in his hands. He'd screwed up royally. He knew that. He'd led her to think one thing and then pulled away when she'd tried to make things more serious, more official between them by going in for a kiss.

He groaned, telling himself it had still been the right thing to do.

For all of them.

He had to believe that.

She would thank him when the time came.

CHAPTER ELEVEN

SHE FELT SICK. Awful. Ever since she'd left the hospital she'd felt as if the whole world had become much darker. She kept forcing herself to eat, even though she didn't want to, knowing that she had to, that otherwise she'd start being sick. Eating was the only thing keeping it at bay.

And she had a shift this morning.

How was she going to be able to work with him? After all he'd put her through?

Okay, maybe she'd read more into it than she should have, but they'd slept together, made a baby. He'd kissed her just a couple of nights ago and it had been the most wonderful, tender, loving kiss she had ever experienced! Of *course* she'd read something into that. Who wouldn't? She'd felt that their kiss had said, *I want you. I care for you. I need you. You mean something to me.*

And she'd allowed those feelings in.

It meant more than being friends, a kiss like that. There'd been meaning in it. They'd been getting to know each other again outside of work. She'd met his daughter. They'd been rekindling their relationship of old, making it into something newer, something better—something that spoke of hope and redemption and possibility.

And love?

She'd be lying if she said she didn't love him. She had *always* loved Logan Riley. She'd just been very good at hiding it, that was all. But that kiss had opened the flood-gates and all those repressed feelings she'd stamped down over the years so that she could move on with her life had come rushing back. She'd been hopeless to fight them.

She'd believed that he would be with her for one of the most stressful events of her life…finding out about this baby… And now?

He'd made it quite clear that they were *not* a couple. That they were *not* together. He hadn't minced his words and they had torn her heart asunder. If she lost this baby because of the grief of that she would never forgive him.

Gritting her teeth, she buzzed through to The Nest and walked down the long corridor towards the staff room. He would be in there. There would be questions from every-one else. Did she feel okay? Was she better?

Would he look at her? Talk to her? Say hello? Ellie didn't know how she would feel about that. Whether she was ready to see him, or whether just looking at him would make her burst into tears all over again.

She'd hardly slept. She'd lain awake all night, staring at the ceiling, her hand resting on her belly which she could swear was definitely already bigger.

There was a roundness to it—a definite swell. She thought that was good. She hadn't got big with Samuel because there had been no amniotic fluid. But she was also worried that this size increase meant something bad—because surely it was too soon to be getting bigger?

At about two in the morning she'd started searching on the internet for what it could mean.

Polyhydramnios was one thing. An excess of amniotic fluid seen only in about one percent of pregnancies. But that didn't mean anything. Bilateral renal agenesis wasn't exactly common, and her son had had that.

Multiple pregnancy? She doubted that very much. There was nothing in her family history to indicate that.

The way the baby was lying? It was still so small! Surely that would have no bearing on things!

It had to be something else. Something she hadn't thought of. Something scary, no doubt—because that was how her life had played out so far, and she knew that whatever it was she was going to be facing it alone, so...

The staff room was full of staff waiting for the handover. Nervously she let her gaze scan the room, but she didn't see Logan and she felt herself relax a little. No matter what had happened between them, she still needed to continue her education.

'Ellie! Hey, how are you feeling? Any better? You look a little pale.'

She smiled at the nurse. 'Just tired, that's all. It was a long night.'

'Well, I hope it's nothing catching.' The nurse smiled.

Was grief catching? Pregnancy certainly wasn't. But grief and hurt and pain might be. It often caught people unawares. Knocked them sideways—wasn't that what they said? Life throwing you a curveball? Having to roll with the punches?

Well, she was fed up with having to do that. What had she done in life that made her deserve all this?

She sat down and Dr Curtis from the night shift stood up at the front. He waited for them to settle and stop talking and then began the hand-over, going over each case, what treatment they'd had overnight, any issues and any red flags. He listed the tests that still needed doing, and the procedures certain babies were due for.

'And as you'll see we have no Dr Riley with us this morning. He's swapped to nights for the next couple of weeks, so we'll just have to cope without him.'

Everyone grumbled—but not Ellie. *Swapped to nights?* Because of what had happened with *them*? Who would be there overnight for Rachel? There must be someone. His parents? A friend? Who? Perhaps there was someone else? Some other relationship he was in and that was why he'd got so vehement with her the other day. Because he'd been juggling two women at the same time. It wouldn't be the first time a man had done that.

She raised a hand. 'He was my learning mentor. Who do I go to now if my shifts haven't been changed to match his?'

'Ah, yes, he mentioned that. You'll now be with me— but you haven't got long left on this placement, and Dr Riley has assured me your training has been proceeding well, so it shouldn't disturb you too much. Okay?'

No. No, it *wasn't* okay. But she nodded anyway. She guessed she'd probably never meant that much to him anyway.

Logan's mother, now back from her travels in Bali, had been really keen to catch up with her granddaughter and had offered to come over each evening and be around through the night, whilst he was at work. She'd been happy to have the company and not be alone at night, what with his dad now being away on a golfing trip to Sri Lanka. His mum hated being alone, so it was a solution that fitted them all.

'I promise it's just for the next couple of weeks or so. You should be home again for when Dad gets back from his trip.'

'Oh, it's no problem! I love being here for you and Rachel—you know that. But is everything all right? I thought they knew you couldn't do nights?'

'They do. It's just… I offered.'

'Oh. Are you sure everything is all right?'

He nodded, but he had to turn away. She could always tell when he was lying. But what was he going to do? Tell her he was trying to give Ellie Jones some space for a bit?

The woman he'd got pregnant? That didn't sound very good, did it?

But he'd done it for Ellie. For her education. He'd screwed up what they had, but he wasn't going to mess with her career. That was important to her. So he'd swapped shifts for her benefit. This way she could continue with her placement without the distraction of him, and concentrate on what she had to do to pass without him ruining everything for her.

Why did he keep doing that to her? He'd left her to go to Edinburgh for his own education and now he was walking away again for the benefit of *hers*!

It was ridiculous! But he would do it because it was best for her. And, despite what he'd done, he did want the best for her. Of course he did. She needed someone who could be there for her one hundred percent, and he couldn't do that if he was distracted by his own feelings for her. She probably didn't understand right now, but she would.

Yes, he loved Ellie. He always had. He'd always cared for her. Deeply. He knew that. It had been hard to walk away from her the first time and he'd fought so hard not to contact her—because what would that have achieved? So he'd told himself he didn't love her because that was better, wasn't it? Easier for his conscience to bear?

And then there'd been Jo, and then Rachel, and then Ellie again, and…

He'd never be able to adequately explain just how he'd felt to have Ellie back in his life again. That first day, seeing her standing there on his ward in The Nest, looking so alone… He'd wondered what that look in her eyes had been about and he got it now. Seeing all those babies after losing her own must have been terrifying. How brave she was to go through this—and now she was pregnant. With *his* child!

He would be there for them both. He would!

But the big question was, would she ever understand the sacrifice he was making?

He was so afraid. Afraid of allowing himself to love her fully, freely, knowing that something could happen to her at any time and rip his heart from his chest and bring him to his knees. He'd been through it with Jo and barely kept going, but he had done so because he'd needed to be a father. To sit by the incubator holding his own daughter in The Nest. The team had been by his side and had been wonderful, but at the end of the day it had all been down to him.

What if something terrible happened to Ellie or the baby? What if this baby had renal agenesis, too? He wasn't brave enough to take a chance on experiencing another loss. How many losses could one person go through before they were unable to function?

These thoughts weighed heavy on his mind as he made his way to work, making sure he saw Ellie leave before he entered the building for his shift. His heart had missed a beat at the sight of her. She looked so forlorn. So lost. So weary. All this had to be weighing heavily on her and he wanted to be there, to wrap his arms around her and tell her that no matter what it would be all right.

But he was afraid to go to her. To make it worse. So he stood back.

His first patient to check on, Baby Wells, was a new admission. Just twenty-five weeks' gestation, tiny as a baby bird, and covered in the usual tubes, monitors and oversized hat. He saw that one of the team had given him a knitted octopus to hold on to. They found that a lot of babies found comfort in knitted toys. They mimicked the feel of the long umbilical cord they'd felt in the safety of the womb.

'Hello…' he said in a low voice to the mother who sat

alongside. 'I'm Dr Logan Riley and I'll be looking after your little one tonight. Does he have a name yet?'

'No. But I've been considering a couple.'

'What are they?'

'I've always liked the name Conor, but I wonder if I ought to name him after his father.'

Logan nodded. He'd read in the notes that the father had passed away. In a way, this baby's mother was in the position he'd found himself in a long, long time ago. He wanted to be able to tell her that it would all work out, but he didn't know that. Not for sure. And it was always best never to make promises you couldn't keep.

'What was his dad's name?'

'Mitchell.'

'Both good names. Strong. Which do you think suits him best?'

She smiled, her eyes welling up. 'Mitchell.'

He offered her a box of tissues. 'Let me know when you've chosen and we can update his records.'

'Okay.' She wiped her nose and dabbed at the under-sides of her eyes. 'You know he died just a few months ago? My husband?'

Logan nodded.

'He was so excited about this pregnancy. We both were. We'd already been through so much—three miscarriages. *Three!* I didn't want to try again. I even went on the pill. But then *he* came along.' She smiled down at her baby. 'Despite everything, I guess he was meant to be, huh?'

Ellie had been on the pill and got pregnant. He couldn't help but think of her.

'Were your miscarriages early on?'

She shook her head. 'No. Second trimester. I had to give birth to them all.'

Logan sank into his seat as he tried to imagine that. What she must have been through.

'But then Mitchell, here—well, he made it to twenty-five weeks and they rushed him up here. Do you have any idea just how much I want to be able to hold a baby of my own in my arms?'

He nodded. 'I think I can imagine.'

'Well, times that by a hundred. A thousand. To lose all those babies and then my husband, and then to go into early labour with this one... I was so scared!'

'But brave, too.' He smiled. How much courage must this woman have found to keep on enduring? Doing it alone? 'How do you think you managed it?'

She smiled. 'You just have to, you know? It's not a question of walking away. You love them and you try your best, no matter what.'

No matter what.

Was that the answer? You just kept going? Because there was no other option? He loved Rachel and he had to love Ellie and the baby, because this staying away, this walking away, had hurt him so badly he could hardly breathe.

Was he doing it for her? Or was he doing it to preserve himself?

I've been selfish!

Ellie needed him! His baby needed him! He should never have walked away! Especially knowing how she'd been abandoned before.

Logan gritted his teeth, wanting to go straight to his office and call her right now. But he couldn't. It was the middle of the night. He felt ashamed of his own selfish behaviour. How would he face her? Apologise? Explain?

'So, it's Mitchell, after all?'

The mother smiled and nodded. Clearly glad to have made the decision.

'I'll change his tags. Let's make it official.'

Ellie was nearly at the end of her first trimester now, and already her waistbands were getting tight. Perhaps it was just all this eating she was doing to stave off the sickness she was feeling? It had to be that, right?

So why aren't I putting on weight everywhere else?

What *was* it? She feared it was some extremely rare condition she didn't know about. Something she hadn't yet come across in her textbooks and research.

Seated in the waiting room of the department, she found herself anxiously fidgeting with the strap of her handbag. She was constantly checking her mobile phone, and twiddling with the hem of her shirt. She was so absorbed that she didn't notice someone come and stand before her until his feet came into view.

She looked up. 'Logan!'

What was he doing here? *Oh, of course. He's here for the baby. Not me. Remember?*

'I wasn't sure you'd come.'

'I said I would.'

Yes, he'd made that quite clear. He wasn't here for her. He was here because he felt a responsibility for putting this probably incredibly ill baby into her womb.

'But I'm also here to explain, if you'll let me.'

Was he really going to string this out even more? What was there left for them to say to one another? Did he not know how hard it was for her to have him here? The man she loved? The man she had in her heart but couldn't have in her arms?

'Oh?'

He sank down into the chair next to her. 'The last time we spoke I said something that I couldn't properly explain.

I was speaking from a place of fear. I acted the way I did because I was trying to protect you from what might come. From the knowledge that I had to be strong for you if everything went wrong.'

He shifted in his seat, made sure she was looking at him and took both her hands in his. She had to hear what he had to say.

'I lost the woman I loved when she was pregnant and I nearly lost my child, too. I've never been so scared in my entire life, Ellie. And when that happened I couldn't imagine going through the same thing again. Knowing how it would hurt you, I took a step back, thinking that if everything went wrong I'd be strong enough to support you—*if* I had some distance. I was bouncing from one thought and feeling to another, like a ball in a pinball machine, and in some stupid, confused, terrified act of trying to distance myself I did what I did and broke your heart. I never meant to. I'm sorry. And I'd like to hope you could learn to forgive me.'

She held her breath, listening to him speak. 'I...'

'I didn't realise until I'd done what I did that you would feel I was abandoning you again, so I've come to tell you that I'm not just here for the baby but for *you* too—whatever happens when we go into that room. I'm here for *us*. If you'll let there *be* an us. And to prove what I mean by that I'd like to do this...'

He got down on one knee and reached into his pocket.

She heard gasps of delight from the other mums-to-be in the room and felt her cheeks colour as he produced a small red velvet box and opened it to reveal a diamond solitaire.

'I love you, Ellie Jones. I always have and I always will. I want you in my life for ever. I want to show the whole world how committed we are. I want to spend the rest of my life showing you every day just how much I love you and how much you mean to me. Will you marry me?'

The room went silent, except for the ringing of a phone at the main desk, and Ellie watched as the receptionist picked up the handset as if in slow motion, her mouth agape, waiting for her answer.

He *loved* her? He'd been *scared*? Well, so had she! Terribly afraid!

But didn't they all do silly things when they were scared? She'd tried to close her whole life off because of what had happened with Samuel and Daniel. She'd been spending all her free hours glued to the internet, trying to discover all the obscure pregnancy-related complications there had ever been so that she could be prepared for each individual occurrence, should it happen.

That wasn't rational behaviour! That was ridiculous! She'd almost driven herself insane, searching for what might be wrong with this pregnancy, when she'd been given no hint that there was anything wrong at all just yet!

And best of all he'd said that he loved her. That he was here for her no matter what. They could both go into that ultrasound room and hear the worst news of their entire lives but he wanted to be by her side for it. He'd been trying to be strong for her by creating some space for himself. That was all. He'd done it all for *her*.

'What about Rachel?'

'I've spoken to Rachel. She knows I'm doing this and she's happy about it. She said, *"At least you won't be lonely any more."* But please don't say yes because you think you'll make Rachel happy, or me happy. Say yes only if you mean it. If you want me as much as I want you. If you *love* me as much as I love you.'

Her heart was pounding in her chest and slowly a smile emerged onto her face. 'Yes! Of course, *yes*!'

The room erupted into noise as he slid the ring onto her finger, and then he was leaning forward to kiss her and hug her.

Words were not enough to explain how she felt in that moment as she stood there, her arms wrapped around the man she loved. Her happiness had multiplied suddenly, exponentially, and if the room had had no lights she felt sure her smile would have lit the place up instead.

They settled into chairs next to each other and she fiddled with the solitaire on her finger. 'It's beautiful...' She kissed him, feeling her heart expand to let him in, feeling the warmth and the strength of his love surround her. Whatever faced them they would do it together.

'Ellie Jones?' said a voice.

A woman stood in the doorway of the ultrasound room. It was her turn.

She turned to face Logan. 'Are we ready for this?'

He squeezed her hand tight and placed another kiss on her lips. 'We can face anything. No matter what.'

Ellie lay down on the bed and undid the button and the zip on her jeans. To be quite frank it was a relief. She'd stuffed herself into them that morning, figuring they would do for the rest of the week, but she'd been regretting that decision ever since she'd left home.

Now she lay there, flinching as cold gel was squirted onto her lower abdomen and the sonographer placed the probe.

She didn't have to reach for Logan's hand. He already held her hand in his and now he kissed it reassuringly. She smiled at him, and then bit her lip. She couldn't see the screen, but she could see the sonographer frowning and her spirits sank.

She mentally prepared herself for the worst. 'What is it? You can tell me.'

The sonographer shook her head. 'I'm...er...this is my first day going solo and I think I just need someone to double-check something for me.'

Ellie *knew* it. She'd known there was something wrong!

'Do you have any history of multiples in your family?' asked the sonographer.

She blinked. Multiples? 'Er... I'm sorry? What...? Er... no.' She glanced at Logan, who shook his head.

'Nor me, as far as I know. Is it twins?'

Ellie turned back to the sonographer, who was shaking her head with a huge smile upon her face.

'I think it *is*!'

Twins!

A multiple pregnancy!

That had to explain why she was so much bigger! She had dismissed that idea simply because there wasn't any history of twins in her family, and quite frankly it had seemed too easy a solution. She'd automatically focused on the dark and the horrible, because that was all she'd ever experienced.

'Twins...?'

'I think so. I'll just get my colleague to confirm...to make sure I'm not missing anything.'

Ellie began to shake. 'Okay...'

The sonographer nipped out of the room and Ellie turned to face Logan. 'Oh, my God! *Twins!*'

He laughed. 'I know! That's *crazy*!'

The sonographer came back with a colleague, who sat down and moved the probe once again before turning the screen and showing them their babies, counting them off— one and two—as she scanned.

'Are they okay? I've been so worried about bilateral renal agenesis. My son had it and—'

'Everything looks okay so far. All good. They're each the size of a singleton baby at this gestation.'

'Oh, my God!' Tears of relief began to flow freely down her cheeks. They were okay! They were healthy! She had *two* babies inside her!

'This will probably explain why your abdomen is a little larger than we'd expect at this stage.'

'Are they identical?' asked Logan.

The sonographer moved the probe. 'See this? They're in individual sacs, so no.'

Logan shook his head in awe. In amazement. He leant forward and kissed Ellie, passing her a tissue for her tears. 'Are you happy?'

'Are you kidding me? I'm *ecstatic*. This day has gone so much better than I could ever have imagined.'

He smiled and kissed her forehead, stroking back her dark hair. 'I'm glad. It's been one of the best days of my life so far.'

'You mean it?'

He smiled. 'Of course I do.'

And then he kissed her again.

EPILOGUE

LOGAN KNELT DOWN to face Rachel outside the hospital room. 'Now, before we go in, tell me the rules again.'

'Be gentle.'

'And...?'

'Wash my hands.'

He smiled. 'Okay. If we press this button on the wall it'll help us do that.'

He demonstrated how to get some antibacterial hand gel from the wall dispenser and rubbed his hands, watching Rachel as she did the same.

'And what else do we need to be?'

Rachel smiled. 'Quiet. Can I see the babies now?'

'Sure.' He elbowed the door open, beaming a smile at Ellie, who sat between two incubators, a blanket over her lap. 'Hey!'

'Rachel!' Ellie beamed a smile and reached out with her hands, curling her little fingers.

She and Rachel had found a new way to give each other hugs that didn't make Rachel feel uncomfortable with bodily contact. They made pinkie promises. Hooking their pinkie fingers around each other's.

'How are you doing, pumpkin?'

'I'm not a pumpkin, Ellie. I'm a little girl.'

She laughed. 'Of course you are. Silly me. I forgot. I saw your beautiful smile and couldn't help myself.'

'Is this my sister and brother?' Rachel peered at each incubator, her expression curious and interested.

They were in The Nest, of course. Not because anything was wrong, but because the twins had been born at thirty-six weeks—early for a singleton pregnancy, but perfect for a twin one. It was purely for monitoring. To make sure they maintained their temperature and oxygen levels and until they learned the sucking reflex for their feeds.

'Yes. This one is Holly and the boy over here is... Well, we wondered if *you'd* like to be the one to give him a name?'

Ellie and Logan had discussed this. There were so many names they both liked, but they wanted Rachel to feel as if she had a part in this new family, and that meant including her in their decisions. Allowing her to name one of the babies was a huge thing, and something they hoped would allow her to feel closer to her new siblings.

Rachel took a good, hard look at him. 'He's very small.'

'He's very young.'

'He looks like a baby.'

They laughed. 'He *is* a baby!'

'Hmm...'

Logan looked at Ellie and smiled as his daughter thought of a good name for their son.

It had been non-stop since they'd found out they were having twins. There'd been extra medical checks and explaining everything to Rachel—including the fact that Ellie would be moving in to their home and that they'd be getting married.

Ellie didn't want to be a pregnant bride, so their wedding wasn't until next year, but the buying of two of everything, whilst they were both working, and Ellie's carrying two babies had been a whirlwind of appointments, scans, shifts at the hospital and scratching their heads over flat-pack furniture.

Ellie had brought Samuel's crib with her. They were going to give it to their son. Whatever he was going to be called.

Logan suddenly had a scary thought. 'Please don't name him anything medical, Rachel. I don't want a son named Aorta, or anything.'

Rachel smiled. 'Don't be silly, Daddy. I know how to choose a boy's name.'

'Oh. Right. Okay.' He couldn't help but smile at her admonishment.

Her little face was screwed up in concentration, and then suddenly her brow unfurrowed and a huge smile came across her face. 'Okay. I know his name!'

'What is it?' Ellie asked, looking at Logan nervously.

'Tobias. Tobias Samuel.' Rachel looked at them both, very pleased with her choice.

Logan nodded and looked at Ellie to see if that was all right. They'd discussed giving their son Samuel's name as a middle name, but for Rachel to choose it… Well, that meant so much more.

'That's perfect, Rachel,' Ellie said, tears of happiness in her eyes. 'Holly and Tobias.'

'We have his present, Daddy—remember?' Rachel grabbed the gift bag from her father's hand and placed it on Ellie's lap. 'We brought him this. For his crib.'

Ellie frowned and opened the bag, and Logan watched as she gasped and tears welled up, reaching in to pull out the blue teddy bear that had sat in Samuel's room all alone for all this time.

Ellie hugged it to her and kissed it as her tears dripped onto the bear's head.

'Have I upset you?' Rachel asked.

'No. No, darling, you haven't. You've made me the happiest and proudest mummy in the whole world.'

And she got up, kissed the bear, and carefully placed it in Tobias's crib.

Where it had always been meant to be.

* * * * *

THE ARMY DOC'S
BABY SECRET

CHARLOTTE HAWKES

MILLS & BOON

To my husband.
I may forget birthday cards
(in my defence, I remembered one last year—
I just forgot to sign it),
but I can dedicate a book to you. xxx

CHAPTER ONE

DR ANTONIA FARRINGDALE was adroit at smelling trouble.

She had first learned it at her father's knee, watching the oft-churning grey expanse of the Atlantic Ocean from the salt-sprayed windows of Westlake lifeboat station, as her mother piloted a boat out for a rescue. Learning to read the signs for when the crew was in for an easy night, or the omens for when they could expect an arduous night of dangerous shouts.

She had honed it as a doctor, often knowing instinctively with her patients when she was hearing horses, and those rare occasions when she was hearing zebras.

And she had perfected it as a battlefield trauma doctor working from twelve-by-twelve tents of field hospitals on missions in whichever conflict-hardened country *du jour* she was in.

Yes, she could certainly smell trouble.

So why, she wondered as she peered uneasily into the hallway at Delburn Bay lifeboat station—a mere hour and a half further up the coast from Westlake, and therefore the closest she'd managed to get herself to *going home* in over a decade—did she smell it so unnervingly strongly, right at this instant?

Immobile yet alert, she stood in her doorway. Scarcely even daring to breathe as her eyes scanned for anything out of the ordinary.

But the sea was agreeably calm beyond the launch slipway, and the corridors were quiet, most of the crew being volunteers who had day jobs but who would be at the station within minutes if they were called to be. There was nothing there which should set her chest thumping the way that it was.

Unless a guilty conscience counted.

Shaking her head as if that would be sufficient to dislodge the censorious thought, Antonia ducked back into the medical supply room, which doubled as her consultation room and office whenever she was on site as the station's new Medical Officer, telling herself it was more likely to be just her overactive imagination.

Telling herself that she had nothing to feel guilty about.

Telling herself…what? That she'd made the right choices—as impossible as they had been—five years ago?

It was true, but it didn't help. It never really had. She still felt like a terrible person.

But then, wasn't that why she was back here? To set the record straight.

Spinning around on the ball of her foot, Antonia strode determinedly back into her office and consultation room even as her mind skittered down the coast to Westlake, back to the past, to the man who had finally brought her back home now. Or, at least, that mere ninety minutes up the coast from home. A man to whom she owed the two biggest apologies of her entire life. Neither of which she had any idea how to even *begin* to make.

Which was why she'd taken a job at Delburn Bay's lifeboat station, rather than back at Westlake. The distance provided her with a much-needed buffer to allow her to pick the words she was going to use when she finally plucked up the courage to drive down the coast and face…*him.*

Ezekiel Jackson.

As though she hadn't already had five years to work out what to say. The drumming in her head intensified, causing her to pinch the bridge of her nose. Not that it helped.

'You're supposed to be working,' Antonia muttered irritably into the silent room. 'Not looking for ghosts.'

Her heeled boots clacked harshly as she strode back to her desk, and she pulled her lips into a grim line as she selected the next file from her pile. Technically she didn't start officially for another month, but it was a voluntary position and they were desperate for someone to settle in. And it was better than being in her father's small house, avoiding his concerned glances and all his unspoken questions, which nonetheless echoed loudly.

Gratefully she slid down into the uncomfortable swivel chair and began to read the notes. Work had always been her salvation. Unsurprising, then, that she was absorbed within minutes.

'So it's true.'

The rich, smouldering, all too familiar voice seemed to charge the room, as Antonia jerked her head up so fast that a *crack* and a stinging sensation ripped through her neck.

She wasn't prepared. She wasn't *ready*.

If a deep chasm had opened up beneath her feet and sent her hurtling down to the earth's dense, super-hot core, it couldn't have made her any more frantic.

Zeke.

Had the air been sucked out of her lungs? Her body? The very room itself? It certainly felt like it. She couldn't breathe, let alone speak, and it was all she could do to keep her mouth clamped shut rather than open and close it like a fish caught out in one of the rock pools out on the sands.

How she managed to stand—to face him—she would never know. Yet suddenly she was on her feet, her fingers braced against the cold, flat wood of her desk to stop the dizziness from winning out. She certainly had no idea how she managed to respond to him.

'True?'

Thank goodness for the open window, which let her suck in deep lungsful of sea air—its salty, tangy taste dancing obliviously on her tongue—as she tried to quell the wave of nausea that crested in her chest.

Damn it if Zeke didn't look every last bit as commanding, and dangerous, and *male*, as she remembered. His hair was longer now. At least, longer than the close-to-the-scalp cut he'd sported as a Special Forces soldier back then. Enough that she might actually be able to feel it between her fingers.

If she wanted to. Which she didn't. Of course she didn't…*because that would be pathetic.*

Desperately, urgently, Antonia reminded herself of that last night, five years ago. He'd been telling her for months that he didn't love her, that he'd never loved her, but that had been the night when she'd finally believed him. Because it hadn't been the words that had convinced her, rather it had been that hard, disgusted look in his cold eyes as they'd bored into her without a trace of softness or love behind them.

Even now, at the mere memory, a pain shot through her heart as though it were folding in on itself.

And then she looked into Zeke's face and suddenly her heart kicked out again, straightening itself out and pounding so loudly within her chest that she was afraid it could be heard.

He was a few years older, maybe, but that face was just as sharp, and masculine, and devastating as it had always been. Those cool blue eyes could still pierce through any soul, and that strong jawline, which she had traced countless times over the years, still housed a mouth that had been her undoing more times than she cared to remember.

Without warning, desire zipped through her, horrifying and thrilling all at the same time. His beaten-up leathers moulded to every broad, muscled inch of him, reminding her of a time when—as teenagers—they had raced the length and breadth of the country on that prized motorbike of his.

Suddenly, she felt like that adoring kid again.

Had she really been so naïve as to believe that the mere passage of time would mean she would no longer be attracted to the man? Had she really told herself that she would be immune?

She'd convinced herself of it, yet now the mere idea that she wouldn't be affected by him was laughable.

Even his silence was dark. Edgy. Lasting only a beat but feeling like an eternity.

'That you're back.'

Another moment of silence. So thick and heavy that she almost imagined she could wear it as a cloak. Maybe one that could chase out the sudden chill that had pervaded her very bones.

Almost against her own volition, Tia let her eyes track lower. Her heart kicked up yet another gear as she fought to control the shallow breaths that jostled inside. Zeke had once been the epitome of a deadly, dangerous, ruinous barracuda.

Something she didn't care to identify pooled low in her belly at the memory of the SBS man with a body that had always defied belief and was worthy of any Rodin or Polycleitus sculpture.

If she didn't know better, she might have thought that nothing had changed. He looked as fit, as honed, as lethal, as ever. And her fingers practically itched to reach out and test it for herself.

Discreetly, she moved her arms behind her back and balled her fists into each other.

And then, finally, she let her gaze travel lower. Down the snug, black motorcycle leathers, which did little to disguise impossibly muscular thighs, and down...

She froze.

For a moment, the fluttering receded as a wave of nausea threatened to close over her head. She couldn't tear her gaze away, couldn't even breathe. Like a swimmer caught in a riptide, fighting to stay focussed and keep their head above the surface.

What had he been saying? Asking her?

Think. Think!

Slowly, so slowly, her brain kicked back into gear. Something about her being back...?

Her tongue took a moment to work loose again.

'It's true,' she confirmed stiffly.

And perhaps needlessly. After all, it was self-evident, wasn't it? Or maybe Zeke was simply giving her the opportunity to rethink her decision and get out of there. Out of Delburn Bay. Out of his corner of the country. Out of his life.

Just as she'd done the last time he'd commanded it.

And if it weren't for Seth, then maybe she would have done just that.

'Although, I'd hardly say I'm back.' She licked her dry lips even as she silently berated herself for such an outward show of nervousness. 'I'm far enough up the coast from Westlake.'

'I think you can call that *back*—' his voice was like a hot cocoa river running through her, and warming her, even as she tried to fight it '—given that it's the closest you've been to *coming home* in around fifteen years.'

Coming home. It sounded so...easy, when dropped from Zeke's lips, and suddenly the realisation terrified her. It meant that home wasn't Westlake where she'd grown up, or Delburn Bay where her father had moved to. Home was where Seth was.

But it was also where Zeke was.

And that absolutely, positively, was not acceptable.

'I disagree,' she lied, aware that folding her arms across her chest was a defensive, negative gesture, yet wholly unable to stop herself.

'No, you don't. You might be here, but you desperately wanted to come all the way to Westlake. You just couldn't bring yourself. It's obvious. You were never very good at lying to me, Tia.'

God, she'd made a monumental mistake coming back here.

It was too soon. She wasn't ready.

'I'm not lying,' she lied, desperation reverberating through every syllable.

Zeke's mouth curled up at one corner, making it seem as if that were actually a bad thing. But she had to concede that he had a point. Which only made it all the more ironic that he'd never realised she'd told him the biggest lie of all.

Before she could answer, he moved into the room—or maybe *prowled* was more accurate—and she couldn't drag her gaze away for even a second. Every bit the most virile, red-blooded, lethally powerful man she'd ever known. Something fluttered low in her belly, like a thousand butterflies all taking flight at once.

She couldn't still want him, still *ache* for him, after all this time. Surely? It was ridiculous. Unconscionable. She couldn't allow it.

She *wouldn't*.

'Then why Delburn Bay, Tia?'

Was she really ready to answer that?

Anyway, *Tia* was the naïve fifteen-year-old girl who had fallen for the handsome, charismatic seventeen-year-old boy the moment they'd volunteered together at Westlake lifeboat station a lifetime ago. *Tia* was the twenty-eight-year-old whose life had changed in a single instant and everything had been turned on its head.

She hadn't been *Tia* for five years.

'It's Antonia now.'

Whether she'd intended it as a distraction or a feeble attempt to take control of the situation, she couldn't be sure. Either way, it fell about as heavily as an anchor on a freight ship.

'The truth, *Tia*,' he pressed her, with deliberate emphasis.

The truth was something she wasn't ready for. But, just like that, just because Zeke had spoken, she was *Tia* again. As though the last five years had never happened.

'How did you know I was here?'

'The lifeboat community is tight-knit. People talk. You should know that.'

She ignored the voice in the back of her head whispering that was precisely why she'd come to Delburn Bay. She'd banked on that same tight-knit community to relay the news to Zeke that she *had* returned.

Just…not so unbelievably quickly.

'Did my father tell you I was here?'

The bark of laughter—if that was what it could be called—was less amused and more incredulous.

'Your father?'

'I'm staying with him. At least, until I find a place of my own.'

'And here I was thinking you were as much *persona non grata* as I am. The man who warned you that I couldn't love you, that I didn't even know what love was, and that we'd never last. Did you tell him you were only too happy to leave, or does he think it was all me?'

She had no idea whether he intended to wound her with the offhand remarks, or not. Probably the former. Then again, she deserved it, even if not for the reason Zeke could have known about. Another surge of guilt coursed through her.

She hadn't exactly been fair to Zeke when she'd reached out to her father—after several years of rebuffing his attempts at offering the proverbial olive branch to her—in order to make amends. Yet another complication of her own making that would, at some point, need resolving. But not today. Today there were more important concerns to address.

Such as, if it hadn't been her father who had contacted him, then Zeke wouldn't know about Seth. *Right?*

An image stole into her head and a wide smile leapt instantly to her lips. It was all she could do to stamp it out.

Her precious Seth.

The happy, funny, in-love-with-life four-year-old boy who *really* mattered in all this, and the one person she would give her life to protect.

Seth—the little boy who had deserved not to be born into the tumultuous aftermath of Zeke's black ops mission gone so harrowingly wrong, and her own part in what had happened that night.

Seth, who deserved to know his father now that Zeke had finally managed to find some peace.

But not yet. Not like this. Not dropping it on Zeke like some kind of bombshell. She had one chance to get this right. Her son deserved for her to get it right. Hell, even Zeke deserved for her to get it right. She would *not* blurt it out now like some kind of weapon against him. Hadn't she done them both enough harm already?

Her entire insides shook at the mere idea of it whilst his intense gaze, pinning her to the spot, seemed to confirm it.

Zeke stared at the ghost in front of him, not wanting to even blink in case she disappeared in that fleeting tenth of a second.

It was incredible.

How many times had he planned on tracking her down this past year? Now that he was finally on track. Now that he could be sure he wouldn't be a burden for her. Now that he finally had something to offer her again.

How Herculean it had been to resist that temptation. After all that had happened between them, and all that he'd said to her, he knew he had no right just to walk back into her life. He couldn't expect to pick back up where they'd left off.

But it hadn't stopped him imagining that maybe, just maybe, there would have been no one else for her but him. The way that there had never been—never would be— anyone else for him but Tia. *His* Tia.

He had no right to any of that. He'd lost that right five years ago when he'd sent her away, and then, when that hadn't worked, had said all those things to her in order to get her to leave him. Harsh, cruel words chosen for maximum wounding, for devastating effect. Words that made him blanch when he thought back to them, even now.

And yet a nonsensical part of him was still galled that she'd bought any of it. That she'd left.

Those five years felt like a lifetime ago, now. So much had changed. *He* had changed. He had healed, mentally and physically, and he had moved on with his life. But he'd never moved on from Tia. He'd carried her with him this whole time, like his private talisman, even her memory enough to galvanise him into action, to try to walk, on days when he might otherwise have curled up in a ball and imagined dying on his black ops mission that fateful night.

Just as two of his buddies had.

Every time he'd wondered why he was still here when they weren't, whether he deserved to still be here when they weren't, he'd thought of Tia, and known he had to try.

Which was why, when he'd finally turned his life

around several years ago, he'd come back to Westlake, where they'd first met as kids. A foolish part of him hoping that somehow it would get back to her that he was here. A selfish part of him imagining that she might turn up, on whatever pretext she liked, just to see him.

He'd never really expected it to happen, and yet now here she was. Looking as glorious, as tempting, as *Tia*, as ever.

It was all he could do not to cross the space between them and haul her to him. To hold her and prove he wasn't simply imagining it.

'You look...well,' she faltered and flushed, her eyes skimming straight down his legs. 'Better than well.'

Had he really been so simple-minded to think she would look at him again without seeing...that?

He wasn't prepared for the familiar pain that shattered through him. A pain he'd thought he had finally beaten into submission eighteen months ago, but which eighteen minutes in this one woman's company seemed to have resurrected with brutal efficiency.

It took all he had not to reach down the leg of his leather biker gear and feel for the lower limb that was no longer there.

That hadn't been there since Tia had cut it off five years and two months ago.

'Are you saying that to make me feel better?' he growled. 'Or you?'

'Zeke... I'm sorry,' she choked out, taking a few stumbling steps towards him. 'You have no idea how sorry.'

'Stop.' His hand flew up, halting both her advice and her words. And his own voice was harsh, razor-sharp even to his own ears. 'I don't want to hear it.'

Not least because she wasn't the one who should be doing any apologising. She shouldn't be sorry for what had happened on that makeshift operating table; she'd carried out the only option left to her. And in doing so, she had saved his life.

The fact that he'd accused her of ruining it meant that any apologies were his to make. He was the one who had pushed her away. She hadn't simply walked out on him, or cast him off faster than a Special Forces wannabe dropped his fifty-pound rucksack after his first fifteen-mile tab. He'd pushed her away. Hard. And without any show of mercy.

His only consolation had been the fact that it was the only way he could save her from feeling guilty or responsible every time she looked at him. The only way he could release her from being burdened with him.

But that had been five years ago, and a lot had changed since then. *He* had changed. How many times had he imagined finding her? Explaining himself to her? But not here, not like this. He needed to do it properly. To show her how he'd turned his life around.

This was the chance he'd been waiting for to get her back. And he wasn't about to blow it.

If only he could work his tongue loose to say a damned word.

'I heard you've been awarded a medal for bravery,' Tia blurted out, clearly unable to stand the silence any longer. 'For saving three crewmen from a sinking ship in heavy seas.'

'I was doing my job.' He could feel himself scowling even as he tried to stop it.

'The newspapers don't seem to think so,' she babbled on but, irrationally, he was more fascinated by the way her pulse was leaping erratically at her throat. 'They're calling you a hero.'

He'd hated the publicity for that. The *hero* nonsense. The public had lauded him for that lifeboat rescue, yet all he could think was that they didn't even know the names of the buddies he'd served with, who had died that night five years ago trying to protect their freedom.

'I think they're right,' she concluded almost shyly, giving him an unexpected flashback to the day his chip-on-the-shoulder seventeen-year-old self had first met the blushing fifteen-year-old he'd had no idea would change his life so dramatically.

He clenched his fists behind his back and fought the unnerving impulse to stride across the room and close that gap between them.

And then what...kiss her? It made no sense. A confusion of questions crowded his brain, screaming for his attention. He fought against the ear-splitting ringing in his head. Strident. Throbbing.

What had he been thinking, coming here? Leaping on his motorbike and hurtling up the stretch of coast from Westlake to Delburn Bay the moment he'd heard she was here?

Like a lovesick teenager, worshipping at her altar. All these...*emotions,* jostling and tumbling inside him. And he had no idea what to do with them all. But then, he always had lost his head when it came to Tia, ever since he'd given into temptation and kissed her on her sixteenth birthday.

Even now he could still remember every detail as they'd stood on the beach, the moonlight glistening off the inky water whilst her party had been in full flow in the beach house a few hundred metres away. A party that he hadn't been invited to because, let's face it, no one nice ever invited his family anywhere, and who could blame them for not wanting any one of four boys dragged up by an alcoholic, aggressive, abusive father?

But Tia had been different.

She'd looked *at* him, rather than *down on* him. She'd told him he was nothing like them, that he was one of the best lifeguards she'd ever seen. And he'd basked in the novelty of her admiration.

The night of her birthday she'd seen him on the beach, pretending not to stare in at everyone else having fun, and she'd come to demand her birthday gift from him. When he'd told her he didn't have one, she'd simply shrugged her shoulders and told him, *Of course you do.*

And then she'd stepped forward, pressing the entire length of her body against his, and she'd lifted her head and kissed him. In that instant she'd found a way past all his armour. Past every single one of the barriers that he'd been erecting for as long as he could remember.

He'd vowed, right there and then, to never let her go. And he wouldn't have...if it hadn't been for that night.

And now she was back. But was she here because she knew he was in Westlake, or had she just moved to be closer to her father?

Or someone else?

The unwanted thought slid through him. What if Tia had moved on? It made him answer more curtly than he had intended.

'I don't give a damn what the newspapers say.'

She licked her lips.

'No... I...don't suppose you do. You never did care what anyone thought.'

He had cared what *she* thought. His Tia. He cared that she was here. And he wanted her back in his life.

But this wasn't how he'd intended to do it. *Any* of it. He'd imagined that if Tia ever returned to his life, he would apologise to her. He would take her to the house he'd built on the plot of land by the Westlake lighthouse— just as their teenage selves had imagined one day doing together—and he would find a way to sit her down and explain what had happened five years ago. To finally find a way to open up to her.

Maybe even to win her back. In time. If he took things slowly enough.

Instead, he'd heard she was here and he'd simply reacted, jumping on his bike and racing up here. He had no idea what to say, or how to start. He could hardly expect her to just jump on the back of his bike, as she'd used to, and let him take her back to Westlake.

He was handling this all wrong. But far from the smooth reunion of his fantasies, *this* reunion was unravelling faster than a ball of para cord dropped down a knife-edge mountainside.

A fist of anger thrust its way back to the forefront of his brain. At himself more than at Tia. Yet still Zeke grabbed at it; he welcomed it. He could deal with *that* emotion far better than this unfamiliar blind panic that threatened to engulf him.

'Anyway,' she was still prattling on unhappily, 'it was impressive, what you did that night. You—'

'Why are you really here, Tia?'

He interrupted her abruptly, his question deliberately curt and jagged, zipping through the air like the verbal equivalent of a Japanese throwing star. He needed to understand what had brought her back; only then could he formulate his best tactical approach.

She blinked and fell silent for a moment.

'My job,' she offered shakily.

'So I heard. Apparently, you're back here as a medical officer for this lifeboat station. What about your career as an army doctor? Does that not appeal to you any longer?'

'I left the army. I'm starting as a locum at the nearby hospital next month, about the same time I officially start volunteering here. I came back because...well, because... I had to.'

She lifted her shoulders helplessly, but the action also caused her chest to rise and fall, the luscious curve of breasts with which he had once been so intimately acquainted snagged his gaze and, for a long moment, he couldn't drag his gaze away.

The hazy cloud of lust was infiltrating him all over. Slipping past his defences as though they were made of mere gauze.

'So you aren't an army doctor any longer. You quit?'

'It's…complicated.'

'That's pathetic.' He snorted, hating the way she was guarded with him even as he understood exactly why she was. 'Even *you* can do better than that, Tia.'

She blinked as though she wasn't quite sure how to answer. Then, abruptly, she straightened her back and tilted her chin into the air. So Tia-like.

'I'm back because I love lifeboats. You seem to forget that I was volunteering down here ever since I was a young teenager. Long before your seventeen-year-old backside came bouncing into town to become a beach lifeguard. Becoming a volunteer medical officer is only following in my father's footsteps. It's how he met my mother—'

She stopped abruptly and he had no idea how he resisted the impulse to go to her.

He knew only too well how Tia's parents had met. He hadn't been around at that time but it was well documented in the lifeboat community, and he'd heard the story often enough. Though never from Tia herself.

Her father had been a medical officer, her mother a coxswain. For twenty years they had volunteered alongside each other, right up until the fateful night when Celia Farringdale had been called out to a shout in heavy seas.

A trawler had lost engines several miles out. Celia's crew had attended, assisting the rescue helicopter to winch to safety all eight men from the stricken vessel, three of whom had been seriously injured. The helicopter had made three trips over several hours, with the lifeboat waiting, protecting, in case they had needed to abandon ship. Just as the last man had been pulled aboard the heli and it had turned for shore, the sea had swelled and crashed causing the lifeboat to roll unpredictably—just as the trawler had been lifted out of the water only to slam down onto the lifeboat's bow. Instantaneous and fatal. None of the lifeboat crew had survived.

Tia had been fourteen. The year before he'd met her for the first time. A kid who had tried so hard to be strong, and untouched by her past, and invincible.

In many ways seeing her had been like holding a mirror up to his own soul.

Was that why now, with emotions playing across her features however much she tried to fight them, Zeke felt like a heel? Enough to make his determination to take things slowly wane for a moment. Enough to let an altogether more welcome sensation invade his body.

Desire.

When refusing to acknowledge it didn't work, he imagined crushing it under the unforgiving sole of his boots.

'I know you have a tie to this place. Your family was part of this community since before you or I were even born,' he offered by way of apology.

She actually gritted her teeth at him.

'I'm not trying to play *who has the greater claim*, Zeke. I'm just saying that…it's understandable why I want to be here.'

She was holding something back; he knew her well enough to be able to tell. But neither could he deny the point she was making. But whatever else either of them might say was curtailed by the sound of movement outside. Clearly an incident was going down.

'So that's why you're back?'

The hesitation was brief. *Blink and you'd miss it.*

'Yes.'

He couldn't explain why it crept through him as it did. *Was she back for someone else?*

But then there was the sound of footsteps and he knew that someone was coming down the corridor. Maybe for Tia.

He'd waited five years for a conversation he'd never been sure would ever take place—and now it was about to be interrupted. Exactly as he'd feared.

Frustration swamped him, making his words harsher, his voice edgier, than he'd intended them to be.

'I don't know, Tia. Maybe I thought you'd returned because you'd read about me in the papers and finally remembered that you were still my *wife*.'

CHAPTER TWO

TIA HURRIED DOWN the hallway, the emergency somehow grounding her.

She'd never been so happy for an interruption as she had been when one of the lifeguards had knocked on the door to tell her that they were dragging a struggling dog walker out of the surf and she might be needed.

Technically, she hadn't started yet but, until they knew what it was or whether the emergency services would need to be called, she could certainly take a look.

The confrontation with Zeke had been harder, so much harder, than she'd imagined it would be. He'd brought her to her knees with just a few curt words. So any further, awkward conversations with Zeke could—mercifully—wait.

Turning the corner, Tia spotted one of the lifeguards guiding a disorientated-looking woman up the steps, a dog leaping around behind them. The woman was moving under her own steam but looked weak.

'This is Marie,' the lifeguard was saying as they approached. 'About forty minutes ago she was walking her dog when it ran into the water a bit too far and got into difficulties. She went into the water to rescue it but got a bit stuck herself so we ran in. We brought her back here for a warm drink and change of clothes and then she seemed okay. Then about five minutes ago, she started to take a turn.'

'So she wasn't this disorientated when you pulled her out?'

'No,' the lifeguard replied. 'She complained of feeling faint about ten minutes later but nothing more. This has got progressively worse since she's been here.'

Tia watched as Zeke moved quickly to the fainting woman's other side, putting her arm around his shoulders.

'She's going to go, Billy,' he warned. 'Put your hand under her thigh and we'll carry her through. Quickly.'

The two men had barely got her to the consulting bed when she stopped breathing.

'Zeke, get her on the bed and get me a defib. Billy—' Tia turned to the lifeguard as he was dropping the woman's rucksack and coat from his shoulder '—call treble nine.'

'Heart attack?' Zeke asked, yanking the cupboard open and producing the defibrillator that Tia hadn't yet had a chance to locate.

'Could be.' Tia ripped open a mechanical ventilating kit and began to administer oxygen to help the woman start breathing again. 'But it may be drug related. Her skin is clammy and I don't like that purple colour.'

'Look there, it's like a rash,' Zeke noted, peering at the woman's arm.

Tia nodded, but her attention turned straight back to her casualty as she saw the woman begin to blink.

'Marie? Marie, are you with me? Good girl. Okay, my name is Tia, I'm a doctor. Have you got any medical conditions?'

'Where's Badge?'

'Is Badge your dog?' Tia guessed, as the woman nodded. 'Badge is fine, he's with our lifeguards now, probably being spoiled rotten.'

As she'd hoped, Marie began to relax.

'So, do you have any medical conditions?'

'None.' She shook her head as best she could with the ventilating mask still over her mouth and nose.

'Has anything like this ever happened to you before?'

Again, Marie shook her head.

'What about this rash?' Tia asked, as Zeke gently lifted the woman's arm to show her.

'Yeah, I get that on my arms or feet sometimes when I've been walking the dog here. It feels itchy and swollen.'

'When you go in the water?' Tia asked, her mind racing.

'I guess. But it goes pretty quickly usually.'

'Okay, I think we might need to run a few tests. An ambulance should be arriving fairly quickly to get you checked out at hospital.'

'Badge…?'

'Is there anyone we can call to get him picked up? He can stay here with us until they get here.'

'My dad. But you really think I need to go to hospital?'

'I suspect you might be suffering from cold urticaria, where your skin has a reaction either to the cold, or to cold water. Given that this is your first serious reaction, I'm guessing it was triggered by plunging into the sea after your dog. Technically, it was most likely the warming phase when you got here and changed clothes. But you do need to get checked out.'

The sound of the ambulance siren reached Tia's ears.

'Zeke…'

'I'll go and bring them,' he pre-empted, already heading out of the door and leaving her alone with her thoughts, which would no doubt be banging down the proverbial door once her patient was safely handed over to the ambulance crew.

Such as the fact that they had fallen into working together with such ease, despite their earlier confrontation.

And the fact that—aside from the reality that he had

sought her out first—she had actually returned to the area with the intention of finding Zeke and finally being able to tell him that he had a son.

So far, she had done neither.

'Don't think our earlier conversation is over, Tia,' he warned softly as they turned away from the ambulance. 'You aren't running away from me this time.'

'I thought I heard Albert mention that you're due on call tonight, at Westlake. That's a ninety-minute drive from here.'

'Don't test me, Tia.' Her skin goosebumped at his grim tone. 'You might have thought Delburn Bay was far enough away from Westlake that I wouldn't know you were here, but you should have known better. And I still want to talk to you.'

She forced herself to meet his eye. She could do this. For Seth.

'And I need to talk to you, too,' she echoed. 'Properly. Like the adults we now are, instead of somehow regressing to those naïve, idealistic, opinionated kids we once were.'

'Is that so?'

If her heart hadn't been lodged somewhere in her throat, the threads of her thoughts threatening to unravel at any moment, she might have laughed at the surprise on his face.

She knew what was coming, and yet somehow she was still here. Still breathing. In and out. In and out.

Not running away this time.

'It is so,' she confirmed at length. 'Zeke, for what it's worth, I'm sorry.'

If she'd kicked him in the guts she didn't think he could look more shocked.

'You have nothing, *nothing*, to be sorry about,' he ground out.

God, if only that were true.

Where did she even start? Her mind spun as she hurried through the lifeboat station and back to her soon-to-be office, needing just a moment alone to compose herself.

As if she hadn't had five years.

As if meeting Zeke, and telling the truth, hadn't been one of the main reasons she'd come so close to home. To finally tell him about her son—*their* son—because it was the right thing to do.

However terrified she might be.

And then they were back in her office, the door closed, and the rest of the world shut out. Tia crossed to the desk, not turning around until she was on the other side of it, using it like some kind of defensive barrier, not that Zeke appeared to have any intention of coming any nearer to her anyway.

They met each other's gaze for a few moments—maybe an eternity—neither of them wanting to be the first to break the silence.

But one of them was going to have to, and, after everything, Tia knew it had to be her. She owed him that much.

'You've changed,' she managed.

'You already said that.' He scowled. 'I believe your words were that I look *better than well*.'

'Right,' she muttered, shaking her head lightly, almost imperceptibly. But he did look well. And changed. Beyond all recognition.

Oh, not in the physical way, of course. Now that the initial shock of their first encounter was behind her, that much was evident. But in terms of the broken man he'd been when she'd last seen and spoken to him. The bleak, black pit he had been in back then. The pit into which—a part of her had never been able to shake the feeling—she'd helped to push him.

Tia's heart pounded so hard in her chest that she was half surprised it didn't batter its way out. Because the truth was that she didn't know Zeke any better than she had as a naïve, adoring kid. This reunion was so much more unpleasant than anything she had feared.

And with what she was about to tell him, it was about to get that much worse.

The storm that raged through Zeke was so much more powerful than that force ten gale that had been blowing all day at sea, so destructive that it threatened to rip him apart. To tear down every last piece of his once broken self that it had taken almost half a decade to put back together.

This wasn't anything like he'd expected today to go.

Meeting Tia again had completely, unexpectedly, unbalanced him. For the last three years he'd been slowly starting to feel more human again. More real. Yet one conversation with Tia and she'd seen through him in an instant.

Without a word she seemed to call him out for being the sham that he was.

He could feel the ground rolling beneath him like the treacherous, shifting sands that lay further out from the bay. Something else roiled inside him. Hope? Uncertainty? Both?

Without warning, the burning, twisting, phantom limb pain that hadn't troubled him for years now threatened to rear itself again. It took everything he had not to reach his hand down and touch his leg.

Where his past met his present. Innocence and reality. Destructible human flesh and the bionics of the future.

He truly was a million-dollar man these days. In more ways than one. A man with whom plenty of women were only too eager to be. But not a single one of them could ever have hoped to come close to the incomparable Antonia Farringdale.

Which was why he'd never bothered with anyone else. Not once.

It was why he was determined to win her back. But he couldn't give her the satisfaction of knowing she had that kind of advantage over him. He wouldn't.

Pushing the phantom pain back, Zeke held eye contact and stared her down. It was all in his head. A mere manifestation of all that he had lost—so much more than just the leg itself—the night what remained of his black ops team had flown him into the single-man makeshift clinic in the middle of no man's land.

And his white-faced wife had been given no choice but to perform an emergency amputation on him.

'So, are the newspapers the real reason you're back? You read about my so-called heroics?'

He hated saying the words; he'd never much cared for public veneration. Not as a young seventeen-year-old lifeguard who had just happened to be on the beach when the mayor's daughter had got caught out by a riptide. Not as a twenty-something decorated marine when he'd made it out of that mission with a limb missing but alive, when two of his buddies had been brought out in body bags. And not in this latest award, as a coxswain who'd just happened to get lucky on a horrible, stormy night.

And yet, as he watched the battle waging within Tia as she fought to keep her cool in the face of his outrageous accusations, a little punch of victory vibrated through his bones. As pathetic as it might be that he took such triumph from the fact that he could still read her, he would take whatever he could right at this moment.

Because little else about her seemed the same. At least, not when he got past the physical similarities. Those brown eyes with the flecks of green, that light brown hair now highlighted with pure gold, that body that made his whole body tighten and his mouth water.

'You heard I was here, and you couldn't stop yourself from racing home to be with me again?' he pushed on, not missing the way her nostrils flared. As though he wasn't entirely wrong and she hated herself for it.

And if that was true, then surely it meant she still felt something for him?

There was still hope.

'I see you aren't denying it.' He grinned, enjoying the way her eyes sparked with anger.

'Denying what?' she challenged. 'Denying wanting to appear in the newspapers with you as your desperate ex-wife?'

'Not ex,' he gritted out. 'We're still married.'

'Fine.' She exhaled deeply, but her voice was that bit tighter, thicker than before. 'Estranged for the last five years, then. Either way, I'm confused.'

'And why is that?'

'Well, let's see.' She lifted her hand as though to tick off her points one at a time. 'First you say I'm in Delburn Bay because I thought it was far enough from Westlake for you not to know I was here. Then you declare that I've come because I've read the papers and wanted a piece of your new-found fame. So which is it to be, Zeke? Because even you can't have it both ways.'

It was that flash of temper, her refusal to cower, which he had fallen in love with all those years ago. And which clawed their way inside him right now. It made him want to pull her to him when he knew he should be taking things slowly.

But it was proving impossible to hold back when she had essentially returned to him after so many years of absence. Especially when she looked at him the way she was doing right now, even if he doubted she realised it. As if she still wanted him, too.

'You didn't answer my question,' he pointed out smoothly.

Tia merely cocked an eyebrow.

'Fancy that.'

The need to claim her as his once more swirled inside him, pounding at him, eroding him. His arms actually ached with the effort of not reaching out to touch her. To place his hands on her shoulders and draw her in. To see if her body still fitted his with as flawlessly as ever. To discover if she was every bit the Tia he remembered.

Would she think he was still the same Zeke who she had married over fifteen years ago? She was certainly the same Tia. Despite that…edge, which he couldn't quite pinpoint.

'You haven't changed,' he told her, taking a step closer. Unable to stop himself.

She braced herself, though he noted she didn't try to move away.

'Don't, Zeke. I have changed, as it happens.' And again, something shot through him too fast for him to grasp. 'More than you can imagine. As, I've no doubt, have you.'

Zeke faltered for a moment, then caught himself. She couldn't be back for the money. Tia couldn't know that he was now a multimillionaire thanks to his company, Z-Black, along with Zane—another of his former marine brothers-in-arms—and Zane's investment mogul brother, Frazer.

He took another step towards her.

'Meaning?'

This time, she did edge away, if only a fraction. And as though her body didn't want to but her head was telling her she had to. She squeezed her eyes shut.

'Meaning, you can't drop me, like you did, and now pick me back up again and expect me to just fall into your arms.'

'I didn't *drop* you.'

'As good as,' she argued shakily. 'We were meant to be partners, Zeke. Husband and wife. But you pushed me away. You didn't trust me.'

He resisted the urge to squeeze his eyes shut; it only made the memories all the more vivid. Real. Even now, very occasionally, he would still wake up in a sweat, reliving that final mission. A mission that had gone south so quickly that his team had had no chance to extract themselves.

The torpedo. The explosion. Then blood in the water all around him, just before everything had gone black. He hadn't even felt the pain at that point.

'I lost everything that night,' he growled, abruptly.

'Yes.' Tia tilted her head up determinedly and met his gaze for the very first time. 'And so did I.'

'Don't go there, Tia.'

Anyone else would have heeded the warning note in his voice. Tia merely swallowed hard, but she stood her ground.

'Why not? Because only you get to own that pain? You don't think I carried it, too?'

'Why do you think I told you to leave?' he bit out. This was insane. It wasn't how he'd imagined things going in any version of meeting up with Tia again. 'I wanted you to be free of it. I released you so that you could walk away and never look back. I've carried it with me for these past five years so that you didn't have to.'

'And yet I have,' she matched him, her eyes shimmering unexpectedly.

Deep within him alarm bells rang, but he couldn't heed them. Couldn't stop himself.

'What? What have you carried, Tia?'

She stopped. Glowering. Emotions charging all over her face. And then, just as suddenly as her temper had flared, she reined it in. The loss was unbearable. He felt her withdrawing and he had no idea how to stop it from happening.

It hurt. Far more than it had any right to.

'I'm sorry,' she choked out, as though she knew how his chest was tightening excruciatingly.

Zeke didn't realise he'd crossed the room to her until she tilted her head to look up at him, her eyes growing darker, her mouth opening just a fraction, her breathing quickening.

And still, Zeke didn't stop himself.

'This can't be why you came home, Tia. It certainly isn't why I drove up here tonight.'

His voice was huskier than it had any right to be. He needed to leave. Now. Tia needed space to think, and he needed to get out of there before he broke all his rules about taking things slowly if they were to stand a chance of piecing their relationship back together.

So why, instead of moving away, was he reaching to take her chin in his fingers, his entire body revelling in the way her breath caught sharply?

CHAPTER THREE

THE URGE TO kiss her pressed in all around Zeke.

He leaned in closer. So close that he could feel her warm breath brushing over his skin. The energy waves bouncing off her and onto him made his entire body goosebump in anticipation.

The whole world had fallen away, and he could see no one—nothing—else, but Tia.

'It's been too long,' he murmured.

She lifted her hands to his sides, then a tiny frown settled over her forehead.

'Your T-shirt's wet.'

'It's from carrying that woman's stuff. It was soaking.'

He felt so on fire right at that moment that it had barely registered.

'It's cold.' Tia sounded concerned, but he couldn't have cared less.

'It's just a T-shirt. You're stalling. But there's nothing to be nervous about. It's just me.'

He dipped his head again.

'Please.' Her voice was a fragile whisper. 'Don't do this, Zeke.'

A token protestation at best.

'Tell me you don't want me to kiss you,' he murmured, his lips closing the gap to hers.

'I…' The sound might as well have been ripped from her throat. And she still didn't move. 'I can't.'

And then, as if suddenly galvanised into action, Tia stumbled backwards. Away from him.

He was an idiot.

He'd frightened her off. Exactly as he'd cautioned himself not to do.

'You can't just expect…' she prattled on. 'I mean…after five years…things have changed.'

'But not the way you feel about me,' he countered smoothly.

She eyed him balefully.

'You're wrong. The way I feel about you *has* changed.'

'Mmm…' He wasn't in the least perturbed. 'You say that, but your body is telling me something quite different.'

'My body evidently doesn't know when to shut up, then,' she snapped.

But her tone was that little bit more brittle than he might have expected. As though there was something he was missing.

Tia raked her hands through her hair in a gesture he recognised only too easily as an indicator of just how wound up she was.

'I can't just fall back into your arms, Zeke. I won't. You don't understand. I… There are things I need to tell you.'

'More apologies for amputating my leg?' he countered. 'I don't need to hear them.'

Moreover, he didn't want to hear them. Especially after all he'd put her through.

And then, suddenly, she seemed to gather herself together and straighten her shoulders.

'I'm not apologising for amputating your damn leg,' she burst out. 'I didn't come back here for that. And I didn't come back here for us. I've moved on, Zeke. Just like you told me to do.'

'If I truly believed that, I would walk away,' he stated flatly, ignoring the way every fibre of his body ignited in protest. 'But I can still read you, Tia. I know you want me.'

She bit her lip but she didn't deny it. He'd known she wouldn't.

'Fine. So, what, then? Do you expect me to put your abrupt return to the area down to curiosity? You've already admitted you read about me in the papers, and knew I was back in Westlake. And suddenly, you're back here. A mere ninety minutes up the coast. And don't tell me it's because your father is here in Delburn, because he has been here for several years now and you haven't been back before.'

'How do you know that?' retorted Tia, giving away more than she intended to.

'Because I've been back at Westlake for the last three years and you haven't been anywhere near the place.'

Without warning, Tia went white. He started forward, concerned she was about to faint, then checked himself as she stared him down. But it was the sheer misery on her face that really got to him.

'You've been here?' she breathed. 'For the past three years? When I read the article in the paper, it never mentioned how long you'd been here.'

'Westlake lifeboats offered me a position as coxswain when they heard I'd left the military,' he ground out, re-alising too late that he might have given himself away by his unintentional admission. 'I needed the job.'

'You said you would never come back here. Ever. You swore it. I read that article in the paper but I never dreamed you'd been here that long.'

'My God, Tia, I was a twenty-year-old kid when I made that stupid vow.'

She didn't need to know that the first thing he'd done when he'd straightened his life back out had been to return to Westlake—the place he'd abhorred as a kid—in the hope that Tia might also return home.

'Does it really surprise you that I'm not that broken, damaged, defeated, shadow of a man you thought I was?'

He ignored the part of him that wondered if she'd been entirely wrong in that conclusion. The part of him that wondered if he would ever get over the guilt he felt that he was still alive when members of his squad—his best buddies—were gone.

Was it something he would *ever* get used to?

'No, it's just. I didn't know. I never imagined...' She shook her head. 'The point is, I didn't come here to re-visit old history.'

'Well, you didn't come back just to make amends with your father,' he carried on grimly, as if it could distract her. 'Up until five years ago we were still a happily married couple and I know that in a decade of marriage you never once took up his olive branches.'

He couldn't be exactly sure what it was that he'd said, but suddenly her face grew harder. More determined. Another spark of the feisty Tia.

'Is this the game we're playing, then, Zeke? You're re-writing history? Claiming that we were a happily married couple?'

Her voice swirled around the room, around him. Shaky, low yet unexpectedly dangerous.

'Weren't we?'

'Constant deployments meant that we rarely spent longer than a week together at a time. So it always felt as though it was fresh, and thrilling, and new. But we weren't a couple as most people would consider that to be. We didn't really share things, at least not our fears, or our flaws.'

'Do many couples?'

'The strongest do.' She shrugged. 'You and I were two

kids running away from our pasts, if for different reasons. And whilst I never thought that that IED defeated you, if we're being fair you were damaged long before then.'

'Say again.' Less of a question, more of a challenge.

But to her credit, Tia didn't back down.

'The fact that you never let your childhood, that… monster who called himself your father, break you was one of the qualities which made you the kind of loyal, dedicated marine who everyone wanted on their squad.'

It was sad how much he actually *ached* to believe her. He nearly did.

Instead, he began a long, slow clap.

'Impressive. Have you been preparing that little show for a while, Tia? You almost had me convinced.'

'But, of course, I didn't,' she threw back without missing a beat. So fiery, so steadfast—the girl he had fallen in love with. 'Because you won't believe me no matter what I say. You never would. You decided what was true for yourself, and anyone else's opinion be damned.'

'I trusted you, too. Once,' he countered pointedly.

'No.' She shook her head. 'You didn't. You were so used to having to rely on yourself, knowing that no one else out there would look out for you, that you found it difficult to let me in.'

'But I did let you in.'

'No, you never did. Because when that last mission went wrong…' She faltered, then regrouped. 'When you ended up losing part of your leg, I was the last person you wanted. You pushed me away. Not just once, Zeke, but again and again.'

This was it. This was his opportunity to say all the things he'd been imagining telling her for half a decade. Instead, he found he couldn't. His head was all over the place, and things were unfolding in a way that didn't match any of the many and varied scenarios that he had envisaged.

He felt reactive. Quite different from the proactivity with which he was usually characterised. And suddenly he found himself falling back on the arguments he'd used back then. When he'd been angry, and desperate, and grieving for the life, the career, he'd had but would never have again. When the only thing he'd felt as though he'd been able to control had been stopping it from impacting on Tia's life too.

'It was for the best.'

'Not for me. Not back then.'

'You didn't need the burden of a cripple.'

'You still believe that's what you are?' she cried out.

'No, of course not.' He'd got past that long ago. The army rehab centre had made sure of it. Wallowing hadn't been an option; the centre had ensured the guys were all up at dawn, making their beds, carrying out daily ablutions, just as they'd all done years before in basic training. It had instilled the work ethic back in them, treating rehab like a training routine, like a job, and tea and sympathy had been far, far down the list.

It was what guys like him—ex-military—had needed. That discipline, those expectations, the rules, had been familiar and comforting.

'Forget I said that.' He hauled off his sodden, icy tee, furious with himself. 'I'm lucky. I got off lightly compared to so many guys.'

What was wrong with him? Why was he acting like the arrogant chip-on-the-shoulder kid he'd thought he'd left behind a long, long time ago?

'Do you still blame me for amputating?'

'Say again?' He stood up incredulously.

He had come to terms years ago with the fact that Tia hadn't had any choice. His role in black ops meant that only a handful of people would ever have known where he was. Tia's commanders would have had no idea that his squad were even within a hundred miles. And his commanders couldn't have changed *her* posting or it would have been a sign that they were planning a black ops mission.

Besides, there had been no reason at all to think that *that* particular mission ran any real risks. It had been a complete curveball to all of them.

But when the IED had gone off and the medevac had come in, her little hearts-and-minds field hospital had been the only one they could have hoped to get to. The fact that she had been the only doctor in that camp was just devastatingly misfortunate.

Then again, she had saved his upper leg, and maybe even his life. If she hadn't amputated above his ankle when she had, then by the time he'd got to the UK he would probably have lost the knee as well. If he'd even survived the journey back, of course.

He knew that. He'd known it by the time he'd got out of physio at the UK hospital, eight months later. Which brought him right back to the question of why was he acting like a belligerent teenager now?

Was it because she was the only person in the world—other than his old man, and he didn't really count—who had made him feel...*less*?

Less of a person. Less of a husband. Less of a *man*. The nightmares he'd had back then—still now—certainly didn't help matters.

'Then why did you push me away?' she croaked out.

How was he supposed to answer that?

Balling up his tee, he stuffed it viciously into his motorbike rucksack and pulled out a clean, fresh one from another compartment, before turning around to face her again. He wasn't prepared for the way her eyes were locked onto him. Or the desire that burned within those darkened irises.

She wanted to know that he didn't blame her for amputating? That he had forgiven her. He could say something, he could try to explain, but he'd never been good with words. He'd always been more of an actions man.

So maybe actions would convince her now.

Deliberately, he crooked his mouth and dropped his arms, delaying pulling on his fresh tee. The sense of triumph swelled as her gaze didn't slide away, instead holding fast. Her pulse leaping a moment at her throat, those flushed patches high on her cheeks, her lips parting a fraction.

His entire body reacted in that very instant. Carnal and primitive.

The next thing Zeke knew he was striding back across the room, snaking one hand around the back of her neck, and hauling her willing mouth to his.

That *thing* that had always been between them—so bright, so electric—blasted back into life with a power that almost knocked him backwards. Making him feel truly alive again.

After all this time.

His mouth feasted on hers, greedily swallowing up her gentle moan of pleasure as she matched his kiss, stroke for stroke, depth for depth. His body exulted in the feel of her against him, her breasts splayed against his chest, her heat against his sex. And still the kiss went on.

For an eternity.

Or longer.

It was almost unconscionable when she stiffened suddenly, lifting her palms to his chest, exerting some pressure.

As unpalatable as it was, he made himself release her. She stumbled back, cast around wildly and fluttered around her desk.

'We can't do that,' she whispered. 'Or…at least…we shouldn't.'

As though she thought that the wooden workspace could

somehow prove a barrier between them, but the fact that she was leaning on it, her hands pressing on it as though subconsciously testing how sturdy it might be, belied her words.

He took a step forward.

'Why shouldn't we? We both want it.'

'Because someone might walk in.' Her ponytail bounced from side to side in agitation, though her lack of denial spoke louder than anything.

He'd always got a kick out of that catch in her voice. Desire laced with a need to at least *appear* to be responsible.

'Then we'll close the blinds.' He twisted the handle with a couple of deft flicks of his wrist.

Her breathing became a fraction shallower.

'Then we hang the sign on the door.' He flipped around the sign that warned people: *Medical Examination in Progress—Do Not Disturb.* 'And finally, we lock the door.'

'It…it doesn't have a lock.' She swallowed hard.

Zeke glanced around, spotted the hard-backed dining chair from the rec room and, spinning it around with one hand, wedged it under the door handle.

'Consider it locked.' He shrugged. 'Any other concerns, Tia?'

She didn't reply immediately, she simply stared at him with overly wide eyes from across the room.

He advanced on her, leisurely, no rush, giving her a chance to object even if he hoped she wouldn't.

'I told you, it's Antonia.' Her voice was thick, loaded. He recognised it only too well and it was like a stroke of her hand against the very hardest part of him.

'Tia,' he repeated easily.

But he didn't know if he was still challenging her, or merely trying to remind her of who she had once been.

Who *he* had once been to her.

Another step, then another. And still she didn't move.

He might have thought she was rooted to the spot but for the faint twist of her body towards him. As though it knew what she wanted, even if her head didn't.

Or was pretending not to.

'Here's your chance, Tia,' he murmured, so close now he could have reached out and touched her.

He knew it was virtually killing her not to melt into him. Her desire was etched into every soft feature on her delicate face. Plus, he was barely staying in control himself. He ached to reach out and touch her with a need that was excruciating. The one thing he was gripping onto so tightly was the knowledge that it was even more excruciating for Tia.

Just as it deserved to be.

She flicked a tongue out over her lips, her voice little more than a whisper.

'My chance?'

'To step away,' he rasped.

The charged silence arced between them and still he steeled himself.

'I'm not moving,' she whispered, her voice cracking.

'No,' he agreed.

The undercurrent rolled. Slowly, almost imperceptibly, she lifted her shoulders to him. A silent plea for him to move.

He held his ground.

'Suddenly I find I want to be sure,' he ground out. 'If you want more, come and get it.'

'Zeke...'

Her eyes gazed at him, tortured. *Another victory,* he told himself, forcing his expression to remain neutral.

'Your choice. I don't want there to be any question about this, Tia.'

For a moment she didn't move but then slowly, seemingly painfully, she lifted her clenched fists off the desk and pushed herself backwards, if only half a step.

Zeke could feel himself teetering on the edge of the abyss, struggling to keep his footing even as he knew he was too far gone. The ground felt as though it were shifting beneath him, even though he knew it was merely in his head.

And then, incredibly, she stepped forwards again. Towards him. Unsteadily. As though her body was acting on its own orders rather than any executed by her brain. But the expression on her face was so painfully familiar it was as though he were igniting from the inside out.

As she finally moved in front of him, going toe to toe, the last of his control went up in spectacular flames.

What the hell was she thinking?

The question flitted briefly into Tia's mind, but then Zeke pinned her against the wall, his deliciously hard body bearing on her with wicked heaviness, and everything liquefied.

The past few hours had been so charged, so heady, that she'd almost lost sense of herself. Thrown back into the past, yet still rooted in the present. It felt surreal.

The first kiss had been like coming home, Tia thought weakly, even as it made her entire body ignite at his touch. But this one had her as though her body was no longer under her own control, reacting to him on an utterly primal level, whilst her brain had no say whatsoever in the matter.

She was vaguely aware that she should object, but instead her hands were threading through his hair, her mouth tingling with every brutal pass of his tongue, her body exalting with the hard, altogether too familiar pressure of Zeke against her.

'Where the hell did you go?' he demanded hoarsely, as though he was barely able to drag his mouth from hers enough to ask. As though he hadn't intended to ask, but instead the words had been ripped from somewhere deep inside.

She didn't know how to respond other than to shake her head minutely and press her lips to his again. Words could only complicate things.

And ruin them.

She just wanted to revel in the kiss that was still pounding through her, hammering along her veins, firing her up as though the last five years had never happened.

Something sloshed around her head, a thought perhaps, maybe a reminder—no, more than that, a *warning*—but she couldn't grasp it. She didn't even want to try that hard.

So instead she simply obeyed as he tilted her head this way and that, testing her, tasting her. He was gentle one moment, demanding the next, his tongue sliding against hers, driving her wild, making her respond every time. It had been too long.

Far too long.

She heard the desperate, needy sound that escaped her lips. She felt the way her fingers clung to him, almost biting into the solid biceps, which time had done nothing to diminish. She experienced the ache—the *yearning*—as it flowed down through her very core, turning everything hot. Molten. Releasing five years of pent-up frustration.

The more roughly he kissed her, the more she pushed back, as if seeing his offering and raising the stakes. It was a dangerous game. A thrilling game. One that she was helpless to stop. Her overriding thought—*need*—was to reacquaint herself with every plane and contour of his body. To make up for all these awful years apart.

Lifting her arms, Tia wrapped them around his neck, shuddering when he let his hands trail down her body with such control that she was certain he was only trying to torment her.

He started with her neck, the backs of his fingers skimming a line down from her jaw to her chest. Tracing the edge of her crisp white shirt right down to the first— perhaps prudishly high—button, then back up the other side, pressing one kiss, then another, and finally a third.

She opened her mouth to say something, anything, but found she couldn't. Her mind was too foggy. And there was the haunting fear that if she said the wrong thing she might break this unexpected spell.

And yet…somewhere…something needled her. Niggled at her.

What was she forgetting?

But then he let his hands wander down her back, dancing over her spine, her hips, until they were cupping her backside and she could do nothing but move with him and press tighter to him.

Heat against steel. Heady and exhilarating.

Just as it had always been with him.

No other man had ever had this effect on her. Not before Zeke, and certainly not after. She'd never even tried. There had never been anyone like him. And that, she told herself, was the only explanation for why she responded to him as if she were a drowning woman and he were the only one who could throw her a lifeline.

She shifted against him urgently, revelling in the sensation of every inch of his sinfully hard body pressed so exquisitely against every inch of her. Exalting as she heard the unmistakable catch of his breathing. Then the hot, still slick feel of his mouth again as she matched his kisses stroke for stroke, urging him on without even a word.

Moving herself against him, until he was reaching for her shirt, making only the briefest attempt to undo the awkward, slippery pearls before cursing softly into her mouth and simply giving one efficient tug. They popped off naughtily, then skittered noisily, feverishly, across the hard floor.

And then Zeke was dropping his hand lazily down the valley between her breasts, his knuckles grazing each soft swell, his tongue teasing swirls over her sensitive skin. Again and again he let his tongue sweep over her, each time stopping short of the nipples that swelled, almost painfully, with the need for him to touch them.

In the dim distance, she could hear her soft moans, her half-uttered pleas, but it was surreal. Like an old dream that she had clung to for so many years. An old memory.

Yes, it had been far, far too long.

And yet…

As her memory clicked over, Tia allowed instinct to kick in. She let her hands glide over Zeke's shoulders, drawing something from their strength, their familiarity. She traced her fingers over the bunched shoulder blades and down the muscled back. She cupped his hard backside just as he had done with her.

And then she very slowly, very deliberately, lifted her hips up to meet him. To press against the hard evidence of his own desire. The way they had done countless times, so many years ago, drawing him in as though it was her who was doing the seducing, not him.

Perhaps that was why he suddenly drew back from her, breaking the kiss and leaving her almost bereft, her eyes flashing open, her hands reaching to cup his cheeks only for him to catch them, and draw them to his chest.

'Zeke…'

'No.' His rebuttal was harsh, ragged. 'My pace. Not yours.'

'I didn't—'

'Stop talking, Tia. Just wait,' he commanded.

She didn't think she could have done anything but obey, just as before, even if she'd wanted to. But the truth was, there was a part of her that was only too happy to stop thinking, stop running, and do exactly what Zeke told her to do.

Then he stopped, his face so tantalisingly close to hers, his gaze holding hers wordlessly, his eyes almost black with desire. When he slid his hands to her waistband, unhooked the buttons and the delicious lick of the zip wound its way into her ears, she thrilled in anticipation.

His hand dropped between them; she could only gasp, her eyelids feeling suddenly heavy as he toyed with her skimpy underwear, which had been like her own private joke with herself.

'Somewhat incongruous with that preppy, oh-so-professional shirt, aren't they?' he accused, but she took a little comfort in the huskiness of his voice, which betrayed him.

'I guess I like to surprise.'

His mouth tautened to a grim line.

'As do I.'

It only dawned on her what he was doing when he dropped abruptly to his knees and pushed her tight suit skirt up to her hips. He intended to make her lose control whilst he held onto his. Hardly fair, or sporting.

'Wait…' she protested, trying to jerk away, but her voice was flimsy at best and, besides, he was more than ready for her. 'That isn't…'

The words died on her lips as Zeke deftly hooked her scrap of lace to the side and anointed her with his mouth, pulling one leg over his shoulder to allow him complete access.

Tia cried out, helpless to do anything but lean back on the edge of her desk and thread her hands through his hair, uncharacteristically longer than she ever remembered. And then her mind stopped thinking anything as he feasted on her, paying homage to her as though he had fantasised about doing this again, for as long as she had.

Even though she knew that, of course, was illogical.

But this wasn't the time for doubts. Not when Zeke was revering her with his hands, his lips, his tongue. Licking into her until her hips were moving of their own accord, dancing to Zeke's sensual, primal tune. His rumbles of approval thrumming through her sex, and making her cry out again and again, barely able to stifle the sounds.

His strokes became deeper and more urgent, as if he couldn't get enough of her, and then... Zeke did that *thing* to her that only he had ever known. A white-hot carnal heat seared through her in seconds, and it was all she could do to bite her lip from screaming out.

Colours danced and exploded as her body shuddered uncontrollably, propelling her inexorably to the edge of the world. Or maybe it was the edge of nothing. And Zeke just kept up his relentless pace, driving her along faster and faster, his hands cupping her bottom all the tighter, to prevent her from backing away. His savage mouth an exquisite weapon against her. Possessing her. Finally finding her again after all these years.

And then he drew the sensitive bud into his mouth and sucked. Hard.

Tia came apart. Spinning and spiralling, going higher and higher, lost inside such an intense pleasure, which only Zeke could have brought her to.

By the time she came back to herself, hastily tugging her skirt back down and pulling the two sides of her now buttonless white shirt together, Zeke was standing halfway across the room. Triumph mingling with an odd black expression, which she couldn't read. But it panicked her.

Her head snapped up as reality crashed in.

Seth!

An image of her—their—son popped into her head. This wasn't how she had intended to tell Zeke. Not after what had just happened. She needed time to think. To re-order her thoughts. To work out how she was supposed to tell him now.

What had she just done?

'Happy now?' she threw at him, her mind still whirring. Racing to catch up. 'Pleased with yourself?'

'Very,' he drawled.

'Because you can still get me to...'

'Orgasm?' he supplied helpfully, but the hard smile didn't quite reach his eyes.

'Yes.' She flushed, telling herself to take deep breaths. 'That.'

'No need to act coy now. Or are you simply aggrieved that I've proved wrong your claim that you no longer have residual feelings for me?'

Zeke was going to be furious when he found out. And what did that say about her that she'd forgotten her son so comprehensively?

'It's...complicated,' she faltered as Zeke frowned.

'How disappointingly clichéd, Tia. I would have expected better from you.'

Anger rolled unexpectedly over her. Possibly more at herself than at Zeke. After all, he didn't know.

'This isn't a game,' she snapped.

His hard smile was more a baring of teeth than anything genuine.

'I don't see why not.'

'No.' She deliberately ignored the voice asking her whose fault that was. 'I imagine that you don't.'

'Then elucidate.'

'Not here.' Tia stalled. 'Especially not after...*this*. But it can't go any further, Zeke. That can't happen. I won't allow it.'

'You're right, it shouldn't have happened.' His tone scratched deep inside her. Gouging at her.

So matter-of-fact, so undaunted, that it made her feel dismissed and unwanted by him all over again. And it hurt more than it had any right to.

As much as she wanted—*needed*—to tell him about Seth, she couldn't. Not after this. Not now, anyway.

She needed time to recompose herself. A night. A couple of days at most.

'I have to go,' she muttered, grabbing her purse and car keys and pushing past him.

Both sick and relieved when he let her go.

Tia had no idea how she got home. One moment she was leaving the lifeboat station, shifting her car into gear and hurtling out of the car park. The next, she was pulling into her father's driveway, blinking away the tears that threatened to spill out over her cheeks the entire eight-minute drive. And as she hurried up to the house her heart lifted at the sight of Seth's face peering out of the window, and his elated grin as he blew her frantic kisses.

She couldn't get her key in the door fast enough as she heard him racing down the hallway, already babbling to her about his day with Grampy. What was it about the prospect of a squeezing hug from her son that promised to settle her churning stomach and the turmoil of the past few hours better than any antacid ever would?

The door was barely open before Seth was dragging her inside, a finger painting in one hand and a sticky piece of toast in the other.

'Look, Mummy, I drew you a tiger catopolly.'

'Wow.' Tia crouched down right there and scooped her son into her arms, inhaling deeply the comforting scent of his freshly washed hair. Right now, she couldn't bear to look in those suddenly too familiar grey-blue eyes. Instead, she smiled brightly and took the picture.

'A big cat tiger, huh?'

'No,' he chuckled. 'A tiger catopolly. They're really fuzzy and there are lots of them on Delburn Island.'

'Oh, that's right, Grampy was taking you on the beach walk today,' she realised, making a great show of admiring the scribbled drawing. 'So this must be a tiger moth caterpillar?'

'Yes,' Seth declared proudly, his eyes sparkling as much as ever, and making her heart constrict. 'A tiger *moth* catopolly.'

'Well, I think it's marvellous,' she declared, shoving any last thoughts of Zeke out of her head.

Reaching out, she began to close the front door when a foot wedged itself in the way.

A big, biker-booted foot.

She almost tipped backwards in her haste to stand up. Instinct making her send her curious son to his grandfather and closing the living room door behind them.

She hadn't even noticed him following her, let alone heard his bike. Yet there it was, parked right on the driveway as though he had every right to be there.

And Zeke, looming and furious, in the doorway. His eyes locked onto the closed door as she gripped the handle as though that could somehow delay the inevitable.

'What the hell, Tia?'

'Zeke…'

She should have told him. Back there in the lifeboat station. It was why she'd come back to Delburn Bay the moment she'd discovered Zeke was in Westlake.

Waiting for the right moment had been a mistake, because there was never going to be the perfect opportunity for giving a person that kind of news. And in delaying, she'd only made things ten times worse. A hundred times.

'I have a son?'

His shocked words were barely audible and still the torment in his tone lacerated her. She couldn't even answer.

Not that he needed her to. Anyone who saw father and son together would instantly see the resemblance. There was no denying the relationship.

Not that she wanted to.

Hadn't she wanted to tell Zeke about his son five years ago, the moment she'd first discovered she was pregnant?

And she would have, if not for that night.

'Jesus, Tia. I have a son.' He started forward. Determination and anger etched onto his face.

She didn't know how she found the strength but suddenly she was blocking his way, her hand pushing back against his shoulders.

'Not here. Not like this. You can't meet him when you're like…this.'

He turned an incredulous black gaze on her. Tia swallowed hard.

'Zeke, I'm sorry. Sorrier than you can ever know. But please. Don't go in there like this. Don't do that to Seth.'

Zeke didn't answer. His eyes slid back to the closed door, to the happy, high-pitched voice inside, assuring her that her son was oblivious to what was going on out in the hallway. The silence spiralled around her, coiling and menacing. It felt like an eternity before anyone spoke again.

'Seth,' Zeke echoed quietly at last. As though he was rolling it around his head. Letting it sink in. Letting it take root.

'Seth,' she repeated quietly. 'And you will meet him. I promise. But…not like this.'

He turned to look at her again. As though he were seeing her for the first time. And it wasn't a good experience. A shiver rippled over her body.

'I have a child? I'm a father? And you kept him from me all this time?'

'I… I can explain.' It sounded so hollow. So inadequate. 'If you give me a chance.'

For another painstakingly long moment, neither of them moved or spoke. And then, abruptly, Zeke stumbled backwards, out of the front door and onto the drive. As if he didn't know where he was going, but was afraid that if he didn't leave now, he might barge her out of the way and walk into that room to see his son.

'Now, Tia. You will explain it to me *now*.'

Without thinking twice Tia released the door handle, snatched up her car keys and followed him out of the door.

She had one chance to get this right. And so help her if she made a mess of it.

CHAPTER FOUR

HE HAD A CHILD.

A son.

Zeke had repeated it a hundred times. A thousand. Scarcely knowing what to make of this incredible revelation. Trying to understand what this…*thing* was that spiralled deep within him, as though it were slowly boring its way out of some pitch-black, fathomless pit he had long pretended didn't still reside inside him.

Yet he suspected he knew exactly what the thing was. It was a flicker of light, even just a spark, but potentially powerful enough to cast a glorious light over his life. Joy. And pride.

He had a *child.*

He, who had long since resigned himself to the fact that he would never be a father. What was the point? When five years ago he'd pushed away the only woman with whom he could ever have imagined himself being?

He had believed he was doing the right thing, the honourable thing. Sparing her from the burden of being with a man so much less than the one she'd married. He'd been a soldier, strong and fit and *whole.* After the accident, he had barely been able to stand looking at himself in the mirror; he certainly hadn't been able to bear seeing her look at him with that expression of…sympathy. As though he was *less than.*

Pushing her away, sparing her from having to take responsibility for him, had been the one thing he could do back then to prove he was still strong. Still fiercely independent. But even so, realising he had succeeded, that his Tia had walked out of his life for good, had hurt beyond anything he could have believed.

Until now.

Had he really pushed her away? Or had she been only too relieved for the excuse to get him out of her life? To ensure his son never knew that he had a failed soldier as a father? The suspicion eroded in like the leaking battery acid on the engine of his very first motorbike.

Had she been pretending all those times she'd visited in the first few months after the accident? Or had she secretly been looking for a way out with the son she'd never told him about?

Because there was no doubt that Seth *was* his son.

And she'd been a couple of months into her medical hearts-and-minds tour of duty when his black ops mission had gone wrong. Which meant the boy had to be around four and a half. Tia would have known she was pregnant. She had to have known.

Surely?

He didn't even need to look across at her to know she was sitting, ramrod straight, in the passenger seat of her car. So typically Tia, at her most defensive. He had no idea what was going on inside her head but he was too angry to ask. A blistering, sizzling fury that tore through him and made it impossible to even speak.

And so here he was, driving her to his house in Westlake because he'd left her with no alternative. Not after he'd seen Seth. He had barked orders at her, rapid and harsh, telling her that he had to be back in Westlake for his duty at the lifeboat station but that he wasn't about to walk away without having a conversation about what he'd just discovered.

When he'd ordered her to come with him—hitting low with the accusation that she owed him that much—he'd nevertheless been surprised when Tia had appeared to capitulate without a word of argument, handing him her car keys before ducking momentarily back inside to ask her father to look after her son—*his own son*—for the evening.

He'd asked her what the keys were for and she'd simply jerked her head towards his bike.

'Well, I can hardly ride on the back of that with you,' she'd muttered awkwardly.

'Because?' he'd demanded irritably, knowing it was irrational to take it as a personal criticism, but unable to do anything else.

And she'd levelled a calm gaze at him, her voice quiet but firm.

'Because we're not kids any more, Zeke. That bike represents my years as a rebel, and a thrill-seeker. Now I'm... I have other responsibilities.'

But it was the words she didn't say that had scraped at him the hardest. That, and the fact that the idea of her body pressed so tightly to his for an hour and a half had been simply unimaginable. Although perhaps it would have given him enough distractions to keep his mind off the all too frequent nightmares that he still endured. The screams, the smell, the sights.

How could he have gone from what had happened between them in her office less than half an hour earlier, from such intense desire then, to such burning anger now? And yet, a part of him couldn't seem to regret how intimate they'd been in that lifeboat station.

So what did that say about him?

Yet for the last ninety minutes, they had sat in a tense, unhappy, charged silence. The same images and questions spinning around in his head, more and more insistent as each minute ticked by. His only comfort was that the closer they came to Westlake—to where she had once lived—the more pent-up she was obviously becoming.

Good. He gripped the steering wheel a little tighter. He wanted her uneasy, off-balance. He suspected it was the only way he was going to get answers to questions she might otherwise deflect all too easily.

But was he imagining it to think that she might possibly have returned to Delburn Bay because she'd felt she owed it to him to tell him about his son?

No.

Tia had had years to find him. To tell him. But she hadn't, so he couldn't afford to let sentiment creep in, or to go soft on her. She had betrayed him. Kept him out of his own child's life for years.

Except that you pushed her away.

Zeke struggled to silence the traitorous voice.

And you wouldn't have been much of a role model for the first few years, would you?

And so he merely kept driving until eventually he was nearing Westlake. First passing the terraced row of tiny fishermen cottages where he had endured years of squalor with the cruel, vindictive, bad-tempered hulk of a man who had spent as much time working hard to avoid getting a job as he had actually going out to do whatever menial job he'd been forced to take.

Then down to the promenade with the larger, more impressive detached houses, which boasted glorious sea views, where Tia had lived with her own kind and protective doctor father. Finally, to the lifeboat station where he was due on call in a matter of hours, and where they had first met when he'd been seventeen and she'd been fifteen. He might have held himself back from going anywhere near her that first year, but she had nonetheless burned too wonderfully brightly for anyone to pretend they didn't notice her.

Becoming a volunteer lifeguard had been Zeke's saving grace as a kid. A stop-gap until he turned eighteen and could join the military, since his old man wouldn't agree to sign papers allowing his kid to join up any earlier. After all, the more Zeke had earned, the less his so-called father had decided *he* had to work.

Even now Zeke could remember the urgency, the desperation, he'd felt, waiting to turn eighteen and swearing to himself that he would never, *ever* return to this part of the country, let alone Westlake.

And then he'd met Tia. Sweet and innocent, but with the kind of steely core and heart of courage that men years older than her hadn't possessed. Especially when it came to being out on a rough sea. The attraction had been instantaneous but he had refused to allow himself to succumb. His respect for the crew—and for Tia's father—had been too great.

When his eighteenth birthday had come, he'd joined up just as he'd always planned. But it was the lure of Tia that had had him returning eighteen months later during a month of leave, a trade in hand and well on his way to his first military promotion.

By the time he'd left they had eloped, marrying in secret, before Tia had embarked on her first year of university, following her father's footsteps in studying for a medical degree.

Now Zeke was deliberately driving her past their very history and it was all too easy to map out. Designed to unsettle her before they even got to his home. The problem was that it was also unsettling him, too.

'Why are we going this way?' she snapped out, as though she couldn't bear it any longer. 'Is this some kind of trip down memory lane intended to make me feel guiltier than I already do?'

'Do you?' he challenged, wishing that a part of him didn't revel in the fact that his Tia was still as astute as ever. 'Feel guilty?'

'What kind of a question is that, Zeke? Of course I do. I never wanted you to find out like this. And I certainly never intended…what happened between us in the lifeboat station this afternoon.'

Any thawing he'd begun feeling towards her disappeared in an instant.

So she didn't regret hiding the truth about his son from him all these years. Just the fact that he'd found out. And that he and Tia had been intimate again.

When the hell was he ever going to learn to stay away from this woman?

'But instead of raking up the past, don't you think we should be looking to the future? Working out where we go from here?'

He battled to harden his heart against her.

'You've had over four years with *our* son,' he ground out bitterly. 'Forgive me if I need a few more minutes to adjust to this revelation.'

'Right,' she murmured, lapsing back into silence.

Along the promenade the grey seas churned and frothed, every now and then smashing against the sea wall and showering their vehicle with a loud, heavy salt shower.

He might have known she wouldn't be able to stay quiet for long.

'It's just that the only thing at this end of the parade is the old lighthouse and…that old piece of waste ground.'

The old waste ground set up from a section of quiet, rocky beach, where the two of them had often gone to be alone when they had finally got together. Where they'd often imagined buying and building a dream home of their own. *When we grow up.*

Well, they'd grown up now. It was just a shame they had never grown up when they'd still been together.

Zeke didn't answer. He just kept going, waiting for the moment when she would be able to see it for herself. The extent of the new life he had managed to build for himself these past few years. His unexpected success—as hollow as it had felt at times, without her to share it with.

The anticipation clung to him like a sodden T-shirt.

And then, beside him, he could sense her sit forward, taking note.

'What the heck is that?' she whispered at length.

The indignation in her tone was only half supressed. He couldn't help but smile, despite everything.

'You don't like it?'

'It's…' She scowled as though the right adjective wouldn't come. Finally she was forced to concede the truth. 'It's stunning. Gallingly so, really. But still, someone really built here?'

'Someone did,' he agreed.

The sheets of curved, tinted glass that made up the entire frontage of the house mirrored the foaming seas and rolling grey clouds flawlessly. The renovated lighthouse just behind.

'Someone who has a *lot* of money, by the looks of it.' Tia sniffed.

Was it fanciful to imagine he knew exactly what was running through her head right at this moment?

'You begrudge them living here?'

She paused.

'I don't begrudge them, exactly. It's just that…a location this special deserved to have gone to someone who would really love it and cherish it, not just someone with enough money to have bought off our historically entrenched council.'

'Someone like you and I, you mean?' he challenged. 'Building that little beach shack home we always talked about building when we were kids?'

She didn't answer, she merely pressed her lips into a thin line, as Zeke schooled himself. Restraining himself from reacting.

So what if she remembered the dreams they'd once had back in the beginning? Less than a couple of hours ago that might have meant something to him. But not now. Not after discovering he had a son who she had kept from him all this time.

Instantly Zeke shut the earlier moment of weakness out and steeled himself again.

Finding out about Seth had changed everything.

He might have spent the past five years rebuilding his life and making himself into a man worthy of Tia again—making it up to her for shutting her out immediately after the accident. Maybe even winning her back.

But that had been before.

Now he had lost out on the first four years of his son's life. Zeke didn't know how to begin to quell the thunder that rolled through him. He didn't know what his next move would be. He didn't even know how to articulate a single one of the questions powering around his head right now.

He only knew that he had no intention of missing a single week more of Seth's life.

He didn't choose to answer. Instead he smoothed his mouth flat and turned onto the private road and began the slight ascent to the house.

'Zeke.' Tia's voice broke into his thoughts as he turned her car up onto the track to his home. 'We can't just wander up here.'

'Pretty sure we can,' he replied grimly.

'I don't think it's just the old road to the lighthouse any more.' She sounded panicked. 'It looks like it's the driveway now.'

'It is. My driveway.'

There was a beat.

Then another.

'I'm sorry, say again?'

He deliberately delayed a moment before complying.

'I live here. This is my home now.'

'You own it?'

'I bought the land and had it built.' He shrugged, deliberately sidestepping her real question. 'So yes, I own it.'

Her confusion was evident, but still he didn't clarify.

Let her wonder.

Let her consider how he had got himself from the mess of a man who couldn't even walk in that rehab centre, to the multimillionaire he was now.

It might give him a moment to begin to get a handle on this racing, flip-flopping tangle of emotions.

Hadn't Tia once called him more of a carefully crafted, honed, precious weapon than a man? A lifetime ago when he'd been about to go on a mission and she'd still been at uni, before she'd joined the army medical corps.

She'd meant it as a good-humoured jibe but it had given him some kind of perverse comfort, and he'd held onto that image for years. Right up until the bomb blast had rendered him broken. Useless. Unsalvageable.

Even now, with all this to show for himself, he was constantly clawed at by vicious nightmares. Regrets. Self-recriminations.

Her heart was hammering so brutally inside her chest that Tia was surprised he couldn't hear it. The place looked like a millionaire's fantasy house by the sea.

If Zeke had intended to unsettle her, he had certainly succeeded. With a shaky arm, she reached out and opened the car door. Getting out and standing up was going to take even more effort.

Toying with her. Leaving her off-balance.

Biting her lip, she followed him across the gravel to the sleek metal and glass door. The place didn't even have a normal lock or key like her house. Instead, he had to have some kind of key fob or pin, because the door opened automatically as he approached.

Not just moneyed, then. But serious money.

Her stomach twisted tightly. With money came contacts, and power. What if he decided to use those resources to get custody of Seth? To provide for him in a way that she couldn't?

Hadn't some former work colleague, Jane, from a few years ago lost joint custody of her two children to her ex-husband? He'd successfully argued something about Jane's career as an A & E doctor meaning long, unpredictable hours whilst he himself had just been promoted in his dependable nine-to-five city job. Plus he'd had a new partner who had cared for a child of her own around the same age.

Tia's mind raced, leaving a plume of fear in its wake.

'Do you live here alone?'

The question was out before she could bite it back, not helped by the way Zeke cast her a look over his shoulder but didn't immediately answer.

On autopilot she followed him as he stepped through a hallway to the lightest, most expansive living room she had ever been in, sleek windows curving from one wall to the other, and from floor to ceiling. Then he spoke.

'There's no one else here, Tia. There never has been. No one who mattered enough to move them in, anyway.'

And she told herself that her heart didn't leap a little. Instead, she forced her legs to carry her across the room to stand in front of those stunning windows and take in the might of Mother Nature at her most volatile.

'There are going to be a lot of shouts in that weather.'

'It has been a force nine gale several miles out there for the past twenty-four hours. The last few teams have been bested.'

She shouldn't say anything. She couldn't give herself away. Tia opened her mouth.

'Be safe out there,' she whispered. 'Don't do anything… typically heroic, Zeke.'

The silence whooshed in on them, like an invisible flood, filling the space and sending them both reeling.

It could have been minutes before they spoke again. It felt like an age.

'You make it sound like you actually care,' he ground out.

'I always cared,' Tia muttered before she could stop herself. 'You were the one who pushed me away, Zeke.'

'Oh, trust me, Tia, it didn't take much pushing.'

Whether it was the coldness of his tone, the injustice of what he was saying, or the fear jostling around inside over her precious son, Tia couldn't be sure, but her temper flared suddenly.

'Oh, no. That's totally unfair. You were the one who said that if I amputated then I would be killing the only life you had ever known as a soldier. You were the one who, for six weeks, told me over and over that you couldn't forgive me. And you were the one who, in that rehab centre, told me that you couldn't bear to look at me and would never, *never*, forgive me.'

'I did it to protect you,' he roared before falling into abrupt silence.

Spinning brusquely, he strode to the couch. She got the sense it was as much to put space between them as anything else, and she was grateful for it. She could barely breathe, let alone think.

The moments ticked by. The silence turning black.

'I did it to release you from the burden of having to be responsible for a cripple. All I'd ever wanted from being a kid was to be a soldier. A marine. I couldn't even get myself out of bed without help.'

'You didn't do it to release me from any burden.' Her heart ached to comfort him, but this was Zeke and she knew him too well. Comforting wouldn't help. She needed to stay strong and meet his accusations head-on. 'You did it because your pride wouldn't let you accept help from me. You didn't trust me enough to let me be there for you. *That's* why you pushed me away, Zeke. No more, no less.'

'You were my wife,' he spat out. 'Who else would I trust?'

Tia was determined to stand fast.

'Which makes it all the more hurtful that you couldn't turn to me, but no less true. If *I* had been the one injured, you would have insisted on never leaving my side. But because it was you, you couldn't bear to have me around. You even told the nursing staff they had to keep me away.'

'You didn't need to see me at that time.'

'Why, Zeke? Because you felt vulnerable and at your lowest? We were married—we should have been a team. We could have been the strongest team. Instead, you never learned to let me in.'

'Of course I let you in. We were married for ten years, for pity's sake. You knew things about me that no one else has ever known.'

'Such as?'

He glowered, clearly hating every second of this line of argument.

'You knew about where I grew up. My old man.'

'Facts, Zeke.' She blew out a deep breath. 'I knew where

you lived because Westlake is a small town and everyone knows everyone. I knew that your dad was a violent, abusive drunk, who took his anger out on you after your mum left, again because everyone knows everyone else's business. But I never knew anything because *you* told me. I never knew how you felt inside, because you never told me.'

She wasn't prepared for the profound sadness that settled inside her, like old dust disturbed from a furniture cover suddenly lifted in a long-abandoned house.

'It was irrelevant,' he gritted out.

'It wasn't.' Tia shook her head. 'That kind of thing makes us who we are. And you never gave me a chance to know that part of you. In truth, Zeke, I don't think we really know each other. We barely ever did.'

'We've known each other for eighteen years,' he snorted.

'You didn't come near me at the beginning because I was fifteen and you decided I was too young,' she pointed out. 'Even though, I hasten to point out, that you were only seventeen back then.'

'Well, we've still been married for the past fifteen years.'

'You can't count the last five of those fifteen years,' Tia argued. 'We've basically spent them apart. The point is that we've never truly understood each other. You never let me in to understand what you thought, or felt, or what made you tick.'

'You already knew all of that. You knew that I was desperate to get out of Westlake. You knew why I joined the army and then the Royal Marines. You knew that my military career was all I had.'

'It wasn't all you had, though,' Tia burst out. 'That's what I'm trying to say but you keep refusing to hear me. You had *me*. You just didn't want me enough.'

She twisted around so he couldn't see the shameful tears

threatening to spill over. Still, his harsh reply was like a dagger to her back.

'That's bull.'

It took her a few moments to steady herself. Another few to turn around and face him.

'We were young, and stupid,' she offered shakily. It sounded feeble but it was simpler than the whole story, and it had the benefit of at least being true. 'In real terms we barely even knew each other. I mean, what were we thinking, running off to get married like that? I was only just eighteen, you weren't even twenty.'

'We thought we were in love.'

And there was the truth, in those little words. *Thought we were.* Not simply *were.* Even though she knew he was right, it still hurt.

'We were selfish. And cruel.'

'You mean I was,' he corrected bitterly. 'Because my old man didn't give a damn about anything I did, and I took you even though I knew that you *did* have a father who cared.'

'I mean *we* were. I certainly don't remember you strong-arming me into anything. In fact, I seem to recall it was my idea. I thought it was romantic and daring.'

His jaw clenched in a way that was achingly familiar, and Tia would have given anything to know what he was thinking in that instant.

'Still,' he ground out eventually. 'We made sure you went to uni. I went back to my training. We weren't completely irresponsible.'

'Do you realise that in those ten years of our marriage, when we weren't separated, we saw each other less than fifteen months? Out of one hundred and twenty months?'

'You're rewriting history.' His eyes glittered coldly from all the way across the room. 'We were living our lives, but we were still together.'

'I don't think it's me who's rewriting things.' She shook her head, warning herself to stay strong. To tell him even half the things she'd imagined telling him these past years. 'I once calculated it.'

'Calculated what?'

She breathed deeply, and in that moment she didn't care if he realised how low she must have been at one time, to work it out.

'I calculated that we, in fact, saw each other less than four hundred and fifty days out of over three thousand, six hundred and fifty.'

He blinked, as though taking it in for a moment. His expression darkening.

'I don't recall you complaining much at the time.'

'No, because it was like a protracted honeymoon every time we saw each other, Zeke. Thrilling and wonderful, filled with passion.'

'And *thrilling* was a problem?'

'Yes!' She threw her arms into the air, as though that could somehow articulate her point better than her words could. 'Because there was nothing remotely realistic about it. We weren't like normal couples who live together and get to know each other's quirks and foibles. Who argue over putting the washing out, or whose turn it is to cook, or whether the toilet seat should be up or down.'

'Seriously?'

'You can scoff—' she shook her head at him '—but you know I'm right. We didn't really know each other at all. We were in love with the idealistic image of the kids who had once fallen for each other. We certainly had no real knowledge of the people we were growing into. Of how our careers, our experiences, were moulding us. You can't really tell me you don't see that.'

She peered at him incredulously, those blue eyes holding

hers with such authority. But then it hit her, the realisation that he knew exactly what she was saying. That he agreed.

They didn't know each other at all.

It was one thing to know the truth on an intellectual level. It was quite another to see it reflected so clearly in Zeke's gaze.

She faltered, stepping backwards as though she'd been dealt a physical blow. The silence closed in again, and this time a bleakness came with it. She felt as though she were a thin plastic bag caught in a squall, blown this way and that.

'None of which explains why you didn't tell me that you were pregnant,' he said suddenly, breaking through the water that was filling her mind and causing her to re-surface. 'Why you've kept my son from me for four years.'

'Zeke.'

'It's funny how the problems of our *protracted honeymoon*, as you called it, only imposed themselves when you realised that my career as a soldier—the thing which had attracted you to me all those years before—was over.'

That wasn't how it had happened but her frustration, and her fears, overtook her.

'My God, Zeke. I was a teenage girl. Show me a teenage girl who isn't swept up by the idea of a strong, good-looking lad intent on becoming some kind of heroic soldier and saving lives? And your monstrous father was what drove you on to be better, and better. It was your way to change who you were and make a difference in the world.'

'And you loved that,' he sneered.

'As a kid…' she heard the desperation in her voice as it rang out '…not as an adult. By the time I was a trauma doctor with several tours under my belt, I knew the reality wasn't anywhere near so poetic.'

'So what *is* the reality, Tia?'

'That nothing would ever be enough for you. You were a maverick, Zeke. Your entire squad was. That was why you got the kind of missions that no one else could ever handle. I may not have known what they were, but I heard the whispers. I knew the rumours.'

'Yet you stayed with me,' he pointed out. 'Because you wanted to be with me. I wasn't just an average bloke you could have met in your student union, I was a marine, and then SBS. I was living life at maximum velocity and you loved that.'

'I was terrified of that,' Tia said quietly. Firmly. 'But I loved *you*. So I accepted that was who you were. Someone who had to keep pushing himself, risking his life, because that was how you had come to define yourself. You guys thought you were invincible, and sometimes you even managed to convince me that you were, too. But then reality would set in, and fear. So, *no*, Zeke, I didn't love it. That last year in particular I watched you walk out the door and expected never to see you again.'

'Then you must have been thanking your lucky stars that I released you from the responsibility of being my wife when I got injured.'

His voice was full of such bitterness and loathing that it clawed inside Tia's chest. She didn't realise she'd sunk onto the rug until she felt the soft material gripped in her hands.

'You really want to know what I thought when you got injured?' she whispered hoarsely, barely recognising her own voice. Every fibre of her being screaming at her to stop talking.

'Why not?' He laughed. A hollow, empty sound. 'It can't be any worse than anything I imagined.'

She swallowed. Sucked in a deep breath. Swallowed again.

'A part of me was relieved,' she managed eventually. So quietly that she wasn't initially sure he'd heard her. But the tense silence in the room told her otherwise. 'A part of me knew that this was the end of your military career—I knew you'd never stay in just to fly a desk—and I was so thankful that I wouldn't have to be scared for you any more.'

'You were glad I was injured,' he echoed. Dark, sharp, lethal.

'No,' she cried, then shrugged helplessly. 'Not exactly. But at least you weren't dead. At least you were still…with me. I thought…maybe…at last…we could finally give our marriage a proper try. But instead, you hated me, you made that abundantly clear. I was the one who had taken your leg and you couldn't forgive me for it.'

He wanted to argue, that much was obvious. He opened his mouth to. But suddenly he couldn't.

It was little comfort.

She had been right. He'd hated her. Not as much as he'd no doubt hated himself, of course.

'You still kept Seth from me,' he choked out at last, but at least he was directing his pain and rage towards her, rather than inward as he might have done during their marriage. Or at least, proper marriage.

He might be mad at her, but he wasn't shutting her out. Surely that had to be a start?

'You had to have known you were pregnant. You would have had every opportunity to tell me. You didn't. You deliberately concealed it. I might have pushed you away, but you were still the one who left. Taking my unborn baby with you.'

'It wasn't like that. I left for both our sakes, Zeke,' she repeated, her voice softer now that she could see he wasn't going to argue with her. 'And for Seth's sake. But please believe me, I never intended to stay away this long.'

He didn't answer, but the expression on his face warned her that he didn't believe her.

'I promise you that I always imagined I'd find you and tell you.'

'When?' Zeke cut in. 'When our son turned eighteen? Got married? Had a family of his own?'

The challenge was clear, but if she hadn't known better, she might have thought she'd heard the briefest of hesitations. As if he might have been on the edge of believing her. As if he had just softened, ever so fractionally, before her eyes.

Not so much that a stranger might notice it, of course. This was Zeke, after all. But she noticed. And it caught her off guard.

But then he shut down on her again, and she knew she must have imagined it.

'You know what, Tia? Forget I asked. I think there have been enough revelations for one night, don't you?'

'I...' She faltered.

'I need time to think. Feel free to leave.'

He stood up, and Tia found herself scrambling to her feet in echo.

'We *will* discuss this further.' Whether he was issuing a threat or a promise, she couldn't be sure. 'I'll come to Delburn Bay when I have a solution.'

Why was he being so cold? What had changed? A chill crept over her skin.

'A solution?'

'Don't disappear,' he continued as if she hadn't even spoken. 'And if you do find your own place, make sure your father knows to tell me *exactly* where that is. I don't intend to have to come searching for you. Or my son.'

He had her halfway out of the door and into her car before she could protest. The darkness of night and whipping wind catching her unawares.

How long had they been in his house? The storm that had been raging way out at sea was clearly beginning to move closer.

'Your motorbike...?' she yelled above the roar.

'I'll collect it another time. I have a car for the meantime.' She followed the jerk of his head towards a sleek double garage more than heard his words. But then he was slamming her door and walking away. Barely stopping to call over his shoulder. 'Goodbye, Tia.'

Mutely, she obeyed, sliding her car fob into the central console and pressing the ignition button and moving inexorably off the drive. She couldn't fight him. She didn't even understand what she was fighting.

Tia was already out of Westlake and on the route home when her mobile rang.

Was it Zeke? Calling to tell her he'd changed his mind? *Dammit, why hadn't she connected to Bluetooth?*

Pulling over into a layby, Tia fumbled through her bag, the phone seeming to slip elusively away from her each time. She certainly wasn't prepared for her father to be calling, asking her if she was okay.

'I'm fine. I'm on my way home, why?'

'That's good,' his reassuring voice crackled over the connection. 'As long as you're safe.'

'What is it?' she asked, unable to shake the sense of disquiet.

'It's nothing. I'll see you when you get back here. Drive safely, and if the weather gets too bad, stop at a motel for the night.'

'What's going on, Dad?' It took all her effort to keep her voice calm. 'Please. Tell me.'

And then she listened as her father reluctantly told her that there had been a major incident at sea and that both Westlake and Delburn Bay lifeboat stations had been called on to attend. They would assist with a search and rescue helicopter already flying out to the scene.

Tia didn't think twice. She confirmed that her father was happy to look after Seth for the night, and then she terminated the call, turning her car around and heading back into Westlake.

If there was a shout now, then Zeke was heading out to it. And after the conversation they'd just had—the emotional state his head must surely be in—she couldn't just leave it at that.

She had to be there. She had to know he was safe.

Whatever that said about the way things were between them, now wasn't the time to worry about it.

CHAPTER FIVE

TIA CLUTCHED THE cool resin countertop of the lifeboat station's compact kitchen and waited for Albert—a volunteer who had been at the station from even before she herself had started there aged a mere fifteen—to terminate the radio call and update them. The last few hours had been unbearable, without a single reprieve, and the atmosphere amongst the other volunteers left behind, concerned for their colleagues and feeling helpless, was sombre, at best.

Her only consolation was the fact that Albert had been so absorbed with the shout that he hadn't had a chance to do more than look shocked at her arrival, then hug her tightly, before focussing in on the emergency.

He certainly hadn't had time to ask her any questions, or, worse, reminisce about the good old days when her mother had been a coxswain and her father the medical officer.

As the old man plodded heavily into the room her heart hammered in her chest, and she fought to try to calm herself.

Even as she had arrived at the station it had been scant relief to hear that the initial report had said that a cargo ship had been slightly listing as a result of some of the hundreds of containers on deck that had shifted in the violent storms. The treacherous conditions at sea had meant that it would most likely take hours before the Delburn and Westlake lifeboats—who had been asked to attend in support of the rescue helicopter taking the lead for the incident—reached the scene.

Now, a few hours later, they were still waiting for news. A temporary loss of radio communications had only heightened the tension all round. Albert cleared his throat, his steadfast, calm voice belied only by the strained lines around his eyes.

'It seems the situation has degenerated. There's about a five-metre swell out there, which has caused the cargo to slide further and made the ship list to such an extent that the portside rails had become submerged. They've lost power and at least two of their crew are already injured.'

'Our guys won't reach them in time,' someone muttered, concerned.

'Zeke has increased his speed to twenty knots to try to ensure that they do.' Albert's frown deepened.

As the murmurs rippled around the room, Tia's grip tightened. As did the fist around her heart. But she couldn't speak. Couldn't even utter a sound.

'They'll never make it.'

'Those seas will be mountainous; the lifeboat will be tossed around like it's a kid's bath toy.'

'They'll be airborne more than they're in the damned water. They're more likely to injure themselves just getting there than anything else.'

Silence reigned for a moment.

'It's typical Zeke, though, ain't it?'

'Well, if anyone can do it, he can.'

'Yeah. If you want someone coming in for you, it'd be him. And his crew.'

She wanted to scream, and shout, and tell them *what did that matter if he got himself killed in the process?* How did she tell her son? How did she even begin to get him to understand? Especially when she barely understood it herself.

But she didn't say a word. She couldn't. And still, the fears encircled her.

It was pitch black out there; even with the lifeboat's searchlights the lads wouldn't be able to see when the waves were coming at them. Ready to hit them. She could only imagine them holding on tightly as they felt their Atlantic class boat climbing each swell, bracing for the moment they plummeted down the other side, smashing back into the unforgiving sea.

That was if they weren't tossed right out of the water altogether. Spun over. Capsized.

A wave of nausea built inside her.

Most of her knew that he would never risk the lives of his crew members. *Never.* But there was that tiny, fearful part of her that knew that the night of his accident had changed him fundamentally. He'd lived but two of his buddies had died.

Tia swallowed hard. Zeke would trade his life for either of theirs in an instant because he didn't value his life enough. His monster of a father had made sure that Zeke had never really known how to value himself at all.

And that was the knowledge that scared her most.

The wait for more news seemed interminable. And then it came through, and Tia almost wished it hadn't.

Zeke and his crew had arrived as the rescue helicopter was trying to get into position to winch up the men from the cargo vessel, one by one. But the wind had been relentless, buffeting the helicopter time and again, and the sea rolling with such power that it had almost smashed the container ship into the helicopter several times. There was no way this wasn't going to end in tragedy.

And so the terrible decision had been made to pull the helicopter back, leaving the crew on board, preparing to abandon ship. Their only choice to leap into the raging waters and pray that the lifeboats would be able to pull them out before they drowned or were slammed into their own ship.

The chances of recovering all of them, or even most, were slim, at best.

It shouldn't have come as a shock to Tia, or any of them sitting there in that station, that Zeke had come up with a different plan. A mad, dangerous plan. But a plan that only a coxswain of Zeke's skill could even hope to pull off.

And exactly the kind of stunt she'd been talking about back at his house, when she'd said he defined himself by how much he was risking of himself, in order to save another life.

He was going to manoeuvre his lifeboat into such a position that he could take a run up to the stricken ship—a vessel thousands of tonnes heavier than Zeke's own, and which could easily be lifted by the seas only to smash down on top of the smaller lifeboat—and get close enough for the terrified crew to leap from their deck onto his.

The nausea rushed Tia all over again.

It was sheer insanity.

But it was the other crew's only chance of surviving. No wonder Zeke was determined to try. Always the hero. But never to himself.

Cramps sliced through Tia's hands as she realised they were locked onto the countertop, clinging on as though it was the only thing keeping her upright at this moment.

It probably was.

When she'd told Zeke earlier of how terrified she'd been that each time he'd walked out of the door of their home, it might be the last time she ever saw him—she'd failed to convey *exactly* how paralysing that fear had been.

How each day, each night, when people knocked on the door or called her, she would momentarily freeze, a part of her wanting to run away just in case they were bearing news she wouldn't want to hear.

Being on tours of duty of her own had almost been a relief. They had been challenging and exhausting, occupying her mind and giving her something else to focus on. Something to stop her from worrying about her husband.

In fact, she hadn't had to worry about Zeke's well-being for five years—although a part of her couldn't pretend that she hadn't thought about him every single day. Every time she'd looked at Seth and seen her son's father.

Now here she was, practically hurtling back in time. Only this was worse, far worse, because now she knew what it felt like to lose him. And however much she told herself she didn't have him to lose any more, the idea of breaking this fragile reconnection they'd just made was almost unpalatable.

Which only confirmed one thing. As soon as Zeke got back safely tonight—and he had to, she couldn't accept any other option—she was going to have to find the courage to answer his questions. To try to explain about Seth.

She wouldn't hide behind the argument that he wasn't going to believe her because *so what* if he didn't? She could hold her head up high and say she had tried. The way she'd always imagined doing.

The way she would have done if her weakness back at the lifeboat station hadn't allowed that…intimacy to occur between them. The way she would have done if he hadn't then followed her home and seen Seth before she'd had a chance to explain.

The radio crackled, making her jump, and everything in her clenched painfully.

How immeasurably cruel would it be that the moment Seth and Zeke had finally found each other, Zeke was taken away from his son again?

And what about you?

Tia hastily crushed the whispering voice, but it was too late. The words, the implications, were already coursing through her entire body as if she herself had toppled into those inky-black ice-cold waters that churned outside in the darkness.

'If you end up killing yourself and leaving Seth broken-hearted, Ezekial Jackson,' she muttered so silently that no one else could hear, 'I swear I'll never forgive you.'

And she told herself it meant nothing when her own heart felt as though it were ready to fragment into a million pieces.

One more practice run at it to make sure he fully understood how the two vessels were likely to interact, Zeke thought, and then he would make the first full attempt to rescue the first crewman from the *Queen Aetna*.

The port side of the cargo ship was now fully submerged, an invisible hazard every time he brought the lifeboat too close. But there was nothing else for it. The crewmen would surely perish if he didn't try something.

His men were harnessed up as per his instructions and each were in their positions, whilst the Delburn Bay lifeboat was holding as steady as they could a little further out, their searchlight trying to illuminate as much as possible for his team.

He always felt the responsibility of getting his guys home safely from shouts, back to their families. And it wasn't always a guarantee when you were in a lifeboat crew—the sea could be a fickle, dangerous mistress. But tonight, it felt as if there was another edge to it. A sharper, more brilliant one.

Tonight, *he* had someone he had to make it home for, too.

He had his son.

And Tia.

No, not Tia. Zeke instantly thrust that thought from his head, ignoring the voice that whispered that it was too late to pretend he didn't still care about her.

But certainly Seth.

Thank goodness they were back home where he knew they were all right. Safe.

Icy cold reality raced back in to douse him, to drag him back to where he was. The conditions were atrocious, the noise of the crashing water drowning out anything else. They were all going to need to be flawless in their hand signals, but he trusted his team. Hadn't he trained most, if not all, of them? Not to mention the very real danger that if he overshot his mark, even by a few metres, the cargo ship could crash down onto the lifeboat's bow.

There was no choice. Lives were on the line.

Then, as the storm blasted around them, Zeke made his first real approach only for the sea to open up in a great, unpredictable, menacing yawn. Both vessels rolled.

Then collided.

It took all of Zeke's skill to extract his lifeboat without any serious damage. A lesser coxswain might have bottled it. But that wasn't him.

It never had been.

Maybe Tia saw it as a flaw, his so-called pig-headedness, but he saw it as a fundamental part of his psyche. He would *never* willingly leave a man behind.

Checking his crew were ready, Zeke manoeuvred himself back into position and set about a second approach.

It was three hours, more than seventy approaches and a lifetime of exhaustion before Zeke and his crew—and the Delburn lifeboat—finally turned and headed back for shore.

Twelve of the fourteen crew from the cargo ship were safe on his boat, whilst the other two, who had missed the jump from their sloping deck to his, had been fished out of the water by Delburn's crew.

Not a single man had been left behind, and for that

Zeke gave silent thanks. When one of the crewmen had got caught up in a rope as the ship had begun to sink, and all the containers had shifted, both crews had thought he was dead.

If two of his lifeboat crew hadn't taken their lives in their hands and taken out the inflatable lifeboat, he certainly would have drowned.

Even launching the inflatable in those conditions had been hair-raising. But now they were facing a new problem—their main casualty needed emergency medical attention that went way beyond the ability of any of his crew.

'Contact the station, see if they can patch us through to emergency services,' he yelled, his eyes not leaving the churning water, still fighting to cut through the heavy swell and get them home safely. 'Maybe they can advise something we can do to help him.'

He focussed back on his own task of piloting the boat; the last thing he expected was to hear his men say that Tia was at Westlake. Fear and something else he couldn't name bit cruelly into him. Like the tentacles of jellyfish hooking into him, locking him in place, stinging painfully every moment. More than they had any right to do.

Why the hell wasn't she back home? Safe with their son?

And then the pain began to recede as a thought slid, unbidden, into his brain. Had she stayed for him?

If so, was it because she cared? Or because she wanted to finally explain herself?

It shouldn't matter to him either way, and yet something crested inside him, like one of the dark, towering waves out there.

Tia listened as the young first aider relayed how the patient had become caught up in some kind of winch rope during the rescue, which had whipped him around causing him to sustain severe chest and arm injuries.

The lad detailed fractured ribs, bleeding and severe lacerations, which they appeared to be stemming. But it was the tachycardia, breathing issues, hypotension and hypoxia that concerned her most.

'I think you're looking at tension pneumothorax. You're going to need to perform a needle decompression, and you're going to need to act fast.'

'I can't.' The voice held a tinge of panic. 'I don't know how to do that.'

'I understand,' Tia soothed, her mind racing over the equipment he might have available to him on the lifeboat. 'But if you don't then he's going to go into cardiac arrest. So I'm going to talk you through it. You're going to be fine. Okay, so first you'll need something that will reach fully into the thoracic cavity. I would suggest a ten-gauge catheter—it's stiff and it will be long enough.'

She waited whilst he shouted out to his colleagues, the noise on the line only giving her the briefest hint at what it must be like for them on the boat, still slamming through the stormy sea.

'I have it.'

'Good, so now you're going to go back to your patient—he's on the floor, right? Okay, clean the area with whatever sterilising solution you have in your kit and then you need to locate the second intercostal space on the same side as the tension pneumo. So find the clavicle and then move down and that will be the second rib. The soft space below it is your second intercostal. Got it?'

She spoke calmly and slowly, trying to keep the kid as confident as possible. It wasn't ideal, but they were hours out to sea. Without the procedure, there was no way the injured man was going to make it back to shore alive.

'Now, you need the mid-clavicular line. Okay? Good lad. Right, I'm going to talk you through it, but, just so you're prepared, you're going to go in perpendicular to the chest wall, and make sure you push in deep enough before you pull the catheter off the needle. You'll know you've succeeded if you get a rush of air. And there's often also a degree of spray as well so just make sure you've got protective gear on.'

Tia heard the crackle on the line, and then he told her to proceed, her whole body tensed up on the kid's behalf. Clearly, brightly, she began, only able to imagine what was going on at the other end of the connection.

It felt like an eternity. And she heard his exclamation of relief at the rush of air. Not long after, the signs of hypotension and shock she had diagnosed began to be alleviated.

She sagged back onto her chair. All that was left now was for them to get back to Westlake.

And for Zeke to come back safely.

CHAPTER SIX

'WHAT THE HELL is wrong with you? You could have been seriously injured. Killed.'

'This is why you never left Westlake last night, even though I sent you home?' Zeke kept his voice remarkably calm and even, knowing it would only irk her all the more. 'So you could stay here to berate me?'

But the truth was, he wasn't just keeping calm for Tia. It was the only way to keep at bay the storm of emotions churning inside himself right at that moment. It was why he didn't even bother to turn around as she slammed her car door and stalked up the drive behind him, her heeled boots crunching hastily on the gravel.

He was only slightly galled to realise that, after all that had been said between them less than six hours ago, he still wanted her. He had to fight the urge to stride up to her and haul her body to his. To remind himself that he was alive. That he'd made it back to land safely.

There had been moments out there, during that shout, when he'd found it impossible to shut out the niggling doubt that—this time—his crew might not make it home. He knew that over the years there had been several times when members of his crew had been concerned. Worried. But he'd never been one of them. He'd believed in fate.

Tonight had been different. Images of Tia, of Seth, had crept into his brain, and with them had come the first tentacles of fear. He'd let himself consider, for the first time in five years, that there was someone worth making it home for.

Two people, in fact.

It was an odd sensation, not exactly unpleasant, but... *strange.*

Why had he never felt this fear back when it had just been him and Tia, off on their own missions? Because there was no doubt that he'd wanted to be with her back then. Yet that worry about not making it home had never existed in the past.

Had Tia been right earlier, when she'd accused him of feeling invincible back then? It was a question that had been circling in the back of his mind ever since she'd said it.

He'd always been so sure of his ability, so proud of his tight-knit squad, that even though he'd known logically that missions could go wrong, in his heart he'd never believed it could happen to *them.*

For the first time, he began to consider how that might have impacted his young wife. But not for long. Tia's voice quickly cut across his musings.

'Well? *Did* you even think about how dangerous what you were doing was?'

'What kind of a question is that? Close the door behind you, Tia, you never know if some raging harridan might follow you in from the street.'

'Very funny. I'm not a raging harridan.'

'I never said you were,' he replied mildly, not even slowing down as he made his way along the corridor, unbuttoning his shirt as he went and hearing her furious, hurried steps tapping down the hallway behind him. 'I merely observed that I wouldn't want one to do so.'

'Of course you did,' she answered snippily, still hot on his heels.

He could pretend it was the adrenalin still racing through him, but he knew that wasn't it. Tia had stayed. For him. And now she was bawling at him because she was concerned.

It should be too little, too late. Yet he was letting her carry on as if he were some starving man and she were throwing him scraps from the bin.

Life was so damned short. It was a fact he already knew well, but tonight had reminded him of it. As if he needed the reminder.

Tia was right: he *had* pushed her away five years ago. He *had* made cruel, devastating, accusations, to drive her from him. Of course, he hadn't known she was pregnant, and he couldn't forgive her for not telling him, but that didn't mean he wasn't determined to be a part of his son's life now that he finally knew Seth existed.

He just hadn't worked out the finer points of *how*, yet. And until he did, all Zeke could do was to keep moving, not stopping long enough for Tia's words—her concern— to get under his skin. To have any real effect.

He just needed to unsettle her long enough to buy himself time to think.

Evidently Tia didn't realise where he was heading until he strode into his en-suite bathroom, dropped his shirt and tee into the laundry basket, and had his hands on his open jeans waistband.

She pulled up sharply as he'd anticipated. Just the way she had less than a day earlier in the lifeboat station. Her eyes lingering a fraction too long, pooling a fraction too dark, before she tore them away and scanned behind her to realise they'd just walked through his bedroom.

'I take it that you intend to join me.' His tone was deceptively conversational. 'I must say it isn't the reaction I'd anticipated, but I guess I'm not complaining.'

For a moment her forehead furrowed in a way that was

achingly familiar, then realisation crossed her features and then, oddly, anger.

'Is this seriously a joke to you?'

Her tone was sharp, but her tongue flickering out over her lips betrayed her.

And fascinated him.

Which made it almost more dangerous than being out in that rolling sea. Suddenly, it didn't seem so wise after all. *Damn her for always finding a way to creep under his skin.* Irritation slammed through him.

'Not in the least. So if you don't want to join me, I suggest you get out.'

If he hadn't been ready, hadn't steeled himself against it, it might have got to him when she flinched as she did. It might have felt like a weight on his soul.

Then, wordlessly, she turned and left the room, leaving him to shower in what he told himself was peace.

He half expected her to have left when he emerged. Told himself it was irritation he felt, not exhilaration, when he saw her still there in his living room. He was glad he'd thought to slip on black jeans to cover the limb. He'd never taken pains to hide it in front of anyone else.

Only Tia could make him feel so irrationally conscious of it. As though he was worried it might make her see him as anything less than fully competent to step up to the role as father to his own son. It was disability he'd spent years proving to the world it didn't have to be. At least tonight had proved him as capable as any other volunteer on that lifeboat. More so.

Though it was galling that he should need to prove anything to her.

'Had your fun?' she asked pointedly, jerking her head up as he approached.

Did he imagine that flicker of weariness in her voice?

Perhaps he did. Perhaps not. Either way, he knew he was done with them taking potshots at each other.

'I'm sure we could go on for what's left of this night firing questions at each other, until that hint of light on the horizon out there stretches into fully fledged morning, but I'm not really sure it's getting us anywhere. Are you?'

'I don't know, Zeke—do you think that could be because you counter all of my questions with one of your own?'

'You don't find that a touch hypocritical?' he pointed out before finally relenting. 'Fine. Yes, I considered the danger, but those men would have been dead without us. Anyone else would have done the same.'

Flames of fury licked at her expression.

'I'm not so sure.'

'Meaning what?'

Lovely as ever, she arched her eyebrows at him.

'Meaning you've always been a risk-taker, Zeke. I think you live for that danger. I think you can't live without it.'

'You're wrong,' he ground out, but something shifted uncomfortably within him. A tiny part of him that suspected she was right.

The silence shrouded them and then, abruptly, the fight went out of her.

'This was a mistake.'

It was the quiet sadness in her tone that really scraped at him.

'What was a mistake?'

'Coming back here. Trying to tell you about Seth.'

It was like a punch to the gut and ray of hope all at once.

'I'm his father. Now I know that he exists I won't let you shut me out of his life ever again. I'll be there for him.'

'You're a liability,' she snapped.

'Say again?' He had never been a violent man—he'd had

enough of that growing up with a father like his—but right now he could have punched a hole through his very walls.

'Tonight was a miracle, Zeke. You got those men to safety and kept your own crew safe. But what would have happened if you'd been just a metre out? Just once? Would everyone have made it back alive then? Would you have made it back alive?'

'But we did.'

'Lord knows how.' Her breath hitched in her throat but she forced it out. 'And what of Seth, your son, then?'

'That didn't happen, Tia.' His voice was low, lethal. It was all he could do to keep his cool.

'This time,' she emphasised. 'But what is your plan, Zeke? To build a relationship with Seth? To get close to him? To get me to agree to tell him who you really are so that he can love you as the father he's always dreamed of?'

'You have a real problem with that, don't you? Why?' he roared.

'Why do you think, Zeke? Because what happens to him, then, next time you go off to pull a stunt like tonight? When, that time, it doesn't work out quite so spectacularly?'

'That's the reality of life, Tia,' he managed, but the words jarred unexpectedly, even to his own ears. 'We can't protect people against horrible things, no matter how much we want to.'

Tia seemed to slump, as though relieved and devastated all at once.

'But I can try to protect my son from as much pain as possible. Especially when it's so inevitable. You have a self-destructive streak, Zeke, you always have had. We both know it. If there's a burning building you would have to be the first one to rush in and risk your life even if the fire service were minutes out.'

'Minutes could make a difference,' he countered, not wanting to concede her point.

'I'm not putting our son through that.' She stood fast.

'You think you can *not* tell him about me?'

'I think it's my duty as his mother to protect him. Whatever noble cause you dress it up as, how can I bring you into his life when I know that one day I will have to get him through the inevitable pain of losing you because the only way you can feel alive is by risking your life?'

'You seemed to have no trouble getting through that so-called pain,' he levelled at her, unable to help himself.

'No trouble?' she cried. 'You told me never to come near you again. That I'd ruined your life and you could never forgive me.'

This was ridiculous; they were going around in circles. But then, maybe that was the point—they had never really learned to talk to one another. They'd never tackled issues or ironed out differences. Maybe Tia was right, they had viewed the whole ten years of their marriage as an extended honeymoon period, never needing to get into the nitty-gritty of relationship bumps in the road because before anything became an issue one or both of them would have been leaving, off on some tour of duty or something.

Except that last time. And then he'd metaphorically drop-kicked her out of his life.

For her own good, Zeke reminded himself fiercely. Yet it didn't drown out the whispering voice that cast doubt. *Or to prevent her from seeing you in any kind of weakened state?*

'I already told you that I said that to protect you. You never once told me that you were carrying our son.'

'You level that at me as an accusation,' Tia cried. 'As though knowing I was pregnant would have changed things. But would it have changed anything, Zeke?'

'Yes.'

'Really? Only, I'm not so sure.'

'Of course it would have,' he bellowed, staring at her incredulously, white-hot anger searing through him. 'It would have changed everything.'

Tia didn't reply, she only watched him. Blinking once. Gently.

A wretched truth began to creep in. Or at least, a suspicion of a truth.

Would it have changed everything? Would it have changed anything?

'Of course it would have,' he repeated.

But this time he was less forceful.

She took a half a step closer to him, though he wasn't even sure she herself was aware of doing so.

'Are you sure?' she pressed softly. 'You told me that you were protecting me. Trying to absolve me of all culpability for amputating in the first place. Trying to free me of the burden that you saw yourself to be. Would you really have changed your mind because of a baby?'

He wanted to repeat that it would. To convince her. But suddenly, he wasn't even sure he was convinced himself.

He'd been a mess in those early months after he'd got back to the UK hospital. He'd only lost his leg but back then it had felt as though his whole life were over. He'd gone from an exceptionally fit Special Forces soldier, risking his life to protect his country, and those he loved, every day, to not even being able to walk, let alone look after himself; the idea of Tia having to run around nursemaiding him had felt too much to bear. Too shameful. Too humiliating.

How would he have felt knowing they had a baby on the way?

Knowing that when their son cried, he wouldn't be able to get up and go to him; couldn't simply stand and reach over the cot to pick him up; couldn't carry him back to Tia for feeding.

All things normal people took for granted.

Hell, he could barely look after himself those first few months, he couldn't have contemplated being able to take care of a baby. Tia would have been running around after their child, and then running around after him.

He couldn't have borne it.

Darkness rippled within him as a pain stabbed through his arm. It took Zeke a moment to realise he'd been clenching his fist tightly, and his wrist—also damaged in the blast five years ago—was screaming in protest.

Releasing Tia from what he'd feared would be a lifetime of feeling trapped had been one thing, but the realisation that he had effectively turned his back on his pregnant wife, his future child? That felt like something different entirely.

'Perhaps that's the truth,' he ground out. 'But I can't know for certain, can I? Because you never afforded me that courtesy. You concealed it from me for months whilst I was in that rehab centre. Visiting me every day despite me telling you—shouting at you—to stay away.'

'Not for months.' Tia sucked in a shaky breath. 'Actually, not at all during that time. I didn't know I was pregnant.'

It was pathetic how hope sprang up so instantly within him. He stomped it down savagely. His tone harsher than ever.

'You were on a tour of duty for three months before I got caught in that IED blast. You would have known.'

'But I didn't.'

'You expect me to believe that?'

'You'll believe whatever you want,' she cried in frustration. 'You always do, Zeke, that's the point. But if you're asking me for the truth, it's that I had no idea. Our jobs pushed us, always training, often in danger, and I was never…regular. You know that. I could go six months without having to worry about anything like that. So I just put it down to the stress of your accident, and the amputation.'

'You visited me in that centre day after day. However many times I told you to stay away, to give me space. You kept coming back.'

Right up until he'd finally found a way to keep her away. The day he'd lied to her and told her that he could never forgive her for what she'd done.

For a long moment they simply stared at each other. Neither of them apparently wanting to talk about that final argument.

'I didn't know.' Her desperation was almost enough to convince him. 'I stayed away because…you were so adamant. Because the nursing staff believed that I was doing more harm than good by visiting. Because I thought if I gave you space, maybe you'd find a way to forgive me for making the only choice I could possibly have made.

'But I swear to you, Zeke, it was only after that I began to suspect I was pregnant.'

'And yet you never came back to me,' he growled.

'How could I? I was afraid that putting additional pressure on you would be damaging. I was warned to let you come to terms with the amputation in your own time.' She flung her arms out helplessly.

'Warned?'

'By the staff at the centre. You were so closed off, it worried everyone. And I was in an impossible situation, Zeke. I wanted to tell you because I hoped it might give you something positive to hold onto, and to work towards. Yet at the same time, I was terrified that you would try to rush your recovery. I was terrified you would push yourself too hard because you felt as though you had to be the one providing for us. For me, and for Seth.'

'That was my job to look after you both. I was his father. I *am* his father.'

The frustration was so thick, so deep, so bitter, he could almost drown in it. And he felt hot, too hot. If he hadn't known better then he might have thought the carefully regulated temperature of his hi-tech home was failing.

'You'd already told me to stay away,' she countered, and he couldn't tell whether she was more furious or sad. 'How could I have loaded that onto you? I figured that I'd give you a bit of space, maybe a couple of weeks, even a month. I thought I had time. But I used to call them. Every day, Zeke. You have to believe that.'

Without warning she moved towards him and placed her hand on his arm.

The effect was electric. Shooting up his arm and through his body in an instant. He could feel her everywhere, and the ache slammed into him with all the force of those metres-high waves on his lifeboat barely a few hours earlier.

'They gave me updates and warned me that you were in a bad place. Survivor's guilt was bandied about for a long while. Hardly a surprise, but it was stopping you from recovering as you should. There was no way you were ready to be told you had a baby on the way. So I knew that staying away from you was the only way you were going to heal. Mentally and physically. Or do you really deny that?'

He hated that she was right.

And he hated the fact that his inability to come to terms with what had happened to him that night had caused Tia to stay away from him. And to keep his son away from him.

Zeke seethed inwardly.

Ultimately, it meant that however much he had congratulated himself on pulling out of that bleak place and setting up a company that he could never have anticipated would take off as it had, he was a failure after all.

Because he'd failed his family.

Stalking the room, he bit back one cruel, damning comeback after another. What was the point in them? The only person who really deserved his condemnation was himself. Tia couldn't hate him any more than he loathed himself right now.

'So I kept calling them each day, until one day I called and they told me you had discharged yourself. They'd thought you would be with me, but you weren't. Of course you weren't,' she choked out, anger and sadness inextricably interlinked.

No, he'd wanted to get as far away from her as possible. Because the temptation to go to her, to be with her, had been too great. He'd feared he might succumb and he'd been determined that the only time he would seek his wife out again would have been when he was strong enough to provide for her again.

He hadn't banked on her leaving her medical career in the army. Effectively disappearing herself. He hadn't for a moment imagined that she'd done so because she had a baby. A son.

His son.

It slammed into him, thrilling and proud, even if somewhat unsettling. And rumbling behind it, unsteadily and weaving a little, a ball of something that felt strangely like joy. He scarcely knew where to start.

'Maybe I *did* need you to stay away from me in order for me to get myself together,' he conceded at last. Ungraciously. 'But you're lying if you say you did it for me. You did it because it suited you, too. Because you didn't want to be around me. Because you didn't want me as father to our baby.'

Everything inside him was coiled up. Waiting. Desperate. Wanting her response.

It was like a fresh kind of hell when she dropped her eyes from his, unable to deny it.

'I didn't want the gung-ho Zeke. The man who basically jumped at any chance to risk his life. I didn't want my child relegated to having to remember his father as some dead hero. I didn't want him to have to wonder—every single day—if you were going to walk through that front door, the way I had to with my mother.'

Tia's voice cracked, and for a moment Zeke almost floundered. He remembered how lost and alone he'd thought she was the first time he met her. It had never occurred to him that she had carried that weight around her neck all those years—right up to becoming a mother herself; perhaps it should have.

'I'm so sorry…' he began, but she turned on him, practically stumbling over angry words in an effort to cut him off.

'I never wanted him to go through the pain I went through the night when she hurried out that door to the shout, kissing me and telling me that she'd be there when I woke in the morning. But she…she never was.'

Something kicked at him. Something he didn't care to name.

'I never realised… I'm so sorry, Tia.'

She dashed a furious hand over her eyes.

'I don't need your sympathy, Zeke. I just wanted you to understand.'

'I do understand now,' he started.

'Not understand why I was frightened back then.' She shook her head wildly. 'I mean to understand why—after your heroics last night—I still don't want you in Seth's life.'

He stood, dumbfounded, feeling as if he'd been sucker-punched. It was impossible even to draw a breath.

'I don't want you to walk into my son's life, and fulfil every childish fantasy he ever had, only to leave it again when something happens to you. Because it *will* happen, Zeke. I came back here because I heard you were here, and I thought you'd changed. But you haven't learned to value your life at all, I see that now.'

How was it possible to feel the loss of something he hadn't even known? And yet he felt it. Acutely. Unbearably. As if his son were being ripped from him, despite the fact that they'd never really had a chance to know each other.

'That's where you're wrong,' he ground out, his mouth feeling wholly alien. 'I *am* Seth's father and I *am* going to be in his life.'

'No.' She snapped her head up. 'I can't allow it. I won't.'

'And *I* won't allow you to shut me out of his life any longer. Not only do I intend to spend time getting to know my son, I intend to take him with me when I leave for France in a few days.'

Her laugh was a sharp, hollow sound.

'This time you really *must* be joking. You think I'm going to let you take him out of the country?'

'I know you are.'

She drew her lips into a thin line. Her eyes narrowing. Ready to fight.

'Over my dead body.'

When had that part of her developed? It wasn't a characteristic of Tia's he'd easily recognised. Yet even through his fury he knew it was appealing to a side of him that had never stopped hankering after *what might have been* between them.

She made to move away. To walk out of his house. Out of his life.

He couldn't let that happen.

Dimly, Zeke was aware that he hadn't fully engaged his brain before his mouth was firing away.

'I don't think that's going to be necessary.' He forced his voice to sound even. 'You're welcome to come with us.'

'I'm not going anywhere.' She snorted. 'And there's no way you're taking my son.'

'*Our* son.'

'Fine. But Seth still isn't going with you.'

'Ever heard of Z-Black, Tia?'

She stopped, her brow furrowing, and he had to fight the urge to reach out and smooth it flat. *Ridiculous.* But she was like a narcotic. An addiction he couldn't seem to kick no matter how hard he tried.

'Who hasn't? At least, in the military world.' She lifted her shoulders. 'What does that have to do with anything, though?'

'What do you know about them?' he pressed.

'Why?'

'Answer me, Tia.'

She glared, then sighed.

'Fine. I know they're renowned for prepping civilians for going into war zones, from foreign correspondents to aid agencies, even corporate individuals for restructure. Z-Black is known as one of the best for training them, showing them how to spot for mines, how to look after themselves, how to work with their close protection teams so they don't actually become a liability themselves.'

'You know quite a bit, then.'

'Yeah, they also train up their own close protection teams for both foreign and domestic scenarios. Rumour has it they're into a heck of a lot more than that, but their guys are immensely loyal and no one on the inside has ever confirmed anything. You work for them?'

'Not exactly.' He could have simply told her, but he wanted to see if she would come to it on her own. If a part of her believed in him enough. 'What do you think the Z and the Black stand for?'

'Black is black ops.' She pursed her lips, moments before her eyes widened. 'The Z...is you?'

'Me. And also the other two founding partners. Brothers, William and Frazer Zane.'

He wasn't surprised when she didn't laugh with him. He could well imagine what was going through her head.

'You couldn't.' She paled. 'You wouldn't use Z-Black to take Seth from me.'

'Then don't make me, Tia. Don't take my son from me.'

It was shocking, inexplicable, this...bond...he felt with a boy he'd seen for barely a few moments. He hardly knew what to make of it. He only knew it was potentially the best news he'd ever heard in his life.

'This house...' she managed, sweeping around as if taking it in all over again. 'You and your partners must be millionaires? You're going to use that against me if I fight you.'

'Multimillionaires,' he corrected. The three of them weren't far off billionaire status, but Tia didn't need to know that right now. 'And I don't want to use anything to fight you, Tia. Just don't back me into a corner where I have no other choice. Seth is my son, too.'

She looked as though she wanted to argue. Perhaps wisely, she bit the words back.

'Why France?'

'That's where our training sites are based. More room. I'm going back to oversee a course and I'm taking my son so that we can start to get to know each other. You don't start work officially for a month. Or so you said before.'

'No, but...'

'Coincidentally, Z-Black currently has a need for a medical trainer with experience out in a hostile environment.' Or, at least, it would after he'd made a phone call. 'Which leaves you with two choices, Tia.' He paused, forced himself to smile, as if he found some perverse pleasure in this awful scenario. 'Either you watch me take my son with me. Or you take this role and come with us as a sort of a family.'

'No,' she whispered, her hand fluttering at her chest.

'Then my son and I will go alone. I have a housekeeper who has nine grandchildren she's forever showing me new photos of. She can show me anything I need to know.'

'You're not taking Seth out of the country without me.'

He hated himself for doing it to her, but there was no way he wasn't going to take the opportunity to get to know his son away from the distractions of everyday life. It was too vital not to get right.

'I'm taking the opportunity to get to know my son. I told you, you're welcome to come too—that option still stands. To my mind, Tia, it's a no-brainer. But then that's just my opinion. The choice, as they say, is yours.'

CHAPTER SEVEN

THE CHATEAU WAS bathed in the most stunning sunset as their black, muscular four-by-four powered up the endless, winding tree-lined driveway. It rose out of its setting of verdant sprawling vineyards in stunning yellow stonework which made it seem warm and welcoming—even the single stunning turret wasn't imposing and hostile, like its owner—whilst the pretty shutters only enhanced the romantic feel of the property.

Yet as the car sped over the uneven ground with a light bump, Tia's heart gave a far more violent jerk. She didn't know what unsettled her the most: the fact that she'd allowed Zeke to command her to bring herself and Seth to live with him whilst he got to know his—their—son, the fact that Z-Black was a private chateau in the south of France, or the fact that he had flown them out on a private plane.

Now they were here her sense of unease only intensified.

It was all a world away from the Zeke she had known, the Zeke she had married, and she couldn't shake the impression that this was his way of showing her exactly that. Proving to her that she didn't know the first thing about him any more.

Maybe it was unintentional. More likely it was a deliberate attempt to unnerve her.

Either way, it was certainly working. She'd been worried enough about the custody angle when she'd seen his home back in Westlake. This was a hundred times worse.

And so she did the only thing she could—she reached for something solid, something which could ground her, something which mattered.

Seth.

'He's still asleep,' she murmured, stroking the soft hair above his brow in the way that always gave her comfort. 'It seems a shame to have to wake him. It has been a tumultuous couple of days.'

Too late, she realised it probably sounded as if she were making a dig at Zeke. She lifted her eyes, opening her mouth to clarify, but the hostile expression that greeted her made her close it again.

'Which is why I've heeded your request not to tell my son who I am,' Zeke ground out before adding darkly, 'Yet.'

Tia swallowed.

'And I appreciate that. I think…it would help for him to get to know you a little before dropping that bombshell on him.'

'The way you dropped it on me, you mean?'

For the second time in as many minutes she opened her mouth only to close it again. Zeke had her boxed in. And he knew it.

They sat in silence for the next few minutes—though it might as well have been years—whilst the vehicle finally pulled up outside the house.

Before she realised it, Zeke had scooped his still-sleeping son up into his arms and was lifting him out of the car and carrying him to the door, with her scurrying to catch up.

Father and son. Leaving her behind. Wasn't this partly what she had feared by coming back into his life? That, or watching him reject Seth as his son. The way he had rejected *her* almost six years ago.

Ironic how she outwardly objected to him ordering her around, demanding that she and Seth join him in France, and yet it was that very commandeering front that made her feel they were wanted. *Required.* She certainly couldn't believe she'd ever considered that Zeke rejecting Seth would be a possibility.

And there it was, the unpredictability that had always been Ezekial Jackson. The reason she had *let* him reject her back then. Not fighting for him, or their fragile marriage, the way a part of her had so desperately longed to do.

Because she'd known that he'd been dealing with enough just coming to terms with losing his leg. Just trying to find a way to piece his life back together and work out a new path for himself, and for his future.

She'd already explained to him the reasons for her keeping Seth a secret, and they were true. But it hadn't stopped a part of her from always railing against the fact that her son didn't know his father, especially one he could be proud of like Zeke.

The fact that he'd started Z-Black certainly explained how he'd dropped off-grid after leaving the rehab's home. And why the first time she'd heard of him was years later when the newspaper had run those reports about Zeke, the hero coxswain.

Despite herself, Tia felt a soft smile toying with her mouth as she followed Zeke upstairs, still cradling Seth in his arms.

There were so many Zeke-like traits that she recognised. As bizarre as it might seem to a casual onlooker, she knew him well enough to understand why a multimillionaire would be working as a coxswain for a lifeboat charity. The sea ran through his blood, much as it did hers. It was who he was, and it was what he loved.

The Westlake connection still baffled her, though. Why had he come back there, of all places, to be a coxswain? He'd hated the place. Barely able to hang around at the scene of his awful childhood once he'd become old enough to join up.

If she hadn't known better she might have fancifully imagined that he'd come back because of the connection to her. To the way they had first met.

Tia hastily shut the idea down. To believe that was foolhardy. He wouldn't have come back for her. Ever. If there was one thing Zeke had never been, it was sentimental. But then, what had that angry young man, dragged up in a town of people who looked down on him, ever, *ever* had to feel sentimental about?

No, he hadn't come back for her. She couldn't allow herself to think that way. She didn't *want* him to have come back for her. It was too raw, too electrifying. She'd spent her entire youth terrified that every time her mother walked out of the front door that would be the last time they would ever see each other, and then it had happened.

Somehow, Zeke—charismatic, indomitable Zeke—had convinced her that he was bulletproof. That he would *always* walk back through their front door.

Until he hadn't. And the pain had been intolerable.

And now he was back to playing the hero, only this time behind the helm of a lifeboat rather than behind the trigger of a rifle.

She wouldn't put herself through that again. More to the point, she wouldn't put Seth through that.

And yet here she was, watching Zeke tenderly carry their son. Like the most precious cargo.

'Where does a fish keep its money?' Seth had gleefully asked during the flight—before exhaustion had finally overwhelmed him.

'I don't know.' Zeke had pondered thoughtfully, and

then proceeded to offer a myriad solutions, each one more absurd than the last and eliciting howls of laughter from a delighted Seth.

In the end, their son had almost been reluctant to answer, knowing it would be the end of the hilarious and outlandish suggestions from the man who had suddenly, unequivocally, entered his little life.

'In the riverbank,' Seth had announced proudly, his tiny chest positively swelling as Zeke had slapped his palm to his forehead and proclaimed how silly he'd been for not realising and then had wonderfully hammed up how impressed he was.

Now, hurrying behind them both to her temporary bedroom, Tia shook her head. As if that could somehow reorder the jumble of thoughts churning around in there, each vying for pole position.

'These are your rooms,' he announced, kicking open the slightly ajar door with one foot and striding inside. 'I'd have given you the tour but I had a feeling you would want to stay with Seth so he doesn't wake up alone in a strange bed. Your luggage will be brought up imminently.'

'This will be just fine,' she murmured, taking in the room, which was probably about the size of a small Parisian apartment. The sheer grandeur of it making her feel gawkish and out of place.

Another reminder that Zeke was now a multimillionaire, who could probably afford to pay the best lawyers to win custody of Seth—if he so chose. He might not have outwardly threatened to do just that, but it was there, simmering below the surface.

It should twist her in knots. But it didn't.

Why?

Because a part of her truly believed, deep down, that Zeke would never do that to her or Seth. Was she being naïve?

She hovered as Zeke laid Seth gently on the bed before

moving to an ornate blanket box and taking out a colourful throw to cover his son.

'This is Seth's room,' Zeke informed her pointedly, before indicating across to the far wall. 'Your rooms are through that adjoining door. Feel free to freshen up, even take a nap. I imagine it has been a fairly stressful seventy-two hours. Dinner will be in two hours in the large dining room. I'll give you the tour after that.'

'So formal for just the three of us?'

'Actually I thought Seth might prefer to eat a little earlier with some of Mme Leroy's grandchildren, since she babysits them from school every day before her daughter can collect them. Just for tonight whilst we discuss the ground rules whilst you are here.'

'I'm to have ground rules?' She smiled a little too tightly, but Zeke ignored her.

'I always hear them having a lot of fun, and then you can get him into bed before you come down. Besides, some of my senior instructors usually dine over here so that they can brief me on the day's events.'

Of course they did. Because work always came first with Zeke. It was one of the qualities that had drawn her to his young self. But it was also one of the ways he'd kept himself closed off from her—even if she'd never appreciated it at the time.

Zeke was deep in conversation with one of the instructors when Tia made her way down the stairs a couple of hours later, yet he was aware of her presence before he even saw her. Tiny hairs on his body standing to attention, as though the entire aura of the room had changed just by her approaching it.

And then she walked in looking like any single one of his fantasies over the last few years despite the fact that she was in nothing more dressed up than a light grey, soft cashmere jumper over a pair of charcoal trousers and those things he was pretty sure they called ballet pumps on her feet.

Her hair was piled up on her head as though she'd thrown it up there having only just got out of bed. A fact that was belied by the faint mandarin scent of shower gel as she glided gracefully up to him.

How he wished he could dismiss the others now and just have the evening with this arresting creature, as every part of him screamed *mine*.

'Gentlemen, I don't believe you've met Dr Antonia Farringdale before.'

'I most certainly have not had that pleasure.'

Zane. He might have known his old marine buddy wouldn't be able to resist her and as ridiculous, as schoolyard, as it was Zeke couldn't help himself—he took a tiny step forward, so subtle it looked simply as though he were shifting his weight from one foot to the other, but enough that his shoulder was tilted towards the newcomer.

The sense of possessiveness that charged through him caught him off guard. He wondered what a body language expert might make of it. He didn't desire Tia. He couldn't possibly. Not after she'd lied to him. *Denied* him, all these years.

He tried to hold onto the fury, the rage, that had almost overtaken him two nights ago when he'd found out that he had a son. *A son.* And yet he found he couldn't. That initial rage had waned the instant she'd left his house in Westlake that first day. All her words, her admissions, rolling around his head.

He hadn't wanted to understand her excuses, let alone believe them, and yet even then he'd known that he didn't matter.

Only Seth mattered.

And feuding parents would be the last thing the four-year-old boy would need.

Yet if it was only about Seth, and not about Tia, then why was it he still couldn't quite bring himself to relinquish his defensive stance as he introduced her to the room? Starting with his old buddy.

'Tia, allow me to introduce Zane, otherwise known as William Zane. One of the other Zs in Z-Black.'

'William.' Tia smiled and the openness and brilliance of it almost knocked Zeke for six.

How had he forgotten how powerful that smile of hers could be?

He ignored the voice that told him that he hadn't forgotten. Not for a moment.

'Zane, please,' his buddy corrected, beaming back.

Making Zeke uncharacteristically long to punch him in the mouth.

'Zane.' Tia inclined her head. 'You guys have got a great place here.'

'Thanks. We're kinda proud of it.'

'It pays the bills.' Zeke grinned, though it turned into more of an uncomfortable baring of teeth. 'Shall we finish introductions and then eat?'

He'd like to have thought that his companions didn't notice—possibly the others didn't—but Zane and Tia eyed him a fraction too long. A fraction too intently. Then the moment passed, and the evening unfolded relatively easily after that, with the meal passing smoothly and the conversation covering the day's events, as it always did.

But for once, Zeke couldn't concentrate.

He felt completely out of control, watching her eat, straining to hear her own soft conversations. Especially those with Zane, a lothario by his buddy's own admission.

'Would you prefer that we all left so that you and your wife could become a little less *estranged*?' Zane murmured, catching Zeke off guard. 'Perhaps I should warn the guys that you might not make it out into the training village tomorrow.'

'Bull,' Zeke gritted out. 'There's nothing between Tia and me. I'll be there.'

But his tone was too thick and too dark; it revealed far too much.

'Yes, I can tell that by the way you're both taking great pains to look anywhere but at each other.' Zane's eyes gleamed with amusement. 'To talk to every other person at this table but one another. Fascinating.'

'Sod off,' Zeke grumbled.

But it was too late. There was something taking flight within him.

Hope.

Forget all his vows to himself that he wasn't going near Tia again. All he wanted was for his business partner and the instructors to be gone so that he could be alone with her.

'I've been toying with a potential new business venture,' he growled. 'We can discuss it in my study after the meal.'

'That desperate to keep your distance from her, huh?' Zane grinned. 'Man, you must have it bad.'

It took everything Zeke had not to let his eyes slide to Tia.

'You're clutching, mate. We'll have a drink and talk business tactics.'

'Can't.' Zane sloshed down a mouthful of red wine. 'I have a cheeky little rendezvous lined up for later. I've been chasing this one for weeks.'

'Bloody hell, Zane. Not one of the staff? I can't lose another one who can't bear to stay around here and see you with another woman.'

'Once, that's happened once.'

'Twice.' Zeke raised an eyebrow.

'Fine, twice. But I always tell them *no strings*.'

'And they always think they can change you into *marriage and kids*. Thing is, Zane, one day one of them will, and you won't know what's hit you.'

'True.' Zane eyed Tia speculatively. 'But now I've seen you two together, and heard you talk about your kid nonstop practically all night, I'm beginning to see why *you've* never once been tempted by the fluttering girls who've thrown themselves at you over the past few years.'

'The two are mutually exclusive,' Zeke growled, only for his buddy to snort loudly.

'Yeah, sure. Anyway, I'll leave you to it.'

And then, Zane was boldly making his excuses, citing an early start and swaggering out of the room, leaving Zeke to mull over his buddy's revelations. Lost in his thoughts, he barely registered the evening drawing to a close until he found himself, finally, alone again with Tia.

'I… I should get Seth and head for bed.' She hovered across the room from him.

He ought to encourage her to go.

'If you're happy to leave Seth a little longer, let me give you that tour.'

She eyed him from under lowered lashes, as though she couldn't decide whether she was going to accompany him or not.

'He's still with Mme Leroy. His sleep this afternoon meant he wasn't ready for bed at the usual time,' she murmured at length. 'Perhaps it's a good opportunity to find my way around the place. It is rather expansive.'

Zeke resisted the urge to take her hand and lead her out. Just.

He started with the rooms closest to where they were, forcing himself to impart a few of the interesting facts that Mme Leroy had insisted on telling him, enjoying the way she laughed, encouraged when she couldn't curb her curiosity about the history of the place any longer and started to ask her own questions.

They moved around the building, slowly warming up to each other again. The thaw that had begun over the last couple of days now accelerating. For a moment, here and there, he could swear they both forgot what had brought them here.

How it had brought them here.

Zeke led Tia out onto the terrace and the pool area.

'I didn't bring a swimsuit.' Tia sounded dismayed.

He bit his tongue before he could suggest she didn't need to worry about wearing one. The very idea of it leaving him hard, and aching.

'I can have someone bring you anything you need.'

It wasn't the right thing to say. A reminder of his money, his power. And the fact that she already didn't trust him.

The thaw slid between them in an instant.

'Thank you.'

It was so damn polite and civil. Like strangers rather than the old married couple they'd been the hour or so before. Tia had been right when she'd said they'd been like perpetual honeymooners during their marriage. They barely knew each other at all.

He forced himself to resume the tour, to carry on walking through the house and working his way from ground floor to first floor, but the ease between them had gone. Until finally he was opening the door to his study and wondering why they were still fighting a lost cause.

Maybe it would be better tomorrow.

'This is where you work,' she breathed, moving across the space to the huge picture windows in front of his desk. 'You can see a lot from up on this floor.'

'I can watch some of the training exercises without anyone feeling they're being overseen.'

'I imagine you're quite off-putting.'

'Mainly for the clients, not so much my men. They're all ex-soldiers with years of experience.'

'I imagine.'

Again, that restrained stiffness.

'Would you like a drink?' He proffered a decanter of amber liquid, even though he rarely bothered to drink much these days.

For a moment he thought she was going to decline, and then she dipped her head.

'Why not?'

He poured the drinks and then, in silence, they stood by the window and watched Seth—their son—at play with the other children, streaking around the garden and tugging balloons and streamers with them.

'This is what you're reading?' she asked abruptly, breaking the silence. 'First World War books?'

'Autobiographies. From Europe and from the Pacific.'

'I've read this one.' She tapped the cover, her smile sad. 'It's quite moving.'

It would break the fragile bridge if he told her he'd already read it so instead he dipped his head thoughtfully.

'I'll bear that in mind.'

'No problem.'

And there it was, that easiness back. So seamlessly.

They were close, both propped against his desk as they watched the domestic scene unfolding before them. It was all too reminiscent of Tia's consultation room back at the lifeboat house. And all he wanted to do was to indulge in a repeat performance.

He didn't dare move.

'He has been asking about his father, you know,' she said softly, almost towards the dark edges of the otherwise summer evening.

He waited, but she didn't seem to want to be any more forthcoming.

'What have you told him?' Zeke asked, when he couldn't bear it any longer.

Did Seth think he was dead? Or an absent father who didn't care?

He clenched his fists in anger.

'I told him the truth,' she murmured. 'That is, as much of the truth as I could manage. I told him that his father was a dedicated, loyal, heroic soldier who had won medals for his bravery. But who had been injured in an accident whilst in a hostile country.'

'So he thinks I'm dead.'

A wave of nausea rushed up inside him before Zeke could stop it.

'I don't know,' Tia answered honestly. 'I never said you were, and neither did he. But I suppose he might think that.'

'And when do I get to tell him who I am?'

She turned her head to look at him. The tension between them locking them both into place.

'I don't know,' she half whispered. 'Give me chance to get my head around it all. Everything has happened so quickly these last few days.'

He had meant to lean in closer in some wild attempt to intimidate her, but he really should have known better. Tia—*his* Tia—had never been the type to back down or cower. So, they sat there, his thigh cleaved to hers. Her head tilted, almost belligerently, up to his. Her arms crossed over her chest hinting at her impatience.

And then he saw the faint pulse on one side of her slender neck. Fast, jerky, certainly not as *in control* as she'd had him believing.

It sideswiped him, apparently knocking any last vestiges of sanity from his head. Before he even knew what he was doing, he had snaked an arm out to circle her all too familiar waist, and hauled her to him.

'Zeke…?'

Her hands braced against his chest, her eyes widening, her breath catching.

'Is this what you came here for?' he bit out, as much to deflect as anything else.

How he loved the way her cheeks flushed—as though suffused with guilt. And the way she wanted him, just like back at the lifeboat station, soared through his body, lifting his spirits and soothing his earlier temper. Or, at least, transforming it into something else entirely.

Desire.

'You could have just told me you wanted me to kiss you again,' he taunted. 'To make you come apart the way I always make you. The way you did back in that consulting room of yours.'

'I never gave that afternoon a second thought.'

It was a valiant attempt, but her voice was too breathy. And he knew her too well. A sensation suspiciously like triumph ripped through him. He bent his head to hers, so close the heat from their breath intertwined, and she shivered deliciously in his arms.

'Liar,' he whispered. 'Tell me I never entered your thoughts.'

For a long moment she didn't move. He wasn't even sure if she'd stopped breathing. Her eyes meeting his, darkening, revealing too many things he knew she didn't want them to.

'You came here for more than just Seth.'

His gaze raked hers, hot and greedy and wanting. Then he leaned into her even closer.

'You came to France for the same reason I invited you,' he ground out. 'Because, as dangerous and nonsensical as it seems to be, you and I can't seem to stay away from each other.'

Before she could answer, he bent his head, unable to

hold himself back any longer from this burning *need* that threatened to overpower him, and claimed her mouth with his own.

Part of him expected Tia to wrench herself away. Another part of him expected her to slap him. Not a single part of him anticipated her groaning and melting against him as if she really couldn't help herself.

In seconds, Zeke had moved their positions, bringing her around so that their bodies were against each other, his hands caressing her back. And she looped her arms around his neck and pulled herself in tighter, as though she could think of no objections.

As though she thrilled to his touch.

His Tia. His wife. *His.*

He ran his hands down her back, teasing and flirting with the sweet curve of her bottom, pulling her into him so that her heat pressed against where he ached for her most, and it did nothing to help his self-control that all he could remember was the way she had tasted the other day in her office, that glorious scent of her sex, slick just for him, and the way she had come apart so perfectly against his mouth.

'Tia,' he groaned, nipping at the sensitive skin of her neck.

His body howled at him to strip her naked, spread her out on his desk and thrust all the way home. To have her screaming his name as she had done every weekend they'd managed to snatch together during their marriage, when they'd barely been able to get out of bed most of the time.

The sex between them had never been an issue.

Belatedly, he realised that this was what she'd meant when she'd said they had barely known each other. They'd mistaken unashamed sex for being emotionally vulnerable. But right now, Zeke couldn't bring himself to care. He just wanted to feel her around him, tight and wet, drawing him inside her until he filled her up.

He hooked his fingers under the hem of her cashmere top and hauled it over her head, the sinfully sexy lace bra making his body constrict all the more painfully. And then he spun her around so that his length was nestled between her buttocks as he cupped her breasts with one hand and undid the zip of her trousers with the other.

He heard her murmur of objection, muffled as she let her head fall back whilst he nuzzled the other side of her neck. Arching her back and pressing her breast into his aching palm.

'So good,' he muttered. 'So damn perfect.'

And then he slid his hand into her trousers and his fingers stroked her sex as though it were the most precious thing he'd ever touched.

The jerk of her hips and her whimper of need was like a lick against his groaning body.

And then just as suddenly as it had begun between them, Tia wrenched herself away. Refastening her trousers and straightening her cashmere top.

Zeke knew what was coming. Was powerless to stop it.

'This can't happen again.'

'You said that last time,' he pointed out nonchalantly, as though her anger couldn't faze him.

'Well, this time, I mean it. We're not kids any more, Zeke. We have responsibilities. I have a son.'

'*We* have a son,' he corrected quietly. Dangerously.

'Indeed you do.' Her eyes flashed just as lethally as she stalked around his study. 'So you should damned well act like it. We're here because you said you wanted to get to know *your* son. But stay away from me, for the rest of this trip.'

CHAPTER EIGHT

'WHAT DO YOU do first?' Tia asked the young lad, her brain fighting to function.

The sun was beating down on them, and with no shade it had already been a long morning of training exercises.

It didn't help that she'd hardly slept in the few nights since that encounter with Zeke. Her mind had been buzzing for days, her body even more so. The worst of it was that, despite everything she had said to him about responsibility, she had imagined going back down to his study and finishing what they had begun.

'Do a blood sweep.' The soldier's voice dragged her back to reality even as he checked down his make-believe patient, moving slow enough to give her time to respond.

'You find blood on his upper-right leg.'

'Check the casualty for holes.'

'You find a gunshot wound,' Tia told him, trying to focus on what was going on around her rather than in her head.

'Okay, I'm going to apply arterial pressure whilst I put a tourniquet around his leg…here.'

'Good—' she nodded '—but you need really solid pressure. Forget your hand, jam your knee right onto it or your casualty is going to bleed out. That's better.'

'How is he doing?' Zeke muttered, coming to stand next to her.

'Okay,' she confirmed, ignoring the way her body pulled tight. As if her skin were too small for her all of a sudden.

'Make sure that tourniquet is really tight. Look.' Zeke moved over to kneel by the trainee, turning up the fabric of his lightweight trousers as he went.

Yet she couldn't help feeling that he had deliberately angled himself so that his body was between her and the bionic limb he was flexing by way of demonstration.

'If my buddies hadn't done that for me, I could easily have lost my whole leg.'

She tried not to take it personally that he didn't mention her part in saving his leg. Or that his voice seemed to be pitched deliberately low. She'd seen and heard him talk about his limb several times to plenty of people over the last few days, but she was sure she wasn't imagining the shift in Zeke's attitude when she was around.

'Tourniquet applied.' The man nodded. 'Checking for other bullet holes.'

'There are no more holes found,' Tia confirmed.

'Does he have radial pulses?'

'He does have radial pulses.' She nodded.

'Okay, I'm calling it in.'

Zeke joined her as she was writing up brief notes and, though it killed her, she leaned over to speak to him confidentially.

'Although he found the gunshot entry point on his casualty's leg, he forgot to turn him over and check for an exit point.' *How could Zeke remain so calm when their arms skimmed each other like that?* 'Also, he never checked for head injuries, or blood in the ears.'

'Mark it down, we'll know to go over it.' Zeke shifted, brushing against her again. Almost more than she could stand.

She took the opportunity to break contact as she circled the trainee and his stand-in casualty.

'You find your casualty is having trouble breathing.'

The trainee paused for a moment before suggesting that his patient was overheating.

Quickly he began to strip his casualty down out of body armour and jacket until he was just in a coat.

'Is that what you were looking for?' Zeke murmured quietly.

'Pretty much.'

'Good. Fine, you seem to have it in hand here. I'll check on the others and then meet you at the house after lunch.'

'Sure.'

She made a mental note to try to avoid the house if Zeke was going to be there after lunch time.

In her peripheral vision she could see him moving away, on to the next team, and concealed her sigh of relief.

If the rest of her month here was going to be this strained then it was going to be hell. But she couldn't give into temptation again, with Zeke.

Zeke stared at the piece of paper in his hand, a whole range of emotions tumbling through him, yet he couldn't seem to grasp hold of a single one of them.

He was still standing in the same spot minutes... weeks...*years* later, when Tia walked into the room. He heard her speak, somewhere in the recesses of his mind, knew she was flustered and apologetic, but nothing registered. Not until she stepped closer, her tone changing to one of curiosity.

'What have you got?'

'A picture.'

'From me,' the lilting, bodiless voice came from the vicinity of the huge brown moleskin office chair. Tia's head jerked and he realised she hadn't even known Seth was in the room, let alone colouring in at Zeke's ornate desk as though it were his own personal colouring station. 'I drew it for him.'

'Oh.'

'It's a rhinoceros,' Seth confirmed, wriggling off the chair. 'I've done another one for Mme Leroy. Can I take it to her?'

She swallowed. Steadied herself, her eyes raking over the picture.

'Sure,' she confirmed after a moment, watching their son leave the room before turning to Zeke, her voice low. 'He loves animals.'

Zeke watched the door close behind the little boy. Marvelled at this incredible person that he—*they*—had created.

'He told me he wants to be a zoo vet, and travel to places like Africa or the Arctic?' Zeke managed.

'Animals have always interested him.' Tia shrugged lightly but he didn't miss the flash of pride in her eyes. 'I don't know if he'll ever become a vet but I'm not about to discourage him. Ask him about the picture and he'll no doubt tell you that it's a popular misconception that the rhinos' ancestor is the triceratops.'

'He already told me.' Zeke wasn't prepared for the grin that suddenly split his face. 'He was really quite adamant about it.'

'Yes, that's Seth.'

'If I remember rightly, his exact words were that a rhino shares about as much DNA with a triceratops as it does with a human.'

'Did he mention that rhinos actually belong to the same order as horses? That's usually one of his favourite facts.'

It was the lopsided smile that got him. Exactly the same smile that had graced the face of his son only an hour earlier, like a tiny glimpse into the purest of souls.

'He did actually—' Zeke laughed quietly '—alongside a whole host of other facts which he had clearly decided

I really ought to know. Then he told me they might have been the original unicorn, so I began to explain that unicorns didn't really exist…'

'I don't imagine that went down well.' She began to chuckle and Zeke's chest pulled unexpectedly tight.

Painful.

How much had he missed that sound over the last few years? How had he forgotten the way it had always slipped through him, making him feel happy? Contented.

Or maybe that was the point. He hadn't forgotten. He'd merely thrust it aside, locked it in the deepest, darkest pit, and pretended that part of his life hadn't existed. Because he hadn't been sure if he deserved such happiness.

He forced himself to smile. But not to *feel* anything more.

'It didn't. He cast a solemn glance at me and informed me, with what sounded a lot like disappointment, that *obviously* unicorns didn't really exist, but that it was possible that rhinos had been behind the original *myth*.'

'Oh, believe me, I know that tone.' Tia laughed again, a deeper sound, which he couldn't pretend he didn't recognise.

It was surreal.

Five years ago they would hardly have been able to stand in this room together without tearing each other's clothes off. Now they were standing here discussing their son.

Their son.

It didn't seem possible.

'You've done an incredible job with Seth,' Zeke managed, suddenly.

The laughter died on her lips as she chewed them uncertainly.

'Thank you.'

'I mean it. He's a bright, happy, confident little boy. I

had no right the other night…threatening a custody battle with you.'

For a moment, she didn't answer.

'I'm sorry, Tia. I really am.'

She still didn't respond, but began to move slowly around the room, dragging her hand over the few trinkets that he allowed to adorn the place. The things that made the place look, if not homely, at least less sparse.

Belatedly, now, he realised they were all items that had been in the home they had once, briefly, shared.

'I'd have thought you would have got rid of these.'

He shrugged but her back was still to him. Probably he should have got rid of them. But he hadn't. What else was there to say?

Because he very much feared that they said too much as it was. That they revealed the sad truth that he hadn't moved on from her, however much he'd claimed to have done. He had a new mansion, a new multimillion-pound business, and a new way to save lives.

But ever since Tia had walked back into his life, he hadn't been able to shake the unsettling feeling that all these achievements had been little more than him marking time.

Waiting for her.

It was pathetic. Infuriating. And regrettably undeniable.

But the more she looked around his study, his private sanctuary, the more he feared she could read into his heart. Before he could think about it, he heard himself speaking again.

'Come out with me tomorrow tonight.'

Less of a request and more of a demand. At least it made Tia turn, and stop analysing his study.

'To where?'

'The Mayor's Charity Ball.'

She narrowed her eyes, assessing him.

'It doesn't sound like your kind of thing.'

He grimaced.

'Z-Black needs a new permit and the mayor isn't convinced. I could do with a little moral support.'

'Since when do you need *any* kind of support?' Tia asked warily.

There was no reason at all for his heart to be hammering so wildly. Like an adolescent boy asking out his crush for the very first time.

'It couldn't do any harm. It's a nice night out, apparently, and you would be my date.'

In an instant, Tia went from smiling to on edge.

'I… I can't.'

'Why not?' It was as though he could almost taste victory only for it to be snatched away from right in front of him.

'Seth, for a start,' she announced, as though convinced it would satisfy any concerns.

'Mme Leroy would love to babysit for the evening.'

'Right. Well. I don't have a dress. Galas haven't really been high on my priority list the last few years.'

'I'll have someone bring a selection over within the hour,' he countered.

She pursed her lips, leaning her hands on the back of the couch and eying him apprehensively.

'Zeke, is this really such a good idea? Won't people… talk?'

'A married couple attending together. Yes, I can see how that would make the headlines.' He laughed, making her feel foolish despite everything.

'Surely you can't really need me there?'

'I do,' he said simply.

And when she blinked at the uncomplicated emotion in his words, something clenched low in his stomach.

He found himself not wanting to give her the chance to back away.

'Go and get ready to collect Seth, Tia, have some time together. I'll set the rest up.'

'I can help for a few moments.'

'Go, Tia,' he growled. 'I'll deal with it.'

And then, before she could argue any more, he strode around the desk, tucked the rhino picture neatly under the glass paperweight on top of his desk, and flicked out his mobile phone, as though his momentum could somehow galvanise Tia, too.

Either way he took it as a small victory when, a few moments later, she turned and headed out of his study.

It felt like less of a victory when he heard his son's shout of delight following a splash and found himself standing at the study window, which overlooked the covered infinity pool, less than ten minutes later, unable to drag his gaze from the sight of his wife stepping out in peacock-blue and executing a graceful dive into the perfectly still waters.

He wanted her with an almost overwhelming intensity.

What the hell was he playing at?

Tia was supposed to be a part of his history, his past. Not something he had to poke at every available opportunity. Like sticking his tongue against a loose tooth when he'd been a kid.

The sooner he remembered that, the better.

'Where's Zeke?' Seth demanded as the two of them headed to the pool together. 'Isn't he coming swimming?'

'No, sweetheart, he had to work.'

'Oh.' Seth peered at her. 'I thought it might have been because he couldn't get his robot leg wet.'

Tia froze, feeling as though her entire body were twisting itself around and around as she turned to her son.

'What do you know about Zeke's leg?'

'Oh, he has one real one and one robot one,' Seth declared. 'Didn't you know?'

'Yes,' she nodded, relieved he clearly didn't know that she had been the one to amputate. 'I did know that, actually. But how do you?'

'I've seen it.'

A gurgle rippled through her. Of course Seth had seen it; Zeke wore shorts out here. It was practical, and suddenly a vivid memory rushed her of the time when, five years ago, the rehab centre had told her to stop worrying about Zeke hiding his leg and give him time, telling her that most of their amputees came to wear their limbs like a badge of honour.

Back then, she'd never believed it would be Zeke.

Every time he'd looked at his legs, he'd had such an expression of loathing. Whether at her for amputating, or at himself for living when his buddies had died, she'd never quite been sure.

It was better than hiding away and feeling somehow 'defective', as Zeke called it.

'Plus, you know, he has taken it off for me.'

Tia snapped her head around to Seth.

'Zeke has taken his leg off for you?'

That was some level of trust. It was ridiculous that she should feel jealous of her son. Or that it rankled so much that Zeke appeared more comfortable to show Seth his amputation than he felt with her.

She tried to shake the foolish notion off, but she couldn't.

'He took it off this morning to show the other kids with robot arms or legs.'

'What other kids?'

'At the sailing school we went to. You remember, Mummy.'

She remembered that Zeke and Seth had been spending some time getting to know each other whilst she was carrying out the medical training that morning. But she'd had no idea Zeke had been planning to take his son to a sailing school. And certainly not that it had been for other amputees. But how utterly Zeke.

It was wonderful that he was bonding with his son, over something he loved so dearly. And it was utterly nonsensical for her to feel excluded.

So why did she?

'I didn't know you were going to a sailing school, that's all.' She plastered a bright smile to her lips. 'I think sailing is a lovely hobby to have.'

'Come with us,' Seth declared suddenly. 'We're going back tomorrow. I think there's going to be a race.'

'I have to lead another medical training exercise,' she realised. 'But Zeke will look after you. Just remember to listen to everything he tells you to do. He's an incredible coxswain.'

'That's the person who steers the ship,' her son told her proudly. 'Zeke explained it to me today. He told me that he set up the sailing school to help children who lost their arms or legs just like he did. Only he was a soldier, Mummy. Like you were. Isn't that cool?'

'Very cool,' she agreed, cranking her tight smile up a notch.

The last thing she wanted was for Seth to think that she objected to him spending time with his father—not that he even knew that was who Zeke was.

Lifting her hand to her head, she massaged her temples. It shouldn't feel this complicated, and she should be pleased that Zeke was sharing such a vital part of his life with his son, and it was clear he was doing it in such a way that Seth thought it all terribly *cool*. But there was a part of her that felt...*odd*.

As though Zeke was able to open his life up to his son in a way he had never been able to do with her.

Even before the accident.

But surely that was insane?

Still, she couldn't escape the disconcerting notion that he had avoided doing anything with his leg since she had arrived. The way he'd been getting out of his wet gear at the lifeboat station that night. The way he'd been at his house when she'd been there. Even here.

As though he was okay with her seeing it if he was dressed, but that he couldn't let her see him with nothing *but* the prosthetic.

Which was ridiculous, given the way he'd made her orgasm with such wild abandon.

But, as she sat at the poolside, her feet dipped into the cool water, Tia pondered the problem and wondered if tomorrow she might now find a way to pop down to the sailing school and see Zeke in action, after all.

Not that she wanted to get closer to Zeke for her own benefit, of course. But it would be a good thing to do now that he was going to be a part of Seth's life.

CHAPTER NINE

'YOUR LITTLE BOY is loving his time here, isn't he?' Netty, one of the other mothers, laughed as she watched Seth run after her own son, both of them shrieking with delight.

Tia also watched the boys play. Seth and Robbie—who had lost his right arm aged two because of meningitis—had apparently become firm friends in the week they had been together. It was a shame that in a few days Netty would be taking him home, her week-long holiday over.

'Seth adores it,' Tia acknowledged. 'And Zeke loved sharing his passion for sailing with him.'

'So you and Zeke are…?'

Tia paused.

'Zeke is Seth's father, if that's what you're asking,' she admitted.

There was something about Netty that was instantly trustworthy, and Tia hadn't had anyone but her father to talk to in a very long time. And because there was no point pretending otherwise. Not when the two of them were heads together as they so often seemed to be.

'But…?' Netty prompted gently.

'But…we've only just…reconnected. And Seth doesn't know.'

'Yet.'

'Right.' She gritted her teeth. 'Yet.'

She sensed rather than saw Netty's sympathetic smile.

'You could do a lot worse than Zeke, you know.' Leaning sideways, she nudged Tia softly in the arm, like a show of solidarity. 'There are plenty of women here who have been trying to land him ever since he founded Look to the Horizon a few years ago. Some of them are even married.'

'And Zeke has…been tempted?'

Netty tipped back her head, her rich laughter almost as gloriously warm as the sun itself.

'Never once, Tia.'

'Oh, right.' *It didn't mean anything. It didn't change anything.*

'And before you ask…sure, I've been tempted. I mean, Zeke's set up this charity to show kids like Robbie that they should never be constrained by what society tells them they should or shouldn't do.'

'As Seth would say, setting up this sailing school is *way cool.*'

'Way cool,' Netty agreed. 'But Zeke also teaches these kids a whole lot more than just sailing. He inspires them to be proud of themselves, and he shows them how to stay mentally strong when people are unkind or impose limitations. He defines the very idea of a kind, caring guy and he's one heck of a role model. And let's face it, he's also fit as hell.'

'True,' Tia agreed, baring her teeth in what she hoped looked like a smile.

'Relax.' Netty laughed again. 'I said I've looked. Who wouldn't? But I've never acted. I got the impression that he was closed off to the possibility of relationships. I always suspected that his heart was taken by some special girl. And here you are.'

'Oh, no. No. It isn't like that at all…' She faltered as Netty reached over and placed her hand on Tia's arm.

'Tia, take it from someone looking at the two of you with no preconceived notions. It is *exactly* like that.'

'He hasn't looked this way once.' She would have swallowed the words down if she could have. But they evaded her attempts to capture them. 'He doesn't even know that I'm here.'

'Trust me, Tia. He knows. Now, stay here, I'm going to get us a refreshing drink. It's roasting out here today.'

Tia murmured a word of thanks, her eyes still on Seth and Robbie, who had already raced back to Zeke and were listening attentively to whatever it was he was teaching them.

Emotion banded around her chest.

This was a side of Zeke she'd always wondered about. If it lurked beneath the surface of their tempestuous, stymied relationship. She'd certainly never known it. Maybe it was meeting too young when his own father's lessons had been too close to the surface, or maybe it was marrying as kids where he'd wanted to prove himself the alpha male; either way it came down to poor timing.

He hadn't even told her directly that this charity was his. When she'd asked him about it he'd simply said that when Z-Black had taken off, he'd realised that he had the chance to build something quite special. Not just teaching a few kids a few skills, but teaching them something as challenging as sailing. Helping them to see it less as a disability. Even just assisting them to get the right prosthetics.

Basically everything that Netty had said, only she'd been full of admiration where Zeke had dismissed his own work.

It was so far removed from the young, arrogant, almost selfish Zeke of old. Like the man she'd always imagined he was, but who he hadn't been. Not back then. He'd been too young. They both had.

Netty was wrong, Tia thought sadly. She didn't have Zeke's heart.

She never had.

* * *

It took a superhuman effort for Zeke not to look across the harbour to where Tia and one of the other mothers sat, apparently deep in conversation.

However much he tried to push her out of his thoughts, she was still there. Setting his body on fire just by being in the same house as him. The same country.

He could still taste her, feel her, picture her. The very thought of her took him out at the knees.

He grimaced at his own dark humour.

Bringing Tia and Seth out here had been supposed to have been about him getting to know the son who she had denied him for the past four and a half years. That was certainly what he'd told himself. The truth was that he couldn't drag himself away from her.

He should resent her for those unilateral decisions she had made. Instead, he still wanted her—just as he had five years ago. Ten years ago. Even fifteen years ago.

He still craved her.

And for Zeke that was a weakness that he despised.

Bringing them out here might have given him an opportunity to develop a relationship with his son, but it had also been because a side of him had desperately wanted Tia to see the success he'd made of his life.

That kid from the dirtiest house in Westlake. The kid who her father had tried to keep her away from. The kid she had chosen to marry.

Though he suspected even that had more to do with the death of her mother—grief propelling her to such an emotional act of rebellion—than the fact that she had truly loved him.

She'd been right when she'd told him that she thought they had been more in love with the idea of each other, than they had truly been in love with the people they were.

'Can we show Seth how to rig the boat again?'

Robbie's excited voice penetrated Zeke's thoughts. Both boys were standing, excited and expectant, in front of him.

'Please, Zeke?' Seth urged, and Zeke wasn't prepared for the longing he felt to hear his son call him *Daddy*.

His son. It was a transformative feeling, this rush of… pride and…love, which poured through him, like nothing he'd ever known before.

'Sure.' Zeke laughed, glad of the distraction. 'Why not?'

It was a good hour before Zeke looked for Tia again. His pulse momentarily accelerated when she wasn't where he'd last seen her—of course she wasn't. Scanning the area, Zeke could only come up empty. She must have gone home without him.

It was ludicrous how let down that made him feel.

He moved around the harbour, interacting with all the kids as he would normally do, Seth and Robbie proudly flanking either side of him. But knowing that Tia had been here and was now gone dampened his mood in a way it surely had no business doing.

He shouldn't expect her to stay; they weren't a family. He didn't know *how* to be a father. He had hardly had a shining example to follow. But he wanted it. He thought he could learn it. Tia might not agree.

The fear clenched at him more than he could have believed possible. A red-hot poker to his belly.

It was only as he crossed the road bridge to the other side that he caught sight of Netty's bobbing head. He had no idea how he managed to make his voice light and easy.

'Have you seen Tia?'

'Hey, boys.' Netty smiled happily. 'I see Robbie and Seth have been having the best time with you, Zeke, so Tia went home. Apparently you have some gala to go to tonight?'

'She left?' He heard the flat tone to his voice, but Netty didn't seem to notice.

'Yeah, she figured Seth was safe with his dad, so she told me she was going to get a shower and get ready.'

'Right.' He nodded on autopilot.

Tia had told Netty that he was Seth's father? It was the first time that she'd told anyone, as far as he knew. His heart thundered in his chest.

'Thanks, Netty.' He reached out for Seth, the little boy confidently gripping his hand.

Father and son.

'Bye, Zeke,' Robbie chanted happily before turning to his mum, chattering nineteen to the dozen.

Leaving Seth and Zeke to return to the chateau.

Home.

Nothing had quite prepared Tia for the almost overwhelming barrage of yelled questions, cameras shoved in her face, and flashbulbs going off blindingly in their eyes, right from the moment they stepped out of their limousine. She might have known the men of the local chateau would be minor celebrities out here. Especially when they looked like Ezekial Jackson and William Zane.

In spite of a whole week of coaching herself to keep her distance from her estranged husband, she plastered a tight, bright smile to her lips and took comfort from the heat of Zeke's steely body pressed against hers, as she gripped his arm tightly. As if she would never let go.

As if she never wanted to.

Even her body, it seemed, had never been more aware of just how close they were walking. Her pulse tapping out a message, like a Morse code warning. Her radial, her carotid, her femoral. Growing ever more intimate—just as Zeke himself might have managed.

'Just a few more steps.' His deep voice suddenly vibrated sensuously against the skin just in front of her tragus as he leaned down close—perhaps too close—to conceal his words from the plethora of mics and cameras. 'You're doing just fine.'

He shouldn't know her, be able to read her, so damned easily.

'Why wouldn't I be?' Somehow, she managed to up the wattage of her public smile, even as she muttered out a response through her teeth.

When he dipped his head towards her again, amusement threaded through his tone, it was all she could do to supress the delicious shiver that chased right through her.

'Of course, my mistake. Antonia Farringdale is never thrown.'

'It's just a ball.' She had never been so glad to reach the end of a carpet and step through doors that finally, mercifully, restored a degree of anonymity from the press on the other side. 'A party by any other name.'

She braced herself, waiting for Zeke to throw back the fact that they had never really attended parties, balls, or even merely nightclubs together.

Ever.

Not as the young, fresh-faced new Royal Marine and his young, university-bound bride. And not as the battle-hardened, secretive SBS and black ops specialist and his second-in-her-class, rising star of an army trauma doctor wife.

They hadn't had time for partying. Any more than they'd had the contacts for social networking. And she'd never once lamented that fact.

Until now.

Standing, suddenly frozen, on the inside of the huge doors, Tia surveyed the scene in front of her. It was like something out of a fairy tale, either animated or acted, it made little difference. It was breathtaking, spellbinding.

Everything and everyone glittered, from the stunning gowns to the tinkling laughter, as though magic had been sprinkled all over. The whole place seemed brighter than reality, more resonant. The colours richer.

And something permeated Tia in that instant. She felt abruptly supercharged. Even the music seemed to slink across the floor all the way from the ballroom, winding itself around her feet first, insinuating its way up her body, until her blood was pumping to the same, compelling rhythm.

'Dance with me.'

She shook her head instinctively, although the temptation to acquiesce was almost suffocating.

'It wasn't a question,' he censured gently.

But the arm he moved around her waist was less gentle, compelling her to move, to stay by his side as he led them, without another word of objection from her, the length of the hall and around the marble pillars to the ballroom itself.

'I don't know how to dance,' she murmured, even as she walked with him.

'You'll remember. You once told me that you used to dance with your father at Christmas events.'

His voice was even, giving nothing away. Panic began to rise inside her.

'The Zeke I knew didn't know how to dance.'

'Now I do.' He shrugged. 'So I guess all you really need to do is follow.'

And then they were on the floor with his one arm circling her waist, his other hand tucking one of her arms to his chest, drawing her to him, and then there was a jolt and everything...changed.

Tia couldn't move, could hardly even breathe. It took her the longest time to realise that the jolt hadn't been the room, but merely some forgotten, aged electricity that had arced between the two of them.

People were dancing, spinning around them like the

multicoloured horses, helicopters and fire engines on the merry-go-round Seth had loved to play on at the park in the last town where they'd lived.

But it was as if she and Zeke were in their own little bubble, right in the centre of them. Staring at each other as if neither of them could work out if they were in their past or their present.

'Are you going to put your other hand on me?' he asked dryly, but there was a rasp to his voice that hadn't been there a few moments ago. 'Or do you intend to dance with your arm dangling awkwardly by your side?'

She didn't answer. She couldn't. She merely lifted her leaden arm and, somehow, placed it on his shoulder.

Even so, it felt surreal when he began moving, leading her smoothly, and she began to follow. As though they had done it a hundred times in the past when the truth was they'd never once danced a ballroom dance together in all their years as a couple.

'Like the waltz we never had,' he muttered unexpectedly in her ear.

'At the wedding celebration that was never ours? We didn't even have a wedding breakfast.'

The words were out before she could swallow them back.

'That's because we had no friends and family to share it with.' His voice lacked any kind of emotion. 'Anyway, we had lunch at the nearest country pub we could find.' He shrugged. 'It was better than burger and fries at the nearest fast-food joint.'

'What the hell were we thinking?' she whispered.

'We weren't,' Zeke answered simply. 'You were rebelling against your father and all his rigid rules. I thought if I had something—someone—back home waiting for me then it meant I would have something to anchor me and keep me safe on every mission.'

It didn't surprise her at all that Zeke never once used

the word *love*. So why did it leave her feeling so raw inside? So scraped out.

Perhaps because the truth was, despite his belief to the contrary, she hadn't married him out of some misplaced sense of rebellion. She had married Zeke because she'd loved him. The only man she had ever loved.

Maybe, shamefully, *still* loved, if she was going to be truly honest with herself.

'We were young,' she managed at last, an attempt at an excuse, which she might not like but was infinitely less painful than the contempt and regret with which he seemed to view their marriage.

'Worse. We were idiots,' Zeke ground out furiously. 'You were right that we were selfish and, because of it, you and your father fell out. I pushed you away. But even more unacceptable of all, our son has been fatherless for his entire life.'

She glanced at him, making no attempt to conceal her shocked expression.

'Is that an apology?' she asked at length.

Zeke gritted his teeth. It had always been a standing joke between them that he hated making apologies. He wondered if she'd ever known it was because growing up his father had beat him until he'd apologised for everything. From the lack of food to the fact it was raining on a day his old man had wanted to walk down to the pub.

'It was an observation,' he hedged after the silence got to him.

'It sounded like an apology to me,' Tia muttered, but he could hear the soft smile in her voice. Could imagine the gentle curve of her sensuous mouth.

He locked his jaw even tighter.

'Take it, then. It's the closest you're going to get to one.'

'Then it will have to do. For now.'

It was too revealing. Too intimate. Yet, Zeke still didn't let her go.

If anything, he crushed her all the more tightly until it was almost painful, although she didn't think he was even aware of it. And, perversely, she didn't say anything, as though the pain could numb some of the guilt she'd felt, for too many years.

Irrationally, her eyes began to prickle and Tia dropped her head to Zeke's shoulder before he could see them.

He tensed for a second, but his steps didn't falter, and then they were whirling across the floor together. As a Tia and Zeke from a different life—a parallel universe—might have done.

As though, if they kept spinning and swirling fast enough, hard enough, long enough, they could spin themselves a new history. A different story. It was inevitable that the moment would end. With all the ceremony of a bubble bursting.

'There's the mayor, Jean-Michel Deram. I have to find Zane—we need to put our case forward now.'

She tried not to read too much into the fact that Zeke actually looked regretful to be leaving her. As though he was enjoying this moment between them as much as she was.

Or was she just being fanciful?

'Shall I come with you? Perhaps turning on a little feminine charm would help to lighten the situation, so he doesn't feel ambushed.'

'I'm fairly certain that in Jean-Michel's world he is accustomed to being *ambushed*, as you call it. But yes, you should come. Thank you.'

And when he looked at her like that—as though they were finally back on the same side when she couldn't remember how they'd got onto opposing sides—she felt as though she were invincible. Just as she had over a decade ago.

CHAPTER TEN

IT WAS ALMOST impossible to keep his mind on business when Tia was sparkling and glowing like that, Zeke realised half an hour later. When he wasn't sure he could recall a single thing he'd uttered since they'd come off the dance floor to put Z-Black's case to Jean-Michel.

She'd known when to hold back when the conversation had flowed, and had instinctively lightened the conversation on the few occasions it had threatened to degenerate into an argument between passion and bureaucracy. All the while keeping them on point, finding a softer way to reiterate whatever point he and Zane had been trying to make a little too forcefully.

Every smile and laugh from Tia seemed to weave a magic spell over their company. She *shimmered.* And he had been wholly unable to drag his gaze away from her. Even when she had excused herself from the negotiations, Zeke had found he was only listening to Jean-Michel with one ear. The other listening out for Tia's tinkling laughter.

He was constantly seeking her out as she moved gracefully through the room, her less than perfect French and evident English accent only appearing to delight the company all the more.

It had started from the moment she'd positively floated down the stairs at the chateau, poured into a dress that was both modest and which made his body tighten so painfully that he wanted to throw her over his shoulder, carry her upstairs to his suite and rip every last shred of material off that sensuous body of hers.

It had continued when they'd been in his expansive four-by-four, which had felt altogether too cramped and suffocating, as the back seat of the car had thrown up all manner of salacious memories from their early marriage that he would do better to forget.

Dancing with her had been a mistake. It had left him hyper-aware of her, and too distracted to focus on the reason he'd even come to this infernal ball in the first instance.

Tia, however, despite her earlier declarations of hating galas and balls, appeared to be the social butterfly of the night. Watching her was mesmerising.

Occasionally a man had got too close, too hands-on, and Zeke had barely been able to stop himself from asserting himself.

But Tia wouldn't have thanked him for his interference. He could almost hear her voice in his head reminding him that she was perfectly capable of looking after herself.

Only he didn't want her to have to.

And then, suddenly, she turned and smiled at him from across the floor. A dazzling, arresting smile that stopped his heart in an instant. Before he could process what she was doing, she had ducked away from the pawing man, and adhered herself to Zeke's side.

He tried not to let his body react. Fighting the instinct to place a possessive arm around her shoulders. It wasn't him she wanted, it was merely his physical protection from her unwanted suitor.

And then, despite his self-cautions, as the man followed her, clearly not taking the hint, Zeke set his glass down and very slowly, very deliberately, set himself between Tia and her harasser.

He had the sense that half the room was watching avidly,

but the man's eyes were still fixed covetously, drunkenly, on Tia and he almost didn't even notice Zeke's unspoken warning.

Almost.

Belatedly, his eyes crossed, and then he jerked his head back as he tried to look up without stumbling backwards.

Zeke crossed his arms over his chest, knowing it made him look all the more imposing. Finally, the man conceded defeat and, spinning around, marched in a not quite straight line in the opposite direction.

For a moment, Zeke watched him go, and then he turned to his wife, and held out his hand and hoped for her sake that she had the good sense not to object.

In his heart she was still his. *His.* There would never be anyone else for him and, whilst she was with him at this chateau, there could never be anyone else for her.

He couldn't have borne it.

It was weak, and shameful, but he couldn't let her go and he couldn't empty his mind of her since that moment back in her consultation room.

Actually, he had never been able to empty his mind of her since he'd turned up for his first day as a lifeguard only to see her scrubbing down the fibreglass sailboats in those little denim shorts and bikini top she'd favoured all those years ago.

Oh, he'd pretended that he'd got over her—even to himself—but he was beginning to realise just how much of a hopeless lie that had been.

And now here she was again, daring him to be his own undoing. Making him walk away from the mayor of the town where his livelihood was based—millionaire or not.

Just to be with her.

'So, shall we finish that dance?'

Her whole body might as well have been on fire, the way that Zeke was looking at her. So directly. As though he was seeing her for who she was—and who she used to be—rather than as the doctor who had done a terrible thing to him.

It was a heady experience, crowding in on her and making her feel naked and vulnerable in front of him. Despite everyone else in the room. As though he owned her, body and soul.

Or perhaps that was just the wanton side of her. The one that Zeke—and only Zeke—had always brought out in her. They had been getting so close these last few weeks, almost like they had once been, maybe it was just inevitable.

Her pulse beat out a rapid tattoo onto her skin, as though trying to warn her not to be so naïve. He wanted his son, and keeping her close, keeping her amenable, was a perfect tactic. And Zeke was nothing if not a tactician; his military training had taught him that much. Always thinking three moves ahead.

Well, this time, so was she.

She wasn't going to let Zeke just do with her as he wanted. She was going to make a few demands of her own. Turn the tables for once and take the lead. Show him that he wasn't as in control as he liked to think he was. At least with her.

She braced herself as he drew her closer to him before telling herself that she couldn't allow him to see how he affected her and instead forced herself to relax into his arms. Forced herself to act as though she were happy to be in his arms. But when his mouth brushed her cheek, she forgot that she was only meant to be playing at it.

He could rescue her. If he wanted to. From a life where she'd resigned herself to never being in love with anyone ever again. From blaming herself for the choices she'd made that night, and the guilt over keeping Seth a secret from him, even though she knew it had been the right decision at the time.

For all their sakes.

Then, as his arm snaked around her back, the heat of his hand searing into the sensitive skin at the hollow of her spine, she watched, transfixed, as his other hand enfolded hers easily. It was all too easy to follow where he led. Floating across the floor as though she were little more than a weightless skein of thread, draped loosely over his arm.

That dark, possessive glint in his eyes shooting right through her and heating her through to her very core. She lost sense of reality, of where they were, of anyone else in the room. They simply moved around the dance floor together, in flawless synchronicity as one piece of music blended into another and another, with nothing else existing for Tia but Zeke. Her husband, and the father of her wonderful son.

And when the music stopped momentarily, the musicians pausing for a brief rest, and Zeke escorted her off the dance floor, forging a direct path through the hastily parting crowds, she accompanied him wordlessly. But her entire body was alive, exulting in the dark, haunted look in his eyes, which she recognised only too well. She'd seen it many times over the years, but that first time had been the night he'd returned to Westlake—after she'd turned eighteen—and she'd stepped out of the calm, moonlit sea to where he'd been standing over her pile of clothes, a concerned expression clouding his features.

She'd laughed as he'd berated her for going into the water alone, at night, holding his coat out to her in some effort to preserve her modesty, and she had tugged it from his hands and thrown it onto the sand, moments before stepping right up to him and pressing her lips against his. His resolve hadn't lasted much longer.

It had been reckless, and exhilarating. Moulding exactly how the future of their relationship would be.

Possibly she should be more mindful that over fifteen

years had passed since that first moment together, and they weren't kids any more. But she wasn't mindful at all. She was only too happy to follow him as he made his way down the imposing hallways, looking for a small, empty room that would suit their needs.

'This will do,' he muttered, poking his head around the fourth door then tugging her inside.

'It will do?' she teased, her laughter floating lightly around them. 'How romantic.'

Zeke rolled his eyes.

'Shut up and kiss me.'

'Willingly,' she agreed, taking one of his hands in each of hers and throwing them around her back as she stepped into the circle of his arms and pressed her lips to his.

Fire roared through her. As he kissed her back, demanding and unyielding as ever, the guttural sound of his approval made desire pool between her legs. He claimed her mouth with his, plundering over and over, using his lips, his tongue, even the rough pad of his thumb, to devastating effect. With no question as to which of them was in control.

She arched against him as if trying to urge him on further, pressing every malleable inch of her lithe body against every muscular, merciless inch of his. But still Zeke seemed determined to prolong her exquisite agony, catching her hands and raising her arms to hold her wrists in one big hand as he allowed his mouth to travel from her mouth to her jawline, but no further.

Tia moved her body, half undulation, half writhe, until Zeke growled at her.

'Be still.'

'I can't,' she gasped, the rawness of his tone scraping deep within her. 'I need more.'

'Then I'll make you.'

Without warning, Zeke crushed his body to hers, trapping her between his solid chest wall and the cold wall behind her. The pressure helping to ease the ache in her straining nipples. And then, finally, he lowered one hand and grazed it over her breasts. Cruelly on the wrong side of the fabric.

'Is this where you want me?' Teasing, taunting. 'Here?'

Tia could only moan and breathe his name. The wild thing inside her clawing its way out.

'Or maybe here?' He skimmed his hand lower over her dress until his knuckles brushed her heat.

'You know exactly where,' she muttered, arching her back then lifting her hips to reconnect with his departing hand.

Instead, she connected with something far more solid, and primal. And Zeke's groan of response galvanised her.

She took advantage of his momentary lack of focus, freeing her hands from his grip above her head and loosening his hold on her. Then, her eyes locking with his, she slowly, deliberately, sank to her knees in front of him.

'Tia…'

'Shhh.' A wicked smile toyed with the corners of her mouth. 'I'm only doing what you did for me barely a few weeks ago.'

Then, sliding her hands to his waistband, she unhooked the suit trousers and drew the zip down in one perfect flourish. It was only as she slid them down his legs, her hands running down the front of his thighs and revelling in the power of the muscles beneath her palms, that Zeke pushed her away from him and took a step back.

'No. This isn't how it's going to go.'

Tia frowned, confused. She stood up and might have stumbled towards him, if he hadn't looked so hostile.

'What isn't?' she challenged shakily.

'This. You. It isn't going to be like that.'

She blinked, her mind whirring. And then the truth began to dawn, ravaging her as it did.

It was about his leg. What she'd done.

'This is about control,' she whispered, horrified. 'You only want me if you're running the show.'

'That's nonsense.'

'It isn't. You want me to give myself up to you completely, and be vulnerable, but you refuse to do the same for me.'

'Forgive me if I thought I was just trying to make you scream in pleasure. I confess I rather like it when you shout out my name as you come apart against my lips.'

She supressed a sinful shiver at the memories his words ignited.

'Yet when I want to give you the same pleasure, you stop me. Because in your book, that would mean letting me be in control. Opening yourself up to me.'

'You're overthinking this,' he warned.

'Is it that you haven't forgiven me, Zeke?' She forced herself to ask the question even though she feared the answer he might give. 'For cutting off your leg? Or for saving your life when no one could save the lives of your buddies?'

It hung there between them, like an axe just waiting to fall. And then Zeke steeled himself, shutting her out as he always had.

'You don't know what you're talking about.'

The words were too harsh, too brutal.

'Or maybe you still don't quite trust me.' She refused to cry. Even though it nearly killed her. 'You're okay with being with me as long as you're running things. Like the other week. But you don't trust me enough to do the same.'

'It isn't that simple,' he gritted out.

'No, you're right. It isn't,' Tia agreed. 'It's not about intimacy, is it? It's about control. As long as you have it over me, that's okay. But not the other way around.'

She wanted to hear him deny it. Longed to. Even as she knew he couldn't.

'You're right.' He dipped his head eventually, without a trace of remorse.

Tia watched as he calmly adjusted his trousers, her entire body shaking as though from the inside out.

But whatever else they might or might not have wanted to say to each other, it was curtailed by the sound of the announcer on the PA system. Introducing the mayor and beginning the speeches.

'I have to go,' he ground out, smoothing down his suit and stepping past her to the door. 'And so do you.'

The irony of it wasn't lost on Tia.

'I can't.'

'You're my guest. You have to,' he commanded sharply.

'I can't. People will see me. They'll *know*.'

His look was both impatient and regretful.

'They won't see anything, Tia. You look…as stunning as ever.'

She shook her head but he snatched up her arm. Not rough enough that it hurt, but firm enough that she couldn't break free.

'The timing is bad, I'll agree. But…*this* wasn't meant to happen. We will talk about it though.'

She baulked. If she felt this embarrassed, and ashamed, and angry now, how would she feel when the numbing shock had worn off?

'I don't want to talk about it.'

'Well, clearly we need to,' Zeke countered. 'But not now. Later. Tomorrow. We'll go for a walk, show Seth those locks, just like I promised.'

Before she could find another objection, he tugged her to him, ran a hand through her tousled hair as though to smooth it, and propelled her out of the room.

CHAPTER ELEVEN

HOW THE HELL had he let this happen?

He'd been thinking the same thing since he'd stood in front of the rowdy, clapping crowd last night when all he'd been able to see had been Tia. Her face white with shock and her eyes wide with pain.

He should never have taken her to the gala. More to the point he should never have danced with her. Or taken her to that room like the irresponsible teenagers they no longer were.

It was galling that she was right, though. That a part of Zeke either didn't forgive her or didn't trust her. Even though he wanted himself to do both.

Even though he wanted to move on with his life and look forwards.

But it wasn't about his leg, as she assumed it was. It was more about the truth that every time he looked at Seth, this wonderful, glorious, little boy that he had never known he wanted, Zeke felt a rushing loss at the years he had missed out on.

And he couldn't help blaming Tia for it.

The fact her decision to walk away without telling him that she was pregnant had been based on what had happened on that mission that night meant, unfortunately, that the two events were bound up in each other for ever.

'So these works were quite a feat of engineering.' He

forced himself to smile at the fascinated boy, who nodded so seriously, sounding out the headers for the tourist information boards, and pointing out the part of the locks that he recognised.

He really was a marvel. His *son*.

Whilst beside them Tia offered a rictus smile and tried to walk as far away from him as she could.

They discussed the works a little longer, with Zeke showing Seth how the series of chains and floodgates would have worked, and Tia moved away, tilting her head up to the sun as though it could conceal the dark shadows on her eyes from lack of sleep, or the lines etched onto her usually smooth features.

And then, finally, they were walking back. Seth skipping obliviously down the dusty canal path, leaving his parents to walk reluctantly together.

'I'm sorry,' Zeke offered at length.

'What for?' He hated that distant, detached quality to her tone. 'For not being able to forgive me, or for not being able to trust me? Or maybe you're only really sorry that I found you out.'

For a moment he didn't answer, and when he did it was more contemplative than anything. The truth only just starting to work its way free in his own mind.

'It isn't about forgiveness,' he began. 'There is nothing to forgive. I know you did the only thing you could when you amputated. If you hadn't then by the time I was flown anywhere else they would have had to amputate above the knee. That's if I had even survived the flight anywhere else.'

'What about your buddies?'

'Duckie and Noel,' Zeke breathed slowly. 'I blamed myself for a long time. You're right—I hated the fact that I was here and they weren't. I wondered what was so damned special about me that I hadn't been killed too.'

'They were just unlucky, Zeke. Desperately, tragically unlucky. It wasn't about you, or them, or anyone else in your squad that night.'

'Logically, I know that. But...you know this well enough, Tia. Logic doesn't always win out.'

'But you *know* it?' she whispered.

'A part of me does.'

'Then last night...?'

'That should never have happened,' he ground out.

The truth was that he suspected it was more to do with *trust* than he had realised. He still sometimes thought of Tia as that young teenage girl, and himself that invincible teenage boy. Whilst he might have long since come to terms with his prosthetic or bionic ancillaries—even learned to embrace them and the new life they had opened up to him—the idea of Tia seeing him as anything less than *whole* still rankled.

Seeing his bionic leg when he was in his everyday environment was one thing, but seeing it in a more intimate setting—when they were about to make love—was something altogether different. Tia was the only person in the world in front of whom he would feel exposed and *less*, if she saw him as he was today.

Yet he suddenly found he couldn't admit to any of it. Because he already knew what her response would be. He knew she would tell him not to be so ridiculous. He could picture her indignation and her frustration; her ponytail would swing wildly from side to side as she emphasised her words. The image made him smile to himself, even as something clenched hard in his chest, like a fist closing around his heart.

She would tell him that, of anyone, she was the person he could trust the most and how he would want to believe her. But he wouldn't.

He couldn't.

Because however much he had achieved with Z-Black, and with Look to the Horizon, he was still the guy who had let her down. And let their son down.

Zeke squared his shoulders, his voice taking on the authoritative tone that had always come to naturally to him, but which felt strained right at this very moment.

'I'm glad you came here, and we had a chance to…iron things out. Before you return to Delburn Bay, we'll agree on our arrangements for the future.'

'Our arrangements?' Tia echoed warily.

'Financial and, more importantly, access to my son.'

'Let me get this straight…'

Staying detached was harder, much harder, than he could have imagined. He was almost grateful as two cyclists suddenly flew around the corner, causing Tia to stop abruptly and Zeke to rush ahead and scoop up Seth.

A split second later Zeke caught sight of the expression on one cyclist's face.

'Get off the path—' he flung Seth to the side, before racing forward as if he could stop the cyclist from mowing down his wife and son '—and get Seth to safety.'

Tia watched in horror as one of the cyclists slumped forward in his saddle and tipped sideways, the bike veering mercifully away from her little boy but then plunging into the canal as the man fell.

A moment ago she'd been almost grateful to them and their breakneck speed, for appearing so abruptly and giving her a moment to collect her scattered thoughts. Last night she'd been angry, and humiliated. She hadn't thought there had been a single thing Zeke would be able to say to her that would have made her feel any better.

But it was what he *hadn't* said this morning that had somehow soothed her soul. He was ashamed of himself, and angry at his own actions. And he was holding back from her, as though it was *him* who needed protecting rather than *her*.

A vulnerability that he had rarely—if ever—shown throughout their marriage. But rather than making her feel safe with a strong man, as she suspected had always been Zeke's intention, it had made her feel shut out, and held at arm's length. He had never let her close enough to see his softer side.

And surely a man so utterly and completely alpha male as Zeke couldn't be dauntless all of the time? Was this a chance to finally get to see the true Ezekial Jackson as he had never allowed her to before? The *whole* man?

Her thoughts had been spinning and whirling so fast all morning. But when he had apologised, stopped talking, she'd seen those shutters slamming down on her all over again, and she'd been powerless to stop it.

She'd grappled for something to say. Anything. But nothing had come.

Now she had a moment's reprieve. She didn't have to think, she simply had to react. Falling back on what she knew best.

Running up the canal path, shouting and signalling to the cyclist who was in front that something had happened to his buddy. And then Zeke sped past her, shouting at her that Seth was safe behind them and shedding his leg moments before he jumped straight into the canal, cutting quickly through the water to where the cyclist was already sinking below the surface.

Spinning around, Tia watched as her son ran up to her, fascinated and not in the least bit afraid.

'Go on, Mummy, you're a doctor. You and Zeke have to save that man's life.'

With a rush of love, Tia turned to obey.

'The walls here are too steep. There's no way to climb

out. Get a rope, or anything to help pull us up,' Zeke yelled as he ducked down to pull the man's head above the water.

It took Tia all of two seconds to locate the nearest moored boat and race across the uneven ground to where its owner was sunbathing, oblivious, on deck. It felt like an eternity as they located a spare rope.

And then Tia was racing back, the other cyclist now lying face down on the edge of the canal, leaning down in a futile attempt to reach his buddy and Zeke—who was doing an incredible job of treading water with the casualty—and help pull them out. But the walls of this part of the canal were too high, and it was clearly proving impossible.

'Grab the rope,' Tia shouted, tying one end around a tree and locking it off before looping the other end and throwing it to Zeke and commanding the second cyclist. *'Aidez-moi…um…tirer.'*

With a last, anguished look at his friend, the man jumped up and hurried over to her, taking hold of the rope between Tia and the canal. His impatience was almost palpable as they both waited for Zeke to finish dropping the loop over his casualty and tie it in place.

'Okay,' he signalled at length, still holding the man's head above water as Tia and the second cyclist began to pull.

It felt like hours but was probably a minute or less before they'd successfully pulled the unresponsive casualty onto dry land, Tia's fingers fumbling to loosen the knot and release the loop for the rope to be thrown back to Zeke.

He couldn't tread water for ever and there was no other way out of this section, but she was going to have to trust the second cyclist to help Zeke. She needed to concentrate on her patient, who she had now ascertained was having a heart attack. There was no choice but to start chest compressions.

'J'ai appelée au secours.'

A strange voice broke Tia's thoughts, and it took a moment for her to realise that it was the woman from the boat.

'I am calling ze help services. They come now.'

'Thank you. *Merci.*'

'Je peux faire quelque'chose d'autre?'

For a moment Tia's head swam, but whilst the words meant little to her the tone was clear. The woman wanted to help. She continued with her chest compressions.

'Defibrillator?' Tia asked, then, hopefully, *'Défibrillateur?'*

'Non, mais il y a un poste de pompage... How you say? A pump-house? Wait... I go.'

Before Tia could answer, the woman had hurried away and she was left with her patient, not even daring to lift her head to check if Zeke was all right. Or her son.

'Seth, baby, are you all right?'

'Yes, Mummy.' Clear, confident. Trusting her.

She couldn't let this man die. Not for him. But also, not in front of her son.

And then, suddenly, Zeke was there, his voice low and reassuring to Seth. And at the same time the woman was back, mercifully with a defibrillator in her hands. Gratefully, Tia took it and turned to Zeke.

'He's having a heart attack. You take over the chest compressions whilst I get this ready. Okay, stand clear.'

It took two shocks and some more CPR before the cyclist's heart was back in normal sinus rhythm, having managed to converse briefly, and laboriously, with his fellow cyclist. Still Tia was grateful when the emergency services arrived as she was stabilising him, the handover going much smoother when Zeke stepped in to translate, a proud Seth tightly gripping his hand.

Father and son. Her chest tightened, almost painfully. She was at serious risk of falling in love with Zeke all over again. And that would be the definition of stupidity, since it was clear he was every bit as determined to keep her at a distance as he had ever been.

The sooner she got her and Seth back to Delburn Bay, the better.

CHAPTER TWELVE

WITH A FINAL intake of breath to quell her nerves, Tia pushed open the anteroom door to the master suite and stepped inside. The odd noises had stopped a while ago, but the draw was still powerful.

In front of her were the panelled double doors to the bedroom, slightly ajar, to her left a single, open panelled door to his walk-in closet. Tia turned to her right where another single, panelled door barely muffled the sounds of a shower.

Tia froze. *This wasn't what she'd bargained for.*

She couldn't have said how long she stood there, unable to move, but suddenly the shower was being turned off and there were sounds of movement inside. She turned awkwardly, almost crashing into the burr walnut table as she tried to leave.

The en-suite bathroom door opened instantly.

'Tia.' He sounded taken aback and she spun back around, an apologetic smile plastered on her lips.

'Zeke...'

Suddenly any hostility that she'd sensed in Zeke dissipated.

'Is Seth okay?' he asked urgently.

'Seth's fine,' she managed.

But any other words were choked off by the sight of him

standing—filling—the doorway, imposing and autocratic as ever despite his state of virtual undress.

Her mouth seemed to simultaneously dry up and yet water. Her eyes wandering greedily over the sight in front of her, from his wet hair, slightly spiky from the shower, to the broad shoulders that seemed to stretch from one door jamb to the other. One muscled arm was braced against the wooden frame, emphasising his solid, honed, tanned chest, which boasted more of an eight-pack than a six-pack, and which tapered to an athletic waist with hips barely holding onto a towel.

'Is he having nightmares?'

She couldn't have said what it was in the question that made the hairs on her arms prick up but it was suddenly as though a fog were beginning to clear in her head.

Nightmares.

Why hadn't she realised it before? She, of all people, a former army doctor.

Tia blinked, trying valiantly to drag her gaze away but she couldn't. Her eyes were locked onto him as though her brain was fervently trying to memorise every last glorious detail to savour for the future.

'Seth is absolutely fine.'

Zeke seemed to relax a little.

'He isn't upset in any way?' The note of urgency had reduced to one of concern. But it was there, nonetheless. 'He's only a kid. It can't have been easy seeing that man have a heart attack in front of him. It's a shock the first time you see arms windmilling like that.'

'Seth isn't upset,' she reassured him. 'We made sure he was far enough back, and I think you and I both kept instinctively putting ourselves between him and the casualty. I don't think he really saw anything at all. If anything, he seems proud.'

She couldn't move; his scanning gaze was rooting her

to where she stood. As though he was trying to work out if she was telling him the truth.

'I'm glad.' Eventually he bobbed his head. A curt, sharp movement that belied his words. 'Thanks for letting me know.'

'Right.' She nodded, hesitating for a moment. 'I should go.'

'You should.'

Neither of them moved. Instead Tia stared, her eyes raking over him again and again, indulging and absorbing. And then they travelled lower. Over the short towel that barely covered his powerful thighs, and down his legs.

Until she could see the one thing he had seemed so hell-bent on keeping from her. The knee and the residual limb. Once she had seen it, she couldn't tear her gaze away.

This was what she had done. Her first ever solo amputation. On her husband. The professional part of herself noted that it had been a good, neat job. The rest of her went hot, then cold, then hot again.

'Seen enough?' His sharp voice pulled her back to reality as he snatched up a temporary crutch from behind the doorway and moved swiftly, smoothly, across the anteroom to where she hadn't noticed an older prosthetic limb by the wall.

Tia watched, transfixed as he slid the liner on, then the fibreglass shell complete with a sleeve art that was so typically Zeke she felt a rush of nostalgia, before he stood forward until the pin fixed into the lock. The click seemed to reverberate around the room, making her jump.

'Where's your bionic limb?' she asked hesitantly.

He paused, as though he wasn't going to answer, then met her gaze and held it. Almost challenging her.

'I wanted to give it a quick clean and check after this afternoon.'

'Right.'

'So, now you've satisfied your curiosity, I suggest you go. Get back to *our* son.'

'Show me.'

The words were out before she could stop them. Zeke's face hardened, his eyes narrowing.

'You want me to show you?'

'Show me how it works.' She nodded. 'You seem to have no problem showing the kids at your charity, or even showing Seth. And I've heard you've turned it into a puppet show at one point to make them all laugh. But whenever I'm around it's different. You shut down, keep me out.'

'You're really making this about you?' he accused her, and for a moment she almost backed down.

But then she remembered that was what Zeke always did: turned it around on others. It possibly worked well in some of his missions.

It wasn't going to work on her. Not any more.

'No, Zeke. I'm making this about you.' She refused to let her eyes slide away. 'The reason I came down here was because I was checking on Seth when I heard noises.'

'Noises?'

She didn't imagine the way his body stiffened up.

'I didn't realise what they were at first but something about them compelled me to come and check it out. It brought me to your suite.'

'Strange?' He cocked his head as though listening out. 'But I don't hear anything now.'

'No,' she agreed. 'But then we wouldn't. Given that you're now awake. You were having a nightmare.'

'You don't know what you're talking about,' he scorned, but the edge to his tone told Tia everything she needed to know.

'You have them a lot. I should have realised. Have I…? Does me being here make it worse?'

'No.'

But he'd paused a fraction too long and she didn't believe him. She told him so.

'No,' Zeke repeated. More firmly this time.

Tia shook her head sadly.

'I heard you. That was what the noise was, wasn't it?'

He glared at her, yet there was something about his expression that was less hostile than she might have expected. Still, she was shocked when he dipped his head in acknowledgement.

'Yes. I had a nightmare. A particularly bad one, I admit it. But…' He tailed off.

Her heart twisted and knotted inside her chest. There was no way she could leave it that way.

'But what, Zeke?' She waited but he didn't answer. 'You accused me of making this about me and I told you I was making it about you. I want to amend that. I'm also making this about us.'

'This has nothing to do with us,' he said coldly. 'There isn't even an *us*.'

It hurt far more than it had a right to. Still Tia refused to back down.

'At some point you're going to have to deal with what happened. We have a son together, and we're going to end up being in each other's lives for good whether you like it or not.'

'I'm well aware of that, Antonia. It's why I brought you out here.'

'You say there's nothing to forgive, yet I don't feel forgiven. It's like every time we take three steps forward somehow your leg gets in the way and we take another two back.'

Belatedly, she realised what she'd said. She opened her mouth to apologise, astounded when a low chuckle reached her ears.

'Pun intended?'

The tension in the room eased instantly. Zeke always had liked a dark sense of humour. She remembered them telling her at the rehab centre that the lads would rag each other mercilessly. Fellow amputees dismantling each other's chairs and hiding the parts or pushing each other around to see who would topple over first.

She'd been horrified, but the response had been that they didn't take it as bullying, they took it as character-building. The kind of camaraderie they had been accustomed to in their units. It was different in the medical corps, but she could see exactly what they'd meant. Why being in that centre had been far better for him than coming home.

But now, if she wanted to finally reach him, then she was going to have to stop being Tia, his estranged wife and mother of his son. And be Tia, a fellow soldier who took no bull.

'I'd like to say I'd intended the pun,' she hazarded, 'but I'm afraid not. I'll think of a better one for next time, though.'

He watched her a moment longer. Intently, as though he was trying to read her very soul. If she'd known how to open it up for him, then she certainly would have.

'Did you blame me for amputating your leg and thereby keeping you alive, when your buddies had died, Zeke?'

He eyed her again, and then, to her surprise, he smiled. A half-apologetic smile, but a smile nonetheless.

'Maybe. I don't know. When I look back on it, nothing I thought back then was rational, so it's possible. I knew I'd pushed you away but a part of me was still angry that you went. I know now that you called the hospital for updates and that you never expected me to discharge myself and go off grid. Just as I understand why you kept the pregnancy from me initially, and I believe you that you intended to tell me as soon as you thought I could handle it. But that's the part that really gets to me. That you thought I couldn't take it. That you thought I was somehow *less*.'

It tore into her chest, squeezing her heart painfully.

'I never, ever considered that you were less of anything.' Her voice cracked but she forced herself to continue. 'You were...*are*... Zeke Jackson. How could you ever be less than that?'

'You wanted to get away from me, Tia. I saw it in your eyes. You keep trying to deny it but I know it was there, just as we keep trying to move on, but it always comes back to that.'

And then she deflated, right there in front of him.

'You're right. I'm sorry, and I hate myself for it, but you're right.'

The noise that escaped his throat was almost animalistic. Like a roar and a pain, all in one.

'But I *can* tell you that it wasn't about the accident, or the leg, or anything like that,' she pushed on. Desperately. Forcefully. 'Not for a second.'

'Then what, Tia?'

'It was about the fear of losing you. The way I had lost my mother. It had always been there, in the back of my mind, but I'd never once imagined that you would be brought to my camp, on my operating table, with no other choice but to perform surgery on you. It's the worst situation to ever be in, Zeke.'

'I can't imagine,' he murmured, and somehow that soothed her.

'I felt so responsible and so lost. You were lying there, bleeding out, and I froze for a moment. I had no damned idea what to do. And in that moment—as ludicrous as it might sound to you, I wanted to shout and scream and rage at you, for putting yourself at risk and putting me in that position.'

For a moment he didn't speak, so many emotions chasing over his rugged features that she could barely keep up, even though she tried. As if he was weighing up her words. Assessing her sincerity.

The silence felt almost suffocating. Tia wanted to shift, to move, to break free. Yet simultaneously she didn't even want to breathe if it risked breaking this spell they seemed to be under.

And then, after what felt like an eternity, he finally answered her.

'You felt powerless,' he said slowly. 'I understand how debilitating that is.'

She didn't want to have to answer him, but she made herself.

'The prospect of losing you was horrific, and then, on top of that, it opened up everything I'd stuffed down and refused to deal with when my mum had died. I thought I could run away, escape it, let it bury itself again.'

'You thought if you could get away from me in that hospital, then you could isolate yourself from everyone and never get hurt again.' His voice was gravelly. Hoarse.

'How stupid, how *selfish*, was that?' She choked back an angry sob, only for Zeke to cup her cheek.

His thumb grazed her jawline, rough, almost assailing. Silencing her.

'It was understandable. Brave, even. Because you didn't pretend we could be something that we weren't. Not back then. You were right not to have told me straight away about the baby. I would never have given myself a chance to heal. I would have felt pressured to provide for you and I would have made both our lives miserable when I couldn't do it.'

'Zeke—'

'I only regret leaving before you had a chance to tell me.' He cut her off as if she hadn't even spoken. 'I thought I was sparing you the burden of me. But I think it was just a way to run away whilst pretending to myself that I wasn't.'

'The survivor's guilt?' she guessed.

He drew in a breath.

'Yes.'

This was it. This was their chance. Zeke was talking to her; she couldn't blow it. And with Zeke, directness was going to be key.

'You know that's the goal, don't you? That's why they make those IEDs exactly the size they do.'

'Of course I know that, Tia.' He exhaled, but this time there was no rancour in his tone.

If anything, she might have even thought there might be a touch of relief in it. But that didn't make sense; he had army buddies—both fellow amputees and not—to talk to.

Could it really be relief at finally being able to talk to *her*?

'I run a company that sends men out there in a private role every day. It's my job to know that. Those IEDs are designed to maim, not kill. If you have someone with their feet or legs blown off, screaming their heads off in pain, it not only ties the men up, but it demoralises too.'

'Is that what the nightmare is?' she asked quietly. 'Hearing the screaming?'

His jaw was locked so tightly she couldn't stop herself from reaching out and cupping her palm against it.

She wasn't prepared when he suddenly lifted his arm and covered her hand with his own.

'Sometimes,' he told her, his voice thick with emotion. 'Sometimes it's the silence. And that can be worse.'

Tia couldn't speak.

'Sometimes it's me being blown up. Sometimes I dream that I'm fine, that I was never blown up, but that I'm standing over someone knowing they're dead. Sometimes it's Duckie, sometimes it's Noel…' He hesitated, but made himself push on. 'Or, when things get really rough, the nightmare is that it's *you*.'

'Me? I wasn't even there.'

'But I lost you all the same.'

'I'm sorry,' she whispered eventually. 'I should have realised. I should have…stayed away.'

His hand, still pressed to hers, held her all the tighter.

'The nightmares aren't worse since you reappeared, Tia,' he choked out. 'I hadn't really considered until now, but they've been getting easier over this past month. That one tonight is the first one I've had since you've been back in my life.'

She tried to contain the joy that leapt to life in her soul. But it was impossible.

'Surely that's good?'

'I usually have at least one bad dream every ten days or so.'

So his nightmares were less since she'd come back into his life.

Tia found that she couldn't focus her mind. Her mind might as well have been stuck inside a hurricane and altogether too many questions were screaming around in there.

The world was shifting around her, shimmering faintly, as though it might be full of possibilities after all. The grip on her hand now tightened, almost painfully. Or perhaps that was the grip on her heart.

It was time to move them forwards. As a couple.

Sliding her hand out from between his palm and her jaw, she led him to the small settee in the room and forced herself to smile.

'Show me,' she murmured, letting her hand sweep over his limb. 'Teach me how it works.'

'Tia,' he berated. 'You know how these things work.'

'Not really.' She shrugged. 'I worked at the other end of this process.'

'The cutting end?' He grinned wryly.

She pulled a rueful expression.

'Show me, Zeke.'

'No. It's too jarring,' he vacillated. 'Hardly…romantic.'

She smiled. A soft teasing smile that she could see twisted inside him.

'So now we're being romantic?'

'Aren't we?' he challenged playfully, and the shimmering hope inside her grew incandescent.

'I guess we are.'

'Then how is showing you my prosthetic, or even my stump, romantic?'

She placed her hand on his thigh where it touched hers, trailing a path down to his knee.

'You still don't see it, do you, Zeke? It's romantic to me.'

'I don't believe that.' He shook his head.

'I know. And that's what makes you an idiot,' but there was no rancour in her words. 'But, for the first time in my life, I would feel like it made you *my* idiot. That you were finally letting me in. That, at last, there were no barriers built between us.'

Tia had no idea what it was—whether her words, or her touch, or maybe just the way she was looking at him—but suddenly everything simply…changed. It was as though he had finally decided to try trusting her and all the tension, all the pain of the last few weeks just dropped away.

It didn't matter any more.

There was just her, and Zeke. And she knew he wanted to be with her in the way she'd been dreaming of for years. As long as he knew that she wanted to just accept him for all that he was, in a way that no one else ever had done in the past.

More importantly, he would need to *want* her to.

She waited, her breathing choppy, loaded. For a long time she couldn't be sure it was even going to happen.

And then abruptly he pressed his forehead to hers, deliberately, roughly, as though, if they could merge as one, she could understand for herself all the things he couldn't easily articulate.

She didn't know what had changed, but she rejoiced that it had.

CHAPTER THIRTEEN

'DO YOU KNOW that these last few weeks have been the first time you've ever really begun to talk to me about your mother, Tia?'

'I'm not sure that's true.' She frowned, knowing that it was.

'It is,' Zeke confirmed. 'You have talked about me shutting you out, but it hasn't just been me. I think that was why we were first drawn to each other all those years ago. We each saw a dark void in the other that we pretended being together could fix. We were both running from our pasts but being together allowed us to act as though we were running *towards* something.'

'Maybe we were.'

'We weren't. You would never have married me if you hadn't been desperate to plug the hole your mother's death had left. Just as I wouldn't have talked you into eloping if I hadn't been trying to prove to myself that someone could want me. Love me.'

She wanted to deny it, but deep down she knew he was right.

'So we did it for the wrong reasons, and we messed things up in the middle. But it brought us Seth. There can be nothing more perfect than our son, surely.

'Tia, I'm trying to say…'

But she didn't want to know what he was trying to say.

She couldn't overcome the unsettling suspicion that it was going to be something she didn't want to hear. Something that might threaten the possibility of them becoming a family, at last.

Grasping his waist with her hands, she angled her head until their lips just brushed, praying that he would meet her halfway. If she couldn't talk him into trusting her, then she was just going to have to show him in the most primal way she could.

For a long moment, he didn't respond. She could feel his warm, ragged breath, tickling her lips, but they were both frozen there. Paralysed.

And then, just as she thought he was going to move away, he kissed her. A kiss to launch a rocket booster into space. And Tia poured everything she was into that kiss. A long, slow burn that unfurled right through her and scorched her from the inside out. Delicious and destructive all at once. She should stop it. But she didn't want to even try. So, instead, she wound her arms around his neck and pressed her entire body against his. Her breasts splayed against his chest, her thighs nestled between his, and Zeke pushing against her belly, so sinfully hard where she was achingly soft.

She rocked against him, slowly and deliberately, revelling in the low growl that escaped his throat, recognising the familiar, mad heat that surged though him, making his whole body tauten against hers. And then she tilted her head, angling for a better fit, and repeating the kiss between them.

Zeke resisted for one moment more, and then…he stopped fighting her. And it was like unleashing a tsunami. His hands cupped her jaw, he deepened the kiss and he merely *took*. Demanded. Whilst Tia gave herself up to him completely.

His mouth plundered hers, feasting on her as though

he couldn't get enough, making her dizzy with a feverish longing. She had no idea how long he kept kissing her, his hands cradling her face then tangling into her hair, sweeping down her back, then grazing up her chest until she was arching wantonly into him.

'Lift up,' he commanded huskily, and when he cradled her backside, instinct made her raise her legs to wind around his hips, shivering as he pulled her so deliciously onto him.

Velvet against steel.

He carried her across the room and to the bed, lowering her down and covering her body with his own, the molten expression in his eyes scorching her from the inside out. Her body shifted over the bed, and her heart thundered in her ears.

Zeke wanted her. Every bit as much as she wanted him. And the mere anticipation was enough to make her begin to lose herself. To wonder, somewhere on the edges of her consciousness, if she would make it out alive this time.

As if he could read her mind, Zeke bent his head and drew one aching nipple into his mouth, like a shot right from her breast and through her body to her very core. He grazed his teeth over the sensitive skin before sucking on it deeply, intense pleasure and exquisite pain all at once.

Tia lost herself completely.

There was nothing but her and Zeke. The way it had been a decade earlier, before real life had begun to get in the way and over-complicate things. When they had let their hearts rule their heads, and when they had acted on glorious impulse and eloped.

When they had simply felt love.

Still, his mouth, his hands, teased her. Tracing whorls over her bare skin, almost reverently, as though he was taking his time to relearn her. Perfect and intoxicating. And every time he teased her, grazing his teeth over her with just the right balance between gentleness and roughness, a fresh jolt of lust clutched at the apex of her legs.

'It's been five years,' she groaned softly. 'Don't you think that's long enough to wait?'

'It's been *over* five years,' he corrected, his hoarseness betraying him. 'I don't intend to rush this like I did back at the lifeboat station.'

Before she could answer, he moved over her again, shedding the last of her clothes and dropping hot, lingering kisses down between her breasts, to her belly button and lower. Much lower.

The storm that had been building between them ever since that first moment in her new office back in Delburn Bay closed in on her with lightning speed. Only that time, Zeke had been in control. Now she was determined that it would be her.

Not just because she wanted to. But because she *had* to. She had to prove to Zeke that she'd meant what she'd said when she'd told him she hadn't cared about his lost leg. That he wasn't any less of a man to her. He never had been.

With a superhuman effort she pressed her hands against his chest.

'My turn,' she whispered, pushing him away and onto his back. Savouring the fact that he let her.

And then she was astride him, her hands acquainting themselves with every solid, contoured muscle of his chest and stomach, as impressive as it always had been. Her mouth following suit, she took her time, letting her hair slide over his skin until he was scarcely able to conceal the way even those defined edges quivered slightly for her.

Carefully, deliberately, Tia worked her way down to his waist, stopping short at the low band where his towel still clung to his hips. He was ready for her, beneath it. Excitement rippled through her. She felt almost wild. But this was about more than just the sex. This was about proving something to him, as well.

Edging backwards, she moved down his legs until she was at his ankles.

'What are you doing?' he demanded gruffly.

'Shh, just wait,' she murmured, meeting his gaze, holding it.

Without breaking eye contact Tia reached up and curled her fingers around the sleeve art, rolling it down with all the reverence that she might have rolled a condom onto his proud, unabashed sex.

'Tia...'

'Trust me?' It was meant to be a command, but it came out more as a soft plea.

Zeke paused, his eyes narrowed a fraction, before offering an almost imperceptible inclination of his head.

Tacit acquiescence.

Still staring into those fathomless blue depths, she reached for his ankle piece and disconnected it, lowering it softly to the floor beside the bed.

'Now what?' he growled, the undercurrent of anger palpable in his tone.

But she was beginning to recognise Zeke again. Finally. And she knew it was more anger at himself, at the discomfort and uncertainty he was feeling right at this moment, than it was directed at her. So it was her job to eradicate it.

He had trusted her this far, anyway, and that was all the encouragement she needed.

'Now...' a seductive smile pulled at the corners of her mouth '...we play.'

Before he could say anything more, Tia moved back up his body, and unhooked the towel, letting it fall either side of his hips, her breath catching in her chest as she finally broke eye contact and let her eyes skim down his incredible body to where he stood, so powerfully male.

She swallowed once. Twice. He was every bit as magnificent as she remembered.

Better.

And he was all *hers*.

It was all she could do not to claim him immediately.

Pressing her lips to his inner thighs, she worked her way, higher and higher, determined not to rush, however much she wanted otherwise. However much she had to taste him, *needed* to.

She jolted when he caught her upper arms with his strong hands, stopping her.

'Tia.' His voice was clipped, raw. 'You don't have to do this.'

'This is exactly your problem, Zeke,' she managed, her husky voice alien even to her. 'You refuse to believe how much I *want* to. Even when the evidence to the contrary is right in front of you.'

And then, before he could object any further, she lowered her head and took him into her mouth.

He was dying.

There was no other way to describe it. This unparalleled pleasure that crashed over him, and all around him.

Her mouth even hotter, cleverer, wickeder than he remembered. And even more urgent than it had been in every one of the futile fantasies he'd harboured in the years since they'd been apart, even whilst he'd thought they would never be together again. As if she, too, had been waiting for this moment. As if she couldn't get enough of him.

She licked him, tasted him, sucked him. The sweetest torture he had ever known. And he could do nothing but lie back and let her, watching her head move over him, letting his fingers tangle in that glorious mass of silken hair of hers. Letting her have her way. Letting her do what she wanted to him.

Tia. *His* Tia.

Claiming him as though she had every right to do so. Turning him inside out. He was building fast. Maybe too fast. Rolling through him like a tornado, a vortex that he couldn't hope to control.

Without warning, she moved her hands to circle his base, her teeth grazing him with the exact amount of pressure before taking him deeper again into her mouth, and Zeke couldn't curb it any longer.

It was like being strapped to a slingshot ride that Tia had suddenly released, leaving him catapulting into space. Crying out her name and who knew what else, as he was shot into a million glorious pieces.

When he came back to himself she was still astride him, watching him. Undisguised victory in those stunning, sparkling eyes. A smirk tugging at one side of her mouth.

'Witch,' he breathed when he could finally speak.

'Why? Because I've just exposed your claims that you have no feelings for the lies they are?'

He could have hurt her. He could have told her that sex and feelings weren't the same thing at all. But suddenly, he didn't want to. He didn't want to dance this power tango any more. He didn't want to fight. He just wanted her.

His Tia.

'Because you have me under your spell,' he muttered, snaking his hands out to hold her as he twisted on the bed so that she was on her back and he was over her. 'Just like you always did.'

Her eyes widened, then darkened.

'Prove it,' she challenged softly, but he didn't mistake the faint quake in her voice, as though she was half frightened.

'Oh, believe me. I intend to.'

He nestled himself between her legs, his mouth finding that sensitive hollow at the base of her neck, which had her arching her back and making the kind of sounds that instantly reignited the insane fire inside him. But he forced himself to take his time, his tongue licking at her salty skin, his hands following the luscious, fascinating curves of her body. Even when she wrapped her long legs around his waist so sensuously, so enticingly, he refused to capitulate.

Carefully he slid his hand down her body, between them, his slightly calloused hand deliberately grazing her soft skin. Tracing patterns and whorls, indulging and teasing.

Slowly, so slowly, he let his fingers creep down, three finger-walks down, then two back up, heightening Tia's anticipation, until she was moving impatiently under him, her breath coming in short, sharp, little gasps.

He moved down over her belly button, the soft swell below, and finally into the neat hair beneath that. All the while, Tia lifted her hips, turned them, in an attempt to get him to touch her where he knew she ached for him most.

Still Zeke teased her. Toyed with her. And himself. Only when he thought she could take no more did he let his fingers inch lower. Lower. To circle all that slick, inviting heat, around and around. To play with that proud button, with long, slow flicks. To slide inside her where she was hot, and swollen, and waiting for him.

Driving her closer and closer to the edge.

He could see the wave reaching its peak inside her. He relished in it.

'Not like this,' she cried suddenly, trying to twist her hips away from him. 'Not this time.'

'Relax.' He lowered his head to her breasts. To the pink, straining buds.

She cried out, then caught herself again.

'I want more, Zeke,' she repeated. 'I want *you*.'

'I'm here,' he growled, deliberately misunderstanding

her. Sucking on her nipple until she was arching up to him again.

'You know what I mean,' she managed, her voice sounding thick, far away, but succeeded in moving her hands down his back to grasp his backside, to pull him to her until his length was pressed against her.

And how he wanted to drive his way inside. Zeke had no idea how he held himself back.

'Say it,' he commanded in a voice he barely recognised.

'You know.' Her head gave a jerky little shake of disbelief.

'Say it. If you really want it.'

'I want you…' She bit her lip shyly. But then, suddenly, a spark leapt into her eyes.

A flash of the old Tia he had lost so long ago. *His* Tia. His *wife*.

'I want you, Zeke, inside me.' Clear, sexy, sure. 'So deep that I don't know where I end and you begin.'

It was like a lightning bolt through his entire body. The words he hadn't expected to ever hear from her again. And he couldn't deny her. He moved so that he hovered at her entrance for a moment, then thrust inside.

Long, deep, hard. Whilst his Tia cried out and lifted her hips to meet him, tightening around him as though to draw him in all the more. He held her tightly to him, withdrawing slightly only to drive back inside her, again and again, until they were both tied up in knots and he didn't think he was going to be able to last much longer.

She was exquisitely perfect. Matching him step for step in this raw, primal dance.

Her body began to tense beneath him, to pull around him, and he reached down between them one more time, and found the hard little bud. This time when he thrust his way home, he flicked his finger and pressed down, and she screamed out his name.

And when she finally hurtled over the edge, falling and tumbling, and shattering into nothingness, he let go and toppled into the blissful abyss with her.

CHAPTER FOURTEEN

THE LIFEBOAT BOUNCED through the heavy seas, every member of the crew on the lookout for the missing yacht.

Given the crashing waves, it was understandable how his antenna had likely been damaged, but it meant locating him was going to be a problem. The search and rescue helicopter was on a shout but had confirmed they would come and help with the search once they were freed up.

Still, Tia thought, peering through the windows, time was going to be a factor, and even though the skipper of the yacht had activated his distress beacon, no one knew what state he was going to be in by now.

'Think I've got him,' a shout went up and Zeke turned the lifeboat in the appropriate direction.

The past couple of weeks had been amazing. Better than anything Tia could have dreamed of, back in France.

Their last week at the chateau had been glorious. Working in the mornings, then being a family afternoons and evenings. Sometimes going together to Look to the Horizon, other times simply going to a local market, or a show, or even just the beach.

Then this week back at Delburn Bay had been wonderful. It had been tempting to move in with Zeke at his house in Westlake when he'd asked, but she'd managed to resist. It seemed premature until Seth knew that Zeke was his father, although she didn't know why they were still holding back.

Perhaps it was because she still didn't know what Zeke had been about to say that night in the chateau, when she'd finally silenced his arguments by making love to him her way.

Or perhaps she was just being over-cautious—Seth was going to have to find out some time—but until she knew exactly how much of a family they were going to be able to be, she didn't want to give her son false expectations.

Or herself.

They'd reached the yacht by now, and even a loudhailer wasn't rousing the skipper.

'I don't want to go alongside in this weather,' Zeke decided. 'Not unless I have to. That yacht is getting thrown around all over the place and the last thing we need is for both boats to be thrown together.'

'I'll go over in an inflatable,' Jonathon, one of the more experienced crewmen, suggested. 'I'll take the tow line across and I can check on the skipper. Then I'll stay below decks with them whilst we start the tow-ride back to Delburn.'

'I'll come with you.' Tia moved alongside Jonathon.

'You stay here for now,' Zeke decided. 'Until we know what state they're in.'

Tia pursed her lips.

'That doesn't make sense. They're likely to be cold and shaken at the very least.'

'Once that yacht is at the end of the line, there's no way to control it or choose which wave it can dodge. It will just have to follow us,' Zeke countered. 'If it goes broadside, that could be the three of you in the water.'

'There was enough of an issue to activate their personal distress beacon. Hypothermia and shock would be my initial concerns. It doesn't make sense to risk the trip across twice.'

She silently willed him to think twice. This was the first shout they'd been on together and if it had been any-body else, she doubted he would have been so reticent. And neither of them wanted their working relationship to be like that.

He scowled briefly, but she could see the exact moment he switched from lover to professional.

'Fine. Get whatever kit you think you could need and we'll see you both over. Once you're there we can shorten the tow if you need anything else, but it's going to be a long ride back.'

'I might be able to temporarily rig the radio somehow through the GPS aerial,' Jonathon suggested.

'Good.' Zeke nodded. 'Okay, get your kit and I'll ma-noeuvre you as close as I can for launch.'

It was twenty minutes later by the time the two of them reached the yacht and climbed on board, with Jonathon securing the tow as she took the exhausted yachtsman—who had been on deck for their landing—back below deck.

His core temperature was low, but he wasn't yet in hy-pothermic shock.

'Okay, let's start by you getting out of your wet gear and into some dry clothes whilst I make you a warm, sweet tea.'

'I'd prefer coffee,' he joked weakly, despite his shiver-ing.

'Glad to see you've still got your sense of humour. Cof-fee it is, then. We can gradually add layers to avoid send-ing you into thermal shock by heating you up too quickly. And I'm going to set up a saline drip just to be on the safe side. We've got a pretty long tow-ride back.'

'Tow line is set up.' Jonathon dropped below for a moment. 'I'm going to stay here for a little longer to make sure it doesn't part. All we can do now is wait.'

'We can't dodge the waves—we could still capsize,' the yachtsman said quietly.

'It's a possibility,' Tia acknowledged after a moment. 'But we've got one of the best coxswains out there. He'll do everything he can to keep us safe.'

'Yeah, he's going to be missed when he goes on that mission of his next week.'

'What mission?' Tia snapped her head up perhaps a little too quickly, but Jonathon had his back to her and didn't notice.

'You'd have thought he'd had enough of it in the military, wouldn't you? But I guess that's his life, he can't stay away. We always pray he'll come back safely.'

Tia faced him, anger swirling around her like some kind of ballroom dancer with a cape. If it hadn't been the last thing he needed right at this moment, he might have taken a moment longer to admire the sheer force of his wife.

'You can't go back there, Zeke.' However firm, and calm, and rational she was clearly trying to sound, her evident desperation was undermining her. 'Look what happened the last time you were in a place that dangerous.'

He felt guilt and elation all at once. As much as he had no desire to hurt her, it was buoying to see how much she cared. He just needed to allay her fears.

'I have to go out there, Tia. These are *my* men, a close-protection squad who *I* have personally trained, and they've just lost their team commander to something as unforeseeable as a motorbike crash. It has shaken them, and for two of these young men this is their first ever job without the full force of the military behind them.'

'And they think you being out there can protect them?'

It was the disdain in her tone that got to him. A dismissal that his father had perfected. A disregard he had sworn he would never again allow anyone to make him feel.

It was as though his very blood were effervescing. His whole body a mass of coiled nerves. His skin almost too tight to contain it.

He couldn't explain the part of him that wanted to roar at her. To tell her, yes, he could protect them all. Because he knew that was illogical. He couldn't guarantee that.

But he'd feel a damn sight better about sending them out there if he was with them.

'You can't protect everyone, you know,' she hurled at him, as if reading his mind. 'You can't stop something from going wrong, if that's what's going to happen. You should know that better than anyone. Or are you saying that if *your* commanders had been there that night, you would never have lost your leg?'

'Of course not.' The admission felt as though it were being ripped from his mouth. His little Tia made her point a little too well. Worse, she might as well be reading his very soul. 'I'm not going out there to protect them. I'm going out there to appraise them.'

'You keep telling yourself that, Zeke.'

'So, you think I should be happy to send them out there to protect the life of a principal who has virtually no military training, yet cower back because it's *safer*?'

'A principal?'

He grasped it as though it were a lifeline.

'The principal,' he repeated. 'The individual who is paying us to protect them out in an environment which is utterly hostile to them.'

'I know what a damn principal is, Zeke.' Tia raised her voice a notch, clearly unable to stop herself. 'But those men you've trained are all former military. The environment isn't hostile to them.'

'I still know it better,' he barked.

'No.' She shook her head. 'You don't. You and I both know that conflict zones are rapidly changing environments. What worked six months ago, a year ago, two years, won't work any more. Tactics change, old exploits stop working, weaknesses get strengthened. It's why the military always choose a selection of troops fresh out of theatre to train the next deployment to go in. Because their intel and experience is the most up to date and relevant.'

'Which is precisely why I go out there several times a year.'

'But not into direct conflict, Zeke. You go into passive conflict zones. You and I both know there's a difference.'

'Is that what you came down here for, Tia? To chastise me? To remind me that I'm disabled now and try to set limits on me as a result? I thought we got past this. Didn't Look to the Horizon teach you anything about my attitude to my capabilities?'

'My God, Zeke, is that what you really think of me?'

He forced himself to stand still. Not to move or even to blink. Merciless. Pitiless. Which made it all the more incredible when he began to finally talk to her.

'I need this, Tia—you must see that?'

'You need it? You're a multimillionaire. You have Z-Black and Look to the Horizon. Why would you need to put yourself through all that again?'

'Because it makes me feel alive. It reminds me who I am, and what I'm capable of.'

'You make it sound as though, if you don't go out there, you'll be someone different.'

He didn't answer immediately, but then he met her confused gaze.

'Maybe that's what I fear.'

He willed her to understand but she only furrowed her brow all the more.

'I don't understand. If it was so important to you, then why not be one of those hundreds of major limb amputation soldiers who have gone back into service? Some even back into war zones.'

He knew what she was thinking. No doubt as an army doctor she'd seen former soldiers hell-bent on getting back to their buddies, to the only life they'd ever known. He certainly had. And she would know how fired up they could be. How single-mindedly they chased down their goals.

Tia had known him for nearly two decades, she would surely imagine that he would have been worse, or better depending on perspective, than any of them.

'But I was SBS. The kind of things we do—the things I *did*—are demanding enough on the human body when it's at its peak. An operative with one leg…that's a liability.'

'Let me guess, you refused to settle for what you would have seen as second best?'

'I was black ops, of course anything else was always going to feel like second best to me.'

'Really?' She wanted to stop but she couldn't. The words—the hurt—were all there. 'Like a family? Like Seth and me?'

'That's a completely different thing, Tia.'

'Is it?' she challenged. 'Only, from where I'm standing, it feels *exactly* like that. Despite everything we said, and faced up to back at the chateau, for some reason you're still punishing yourself.'

'And you know all this, do you?' He was contemptuous, valiantly trying to ignore the fear that ran beneath the surface, that she might just be right. 'Just because we've been sleeping together for a couple of weeks? Just because I finally let you see my stump?'

She blanched.

It should have felt more of a victory.

'We're going around in circles,' she mumbled at last.

'Every time I think we've sorted it out, somehow it finds a way to resurrect itself.'

'Maybe that's because I'll never get away from it, Tia. It's who I am. You should know that by now.'

'You need to change,' she announced suddenly.

He didn't know what it was about her tone, but a shiver moved over his entire body.

'Why do I need to change, Tia? For me? Or for you?'

'For my son.'

'*Our* son,' he corrected furiously, a coldness washing through him as she shook her head.

'No.'

It hung between them, casting a shadow that looked bizarrely menacing.

'Yes, Tia. *Our* son. You don't get to shut me out.'

It was the sudden silence that scraped at him, he realised. The awful, bleak, dangerous lack of sound as Tia stared at him wordlessly.

And this time when she spoke, it was the careful, quiet, deadly way she controlled her voice that made the hairs on the back of his arms stand to attention.

'I do. Or, at least, I will do everything within my earthly power to do so.'

'Say again?' His tone was lethal.

'I won't agree to you telling Seth who you are if you go out there.'

'You're threatening me.' He was incredulous.

'I'm warning you,' she corrected. And then, without warning, a sadness crept into her words.

'You aren't listening to me. I told you what I went through with my mum. With you. I can't put my child through that, Zeke. I *won't*.'

Tia stopped, choking on her words and her tears, unable to go on.

She didn't need to. Zeke could hear them, loud and clear, and destructive, echoing around his head.

He had no idea how long they stood there, glaring at each other, her stifled sounds slowly subsiding.

'This is who I am, Tia. This is what I do. It gives me purpose.'

'You have Z-Black,' she croaked. 'Look to the Horizon.'

'I told you, they aren't enough.'

'Seth should be enough. He is four years old.' She dropped her head, the whispered words barely audible. 'He won't cope with losing his father. He won't understand it.'

'We'll explain it to him…' Zeke began, but he already knew that he never would.

'I don't think *I* can understand it…' she choked out. 'You were *the one*, Zeke. You were always *the one*. There has never been anyone else for me but you, and there never will be.'

Had his chest exploded, right there and then? It felt as if it should have. He had no idea how he managed to stay calm.

'Is that so?'

She swallowed before saying anything more.

'But I can't be with you, Zeke. Not if you go back out on missions again.'

Her words were like a hidden propeller slicing into him again and again. Wounding him, damaging him. He was caught in the momentum and there was no escape.

'Tia, you have to understand why this is so important.'

'I do,' she gasped, as though fighting for every breath. 'I truly do. But you also have to understand that we can't lose you, Zeke.'

Her words struck him, their impact feeling much the same as the time he'd been struck in the Kevlar-protected chest by a shotgun round. How he'd stayed upright was beyond him.

'You won't.'

'You can't guarantee that.'

'And I can't guarantee that I wouldn't walk out of that door and be hit by a speeding motorist.'

'It isn't the same and you know it. One is a pure freak accident. The other…you're deliberately putting yourself into a hostile environment. I can't have Seth living like that. Always watching the door and wondering.'

'You're telling me not to go.'

'No.' She shook her head sadly. 'I'm desperately hoping that you won't *want* to, any more.'

It was like a black, oily slick, spreading through his body, into his brain, clogging his mouth.

Something in him wanted to oblige. He could feel his throat tightening and loosening as though preparing for the words, but they never came.

All he could do was shake his head. Once. Brusquely. As though that might ease the white light pain slicing through his head.

He heard the sob thicken her throat even as she pushed her words past it, valiantly holding herself together.

'That's what I thought.' The words so sorrowful, so wispy, that he barely heard them before the wind whipped them away.

And when she stumbled away from him, he didn't try to stop her.

CHAPTER FIFTEEN

As THE LIGHTWEIGHT, fast vessel powered its way through the churning waters, Tia held tightly to the grab-rail and scanned the expanse of water, along with the other three crew members.

There was no sign of their Mayday call-out—a young girl whose dinghy had apparently been swept out of the bay—and Tia's last shout with Delburn Bay's lifeboat crew.

With everything that had happened with Zeke, staying here was no longer an option. The place held almost as many memories for her as Westlake. It was time for a fresh start, in a completely new place. And even if her heart was breaking, she had no time to indulge it; her son needed her to be strong.

He needed her to be good enough to make up the role of two parents. And she wouldn't let him down.

'There, what's that just off your bow?' she yelled, suddenly spotting a movement on the jagged rocks below the towering cliffs that lined up either side of the bay. 'Red-heart's Point.'

The crew all peered harder, the glare of the sun off the water hampering their efforts. But eventually Billy, the lifeguard she had met that first day in the office, bobbed his head in agreement.

'There's someone on those rocks and it looks like

they're trying to hail us. Have we got any more intel on the scenario?'

'Nothing. I'm taking her in,' the helmsman concurred, as he turned the boat and headed towards the cliffs.

Tia pursed her lips. This was a dangerous stretch of coast. The water was never very deep and the wrecks of multiple fishing boats posed an additional danger to the hull of their lifeboat. But there was no way down to, or up from, the beach at Redheart's Point. And twice a day it got swallowed up by the tide. Whoever was waving to them would have no way off their rapidly shrinking beach if her lifeboat crew didn't get in to them.

Dan, their helmsman, made several attempts, but the swell kept lifting and buffeting them, threatening to smash them against the small jagged rocks that occasionally tipped their sharp heads above the swirling water, like razor fish coming to the surface of the sand.

'We could veer out?' Billy suggested.

Dan shook his head.

'There's too much submerged just below the boat. It's too great a risk.'

'I don't mind getting in and heading onto the beach,' Tia suggested.

'You stay here,' Vinny, the third crew member, jumped in immediately. 'It's bad enough that you're leaving. We can't have anything happening to you, as well.'

'Funny.' Tia punched him lightly on the arm, but it was heartening to hear she would be missed. Her ego could do with a bit of massaging at the moment.

'Wait, let these three waves go and then I'll get you as close as possible.' Dan delayed his crewman. 'We'll come in as soon as you radio us.'

'Stay safe,' Tia instructed as Vinny began to scramble over the side.

They watched as he braced himself and dropped into the water.

'"Smoke me a kipper,"' he quoted, taking the bag Billy was passing him and getting clear of the boat before a wave smashed him against it.

Tia watched, her heart racing, as he made slow progress through the swell, almost being knocked off his feet twice in the first minute alone.

As hairy as it was, though, Tia welcomed the challenge. It was better than being consumed with thoughts of Zeke, and how she and Seth hadn't been enough to keep him home. Keep him safe.

Suddenly, Dan edged up in his seat.

'I think there are two casualties.'

'Say again?' Moving across the boat, Tia put her head by his shoulder to follow the direction of his hand.

'There. Beyond the girl who was signalling. Is that another figure on the rocks? Lying down?'

'I see it.' Tia nodded. 'Definitely another person. Dan, I have to go with Vinny, and I'm going to take the spinal board.'

'Then I'm going with you.' Billy jerked upright so fast the boat rocked. 'There's no way you can get through that surf with a kit bag and a seven-foot board on your own.'

'Fine.' Tia nodded. 'Okay, Dan? Good, let's go.'

It took another twelve chilling minutes before she was grasping Vinny's hand and he was hauling her and the spinal board onto the rocky beach. Billy was seconds behind.

'Tread carefully,' Vinny warned. 'These rocks are particularly slippery. Okay, so casualties are Rebecca, eighteen, and her sixteen-year-old sister, Amy. They were both in the dinghy when it got caught by the wind and swept out of the bay. They ended up just off the shore here where the tide drove them to these rocks.'

Tia followed Vinny across the rocks as quickly and carefully as she could, with both Vinny and Billy carrying the board.

'They got caught up in a swell just as they were coming in and the dinghy capsized. Amy was thrown cleanly into the water, but Rebecca was thrown onto something. She made it ashore but she's complaining of severe pain in her neck. They've tried to lie her down as flat as they can, but it's just not possible on the rocks.'

'Okay, thanks.' Tia hurried over to the sisters. 'Hi, Amy, is it? My colleague Billy is going to check you out. I'm Tia, I'm a doctor. I'm going to look after your sister. Rebecca, can you tell me where it hurts?'

Carefully, Tia carried out a check of Rebecca, ascertaining pain in the girl's left buttock and leg and an inability to move her left leg.

'Okay, Rebecca, flower, you're doing really well. I'm going to give you something to help with the pain and then we're going to try to get you onto a spinal board. I'm going to have to cut away your wet clothes as well.'

She glanced over to where Billy was holding up a blanket to afford the sister a degree of privacy whilst she also got out of her wet things and into the insulating bag that he had pulled out of his kit.

His signal reassured Tia that, other than treatment to prevent hypothermia, he was confident there were no other medical concerns with the younger girl.

She turned to Vinny. 'I'm going to administer some pain relief and let Dan know to scramble the coastguard's search and rescue heli. I don't want to risk trying to transfer her via board and boat, with her paralysis and neurological deficit. Can you look after Rebecca here, and then we'll get Billy to help us put her on a spinal board?'

'Yeah. Guess your last day is going out with a bang,

then.' He lifted his eyebrows. 'Not exactly what you had in mind when you came in this morning?'

'Not at all.' Tia exhaled. 'But as long as we get them away safely, that's all that matters.'

When the door opened, she didn't even bother to turn around. It would only be another person asking why she was leaving, telling her that she should stay.

She didn't want to hear either. There was only one person she'd ever wanted to hear from. And he hadn't wanted to say the words.

'I hear you're leaving.'

Tia froze. The familiar, uncompromisingly male voice rooting her to the spot. It took her a few long moments to answer.

'Yes.'

Another silence stretched between them.

'You shouldn't. You're good here. You fit in.'

Each sentence was like a lash, whipping her with its polite evenness. Wholly unemotional.

'I can be a medical advisor somewhere else. Coming back here was…a bad idea.'

'Coming back here was brave,' he corrected.

'No, it was foolish.'

And desperate, not that she was about to add that last bit. Instead, she wondered if the silence that once again descended were a black cloak, would she be able to lose herself for good?

Instead, Tia forced herself to turn around. She wasn't prepared for the way her heart slammed against her chest wall.

His voice might be inscrutable, collected, but his appearance was anything but.

Dark shadows ringed eyes that didn't look as though they'd slept in days whilst an even darker shadow veiled his jaw; making it seem even more square, even more male, than ever. Irrationally, she ached to reach out and touch it, to let it graze her soft skin as though the abrasion could make her *feel* something, anything, after a month of feeling numb.

She had no idea how she pulled herself together.

'If it wasn't foolish, then tell me what it was, Zeke.' She was proud of the way her voice didn't crack and completely betray her. 'What are you doing back here? I thought you were going for three months, not one. Or is this a couple of days' break to check on your business?'

Without warning, he raked his hand through his hair. It was a gesture so unsure, so unfamiliar, so wholly un-Zeke-like that it made her breath catch in her throat.

'I love you.'

'I know,' she whispered. 'Just not enough.'

'Enough that I'm not going back.'

It was so simple, so sure, so unexpected, that she felt as though she must be swaying, right there where she stood. And how she stayed upright defied belief. She had to caution her fickle heart.

'This time. But what about next time, or the one after that?'

'Enough that I will never leave you—or Seth—again. I will never go back into a conflict zone.'

The words tossed into the air, like the spray from the sea as it crashed wave after wave down on the shoreline outside the window, beyond where Zeke stood. And Tia found she was staring at it as though she were reading the words in the surf rather than hearing them coming from his mouth itself.

It was surreal. And perfect. And almost too much to hope for.

'I want to believe you,' she muttered softly, 'so much.'

'You should.'

Tia hesitated. She felt raw, scraped through. Emotionally wrung out like an exhausted swimmer caught in a riptide and barely able to keep their head above water whilst they prayed for help to arrive.

'Why?' she whispered at last.

'Because you were right, I was pushing myself, trying to prove myself to a ghost of a man to whom I should never have even given a second thought. It gave me a battle to distract myself. Without it, I might have just given up.'

She couldn't imagine Zeke, so ruthless, so strong, ever giving up on anything.

Except her.

And now he was telling her that he hadn't even done that.

'What changed?'

'You. Telling me that I didn't need all of *that* to feel alive. Showing me that I had you. And Seth. A family.'

'I told you that a month ago. You left anyway.'

'Because I was an idiot.'

'You were,' she agreed, then offered an unexpected, if weak, smile. 'But you aren't the only one. You were right, you know?'

'I was right? I like the sound of that.'

'Don't get used to it,' she tried to joke feebly. 'But you accused me once of being just as closed off as you. There I was, blaming you for shutting me out and not trusting me. But I was doing exactly the same to you.'

'Your mother.'

'Yes.' She nodded, trying to swallow down the painful lump currently wedged in her throat. 'Her death devastated me, we were so close. I needed to talk about her and honour her, but my father found it too painful, and so I had to stay silent. I felt as though we were pretending she didn't exist and I know I resented him for it.'

'So dating me *was* a way to rebel.' He didn't sound sad, or angry, but that didn't make her feel any better.

'I suppose it was a bit of that. It was my way of getting my own back on him. But it was also a bit of the other thing you once said. The "running away from our pasts" bit.'

'And are you still doing that?'

Taut lines radiated from his face. Her answer mattered to him.

It mattered to her, as well.

'No, I'm not. At least, I'm trying not to. When I lost you, I knew I needed to make a change. I finally asked my father about my mother and he started to tell me. Only a little at first—it isn't easy for him and after all this time it isn't easy for me either—but enough. Then the next time I visited, he had a few photos and some little anecdotes to go with it.'

'I'm so glad, Tia.'

'Yes.' His obvious care made her feel more cherished than he'd ever made her feel before. 'It's going to take time, but we're getting there. Soon I can start sharing little memories with Seth. I think he should know a little about my mother and how much of a hero she was.'

'I think he would like that.'

'And…and I'd like to start sharing what I've learned with you, too. Maybe even work on getting a plaque dedicated to her and her crew.'

'They want one, you know. At Westlake. There are a couple of old-timers there who even still remember working with her. But your father always shot the idea down.'

It was almost too much. She swallowed once. Twice. But the heavy ball of emotion was still there, lodged in her throat.

'I didn't know,' she admitted. 'But it sounds lovely.'

'It is. But don't rush at it, Tia. Go at your own pace. The crew will understand. Everyone will.'

'Thank you, I...just thank you,' she managed. 'So you've really come home?'

'For good. The only travelling I intend to do now is to the chateau. I've done my bit. I've laid down my life for people for years. Now the only people I'm prepared to give my life for are my wife and son.'

'Do you really mean that?'

'I spent five years buried beneath my despair, using my company and my charity to distract me from what I didn't want to face. But this past month without you, or Seth, was worse than all of that put together. You make me a better version of myself, Tia. The kind of man I never knew I wanted to become.'

'And it took you a month to realise that?'

'Not quite. But I had to get a new guy out and bring him up to speed. He's the new team leader now. The wait damn near killed me.'

'If you'd listened to me in the first place, you wouldn't have had to,' she teased, scarcely able to believe what he was saying. 'You *are* an idiot.'

'But I seem to remember you telling me a few weeks ago that I could be *your* idiot.'

'You remember that, huh?' She laughed, a shaky but genuine sound.

Her eyes prickled and something inside her began to unfurl and warm her, the heat penetrating right through to her icy bones.

'I will never forget it again,' he promised her solemnly, finally closing the gap between them and taking her face in his hands. 'Will you?'

'Never,' she breathed, placing her hands flat on Zeke's solid chest to reassure herself that she wasn't dreaming.

'Kiss me,' he commanded. 'So I know this is real.'

As though he had read her mind.

And Tia was only too happy to oblige. She pushed herself up onto her toes, her hands gliding up the reassuringly hard ridges and planes and winding around Zeke's neck. She shivered as their lips met, his mouth so demanding, crushing hers so that pleasure and pain intertwined. Finally she melted as he pulled her body to his, fitting it to him as though they had been handcrafted to be together.

For ever.

'I only have one amendment to make to your promise to lay down your life for no one else but Seth and me,' she murmured softly when they finally resurfaced a lifetime later.

'Really?' he managed abstractly. His teeth nipped at her neck, his hands moving over her as though he was trying to assure himself he hadn't forgotten a single detail whilst he'd been away. 'And what's that?'

'That you'll also protect any sister or brother Seth might have.'

Zeke stopped, his head lifting slowly and his eyes coming to meet hers. There was no doubting the love shining from them. So bright, so strong, it was almost blinding.

'You want another baby with me?' He sounded almost awed.

'I do. Don't you?'

'More than anything,' he assured her gruffly. 'When do you want to start? This year? Next?'

'How about now? Or at least…when we get home?'

'Home?'

'To Westlake. There's a house on a plot overlooking the sea, where I always wanted to live.'

'Convenient.'

'I thought so.'

And then he groaned slightly with the effort of pulling away from her, enveloped her hand in his, and finally took her home.

* * * * *

COMING SOON!

We really hope you enjoyed reading this book. If you're looking for more romance, be sure to head to the shops when new books are available on

Thursday 25th July

To see which titles are coming soon, please visit **millsandboon.co.uk/nextmonth**

MILLS & BOON

Coming next month

DR RIGHT FOR THE SINGLE MUM
Alison Roberts

'I learned then that you just had to get on with it,' Laura
said, her voice soft enough to make Tom lift his gaze to
catch hers. 'You get to choose some of the cards you play
with in the game of life but others just get dealt out, don't
they? There's nothing you can do about that except to
play the absolute best game you can. And you have to
fight for the people you love. For yourself, too.'

It was impossible to look away from those warm,
brown eyes. She totally believed in what she was saying.
Laura McKenzie was quite prepared to fight to the death
for someone she loved. There was real passion there,
mixed with that courage and determination. He was seeing
a whole new side to the person he was so comfortable to
work with and it was more than a little disconcerting
because it was making him curious. Apart from being an
amazing nurse and clearly a ferociously protective single
mother, just who was Laura McKenzie? No... It was none
of his business, was it?

The half-smile that tugged at one corner of her mouth
made it seem as if she could read his thoughts and sympathised with his small dilemma.

But she was just finishing off her surprisingly passionate
little speech. 'I guess that's the same thing, isn't it? If
you're fighting for yourself that means you can't do
anything other than to fight for the people you love.'

Okay… That did it. Tom had to back off fast before he got sucked into a space he had vowed never to enter again. He didn't want to think about what it was like to live in a space where you could love other people so much they became more important than anything else in life. That space that was too dangerous because, when you lost those people, you were left with what felt like no life at all…

He had to break that eye contact. And he had to move. Making a noise that was somewhere between a sound of agreement and clearing his throat, Tom slid off the corner of his desk.

'I'd better get back to the department.' He opened the door and there was an instant sense of relief. Escape was within touching distance. 'As I said, we'll work around whatever you need. Send me a copy of the chemotherapy calendar and I'll make sure Admin's on board for when you're rostered.'

Laura nodded as she got out of her chair. 'Thank you very much.'

Her formality was just what Tom needed to make things seem a little more normal. 'It's the least I can do,' he said. 'The least we can do. You're a valued member of this department, Laura. We'll all do everything we can to support you.'

Continue reading
DR RIGHT FOR THE SINGLE MUM
Alison Roberts

Available next month
www.millsandboon.co.uk

Want even more
ROMANCE?

Join our bookclub today!